## Also by Rick Riordan

### Percy Jackson and the Olympians

Book One: *The Lightning Thief*
Book Two: *The Sea of Monsters*
Book Three: *The Titan's Curse*
Book Four: *The Battle of the Labyrinth*
Book Five: *The Last Olympian*

*The Demigod Files*

*Percy Jackson's Greek Gods*, illustrated by John Rocco
*Percy Jackson's Greek Heroes*, illustrated by John Rocco

*The Lightning Thief: The Graphic Novel*
*The Sea of Monsters: The Graphic Novel*
*The Titan's Curse: The Graphic Novel*

### The Kane Chronicles

Book One: *The Red Pyramid*
Book Two: *The Throne of Fire*
Book Three: *The Serpent's Shadow*

*The Red Pyramid: The Graphic Novel*
*The Throne of Fire: The Graphic Novel*

### The Heroes of Olympus

Book One: *The Lost Hero*
Book Two: *The Son of Neptune*
Book Three: *The Mark of Athena*
Book Four: *The House of Hades*
Book Five: *The Blood of Olympus*

*The Demigod Diaries*

*The Lost Hero: The Graphic Novel*

### Magnus Chase and the Gods of Asgard

Book One: *The Sword of Summer*

THE HEROES  OF OLYMPUS

# THE BLOOD OF OLYMPUS

## RICK RIORDAN

DISNEP • HYPERION

LOS ANGELES   NEW YORK

First Edition, October 2014

3 5 7 9 10 8 6 4 2

FAC-026988-16060

Printed in the United States of America

Library of Congress Cataloging-in-Publication Data
Riordan, Rick.
The blood of Olympus / Rick Riordan.—First edition.
pages cm.—(The heroes of Olympus ; book 5)
Summary: "The Greek and Roman demigods must simultaneously prevent the Earth Mother, Gaea, from waking and stop war from breaking out at Camp Half-Blood"—Provided by publisher.
ISBN 978-1-4231-4673-5 (hardback)
[1. Mythology, Greek—Fiction. 2. Mythology, Roman—Fiction. 3. Gaia (Greek deity)—Fiction.] I. Title.
PZ7.R4829Bl 2014
[Fic]—dc23        2014017392

Reinforced binding

Visit www.DisneyBooks.com

SUSTAINABLE FORESTRY INITIATIVE   Certified Sourcing
www.sfiprogram.org
SFI-00993

THIS LABEL APPLIES TO TEXT STOCK

*To my wonderful readers.*
*Sorry about that apology for that last cliffhanger.*
*I'll try to avoid cliffhangers in this book.*
*Well, except for maybe a few small ones . . .*
*because I love you guys.*

*Seven half-bloods shall answer the call,*
*To storm or fire the world must fall.*
*An oath to keep with a final breath,*
*And foes bear arms to the Doors of Death.*

# THE BLOOD
# OF OLYMPUS

# I

# JASON

**JASON HATED BEING OLD.**

His joints hurt. His legs shook. As he tried to climb the hill, his lungs rattled like a box of rocks.

He couldn't see his face, thank goodness, but his fingers were gnarled and bony. Bulging blue veins webbed the backs of his hands.

He even had that old man smell—mothballs and chicken soup. How was that possible? He'd gone from sixteen to seventy-five in a matter of seconds, but the old man smell happened instantly, like *boom*. Congratulations! You stink!

"Almost there." Piper smiled at him. "You're doing great."

Easy for her to say. Piper and Annabeth were disguised as lovely Greek serving maidens. Even in their white sleeveless gowns and laced sandals, they had no trouble navigating the rocky path.

Piper's mahogany hair was pinned up in a braided spiral. Silver bracelets adorned her arms. She resembled an ancient statue of her mom, Aphrodite, which Jason found a little intimidating.

Dating a beautiful girl was nerve-racking enough. Dating a girl whose mom was the goddess of love . . . well, Jason was always afraid he'd do something unromantic, and Piper's mom would frown down from Mount Olympus and change him into a feral hog.

Jason glanced uphill. The summit was still a hundred yards above.

"Worst idea ever." He leaned against a cedar tree and wiped his forehead. "Hazel's magic is too good. If I have to fight, I'll be useless."

"It won't come to that," Annabeth promised. She looked uncomfortable in her serving-maiden outfit. She kept hunching her shoulders to keep the dress from slipping. Her pinned-up blond bun had come undone in the back and her hair dangled like long spider legs. Knowing her hatred of spiders, Jason decided not to mention that.

"We infiltrate the palace," she said. "We get the information we need, and we get out."

Piper set down her amphora, the tall ceramic wine jar in which her sword was hidden. "We can rest for a second. Catch your breath, Jason."

From her waist cord hung her cornucopia—the magic horn of plenty. Tucked somewhere in the folds of her dress was her knife, Katoptris. Piper didn't look dangerous, but if the need arose, she could dual-wield Celestial bronze blades or shoot her enemies in the face with ripe mangoes.

Annabeth slung her own amphora off her shoulder. She

too had a concealed sword; but even without a visible weapon, she looked deadly. Her stormy gray eyes scanned the surroundings, alert for any threat. If any dude asked Annabeth for a drink, Jason figured she was more likely to kick the guy in the *bifurcum*.

He tried to steady his breathing.

Below them, Afales Bay glittered, the water so blue it might've been dyed with food coloring. A few hundred yards offshore, the *Argo II* rested at anchor. Its white sails looked no bigger than postage stamps, its ninety oars like toothpicks. Jason imagined his friends on deck following his progress, taking turns with Leo's spyglass, trying not to laugh as they watched Grandpa Jason hobble uphill.

"Stupid Ithaca," he muttered.

He supposed the island was pretty enough. A spine of forested hills twisted down its center. Chalky white slopes plunged into the sea. Inlets formed rocky beaches and harbors where red-roofed houses and white stucco churches nestled against the shoreline.

The hills were dotted with poppies, crocuses, and wild cherry trees. The breeze smelled of blooming myrtle. All very nice—except the temperature was about a hundred and five degrees. The air was as steamy as a Roman bathhouse.

It would've been easy for Jason to control the winds and fly to the top of the hill, but *nooo*. For the sake of stealth, he had to struggle along as an old dude with bad knees and chicken-soup stink.

He thought about his last climb, two weeks ago, when Hazel and he faced the bandit Sciron on the cliffs of Croatia.

At least then Jason had been at full strength. What they were about to face would be much worse than a bandit.

"You sure this is the right hill?" he asked. "Seems kind of—I don't know—*quiet.*"

Piper studied the ridgeline. Braided in her hair was a bright blue harpy feather—a souvenir from last night's attack. The feather didn't exactly go with her disguise, but Piper had earned it, defeating an entire flock of demon chicken ladies by herself while she was on duty. She downplayed the accomplishment, but Jason could tell she felt good about it. The feather was a reminder that she wasn't the same girl she'd been last winter, when they'd first arrived at Camp Half-Blood.

"The ruins are up there," she promised. "I saw them in Katoptris's blade. And you heard what Hazel said. 'The biggest—'"

"'The biggest gathering of evil spirits I've ever sensed,'" Jason recalled. "Yeah, sounds awesome."

After battling through the underground temple of Hades, the last thing Jason wanted was to deal with more evil spirits. But the fate of the quest was at stake. The crew of the *Argo II* had a big decision to make. If they chose wrong, they would fail, and the entire world would be destroyed.

Piper's blade, Hazel's magical senses, and Annabeth's instincts all agreed—the answer lay here in Ithaca, at the ancient palace of Odysseus, where a horde of evil spirits had gathered to await Gaea's orders. The plan was to sneak among them, learn what was going on, and decide the best course of action. Then get out, preferably alive.

Annabeth readjusted her golden belt. "I hope our disguises hold up. The suitors were nasty customers when they were alive. If they find out we're demigods—"

"Hazel's magic will work," Piper said.

Jason tried to believe that.

*The suitors:* a hundred of the greediest, evilest cutthroats who'd ever lived. When Odysseus, the Greek king of Ithaca, went missing after the Trojan War, this mob of B-list princes had invaded his palace and refused to leave, each one hoping to marry Queen Penelope and take over the kingdom. Odysseus managed to return in secret and slaughter them all—your basic happy homecoming. But if Piper's visions were right, the suitors were now back, haunting the place where they'd died.

Jason couldn't believe he was about to visit the actual palace of Odysseus—one of the most famous Greek heroes of all time. Then again, this whole quest had been one mindblowing event after another. Annabeth herself had just come back from the eternal abyss of Tartarus. Given that, Jason decided maybe he shouldn't complain about being an old man.

"Well . . ." He steadied himself with his walking stick. "If I *look* as old as I feel, my disguise must be perfect. Let's get going."

As they climbed, sweat trickled down his neck. His calves ached. Despite the heat, he began to shiver. And try as he might, he couldn't stop thinking about his recent dreams.

Ever since the House of Hades, they'd gotten more vivid. Sometimes Jason stood in the underground temple of

Epirus, the giant Clytius looming over him, speaking in a chorus of disembodied voices: *It took all of you together to defeat me. What will you do when the Earth Mother opens her eyes?*

Other times Jason found himself at the crest of Half-Blood Hill. Gaea the Earth Mother rose from the ground—a swirling figure of soil, leaves, and stones.

*Poor child.* Her voice resonated across the landscape, shaking the bedrock under Jason's feet. *Your father is first among the gods, yet you are always second best—to your Roman comrades, to your Greek friends, even to your family. How will you prove yourself?*

His worst dream started in the courtyard of the Sonoma Wolf House. Before him stood the goddess Juno, glowing with the radiance of molten silver.

*Your life belongs to me,* her voice thundered. *An appeasement from Zeus.*

Jason knew he shouldn't look, but he couldn't close his eyes as Juno went supernova, revealing her true godly form. Pain seared Jason's mind. His body burned away in layers like an onion.

Then the scene changed. Jason was still at the Wolf House, but now he was a little boy—no more than two years old. A woman knelt before him, her lemony scent so familiar. Her features were watery and indistinct, but he knew her voice: bright and brittle, like the thinnest layer of ice over a fast stream.

*I will be back for you, dearest,* she said. *I will see you soon.*

Every time Jason woke up from that nightmare, his face was beaded with sweat. His eyes stung with tears.

Nico di Angelo had warned them: the House of Hades would stir their worst memories, make them see things and hear things from the past. Their ghosts would become restless.

Jason had hoped that *particular* ghost would stay away, but every night the dream got worse. Now he was climbing to the ruins of a palace where an army of ghosts had gathered.

*That doesn't mean* she'll *be there*, Jason told himself.

But his hands wouldn't stop trembling. Every step seemed harder than the last.

"Almost there," Annabeth said. "Let's—"

*BOOM!* The hillside rumbled. Somewhere over the ridge, a crowd roared in approval, like spectators in a coliseum. The sound made Jason's skin crawl. Not so long ago, he'd fought for his life in the Roman Colosseum before a cheering ghostly audience. He wasn't anxious to repeat the experience.

"What was that explosion?" he wondered.

"Don't know," Piper said. "But it sounds like they're having fun. Let's go make some dead friends."

# JASON

NATURALLY, the situation was worse than Jason expected.

It wouldn't have been any fun otherwise.

Peering through the olive bushes at the top of the rise, he saw what looked like an out-of-control zombie frat party.

The ruins themselves weren't that impressive: a few stone walls, a weed-choked central courtyard, a dead-end stairwell chiseled into the rock. Some plywood sheets covered a pit and a metal scaffold supported a cracked archway.

But superimposed over the ruins was another layer of reality—a spectral mirage of the palace as it must have appeared in its heyday. Whitewashed stucco walls lined with balconies rose three stories high. Columned porticoes faced the central atrium, which had a huge fountain and bronze braziers. At a dozen banquet tables, ghouls laughed and ate and pushed one another around.

Jason had expected about a hundred spirits, but twice that many were milling about, chasing spectral serving girls, smashing plates and cups, and basically making a nuisance of themselves.

Most looked like Lares from Camp Jupiter—transparent purple wraiths in tunics and sandals. A few revelers had decayed bodies with gray flesh, matted clumps of hair, and nasty wounds. Others seemed to be regular living mortals— some in togas, some in modern business suits or army fatigues. Jason even spotted one guy in a purple Camp Jupiter T-shirt and Roman legionnaire armor.

In the center of the atrium, a gray-skinned ghoul in a tattered Greek tunic paraded through the crowd, holding a marble bust over his head like a sports trophy. The other ghosts cheered and slapped him on the back. As the ghoul got closer, Jason noticed that he had an arrow in his throat, the feathered shaft sprouting from his Adam's apple. Even more disturbing: the bust he was holding . . . was that *Zeus?*

It was hard to be sure. Most Greek god statues looked similar. But the bearded, glowering face reminded Jason very much of the giant Hippie Zeus in Cabin One at Camp Half-Blood.

"Our next offering!" the ghoul shouted, his voice buzzing from the arrow in his throat. "Let us feed the Earth Mother!"

The partyers yelled and pounded their cups. The ghoul made his way to the central fountain. The crowd parted, and Jason realized the fountain wasn't filled with water. From the three-foot-tall pedestal, a geyser of sand spewed upward, arcing into an umbrella-shaped curtain of white particles before spilling into the circular basin.

The ghoul heaved the marble bust into the fountain. As

soon as Zeus's head passed through the shower of sand, the marble disintegrated like it was going through a wood chipper. The sand glittered gold, the color of ichor—godly blood. Then the entire mountain rumbled with a muffled *BOOM*, as if belching after a meal.

The dead partygoers roared with approval.

"Any more statues?" the ghoul shouted to the crowd. "No? Then I guess we'll have to wait for some *real* gods to sacrifice!"

His comrades laughed and applauded as the ghoul plopped himself down at the nearest feast table.

Jason clenched his walking stick. "That guy just disintegrated my dad. Who does he think he *is*?"

"I'm guessing that's Antinous," said Annabeth, "one of the suitors' leaders. If I remember right, it was Odysseus who shot him through the neck with that arrow."

Piper winced. "You'd think that would keep a guy down. What about all the others? Why are there so many?"

"I don't know," Annabeth said. "Newer recruits for Gaea, I guess. Some must've come back to life before we closed the Doors of Death. Some are just spirits."

"Some are ghouls," Jason said. "The ones with the gaping wounds and the gray skin, like Antinous . . . I've fought their kind before."

Piper tugged at her blue harpy feather. "Can they be killed?"

Jason remembered a quest he'd taken for Camp Jupiter years ago in San Bernardino. "Not easily. They're strong and fast and intelligent. Also, they eat human flesh."

"Fantastic," Annabeth muttered. "I don't see any option

except to stick to the plan. Split up, infiltrate, find out why they're here. If things go bad—"

"We use the backup plan," Piper said.

Jason hated the backup plan.

Before they left the ship, Leo had given each of them an emergency flare the size of a birthday candle. Supposedly, if they tossed one in the air, it would shoot upward in a streak of white phosphorus, alerting the *Argo II* that the team was in trouble. At that point, Jason and the girls would have a few seconds to take cover before the ship's catapults fired on their position, engulfing the palace in Greek fire and bursts of Celestial bronze shrapnel.

Not the safest plan, but at least Jason had the satisfaction of knowing that he could call an air strike on this noisy mob of dead guys if the situation got dicey. Of course, that was assuming he and his friends could get away. *And* assuming Leo's doomsday candles didn't go off by accident—Leo's inventions sometimes did that—in which case the weather would get much hotter, with a ninety percent chance of fiery apocalypse.

"Be careful down there," he told Piper and Annabeth.

Piper crept around the left side of the ridge. Annabeth went right. Jason pulled himself up with his walking stick and hobbled toward the ruins.

He flashed back to the last time he'd plunged into a mob of evil spirits, in the House of Hades. If it hadn't been for Frank Zhang and Nico di Angelo . . .

Gods . . . *Nico.*

Over the past few days, every time Jason sacrificed a portion of a meal to Jupiter, he prayed to his dad to help Nico. That kid had gone through so much, and yet he had volunteered for the most difficult job: transporting the Athena Parthenos statue to Camp Half-Blood. If he didn't succeed, the Roman and Greek demigods would slaughter each other. Then, no matter what happened in Greece, the *Argo II* would have no home to return to.

Jason passed through the palace's ghostly gateway. He realized just in time that a section of mosaic floor in front of him was an illusion covering a ten-foot-deep excavation pit. He sidestepped it and continued into the courtyard.

The two levels of reality reminded him of the Titan stronghold on Mount Othrys—a disorienting maze of black marble walls that randomly melted into shadow and solidified again. At least during that fight Jason had had a hundred legionnaires at his side. Now all he had was an old man's body, a stick, and two friends in slinky dresses.

Forty feet ahead of him, Piper moved through the crowd, smiling and filling wineglasses for the ghostly revelers. If she was afraid, she didn't show it. So far the ghosts weren't paying her any special attention. Hazel's magic must have been working.

Over on the right, Annabeth collected empty plates and goblets. She wasn't smiling.

Jason remembered the talk he'd had with Percy before leaving the ship.

Percy had stayed aboard to watch for threats from the sea,

but he hadn't liked the idea of Annabeth going on this expedition without him—especially since it would be the first time they were apart since returning from Tartarus.

He'd pulled Jason aside. "Hey, man . . . Annabeth would kill me if I suggested she needed anybody to protect her."

Jason laughed. "Yeah, she would."

"But look out for her, okay?"

Jason squeezed his friend's shoulder. "I'll make sure she gets back to you safely."

Now Jason wondered if he could keep that promise.

He reached the edge of the crowd.

A raspy voice cried, "IROS!"

Antinous, the ghoul with the arrow in his throat, was staring right at him. "Is that you, you old beggar?"

Hazel's magic did its work. Cold air rippled across Jason's face as the Mist subtly altered his appearance, showing the suitors what they expected to see.

"That's me!" Jason said. "Iros!"

A dozen more ghosts turned toward him. Some scowled and gripped the hilts of their glowing purple swords. Too late, Jason wondered if Iros was an enemy of theirs, but he'd already committed to the part.

He hobbled forward, putting on his best cranky old man expression. "Guess I'm late to the party. I hope you saved me some food?"

One of the ghosts sneered in disgust. "Ungrateful old panhandler. Should I kill him, Antinous?"

Jason's neck muscles tightened.

Antinous regarded him for a three count, then chuckled. "I'm in a good mood today. Come, Iros, join me at my table."

Jason didn't have much choice. He sat across from Antinous while more ghosts crowded around, leering as if they expected to see a particularly vicious arm-wrestling contest.

Up close, Antinous's eyes were solid yellow. His lips stretched paper-thin over wolfish teeth. At first, Jason thought the ghoul's curly dark hair was disintegrating. Then he realized a steady stream of dirt was trickling from Antinous's scalp, spilling over his shoulders. Clods of mud filled the old sword gashes in the ghoul's gray skin. More dirt spilled from the base of the arrow wound in his throat.

*The power of Gaea,* Jason thought. *The earth is holding this guy together.*

Antinous slid a golden goblet and a platter of food across the table. "I didn't expect to see you here, Iros. But I suppose even a beggar can sue for retribution. Drink. Eat."

Thick red liquid sloshed in the goblet. On the plate sat a steaming brown lump of mystery meat.

Jason's stomach rebelled. Even if ghoul food didn't kill him, his vegetarian girlfriend probably wouldn't kiss him for a month.

He recalled what Notus the South Wind had told him: *A wind that blows aimlessly is no good to anyone.*

Jason's entire career at Camp Jupiter had been built on careful choices. He mediated between demigods, listened to all sides of an argument, found compromises. Even when he chafed against Roman traditions, he thought before he acted. He wasn't impulsive.

Notus had warned him that such hesitation would kill him. Jason had to stop deliberating and take what he wanted. If he was an ungrateful beggar, he had to *act* like one.

He ripped off a chunk of meat with his fingers and stuffed it in his mouth. He guzzled some red liquid, which thankfully tasted like watered-down wine, not blood or poison. Jason fought the urge to gag, but he didn't keel over or explode.

"Yum!" He wiped his mouth. "Now tell me about this . . . what did you call it? Retribution? Where do I sign up?"

The ghosts laughed. One pushed his shoulder and Jason was alarmed that he could actually *feel* it.

At Camp Jupiter, Lares had no physical substance. Apparently these spirits *did*—which meant more enemies who could beat, stab, or decapitate him.

Antinous leaned forward. "Tell me, Iros, what do you have to offer? We don't need you to run messages for us like in the old days. Certainly you aren't a fighter. As I recall, Odysseus crushed your jaw and tossed you into the pigsty."

Jason's neurons fired. *Iros* . . . the old man who'd run messages for the suitors in exchange for scraps of food. Iros had been sort of like their pet homeless person. When Odysseus came home, disguised as a beggar, Iros thought the new guy was moving in on his territory. The two had started arguing . . .

"You made Iros—" Jason hesitated. "You made *me* fight Odysseus. You bet money on it. Even when Odysseus took off his shirt and you saw how muscular he was . . . you still made me fight him. You didn't care if I lived or died!"

Antinous bared his pointed teeth. "Of course I didn't care.

I still don't! But you're here, so Gaea must have had a reason to allow you back into the mortal world. Tell me, why are you worthy of a share in our spoils?"

"What spoils?"

Antinous spread his hands. "The entire world, my friend. The first time we met here, we were only after Odysseus's land, his money, and his wife."

"Especially his wife!" A bald ghost in ragged clothes elbowed Jason in the ribs. "That Penelope was a hot little honey cake!"

Jason caught a glimpse of Piper serving drinks at the next table. She discreetly put her finger to her mouth in a *gag me* gesture, then went back to flirting with dead guys.

Antinous sneered. "Eurymachus, you whining coward. You never stood a *chance* with Penelope. I remember you blubbering and pleading for your life with Odysseus, blaming everything on me!"

"Lot of good it did me." Eurymachus lifted his tattered shirt, revealing an inch-wide hole in the middle of his spectral chest. "Odysseus shot me in the heart, just because I wanted to marry his wife!"

"At any rate . . ." Antinous turned to Jason. "We have gathered now for a much bigger prize. Once Gaea destroys the gods, we will divide up the remnants of the mortal world!"

"Dibs on London!" yelled a ghoul at the next table.

"Montreal!" shouted another.

"Duluth!" yelled a third, which momentarily stopped the conversation as the other ghosts gave him confused looks.

The meat and wine turned to lead in Jason's stomach.

"What about the rest of these . . . guests? I count at least two hundred. Half of them are new to me."

Antinous's yellow eyes gleamed. "All of them are suitors for Gaea's favor. All have claims and grievances against the gods or their pet heroes. That scoundrel over there is Hippias, former tyrant of Athens. He got deposed and sided with the Persians to attack his own countrymen. No morals whatsoever. He'd do anything for power."

"Thank you!" called Hippias.

"That rogue with the turkey leg in his mouth," Antinous continued, "that's Hasdrubal of Carthage. He has a grudge to settle with Rome."

"Mhhmm," said the Carthaginian.

"And Michael Varus—"

Jason choked. *"Who?"*

Over by the sand fountain, the dark-haired guy in the purple shirt and legionnaire armor turned to face them. His outline was blurred, smoky, and indistinct, so Jason guessed he was some form of spirit, but the legion tattoo on his forearm was clear enough: SPQR, the double-faced head of the god Janus, and six score-marks for years of service. On his breastplate hung the badge of praetorship and the emblem of the Fifth Cohort.

Jason had never met Michael Varus. The infamous praetor had died in the 1980s. Still, Jason's skin crawled when he met Varus's gaze. Those sunken eyes seemed to bore right through Jason's disguise.

Antinous waved dismissively. "He's a Roman demigod. Lost his legion's eagle in . . . Alaska, was it? Doesn't matter. Gaea lets him hang around. He insists he has some insight into defeating Camp Jupiter. But you, Iros—you still haven't answered my question. Why should *you* be welcome among us?"

Varus's dead eyes had unnerved Jason. He could feel the Mist thinning around him, reacting to his uncertainty.

Suddenly Annabeth appeared at Antinous's shoulder. "More wine, my lord? Oops!"

She spilled the contents of a silver pitcher down the back of Antinous's neck.

"Gahh!" The ghoul arched his spine. "Foolish girl! Who let you back from Tartarus?"

"A Titan, my lord." Annabeth dipped her head apologetically. "May I bring you some moist towelettes? Your arrow is dripping."

"Begone!"

Annabeth caught Jason's eye—a silent message of support—then she disappeared in the crowd.

The ghoul wiped himself off, giving Jason a chance to collect his thoughts.

He was Iros . . . former messenger of the suitors. Why would he be here? Why should they accept him?

He picked up the nearest steak knife and stabbed it into the table, making the ghosts around him jump.

"Why should you welcome me?" Jason growled. "Because I'm still running messages, you stupid wretches! I've just come from the House of Hades to see what you're up to!"

That last part was true, and it seemed to give Antinous pause. The ghoul glared at him, wine still dripping from the arrow shaft in his throat. "You expect me to believe Gaea sent you—a beggar—to check up on us?"

Jason laughed. "I was among the last to leave Epirus before the Doors of Death were closed! I saw the chamber where Clytius stood guard under a domed ceiling tiled with tombstones. I walked the jewel-and-bone floors of the Necromanteion!"

That was also true. Around the table, ghosts shifted and muttered.

"So, Antinous . . ." Jason jabbed a finger at the ghoul. "Maybe *you* should explain to me why *you're* worthy of Gaea's favor. All I see is a crowd of lazy, dawdling dead folk enjoying themselves and not helping the war effort. What should I tell the Earth Mother?"

From the corner of his eye, Jason saw Piper flash him an approving smile. Then she returned her attention to a glowing purple Greek dude who was trying to make her sit on his lap.

Antinous wrapped his hand around the steak knife Jason had impaled in the table. He pulled it free and studied the blade. "If you come from Gaea, you must know we are here under orders. Porphyrion decreed it." Antinous ran the knife blade across his palm. Instead of blood, dry dirt spilled from the cut. "You do know Porphyrion . . . ?"

Jason struggled to keep his nausea under control. He remembered Porphyrion just fine from their battle at the Wolf House. "The giant king—green skin, forty feet tall, white eyes, hair braided with weapons. Of course I know him. He's a lot more impressive than *you*."

He decided not to mention that the last time he'd seen the giant king, Jason had blasted him in the head with lightning.

For once, Antinous looked speechless, but his bald ghost friend Eurymachus put an arm around Jason's shoulders.

"Now, now, friend!" Eurymachus smelled like sour wine and burning electrical wires. His ghostly touch made Jason's rib cage tingle. "I'm sure we didn't mean to question your credentials! It's just, well, if you've spoken with Porphyrion in Athens, you *know* why we're here. I assure you, we're doing exactly as he ordered!"

Jason tried to mask his surprise. *Porphyrion in Athens.*

Gaea had promised to pull up the gods by their roots. Chiron, Jason's mentor at Camp Half-Blood, had assumed that meant that the giants would try to rouse the earth goddess at the original Mount Olympus. But now . . .

"The Acropolis," Jason said. "The most ancient temples to the gods, in the middle of Athens. That's where Gaea will wake."

"Of course!" Eurymachus laughed. The wound in his chest made a popping sound, like a porpoise's blowhole. "And to get there, those meddlesome demigods will have to travel by sea, eh? They know it's too dangerous to fly over land."

"Which means they'll have to pass this island," Jason said.

Eurymachus nodded eagerly. He removed his arm from Jason's shoulders and dipped his finger in his wineglass. "At that point, they'll have to make a choice, eh?"

On the tabletop, he traced a coastline, red wine glowing unnaturally against the wood. He drew Greece like a misshapen hourglass—a large dangly blob for the northern mainland, then another blob below it, almost as large—the big chunk of land known as the Peloponnese. Cutting between them was a narrow line of sea—the Straits of Corinth.

Jason hardly needed a picture. He and the rest of the crew had spent the last day at sea studying maps.

"The most direct route," Eurymachus said, "would be due east from here, across the Straits of Corinth. But if they try to go that way—"

"Enough," Antinous snapped. "You have a loose tongue, Eurymachus."

The ghost looked offended. "I wasn't going to tell him everything! Just about the Cyclopes armies massed on either shore. And the raging storm spirits in the air. And those vicious sea monsters Keto sent to infest the waters. And of course if the ship got as far as Delphi—"

"Idiot!" Antinous lunged across the table and grabbed the ghost's wrist. A thin crust of dirt spread from the ghoul's hand, straight up Eurymachus's spectral arm.

"No!" Eurymachus yelped. "Please! I—I only meant—"

The ghost screamed as the dirt covered his body like a shell, then cracked apart, leaving nothing but a pile of dust. Eurymachus was gone.

Antinous sat back and brushed off his hands. The other suitors at the table watched him in wary silence.

"Apologies, Iros." The ghoul smiled coldly. "All you need to know—the ways to Athens are well guarded, just as we promised. The demigods would either have to risk the straits, which are impossible, or sail around the entire Peloponnese, which is hardly much safer. In any event, it's unlikely they will survive long enough to *make* that choice. Once they reach Ithaca, we will know. We will stop them here, and Gaea will see how valuable we are. You can take that message back to Athens."

Jason's heart hammered against his sternum. He'd never seen anything like the shell of earth that Antinous had summoned to destroy Eurymachus. He didn't want to find out if that power worked on demigods.

Also, Antinous sounded confident that he could detect the *Argo II.* Hazel's magic seemed to be obscuring the ship so far, but there was no telling how long that would last.

Jason had the intel they'd come for. Their goal was Athens. The safer route, or at least the *not impossible* route, was around the southern coast. Today was July 20. They only had twelve days before Gaea planned to wake, on August 1, the ancient Feast of Hope.

Jason and his friends needed to leave while they had the chance.

But something else bothered him—a cold sense of foreboding, as if he hadn't heard the worst news yet.

Eurymachus had mentioned Delphi. Jason had secretly hoped to visit the ancient site of Apollo's Oracle, maybe get some insight into his personal future, but if the place had been overrun by monsters . . .

He pushed aside his plate of cold food. "Sounds like everything is under control. For your sake, Antinous, I hope so. These demigods are resourceful. They closed the Doors of Death. We wouldn't want them sneaking past you, perhaps getting help from Delphi."

Antinous chuckled. "No risk of that. Delphi is no longer in Apollo's control."

"I—I see. And if the demigods sail the long way around the Peloponnese?"

"You worry too much. That journey is *never* safe for demigods, and it's much too far. Besides, Victory runs rampant in Olympia. As long as that's the case, there is no way the demigods can win this war."

Jason didn't understand what that meant either, but he nodded. "Very well. I will report as much to King Porphyrion. Thank you for the, er, meal."

Over at the fountain, Michael Varus called, "Wait."

Jason bit back a curse. He'd been trying to ignore the dead praetor, but now Varus walked over, surrounded in a hazy white aura, his deep-set eyes like sinkholes. At his side hung an Imperial gold *gladius*.

"You must stay," Varus said.

Antinous shot the ghost an irritated look. "What's the problem, legionnaire? If Iros wants to leave, let him. He smells bad!"

The other ghosts laughed nervously. Across the courtyard, Piper shot Jason a worried glance. A little farther away, Annabeth casually palmed a carving knife from the nearest platter of meat.

Varus rested his hand on the pommel of his sword. Despite the heat, his breastplate was glazed with ice. "I lost my cohort *twice* in Alaska—once in life, once in death to a *Graecus* named Percy Jackson. Still I have come here to answer Gaea's call. Do you know why?"

Jason swallowed. "Stubbornness?"

"This is a place of longing," Varus said. "All of us are drawn here, sustained not only by Gaea's power, but also by our strongest desires. Eurymachus's greed. Antinous's cruelty."

"You flatter me," the ghoul muttered.

"Hasdrubal's hatred," Varus continued. "Hippias's bitterness. My ambition. And you, *Iros*. What has drawn you here? What does a beggar most desire? Perhaps a home?"

An uncomfortable tingle started at the base of Jason's skull—the same feeling he got when a huge electrical storm was about to break.

"I should be going," he said. "Messages to carry."

Michael Varus drew his sword. "My father is Janus, the god of two faces. I am used to seeing through masks and deceptions. Do you know, Iros, why we are so sure the demigods will not pass our island undetected?"

Jason silently ran through his repertoire of Latin cuss words. He tried to calculate how long it would take him to get out his emergency flare and fire it. Hopefully he could buy enough time for the girls to find shelter before this mob of dead guys slaughtered him.

He turned to Antinous. "Look, are you in charge here or not? Maybe you should muzzle your Roman."

The ghoul took a deep breath. The arrow rattled in his throat. "Ah, but this might be entertaining. Go on, Varus."

The dead praetor raised his sword. "Our desires reveal us. They show us for who we really are. Someone has come for you, Jason Grace."

Behind Varus, the crowd parted. The shimmering ghost of a woman drifted forward, and Jason felt as if his bones were turning to dust.

"My dearest," said his mother's ghost. "You have come home."

# JASON

**SOMEHOW HE KNEW HER.** He recognized her dress—a flowery green-and-red wraparound, like the skirt of a Christmas tree. He recognized the colorful plastic bangles on her wrists that had dug into his back when she hugged him good-bye at the Wolf House. He recognized her hair, an over-teased corona of dyed blond curls, and her scent of lemons and aerosol.

Her eyes were blue like Jason's, but they gleamed with fractured light, like she'd just come out of a bunker after a nuclear war—hungrily searching for familiar details in a changed world.

"Dearest." She held out her arms.

Jason's vision tunneled. The ghosts and ghouls no longer mattered.

His Mist disguise burned off. His posture straightened. His joints stopped aching. His walking stick turned back into an Imperial gold *gladius*.

The burning sensation didn't stop. He felt as if layers of his life were being seared away—his months at Camp Half-Blood, his years at Camp Jupiter, his training with Lupa the wolf goddess. He was a scared and vulnerable two-year-old again. Even the scar on his lip, from when he'd tried to eat a stapler as a toddler, stung like a fresh wound.

"Mom?" he managed.

"Yes, dearest." Her image flickered. "Come, embrace me."

"You're—you're not real."

"Of course she is real." Michael Varus's voice sounded far away. "Did you think Gaea would let such an important spirit languish in the Underworld? She is your mother, Beryl Grace, star of television, sweetheart to the king of Olympus, who rejected her not once but twice, in both his Greek and Roman aspects. She deserves justice as much as any of us."

Jason's heart felt wobbly. The suitors crowded around him, watching.

*I'm their entertainment,* Jason realized. The ghosts probably found this even more amusing than two beggars fighting to the death.

Piper's voice cut through the buzzing in his head. "Jason, look at me."

She stood twenty feet away, holding her ceramic amphora. Her smile was gone. Her gaze was fierce and commanding—as impossible to ignore as the blue harpy feather in her hair. "That isn't your mother. Her voice is working some kind of magic on you—like charmspeak, but more dangerous. Can't you sense it?"

"She's right." Annabeth climbed onto the nearest table.

She kicked aside a platter, startling a dozen suitors. "Jason, that's only a remnant of your mother, like an *ara*, maybe, or—"

"A remnant!" His mother's ghost sobbed. "Yes, look what I have been reduced to. It's Jupiter's fault. He abandoned us. He wouldn't help me! I didn't want to leave you in Sonoma, my dear, but Juno and Jupiter gave me no choice. They wouldn't allow us to stay together. Why fight for them now? Join these suitors. Lead them. We can be a family again!"

Jason felt hundreds of eyes on him.

This has been the story of my life, he thought bitterly. Everyone had always watched him, expecting him to lead the way. From the moment he'd arrived at Camp Jupiter, the Roman demigods had treated him like a prince in waiting. Despite his attempts to alter his destiny—joining the worst cohort, trying to change the camp traditions, taking the least glamorous missions, and befriending the least popular kids— he had been made praetor anyway. As a son of Jupiter, his future had been assured.

He remembered what Hercules had said to him at the Straits of Gibraltar: *It's not easy being a son of Zeus. Too much pressure. Eventually, it can make a guy snap.*

Now Jason was here, drawn as taut as a bowstring.

"You left me," he told his mother. "That wasn't Jupiter or Juno. That was *you.*"

Beryl Grace stepped forward. The worry lines around her eyes, the pained tightness in her mouth reminded Jason of his sister, Thalia.

"Dearest, I told you I would come back. Those were my last words to you. Don't you remember?"

Jason shivered. In the ruins of the Wolf House his mother had hugged him one last time. She had smiled, but her eyes were full of tears.

*It's all right,* she had promised. But even as a little kid, Jason had known it wasn't all right. *Wait here. I will be back for you, dearest. I will see you soon.*

She hadn't come back. Instead, Jason had wandered the ruins, crying and alone, calling for his mother and for Thalia—until the wolves came for him.

His mother's unkept promise was at the core of who he was. He'd built his whole life around the irritation of her words, like the grain of sand at the center of a pearl.

*People lie. Promises are broken.*

That was why, as much as it chafed him, Jason followed rules. He kept his promises. He never wanted to abandon anyone the way he'd been abandoned and lied to.

Now his mom was back, erasing the one certainty Jason had about her—that she'd left him forever.

Across the table, Antinous raised his goblet. "So pleased to meet you, son of Jupiter. Listen to your mother. You have many grievances against the gods. Why not join us? I gather these two serving girls are your friends? We will spare them. You wish to have your mother remain in the world? We can do that. You wish to be a king—"

"No." Jason's mind was spinning. "No, I don't belong with you."

Michael Varus regarded him with cold eyes. "Are you so sure, my fellow praetor? Even if you defeat the giants and Gaea, would you return home like Odysseus did? Where *is* your home now? With the Greeks? With the Romans? No one will accept you. And *if* you get back, who's to say you won't find ruins like this?"

Jason scanned the palace courtyard. Without the illusory balconies and colonnades, there was nothing but a heap of rubble on a barren hilltop. Only the fountain seemed real, spewing forth sand like a reminder of Gaea's limitless power.

"You were a legion officer," he told Varus. "A leader of Rome."

"So were you," Varus said. "Loyalties change."

"You think I belong with *this* crowd?" Jason asked. "A bunch of dead losers waiting for a free handout from Gaea, whining that the world owes them something?"

Around the courtyard, ghosts and ghouls rose to their feet and drew weapons.

"Beware!" Piper yelled at the crowd. "Every man in this palace is your enemy. Each one will stab you in the back at the first chance!"

Over the last few weeks, Piper's charmspeak had become truly powerful. She spoke the truth, and the crowd believed her. They looked sideways at one another, hands clenching the hilts of their swords.

Jason's mother stepped toward him. "Dearest, be sensible. Give up your quest. Your *Argo II* could never make the trip to Athens. Even if it did, there's the matter of the Athena Parthenos."

A tremor passed through him. "What do you mean?"

"Don't feign ignorance, my dearest. Gaea knows about

your friend Reyna, and Nico the son of Hades, and the satyr Hedge. To kill them, the Earth Mother has sent her most dangerous son—the hunter who never rests. But you don't have to die."

The ghouls and ghosts closed in—two hundred of them facing Jason in anticipation, as if he might lead them in the national anthem.

*The hunter who never rests.*

Jason didn't know who that was, but he had to warn Reyna and Nico.

Which meant he had to get out of here alive.

He looked at Annabeth and Piper. Both stood ready, waiting for his cue.

He forced himself to meet his mother's eyes. She looked like the same woman who'd abandoned him in the Sonoma woods fourteen years ago. But Jason wasn't a toddler anymore. He was a battle veteran, a demigod who'd faced death countless times.

And what he saw in front of him wasn't his mother—at least, not what his mother *should* be—caring, loving, selflessly protective.

*A remnant,* Annabeth had called her.

Michael Varus had told him that the spirits here were sustained by their strongest desires. The spirit of Beryl Grace literally *glowed* with need. Her eyes demanded Jason's attention. Her arms reached out, desperate to possess him.

"What do you want?" he asked. "What brought you here?"

"I want life!" she cried. "Youth! Beauty! Your father could

have made me immortal. He could have taken me to Olympus, but he abandoned me. You can set things right, Jason. You are my proud warrior!"

Her lemony scent turned acrid, as if she were starting to burn.

Jason remembered something Thalia had told him. Their mother had become increasingly unstable, until her despair drove her crazy. She had died in a car accident, the result of her driving while drunk.

The watered wine in Jason's stomach churned. He decided that if he lived through this day, he would never drink alcohol again.

"You're a *mania*," Jason decided, the word coming to him from his studies at Camp Jupiter long ago. "A spirit of insanity. That's what you've been reduced to."

"I am all that remains," Beryl Grace agreed. Her image flickered through a spectrum of colors. "Embrace me, son. I am all you have left."

The memory of the South Wind spoke in his mind: *You can't choose your parentage. But you can choose your legacy.*

Jason felt like he was being reassembled, one layer at a time. His heartbeat steadied. The chill left his bones. His skin warmed in the afternoon sun.

"No," he croaked. He glanced at Annabeth and Piper. "My loyalties haven't changed. My family has just expanded. I'm a child of Greece and Rome." He looked back at his mother for the last time. "I'm no child of yours."

He made the ancient sign of warding off evil—three

fingers thrust out from the heart—and the ghost of Beryl Grace disappeared with a soft hiss, like a sigh of relief.

The ghoul Antinous tossed aside his goblet. He studied Jason with a look of lazy disgust. "Well, then," he said, "I suppose we'll just kill you."

All around Jason, the enemies closed in.

# IV

# JASON

THE FIGHT WAS GOING GREAT—until he got stabbed.

Jason slashed his *gladius* in a wide arc, vaporizing the nearest suitors; then he vaulted onto the table and jumped right over Antinous's head. In midair he willed his blade to extend into a javelin—a trick he'd never tried with this sword—but somehow he knew it would work.

He landed on his feet holding a six-foot-long *pilum*. As Antinous turned to face him, Jason thrust the Imperial gold point through the ghoul's chest.

Antinous looked down incredulously. "You—"

"Enjoy the Fields of Punishment." Jason yanked out his *pilum* and Antinous crumbled to dirt.

Jason kept fighting, spinning his javelin—slicing through ghosts, knocking ghouls off their feet.

Across the courtyard, Annabeth fought like a demon too. Her drakon-bone sword scythed down any suitors stupid enough to face her.

Over by the sand fountain, Piper had also drawn her sword—the jagged bronze blade she'd taken from Zethes the Boread. She stabbed and parried with her right hand, occasionally shooting tomatoes from the cornucopia in her left, while yelling at the suitors, "Save yourselves! I'm too dangerous!"

That must have been exactly what they wanted to hear, because her opponents kept running away, only to freeze in confusion a few yards downhill, then charge back into the fight.

The Greek tyrant Hippias lunged at Piper, his dagger raised, but Piper blasted him point-blank in the chest with a lovely pot roast. He tumbled backward into the fountain and screamed as he disintegrated.

An arrow whistled toward Jason's face. He blew it aside with a gust of wind, then cut through a line of sword-wielding ghouls and noticed a dozen suitors regrouping by the fountain to charge Annabeth. He lifted his javelin to the sky. A bolt of lightning ricocheted off the point and blasted the ghosts to ions, leaving a smoking crater where the earthen fountain had been.

Over the last few months, Jason had fought many battles, but he'd forgotten what it was like to feel *good* in combat. Of course he was still afraid, but a huge weight had been lifted from his shoulders. For the first time since waking up in Arizona with his memories erased, Jason felt *whole*. He knew who he was. He had chosen his family, and it had nothing to do with Beryl Grace or even Jupiter. His family included all the demigods who fought at his side, Roman and Greek, new friends and old. He wasn't going to let anyone break his family apart.

He summoned the winds and tossed three ghouls off the side of the hill like rag dolls. He skewered a fourth, then willed his javelin to shrink back to a sword and hacked through another group of spirits.

Soon no more enemies faced him. The remaining ghosts began to disappear on their own. Annabeth cut down Hasdrubal the Carthaginian, and Jason made the mistake of sheathing his sword.

Pain flared in his lower back—so sharp and cold he thought Khione the snow goddess had touched him.

Next to his ear, Michael Varus snarled, "Born a Roman, die a Roman."

The tip of a golden sword jutted through the front of Jason's shirt, just below his rib cage.

Jason fell to his knees. Piper's scream sounded miles away. He felt like he'd been immersed in salty water—his body weightless, his head swaying.

Piper charged toward him. He watched with detached emotion as her sword passed over his head and cut through Michael Varus's armor with a metallic *ka-chunk*.

A burst of cold parted Jason's hair from behind. Dust settled around him, and an empty legionnaire's helmet rolled across the stones. The evil demigod was gone—but he had made a lasting impression.

"Jason!" Piper grabbed his shoulders as he began to fall sideways. He gasped as she pulled the sword out of his back.

Then she lowered him to the ground, propping his head against a stone.

Annabeth ran to their side. She had a nasty cut on the side of her neck.

"Gods." Annabeth stared at the wound in Jason's gut. "Oh, gods."

"Thanks," Jason groaned. "I was afraid it might be bad."

His arms and legs started to tingle as his body went into crisis mode, sending all the blood to his chest. The pain was dull, which surprised him, but his shirt was soaked red. The wound was smoking. He was pretty sure sword wounds weren't supposed to smoke.

"You're going to be fine." Piper spoke the words like an order. Her tone steadied his breathing. "Annabeth, ambrosia!"

Annabeth stirred. "Yeah. Yeah, I got it." She ripped through her supply pouch and unwrapped a piece of godly food.

"We have to stop the bleeding." Piper used her dagger to cut fabric from the bottom of her dress. She ripped the cloth into bandages.

Jason dimly wondered how she knew so much first aid. She wrapped the wounds on his back and stomach while Annabeth pushed tiny bites of ambrosia into his mouth.

Annabeth's fingers trembled. After all the things she'd been through, Jason found it odd that she would freak out now while Piper acted so calm. Then it occurred to him— Annabeth could *afford* to be scared for him. Piper couldn't. She was completely focused on trying to save him.

Annabeth fed him another bite. "Jason, I—I'm sorry. About your mom. But the way you handled it . . . that was so brave."

Jason tried not to close his eyes. Every time he did, he saw his mom's spirit disintegrating.

"It wasn't her," he said. "At least, no part of her I could save. There was no other choice."

Annabeth took a shaky breath. "No other *right* choice, maybe, but . . . a friend of mine, Luke. His mom . . . similar problem. He didn't handle it as well."

Her voice broke. Jason didn't know much about Annabeth's past, but Piper glanced over in concern.

"I've bandaged as much as I can," she said. "Blood is still soaking through. And the smoke. I don't get that."

"Imperial gold," Annabeth said, her voice quavering. "It's deadly to demigods. It's only a matter of time before—"

"He'll be all right," Piper insisted. "We've got to get him back to the ship."

"I don't feel that bad," Jason said. And it was true. The ambrosia had cleared his head. Warmth was seeping back into his limbs. "Maybe I could fly. . . ."

Jason sat up. His vision turned a pale shade of green. "Or maybe not. . . ."

Piper caught his shoulders as he keeled sideways. "Whoa, Sparky. We need to contact the *Argo II*, get help."

"You haven't called me Sparky in a long time."

Piper kissed his forehead. "Stick with me and I'll insult you all you want."

Annabeth scanned the ruins. The magic veneer had faded,

leaving only broken walls and excavation pits. "We could use the emergency flares, but—"

"No," Jason said. "Leo would blast the top of the hill with Greek fire. Maybe if you guys helped me, I could walk—"

"Absolutely not," Piper objected. "That would take too long." She rummaged in her belt pouch and pulled out a compact mirror. "Annabeth, you know Morse code?"

"Of course."

"So does Leo." Piper handed her the mirror. "He'll be watching from the ship. Go to the ridge—"

"And flash him!" Annabeth's face reddened. "That came out wrong. But yeah, good idea."

She ran to the edge of the ruins.

Piper pulled out a flask of nectar and gave Jason a sip. "Hang in there. You are *not* dying from a stupid body piercing."

Jason managed a weak smile. "At least it wasn't a head injury this time. I stayed conscious the entire fight."

"You defeated like two hundred enemies," Piper said. "You were *scary* amazing."

"You guys helped."

"Maybe, but . . . Hey, stay with me."

Jason's head started to droop. The cracks in the stones came into sharper focus.

"Little dizzy," he muttered.

"More nectar," Piper ordered. "There. Taste okay?"

"Yeah. Yeah, fine."

In fact the nectar tasted like liquid sawdust, but Jason kept that to himself. Ever since the House of Hades, when he'd resigned his praetorship, ambrosia and nectar didn't taste like his favorite foods from Camp Jupiter. It was as if the memory of his old home no longer had the power to heal him.

*Born a Roman, die a Roman,* Michael Varus had said.

He looked at the smoke curling from his bandages. He had worse things to worry about than blood loss. Annabeth was right about Imperial gold. The stuff was deadly to demigods as well as monsters. The wound from Varus's blade would do its best to eat away at Jason's life force.

He'd seen a demigod die like that once before. It hadn't been fast or pretty.

*I can't die,* he told himself. *My friends are depending on me.*

Antinous's words rang in his ears—about the giants in Athens, the impossible trip facing the *Argo II,* the mysterious hunter Gaea had sent to intercept the Athena Parthenos.

"Reyna, Nico, and Coach Hedge," he said. "They're in danger. We need to warn them."

"We'll take care of it when we get back to the ship," Piper promised. "Your job right now is to relax." Her tone was light and confident, but her eyes brimmed with tears. "Besides, those three are a tough group. They'll be fine."

Jason hoped she was right. Reyna had risked so much to help them. Coach Hedge was annoying sometimes, but he'd been a loyal protector for the entire crew. And Nico . . . Jason felt especially worried about him.

Piper brushed her thumb against the scar on his lip. "Once the war is over . . . everything will work out for Nico. You've done what you could, being a friend to him."

Jason wasn't sure what to say. He hadn't told Piper anything about his conversations with Nico. He'd kept di Angelo's secret.

Still . . . Piper seemed to sense what was wrong. As a daughter of Aphrodite, maybe she could tell when somebody was struggling with heartache. She hadn't pressured Jason to talk about it, though. He appreciated that.

Another wave of pain made him wince.

"Concentrate on my voice." Piper kissed his forehead. "Think about something good. Birthday cake in the park in Rome—"

"That was nice."

"Last winter," she suggested. "The s'mores fight at the campfire."

"I totally got you."

"You had marshmallows in your hair for days!"

"I did not."

Jason's mind drifted back to better times.

He just wanted to stay there—talking with Piper, holding her hand, not worrying about giants or Gaea or his mother's madness.

He knew they should get back to the ship. He was in bad shape. They had the information they'd come for. But as he lay there on the cool stones, Jason felt a sense of incompleteness. The story of the suitors and Queen Penelope . . . his thoughts about family . . . his recent dreams. Those things all swirled around in his head. There was something more to this place—something he'd missed.

Annabeth came back limping from the edge of the hill.

"Are you hurt?" Jason asked her.

Annabeth glanced at her ankle. "It's fine. Just the old break from the Roman caverns. Sometimes when I'm stressed . . . That's not important. I signaled Leo. Frank's going to change form, fly up here, and carry you back to the ship. I need to make a litter to keep you stable."

Jason had a terrifying image of himself in a hammock, swinging between the claws of Frank the giant eagle, but he decided it would be better than dying.

Annabeth set to work. She collected scraps left behind by the suitors—a leather belt, a torn tunic, sandal straps, a red blanket, and a couple of broken spear shafts. Her hands flew across the materials—ripping, weaving, tying, braiding.

"How are you doing that?" Jason asked in amazement.

"Learned it during my quest under Rome." Annabeth kept her eyes on her work. "I'd never had a reason to try weaving before, but it's handy for certain things, like getting away from spiders. . . ."

She tied off one last bit of leather cord and *voilà*—a stretcher large enough for Jason, with spear shafts as carrying handles and safety straps across the middle.

Piper whistled appreciatively. "The next time I need a dress altered, I'm coming to you."

"Shut up, McLean," Annabeth said, but her eyes glinted with satisfaction. "Now, let's get him secured—"

"Wait," Jason said.

His heart pounded. Watching Annabeth weave the make-shift bed, Jason had remembered the story of Penelope—how she'd held out for twenty years, waiting for her husband Odysseus to return.

"A bed," Jason said. "There was a special bed in this palace."

Piper looked worried. "Jason, you've lost a lot of blood."

"I'm not hallucinating," he insisted. "The marriage bed was sacred. If there was *any* place you could talk to Juno . . ." He took a deep breath and called, "Juno!"

Silence.

Maybe Piper was right. He wasn't thinking clearly.

Then, about sixty feet away, the stone floor cracked. Branches muscled through the earth, growing in fast motion until a full-sized olive tree shaded the courtyard. Under a canopy of gray-green leaves stood a dark-haired woman in a white dress, a leopard-skin cape draped over her shoulders. Her staff was topped with a white lotus flower. Her expression was cool and regal.

"My heroes," said the goddess.

"Hera," Piper said.

"Juno," Jason corrected.

"Whatever," Annabeth grumbled. "What are you doing here, Your Bovine Majesty?"

Juno's dark eyes glittered dangerously. "Annabeth Chase. As charming as ever."

"Yeah, well," Annabeth said, "I just got back from *Tartarus*, so my manners are a little rusty, especially toward goddesses who wiped my boyfriend's memory, made him disappear for months, and then—"

"Honestly, child. Are we going to rehash this again?"

"Aren't you supposed to be suffering from split personality disorder?" Annabeth asked. "I mean—more so than usual?"

"Whoa," Jason interceded. He had plenty of reasons to hate Juno, but they had other issues to deal with. "Juno, we need your help. We—" Jason tried to sit up and immediately regretted it. His insides felt like they were being twirled on a giant spaghetti fork.

Piper kept him from falling over. "First things first," she said. "Jason is hurt. Heal him!"

The goddess knit her eyebrows. Her form shimmered unsteadily.

"Some things even the gods cannot heal," she said. "This wound touches your soul as well as your body. You must fight it, Jason Grace . . . you *must* survive."

"Yeah, thanks," he said, his mouth dry. "I'm trying."

"What do you mean, the wound touches his soul?" Piper demanded. "Why can't you—"

"My heroes, our time together is short," Juno said. "I am grateful that you called upon me. I have spent weeks in a state of pain and confusion . . . my Greek and Roman natures warring against each other. Worse, I've been forced to hide from Jupiter, who searches for me in his misguided wrath, believing that *I* caused this war with Gaea."

"Gee," Annabeth said, "why would he think that?"

Juno flashed her an irritated look. "Fortunately, this place is sacred to me. By clearing away those ghosts, you have purified it and given me a moment of clarity. I will be able to speak with you—if only briefly."

"Why is it sacred . . . ?" Piper's eyes widened. "Oh. The marriage bed!"

"Marriage bed?" Annabeth asked. "I don't see any—"

"The bed of Penelope and Odysseus," Piper explained. "One of its bedposts was a living olive tree, so it could never be moved."

"Indeed." Juno ran her hand along the olive tree's trunk. "An immovable marriage bed. Such a beautiful symbol! Like Penelope, the most faithful wife, standing her ground, fending off a hundred arrogant suitors for years because she knew her husband would return. Odysseus and Penelope—the epitome of a perfect marriage!"

Even in his dazed state, Jason was pretty sure he remembered stories about Odysseus falling for other women during his travels, but he decided not to bring that up.

"Can you advise us, at least?" he asked. "Tell us what to do?"

"Sail around the Peloponnese," said the goddess. "As you suspect, that is the only possible route. On your way, seek out the goddess of victory in Olympia. She is out of control. Unless you can subdue her, the rift between Greek and Roman can never be healed."

"You mean Nike?" Annabeth asked. "How is she out of control?"

Thunder boomed overhead, shaking the hill.

"Explaining would take too long," Juno said. "I must flee before Jupiter finds me. Once I leave, I will not be able to help you again."

Jason bit back a retort: *When did you help me the first time?*

"What else should we know?" he asked.

"As you heard, the giants have gathered in Athens. Few gods will be able to help you on your journey, but I am not the only Olympian who is out of favor with Jupiter. The twins have also incurred his wrath."

"Artemis and Apollo?" Piper asked. "Why?"

Juno's image began to fade. "If you reach the island of Delos, they might be prepared to help you. They are desperate enough to try anything to make amends. Go now. Perhaps we will meet again in Athens, if you succeed. If you do not . . ."

The goddess disappeared, or maybe Jason's eyesight simply failed. Pain rolled through him. His head lolled back. He saw a giant eagle circling high above. Then the blue sky turned black, and Jason saw nothing at all.

# V

# REYNA

DIVE-BOMBING A VOLCANO was *not* on Reyna's bucket list.

Her first view of southern Italy was from five thousand feet in the air. To the west, along the crescent of the Gulf of Naples, the lights of sleeping cities glittered in the predawn gloom. A thousand feet below her, a half-mile-wide caldera yawned at the top of a mountain, white steam pluming from the center.

Reyna's disorientation took a moment to subside. Shadow-travel left her groggy and nauseous, as if she'd been dragged from the cold waters of the *frigidarium* into the sauna at a Roman bathhouse.

Then she realized she was suspended in midair. Gravity took hold, and she began to fall.

"Nico!" she yelled.

"Pan's pipes!" cursed Gleeson Hedge.

"Whaaaaa!" Nico flailed, almost slipping out of Reyna's grip. She held tight and grabbed Coach Hedge by the shirt collar as he started to tumble away. If they got separated now, they were dead.

They plummeted toward the volcano as their largest piece of luggage—the forty-foot-tall Athena Parthenos—trailed after them, leashed to a harness on Nico's back like a very ineffective parachute.

"That's Vesuvius below us!" Reyna shouted over the wind. "Nico, teleport us out of here!"

His eyes were wild and unfocused. His dark feathery hair whipped around his face like a raven shot out of the sky. "I—I can't! No strength!"

Coach Hedge bleated. "News flash, kid! Goats can't fly! Zap us out of here or we're gonna get flattened into an Athena Parthenos omelet!"

Reyna tried to think. She could accept death if she had to, but if the Athena Parthenos was destroyed, their quest would fail. Reyna *could not* accept that.

"Nico, shadow-travel," she ordered. "I'll lend you my strength."

He stared at her blankly. "How—"

*"Do it!"*

She tightened her grip on his hand. The torch-and-sword symbol of Bellona on her forearm grew painfully hot, as if it were being seared into her skin for the first time.

Nico gasped. Color returned to his face. Just before they hit the volcano's steam plume, they slipped into shadows.

The air turned frigid. The sound of the wind was replaced by a cacophony of voices whispering in a thousand languages. Reyna's insides felt like a giant *piragua*—cold syrup trickled over crushed ice—her favorite treat from her childhood in Viejo San Juan.

She wondered why that memory would surface now, when she was on the verge of death. Then her vision cleared. Her feet rested on solid ground.

The eastern sky had begun to lighten. For a moment Reyna thought she was back in New Rome. Doric columns lined an atrium the size of a baseball diamond. In front of her, a bronze faun stood in the middle of a sunken fountain decorated with mosaic tile.

Crape myrtles and rosebushes bloomed in a nearby garden. Palm trees and pines stretched skyward. Cobblestone paths led from the courtyard in several directions—straight, level roads of good Roman construction, edging low stone houses with colonnaded porches.

Reyna turned. Behind her, the Athena Parthenos stood intact and upright, dominating the courtyard like a ridiculously oversized lawn ornament. The little bronze faun in the fountain had both his arms raised, facing Athena, so he seemed to be cowering in fear of the new arrival.

On the horizon, Mount Vesuvius loomed—a dark, humpbacked shape now several miles away. Thick pillars of steam curled from the crest.

"We're in Pompeii," Reyna realized.

"Oh, that's not good," Nico said, and immediately collapsed.

"Whoa!" Coach Hedge caught him before he hit the ground. The satyr propped him against Athena's feet and loosened the harness that attached Nico to the statue.

Reyna's own knees buckled. She'd expected some back-lash; it happened every time she shared her strength. But she hadn't anticipated so much raw anguish from Nico di Angelo. She sat down heavily, just managing to stay conscious.

*Gods of Rome.* If this was only a portion of Nico's pain . . . how could he bear it?

She tried to steady her breathing while Coach Hedge rummaged through his camping supplies. Around Nico's boots, the stones cracked. Dark seams radiated outward like a shotgun blast of ink, as if Nico's body were trying to expel all the shadows he'd traveled through.

Yesterday had been worse: an entire meadow withering, skeletons rising from the earth. Reyna wasn't anxious for that to happen again.

"Drink something." She offered him a canteen of unicorn draught—powdered horn mixed with sanctified water from the Little Tiber. They'd found it worked on Nico better than nectar, helping to cleanse the fatigue and darkness from his system with less danger of spontaneous combustion.

Nico gulped it down. He still looked terrible. His skin had a bluish tint. His cheeks were sunken. Hanging at his side, the scepter of Diocletian glowed angry purple, like a radioactive bruise.

He studied Reyna. "How did you do that . . . that surge of energy?"

Reyna turned her forearm. The tattoo still burned like hot wax: the symbol of Bellona, SPQR, with four lines for her years of service. "I don't like to talk about it," she said, "but it's a power from my mother. I can impart strength to others."

Coach Hedge looked up from his rucksack. "Seriously? Why haven't you hooked me up, Roman girl? I want super-muscles!"

Reyna frowned. "It doesn't work like that, Coach. I can only do it in life-and-death situations, and it's more useful in large groups. When I command troops, I can share whatever attributes I have—strength, courage, endurance—multiplied by the size of my forces."

Nico arched an eyebrow. "Useful for a Roman praetor."

Reyna didn't answer. She preferred not to speak of her power for exactly this reason. She didn't want the demigods under her command to think she was controlling them, or that she'd become a leader because she had some special magic. She could only share the qualities she already possessed, and she couldn't help anyone who wasn't worthy of being a hero.

Coach Hedge grunted. "Too bad. Super-muscles would be nice." He went back to sorting through his pack, which seemed to hold a bottomless supply of cooking utensils, survivalist gear, and random sports equipment.

Nico took another swig of unicorn draught. His eyes were heavy with exhaustion, but Reyna could tell he was fighting to stay awake.

"You stumbled just now," he noted. "When you use your power . . . do you get some sort of, um, feedback from me?"

"It's not mind-reading," she said. "Not even an empathy link. Just . . . a temporary wave of exhaustion. Primal emotions. Your pain washes over me. I take on some of your burden."

Nico's expression became guarded.

He twisted the silver skull ring on his finger, the same way Reyna did with *her* silver ring when she was thinking. Sharing a habit with the son of Hades made her uneasy.

She'd felt more pain from Nico in their brief connection than she had from her entire legion during the battle against the giant Polybotes. It had drained her worse than the *last* time she'd used her power, to sustain her pegasus Scipio during their journey across the Atlantic.

She tried to push away that memory. Her brave winged friend, dying from poison, his muzzle in her lap, looking at her trustingly as she raised her dagger to end his misery . . . Gods, no. She couldn't dwell on that or it would break her.

But the pain she'd felt from Nico was sharper.

"You should rest," she told him. "After two jumps in a row, even with a little help . . . you're lucky to be alive. We'll need you to be ready again by nightfall."

She felt bad asking him to do something so impossible. Unfortunately, she'd had a lot of practice pushing demigods beyond their limits.

Nico clenched his jaw and nodded. "We're stuck here now." He scanned the ruins. "But Pompeii is the *last* place I would've chosen to land. This place is full of *lemures*."

"Lemurs?" Coach Hedge seemed to be making some sort of snare out of kite string, a tennis racket, and a hunting knife. "You mean those cute fuzzy critters—"

"*No.*" Nico sounded annoyed, like he got that question a lot. "*Lemures.* Unfriendly ghosts. All Roman cities have them, but in Pompeii—"

"The whole city was wiped out," Reyna remembered. "In 79 c.e., Vesuvius erupted and covered the town in ash."

Nico nodded. "A tragedy like that creates a *lot* of angry spirits."

Coach Hedge eyed the distant volcano. "It's steaming. Is that a bad sign?"

"I—I'm not sure." Nico picked at a hole in the knee of his black jeans. "Mountain gods, the *ourae*, can sense children of Hades. It's possible that's why we were pulled off course. The spirit of Vesuvius might have been intentionally trying to kill us. But I doubt the mountain can hurt us this far away. Working up to a full eruption would take too long. The immediate threat is all around us."

The back of Reyna's neck tingled.

She'd grown used to Lares, the friendly spirits at Camp Jupiter, but even *they* made her uneasy. They didn't have a good understanding of personal space. Sometimes they'd walk right through her, leaving her with vertigo. Being in Pompeii gave Reyna the same feeling, as if the whole city was one big ghost that had swallowed her whole.

She couldn't tell her friends how much she feared ghosts, or why she feared them. The whole reason she and her sister had run away from San Juan all those years ago . . . that secret had to stay buried.

"Can you keep them at bay?" she asked.

Nico turned up his palms. "I've sent out that message: *Stay away*. But once I'm asleep, it won't do us much good."

Coach Hedge patted his tennis-racket-knife contraption.

"Don't worry, kid. I'm going to line the perimeter with alarms and snares. Plus, I'll be watching over you the whole time with my baseball bat."

That didn't seem to reassure Nico, but his eyes were already half-closed. "Okay. But . . . go easy. We don't want another Albania."

"No," Reyna agreed.

Their first shadow-travel experience together, two days ago, had been a total fiasco, possibly the most humiliating episode in Reyna's long career. Perhaps someday, if they survived, they would look back on it and laugh, but not now. The three of them had agreed never to speak of it. What happened in Albania would *stay* in Albania.

Coach Hedge looked hurt. "Fine, whatever. Just rest, kid. We got you covered."

"All right," Nico relented. "Maybe a little . . ." He managed to take off his aviator jacket and wad it into a pillow before he keeled over and began to snore.

Reyna marveled at how peaceful he looked. The worry lines vanished. His face became strangely angelic . . . like his surname, *di Angelo*. She could almost believe he was a regular fourteen-year-old boy, not a son of Hades who had been pulled out of time from the 1940s and forced to endure more tragedy and danger than most demigods would in a lifetime.

When Nico had arrived at Camp Jupiter, Reyna didn't trust him. She'd sensed there was more to his story than being an ambassador from his father, Pluto. Now, of course, she knew the truth. He was a *Greek* demigod—the first person in living memory, perhaps the first *ever*, to go back and forth between the Roman and Greek camps without telling either group that the other existed.

Strangely, that made Reyna trust Nico more.

Sure, he wasn't Roman. He'd never hunted with Lupa or endured the brutal legion training. But Nico had proven himself in other ways. He'd kept the camps' secrets for the best of reasons, because he feared a war. He had plunged into Tartarus alone, *voluntarily*, to find the Doors of Death. He'd been captured and imprisoned by giants. He had led the crew of the *Argo II* into the House of Hades . . . and now he had accepted yet another terrible quest: risking himself to haul the Athena Parthenos back to Camp Half-Blood.

The pace of the journey was maddeningly slow. They could only shadow-travel a few hundred miles each night, resting during the day to let Nico recover; but even that required more stamina from Nico than Reyna would have thought possible.

He carried so much sadness and loneliness, so much heartache. Yet he put his mission first. He persevered. Reyna respected that. She understood that.

She'd never been a touchy-feely person, but she had the strangest desire to drape her cloak over Nico's shoulders and tuck him in. She mentally chided herself. He was a comrade, not her little brother. He wouldn't appreciate the gesture.

"Hey." Coach Hedge interrupted her thoughts. "You need sleep too. I'll take first watch and cook some grub. Those ghosts shouldn't be too dangerous now that the sun's coming up."

Reyna hadn't noticed how light it was getting. Pink and turquoise clouds striped the eastern horizon. The little bronze faun cast a shadow across the dry fountain.

"I've read about this place," Reyna realized. "It's one of the best-preserved villas in Pompeii. They call it the House of the Faun."

Gleeson glanced at the statue with distaste. "Yeah, well, today it's the House of the *Satyr.*"

Reyna managed a smile. She was starting to appreciate the differences between satyrs and fauns. If she ever fell asleep with a *faun* on duty, she'd wake up with her supplies stolen, a mustache drawn on her face, and the faun long gone. Coach Hedge was different—mostly *good* different, though he did have an unhealthy obsession with martial arts and baseball bats.

"All right," she agreed. "You take first watch. I'll put Aurum and Argentum on guard duty with you."

Hedge looked like he wanted to protest, but Reyna whistled sharply. The metallic greyhounds materialized from the ruins, racing toward her from different directions. Even after so many years, Reyna had no idea where they came from or where they went when she dismissed them, but seeing them lifted her spirits.

Hedge cleared his throat. "You *sure* those aren't Dalmatians? They look like Dalmatians."

"They're greyhounds, Coach." Reyna had no idea why Hedge feared Dalmatians, but she was too tired to ask right now. "Aurum, Argentum, guard us while I sleep. Obey Gleeson Hedge."

The dogs circled the courtyard, keeping their distance from the Athena Parthenos, which radiated hostility toward everything Roman.

Reyna herself was only now getting used to it, and she was pretty sure the statue did not appreciate being relocated in the middle of an ancient Roman city.

She lay down and pulled her purple cloak over herself. Her fingers curled around the pouch at her belt, where she kept the silver coin Annabeth had given her before they parted company in Epirus.

*It's a sign that things can change,* Annabeth had told her. *The Mark of Athena is yours now. Maybe the coin will bring you luck.*

Whether that luck would be good or bad, Reyna wasn't sure.

She took one last look at the bronze faun cowering before the sunrise and the Athena Parthenos. Then she closed her eyes and slipped into dreams.

# V I

# REYNA

**MOST OF THE TIME**, Reyna could control her nightmares.

She had trained her mind to start all her dreams in her favorite place—the Garden of Bacchus on the tallest hill in New Rome. She felt safe and tranquil there. When visions invaded her sleep—as they always did with demigods—she could contain them by imagining they were reflections in the garden's fountain. This allowed her to sleep peacefully and avoid waking up the next morning in a cold sweat.

Tonight, however, she wasn't so lucky.

The dream began well enough. She stood in the garden on a warm afternoon, the arbor heavy with blooming honeysuckle. In the central fountain, the little statue of Bacchus spouted water into the basin.

The golden domes and red-tiled roofs of New Rome spread out below her. Half a mile west rose the fortifications of Camp Jupiter. Beyond that, the Little Tiber curved gently around the valley, tracing the edge of the Berkeley Hills, hazy and golden in the summer light.

Reyna held a cup of hot chocolate, her favorite drink.

She exhaled contentedly. This place was worth defending—for herself, for her friends, for all demigods. Her four years at Camp Jupiter hadn't been easy, but they'd been the best time of Reyna's life.

Suddenly the horizon darkened. Reyna thought it might be a storm. Then she realized a tidal wave of dark loam was rolling across the hills, turning the skin of the earth inside out, leaving nothing behind.

Reyna watched in horror as the earthen tide reached the edge of the valley. The god Terminus sustained a magical barrier around the camp, but it slowed the destruction for only a moment. Purple light sprayed upward like shattered glass, and the tide poured through, shredding trees, destroying roads, wiping the Little Tiber off the map.

It's a vision, Reyna thought. I can control this.

She tried to change the dream. She imagined that the destruction was only a reflection in the fountain, a harmless video image, but the nightmare continued in full vivid scope.

The earth swallowed the Field of Mars, obliterating every trace of forts and trenches from the war games. The city's aqueduct collapsed like a line of children's blocks. Camp Jupiter itself fell—watchtowers crashing down, walls and barracks disintegrating. The screams of demigods were silenced, and the earth moved on.

A sob built in Reyna's throat. The gleaming shrines and

monuments on Temple Hill crumbled. The coliseum and the hippodrome were swept away. The tide of earth reached the Pomerian line and roared straight into the city. Families ran through the forum. Children cried in terror.

The Senate House imploded. Villas and gardens disappeared like crops under a tiller. The tide churned uphill toward the Garden of Bacchus—the last remnant of Reyna's world.

*You left them helpless, Reyna Ramírez-Arellano.* A woman's voice issued from the black terrain. *Your camp will be destroyed. Your quest is a fool's errand. My hunter comes for you.*

Reyna tore herself from the garden railing. She ran to the fountain of Bacchus and gripped the rim of the basin, staring desperately into the water. She willed the nightmare to become a harmless reflection.

*THUNK.*

The basin broke in half, split by an arrow the size of a rake. Reyna stared in shock at the raven-feather fletching, the shaft painted red, yellow, and black like a coral snake, the Stygian iron point embedded in her gut.

She looked up through a haze of pain. At the edge of the garden, a dark figure approached—the silhouette of a man whose eyes shone like miniature headlamps, blinding Reyna. She heard the scrape of iron against leather as he drew another arrow from his quiver.

Then her dream changed.

The garden and the hunter vanished, along with the arrow in Reyna's stomach.

She found herself in an abandoned vineyard. Stretched out

before her, acres of dead grapevines hung in rows on wooden lattices, like gnarled miniature skeletons. At the far end of the fields stood a cedar-shingled farmhouse with a wraparound porch. Beyond that, the land dropped off into the sea.

Reyna recognized this place: the Goldsmith Winery on the north shore of Long Island. Her scouting parties had secured it as a forward base for the legion's assault on Camp Half-Blood.

She had ordered the bulk of the legion to remain in Manhattan until she told them otherwise, but obviously Octavian had disobeyed her.

The entire Twelfth Legion was camped in the northernmost field. They'd dug in with their usual military precision—ten-foot-deep trenches and spiked earthen walls around the perimeter, a watchtower on each corner armed with ballistae. Inside, tents were arranged in neat rows of white and red. The standards of all five cohorts curled in the wind.

The sight of the legion should have lifted Reyna's spirits. It was a small force, barely two hundred demigods, but they were well trained and well organized. If Julius Caesar came back from the dead, he would've had no trouble recognizing Reyna's troops as worthy soldiers of Rome.

But they had no business being so close to Camp Half-Blood. Octavian's insubordination made Reyna clench her fists. He was intentionally provoking the Greeks, hoping for battle.

Her dream vision zoomed to the porch of the farmhouse, where Octavian sat in a gilded chair that looked suspiciously like a throne. Along with his senatorial purple-lined toga, his centurion badge, and his augur's knife, he had adopted a new honor: a white cloth mantle over his head, which marked him as *pontifex maximus*, high priest to the gods.

Reyna wanted to strangle him. No demigod in living memory had taken the title *pontifex maximus*. By doing so, Octavian was elevating himself almost to the level of emperor.

To his right, reports and maps were strewn across a low table. To his left, a marble altar was heaped with fruit and gold offerings, no doubt for the gods. But to Reyna it looked like an altar to Octavian himself.

At his side, the legion's eagle bearer, Jacob, stood at attention, sweating in his lion-skin cloak as he held the staff with the golden eagle standard of the Twelfth.

Octavian was in the midst of an audience. At the base of the stairs knelt a boy in jeans and a rumpled hoodie. Octavian's fellow centurion of the First Cohort, Mike Kahale, stood to one side with his arms crossed, glowering with obvious displeasure.

"Well, now." Octavian scanned a piece of parchment. "I see here you are a legacy, a descendant of Orcus."

The boy in the hoodie looked up, and Reyna caught her breath. *Bryce Lawrence.* She recognized his mop of brown hair, his broken nose, his cruel green eyes and smug, twisted smile.

"Yes, my lord," Bryce said.

"Oh, I'm not a *lord*." Octavian's eyes crinkled. "Just a centurion, an augur, and a humble priest doing his best to serve the gods. I understand you were dismissed from the legion for . . . ah, disciplinary problems."

Reyna tried to shout, but she couldn't make a sound. Octavian knew perfectly well why Bryce had been kicked out. Much like his godly forefather, Orcus, the underworld god of punishment, Bryce was completely remorseless. The little psychopath had survived his trials with Lupa just fine, but as soon as he arrived at Camp Jupiter he had proved to be untrainable. He had tried to set a cat on fire for fun. He had stabbed a horse and sent it stampeding through the Forum. He was even suspected of sabotaging a siege engine and getting his own centurion killed during the war games.

If Reyna had been able to prove it, Bryce's punishment would've been death. But because the evidence was circumstantial, and because Bryce's family was rich and powerful with lots of influence in New Rome, he'd gotten off with the lighter sentence of banishment.

"Yes, Pontifex," Bryce said slowly. "But, if I may, those charges were unproven. I am a loyal Roman."

Mike Kahale looked like he was doing his best not to throw up.

Octavian smiled. "I believe in second chances. You've responded to my call for recruits. You have the proper credentials and letters of recommendation. Do you pledge to follow my orders and serve the legion?"

"Absolutely," said Bryce.

"Then you are reinstated *in probatio*," Octavian said, "until you have proven yourself in combat."

He gestured at Mike, who reached in his pouch and fished out a lead *probatio* tablet on a leather cord. He hung the cord around Bryce's neck.

"Report to the Fifth Cohort," Octavian said. "They could use some new blood, some fresh perspective. If your centurion Dakota has any problem with that, tell him to talk to me."

Bryce smiled like he'd just been handed a sharp knife. "My pleasure."

"And, Bryce." Octavian's face looked almost ghoulish under his white mantle—his eyes too piercing, his cheeks too gaunt, his lips too thin and colorless. "However much money, power, and prestige the Lawrence family carries in the legion, remember that *my* family carries more. I am *personally* sponsoring you, as I am sponsoring all the other new recruits. Follow my orders, and you'll advance quickly. Soon I may have a little job for you—a chance to prove your worth. But cross me, and I will not be as lenient as Reyna. Do you understand?"

Bryce's smile faded. He looked like he wanted to say something, but he changed his mind. He nodded.

"Good," Octavian said. "Also, get a haircut. You look like one of those *Graecus* scum. Dismissed."

After Bryce left, Mike Kahale shook his head. "That makes two dozen now."

"It's good news, my friend," Octavian assured him. "We need the extra manpower."

"Murderers. Thieves. Traitors."

"Loyal demigods," Octavian said, "who owe their position to *me*."

Mike scowled. Until Reyna had met him, she'd never understood why people called biceps *guns*, but Mike's arms were as thick as bazooka barrels. He had broad features, a toasted-almond complexion, onyx hair, and proud dark eyes, like the old Hawaiian kings. She wasn't sure how a high school linebacker from Hilo had wound up with Venus for a mom, but no one in the legion gave him any grief about that—not once they saw him crush rocks with his bare hands.

Reyna had always liked Mike Kahale. Unfortunately, Mike was *very* loyal to his sponsor. And his sponsor was Octavian.

The pontifex rose and stretched. "Don't worry, old friend. Our siege teams have the Greek camp surrounded. Our eagles have complete air superiority. The Greeks aren't going anywhere until we're ready to strike. In eleven days, all my forces will be in place. My little surprises will be prepared. On August first, the Feast of Spes, the Greek camp will fall."

"But Reyna said—"

"We've been through this." Octavian slid his iron dagger from his belt and threw it at the table, where it impaled a map of Camp Half-Blood. "Reyna has forfeited her position. She went to the ancient lands, which is against the *law*."

"But the Earth Mother—"

"—has been stirring *because* of the war between the Greek and Roman camps, yes? The gods are incapacitated, yes? And how do we solve that problem, Mike? We eliminate the division. We wipe out the Greeks. We return the gods to their proper manifestation as *Roman*. Once the gods are restored to their full power, Gaea will not dare rise. She will sink back into her slumber. We demigods will be strong and unified, as we were in the old days of the empire. Besides, the first day of August is most auspicious—the month named after my ancestor Augustus. And you know how he united the Romans?"

"He seized power and became emperor," Mike rumbled.

Octavian waved aside the comment. "Nonsense. He saved Rome by becoming *First Citizen*. He wanted peace and prosperity, not power! Believe me, Mike, I intend to follow his example. I will save New Rome, and when I do, I will remember my friends."

Mike shifted his considerable bulk. "You sound certain. Has your gift of prophecy—"

Octavian held up his hand in warning. He glanced at Jacob the eagle bearer, who was still standing at attention behind him. "Jacob, you're dismissed. Why don't you go polish the eagle or something?"

Jacob's shoulders slumped in relief. "Yes, Augur. I mean Centurion! I mean *Pontifex*! I mean—"

"Go."

"I'll go."

Once Jacob had hobbled off, Octavian's face clouded. "Mike, I told you not to speak of my, ah, problem. But to answer your question: no, there still seems to be some *interference* with Apollo's usual gift to me." He glanced resentfully at a pile of mutilated stuffed animals heaped in the corner of the porch. "I can't see the future. Perhaps that false Oracle at Camp Half-Blood is working some sort of witchcraft. But as I've told you before, in strictest confidence, Apollo spoke to me *clearly* last year at Camp Jupiter! He personally blessed my endeavors. He promised I would be remembered as the savior of the Romans."

Octavian spread his arms, revealing his harp tattoo, the symbol of his godly forefather. Seven slash marks indicated his years of service—more than any presiding officer, including Reyna.

"Never fear, Mike. We will crush the Greeks. We will stop Gaea and her minions. Then we'll take that harpy the Greeks have been harboring—the one who memorized our Sibylline Books—and we'll force her to give us the knowledge of our ancestors. Once that happens, I'm sure Apollo will restore my gift of prophecy. Camp Jupiter will be more powerful than ever. We will *rule* the future."

Mike's scowl didn't lessen, but he raised his fist in salute. "You're the boss."

"Yes, I am." Octavian pulled his dagger from the table. "Now, go check on those two dwarfs you captured. I want them properly terrified before I interrogate them again and dispatch them to Tartarus."

The dream faded.

"Hey, wake up." Reyna's eyes fluttered open. Gleeson Hedge was leaning over her, shaking her shoulder. "We got trouble."

His grave tone got her blood moving.

"What is it?" She struggled to sit up. "Ghosts? Monsters?"

Hedge scowled. "Worse. *Tourists.*"

# VII

# REYNA

**THE HORDES HAD ARRIVED.**

In groups of twenty or thirty, tourists swarmed through the ruins, milling around the villas, wandering the cobblestone paths, gawking at the colorful frescoes and mosaics.

Reyna worried how the tourists would react to a forty-foot-tall statue of Athena in the middle of the courtyard, but the Mist must have been working overtime to obscure the mortals' vision.

Each time a group approached, they'd stop at the edge of the courtyard and stare in disappointment at the statue. One British tour guide announced, "Ah, scaffolding. It appears this area is undergoing restoration. Pity. Let's move along."

And off they went.

At least the statue didn't rumble, "DIE, UNBELIEVERS!" and zap the mortals to dust. Reyna had once dealt with a statue of the goddess Diana like that. It hadn't been her most relaxing day.

She recalled what Annabeth had told her about the Athena Parthenos: its magical aura both attracted monsters and kept them at bay. Sure enough, every so often, out of the corner of her eye, Reyna would spot glowing white spirits in Roman clothes flitting among the ruins, frowning at the statue in consternation.

"Those *lemures* are everywhere," Gleeson muttered. "Keeping their distance for now—but come nightfall, we'd better be ready to move. Ghosts are always worse at night."

Reyna didn't need to be reminded of that.

She watched as an elderly couple in matching pastel shirts and Bermuda shorts tottered through a nearby garden. She was glad they didn't come any closer. Around the camp, Coach Hedge had rigged all sorts of trip wires, snares, and oversized mousetraps that wouldn't stop any self-respecting monster, but they might very well bring down a senior citizen.

Despite the warm morning, Reyna shivered from her dreams. She couldn't decide which was more terrifying—the impending destruction of New Rome, or the way Octavian was poisoning the legion from the inside.

*Your quest is a fool's errand.*

Camp Jupiter needed her. The Twelfth Legion needed her. Yet Reyna was halfway across the world, watching a satyr cook Eggo blueberry waffles on a stick over an open fire.

She wanted to talk about her nightmares, but she decided to wait until Nico woke up. She wasn't sure she'd have the courage to describe them twice.

Nico kept snoring. Reyna had discovered that once he fell asleep, it took a *lot* to wake him up. The coach could do a goat-hoof tap dance around Nico's head, and the son of Hades wouldn't even budge.

"Here." Hedge offered her a plate of flame-broiled Eggos with fresh sliced kiwi and pineapple. It all looked surprisingly good.

"Where are you getting these supplies?" Reyna marveled.

"Hey, I'm a satyr. We're *very* efficient packers." He took a bite of waffle. "We also know how to live off the land!"

As Reyna ate, Coach Hedge took out a notepad and started to write. When he was finished, he folded the paper into an airplane and tossed it into the air. A breeze carried it away.

"A letter to your wife?" Reyna guessed.

Under the rim of his baseball cap, Hedge's eyes were bloodshot. "Mellie's a cloud nymph. Air spirits send stuff by paper airplane all the time. Hopefully her cousins will keep the letter going across the ocean until it finds her. It's not as fast as an Iris-message, but, well, I want our kid to have some record of me, in case, you know . . ."

"We'll get you home," Reyna promised. "You will see your kid."

Hedge clenched his jaw and said nothing.

Reyna was pretty good at getting people to talk. She considered it essential to know her comrades-in-arms. But she'd had a tough time convincing Hedge to open up about his wife, Mellie, who was close to giving birth back at Camp Half-Blood. Reyna had trouble imagining the coach as a father, but she understood what it was like to grow up without parents. She wasn't going to let that happen to Coach Hedge's child.

"Yeah, well . . ." The satyr bit off another piece of Eggo,

including the stick he'd toasted it on. "I just wish we could move faster." He chin-pointed to Nico. "I don't see how this kid is going to last one more jump. How many more will it take us to get home?"

Reyna shared his concern. In only eleven days, the giants planned to awaken Gaea. Octavian planned to attack Camp Half-Blood on the same day. That couldn't be a coincidence. Perhaps Gaea was whispering in Octavian's ear, influencing his decisions subconsciously. Or worse: Octavian was actively in league with the earth goddess. Reyna didn't want to believe that even Octavian would knowingly betray the legion, but after what she'd seen in her dreams, she couldn't be sure.

She finished her meal as a group of Chinese tourists shuffled past the courtyard. Reyna had been awake for less than an hour, and already she was restless to get moving.

"Thanks for breakfast, Coach." She got to her feet and stretched. "If you'll excuse me, where there are tourists, there are bathrooms. I need to use the little praetors' room."

"Go ahead." The coach jangled the whistle that hung around his neck. "If anything happens, I'll blow."

Reyna left Aurum and Argentum on guard duty and strolled through the crowds of mortals until she found a visitor center with restrooms. She did her best to clean up, but she found it ironic that she was in an actual Roman city and couldn't enjoy a nice hot Roman bath. She had to settle for paper towels, a broken soap dispenser, and an asthmatic hand dryer. And the toilets . . . the less said about those, the better.

As she was walking back, she passed a small museum with a window display. Behind the glass lay a row of plaster figures, all frozen in the throes of death. A young girl was curled in a fetal position. A woman lay twisted in agony, her mouth open to scream, her arms thrown overhead. A man knelt with his head bowed, as if accepting the inevitable.

Reyna stared with a mixture of horror and revulsion. She'd read about such figures, but she'd never seen them in person. After the eruption of Vesuvius, volcanic ash had buried the city and hardened to rock around dying Pompeians. Their bodies had disintegrated, leaving behind human-shaped pockets of air. Early archaeologists had poured plaster into the holes and made these casts—creepy replicas of Ancient Romans.

Reyna found it disturbing, *wrong*, that these people's dying moments were on display like clothes in a shop window, yet she couldn't look away.

All her life she'd dreamed about coming to Italy. She had assumed it would never happen. The ancient lands were forbidden to modern demigods; the area was simply too dangerous. Nevertheless, she wanted to follow in the footsteps of Aeneas, son of Aphrodite, the first demigod to settle here after the Trojan War. She wanted to see the original Tiber River, where Lupa the wolf goddess saved Romulus and Remus.

But Pompeii? Reyna had never wanted to come here. The site of Rome's most infamous disaster, an entire city swallowed by the earth . . . After Reyna's nightmares, that hit a little too close to home.

So far in the ancient lands, she'd only seen one place on her wish list: Diocletian's Palace in Split, and even that visit had hardly gone the way she'd imagined. Reyna used to dream about going there with Jason to admire their favorite emperor's home. She pictured romantic walks with him through the old city, sunset picnics on the parapets.

Instead, Reyna had arrived in Croatia not with him, but with a dozen angry wind spirits on her tail. She'd fought her way through ghosts in the palace. On her way out, gryphons had attacked, mortally wounding her pegasus. The closest she'd gotten to Jason was finding a note he'd left for her under a bust of Diocletian in the basement.

She would only have painful memories of that place.

*Don't be bitter,* she chided herself. *Aeneas suffered too. So did Romulus, Diocletian, and all the rest. Romans don't complain about hardship.*

Staring at the plaster death figures in the museum window, she wondered what they had been thinking as they curled up to die in the ashes. Probably not: *Well, we're Romans! We shouldn't complain!*

A gust of wind blew through the ruins, making a hollow moan. Sunlight flashed against the window, momentarily blinding her.

With a start, Reyna looked up. The sun was directly overhead. How could it be noon already? She'd left the House of the Faun just after breakfast. She'd only been standing here a few minutes . . . hadn't she?

She tore herself from the museum display and hurried off, trying to shake the feeling that the dead Pompeians were whispering behind her back.

The rest of the afternoon was unnervingly quiet.

Reyna kept watch while Coach Hedge slept, but there

was nothing much to guard against. Tourists came and went. Random harpies and wind spirits flew by overhead. Reyna's dogs would snarl in warning, but the monsters didn't stop to fight.

Ghosts skulked around the edges of the courtyard, apparently intimidated by the Athena Parthenos. Reyna couldn't blame them. The longer the statue stood in Pompeii, the more anger it seemed to radiate, making Reyna's skin itchy and her nerves raw.

Finally, just after sunset, Nico woke. He wolfed down an avocado and cheese sandwich, the first time he'd shown a decent appetite since leaving the House of Hades.

Reyna hated to ruin his dinner, but they didn't have much time. As the daylight faded, the ghosts started moving closer and in greater numbers.

She told him about her dreams: the earth swallowing Camp Jupiter, Octavian closing in on Camp Half-Blood, and the hunter with the glowing eyes who had shot Reyna in the gut.

Nico stared at his empty plate. "This hunter . . . a giant, maybe?"

Coach Hedge grunted. "I'd rather not find out. I say we keep moving."

Nico's mouth twitched. "*You* are suggesting we avoid a fight?"

"Listen, cupcake, I like a smackdown as much as the next guy, but we've got enough monsters to worry about without some bounty hunter giant tracking us across the world. I don't like the sound of those huge arrows."

"For once," Reyna said, "I agree with Hedge."

Nico unfolded his aviator jacket. He put his finger through an arrow hole in the sleeve.

"I could ask for advice." Nico sounded reluctant. "Thalia Grace . . ."

"Jason's sister," Reyna said.

She'd never met Thalia. In fact, she'd only recently learned Jason *had* a sister. According to Jason, she was a Greek demigod, a daughter of Zeus, who led a group of Diana's . . . no, Artemis's followers. The whole idea made Reyna's head spin.

Nico nodded. "The Hunters of Artemis are . . . well, *hunters*. If anybody knew about this giant hunter guy, Thalia would. I could try sending her an Iris-message."

"You don't sound very excited about the idea," Reyna noticed. "Are you two . . . on bad terms?"

"We're fine."

A few feet away, Aurum snarled quietly, which meant Nico was lying.

Reyna decided not to press.

"I should also try to contact my sister, Hylla," she said. "Camp Jupiter is lightly defended. If Gaea attacks there, perhaps the Amazons could help."

Coach Hedge scowled. "No offense, but, uh . . . what's an army of Amazons going to do against a wave of dirt?"

Reyna fought down a sense of dread. She suspected Hedge was right. Against what she'd seen in her dreams, the only defense would be to prevent the giants from waking Gaea. For that, she had to put her trust in the crew of the *Argo II*.

The daylight was almost gone. Around the courtyard,

ghosts were forming a mob—hundreds of glowing Romans carrying spectral clubs or stones.

"We can talk more after the next jump," Reyna decided. "Right now, we need to get out of here."

"Yeah." Nico stood. "I think we can reach Spain this time if we're lucky. Just let me—"

The mob of ghosts vanished, like a mass of birthday candles blown out in a single breath.

Reyna's hand went to her dagger. "Where did they go?"

Nico's eyes flitted across the ruins. His expression was not reassuring. "I—I'm not sure, but I don't think it's a good sign. Keep a lookout. I'll get harnessed up. Should only take a few seconds."

Gleeson Hedge rose to his hooves. *"A few seconds you do not have."*

Reyna's stomach curled into a tiny ball.

Hedge spoke with a woman's voice—the same one Reyna had heard in her nightmare.

She drew her knife.

Hedge turned toward her, his face expressionless. His eyes were solid black. *"Be glad, Reyna Ramírez-Arellano. You will die as a Roman. You will join the ghosts of Pompeii."*

The ground rumbled. All around the courtyard, spirals of ash swirled into the air. They solidified into crude human figures—earthen shells like the ones in the museum. They stared at Reyna, their eyes ragged holes in faces of rock.

*"The earth will swallow you,"* Hedge said in the voice of Gaea. *"Just as it swallowed them."*

# VIII

# REYNA

"THERE ARE TOO MANY OF THEM." Reyna wondered bitterly how many times she'd said that in her demigod career.

She should have a button made and wear it around to save time. When she died, the words would probably be written on her tombstone: *There were too many of them.*

Her greyhounds stood on either side of her, growling at the earthen shells. Reyna counted at least twenty, closing in from every direction.

Coach Hedge continued to speak in a very womanly voice: *"The dead always outnumber the living. These spirits have waited centuries, unable to express their anger. Now I have given them bodies of earth."*

One earthen ghost stepped forward. It moved slowly, but its footfall was so heavy it cracked the ancient tiles.

"Nico?" Reyna called.

"I can't control them," he said, frantically untangling his

harness. "Something about the rock shells, I guess. I need a couple of seconds to concentrate on making the shadow-jump. Otherwise I might teleport us into another volcano."

Reyna cursed under her breath. There was no way she could fight off so many by herself while Nico prepared their escape, especially with Coach Hedge out of commission. "Use the scepter," she said. "Get me some zombies."

*"It will not help,"* Coach Hedge intoned. *"Stand aside, Praetor. Let the ghosts of Pompeii destroy this Greek statue. A true Roman would not resist."*

The earthen ghosts shuffled forward. Through their mouth holes, they made hollow whistling noises, like someone blowing across empty soda bottles. One stepped on the coach's dagger-tennis-racket trap and smashed it to pieces.

From his belt, Nico pulled the scepter of Diocletian. "Reyna, if I summon *more* dead Romans . . . who's to say they won't join this mob?"

*"I* say. I am a praetor. Get me some legionnaires, and I'll control them."

*"You shall perish,"* said the coach. *"You shall never—"*

Reyna smacked him on the head with the pommel of her knife. The satyr crumpled.

"Sorry, Coach," she muttered. "That was getting tiresome. Nico—zombies! Then concentrate on getting us out of here."

Nico raised his scepter and the ground trembled.

The earthen ghosts chose that moment to charge. Aurum leaped at the nearest one and literally bit the creature's head off with his metal fangs. The rock shell toppled backward and shattered.

Argentum was not so lucky. He sprang at another ghost, which swung its heavy arm and bashed the greyhound in his face. Argentum went flying. He staggered to his feet. His head was twisted forty-five degrees to the right. One of his ruby eyes was missing.

Anger hammered in Reyna's chest like a hot spike. She'd already lost her pegasus. She was *not* going to lose her dogs too. She slashed her knife through the ghost's chest, then drew her *gladius*. Strictly speaking, fighting with two blades wasn't very Roman, but Reyna had spent time with pirates. She'd picked up more than a few tricks.

The earthen shells crumbled easily, but they hit like sledgehammers. Reyna didn't understand how, but she knew she couldn't afford to take even one blow. Unlike Argentum, she wouldn't survive getting her head knocked sideways.

"Nico!" She ducked between two earthen ghosts, allowing them to smash each other's heads in. "Any time now!"

The ground split open down the center of the courtyard. Dozens of skeletal soldiers clawed their way to the surface. Their shields looked like giant corroded pennies. Their blades were more rust than metal. But Reyna had never been so relieved to see reinforcements.

"Legion!" she shouted. *"Ad aciem!"*

The zombies responded, pushing through the earthen ghosts to form a battle line. Some fell, crushed by stone fists. Others managed to close ranks and raise their shields.

Behind her, Nico cursed.

Reyna risked a backward glance. The scepter of Diocletian was smoking in Nico's hands.

"It's fighting me!" he yelled. "I don't think it likes summoning Romans to fight other Romans!"

Reyna knew that Ancient Romans had spent at least half their time fighting each other, but she decided not to bring that up. "Just secure Coach Hedge. Get ready to shadow-travel! I'll buy you some—"

Nico yelped. The scepter of Diocletian exploded into pieces. Nico didn't look hurt, but he stared at Reyna in shock. "I—I don't know what happened. You've got a few minutes, tops, before your zombies disappear."

"Legion!" Reyna shouted. *"Orbem formate! Gladium signe!"*

The zombies circled the Athena Parthenos, their swords ready for close-quarters fighting. Argentum dragged the unconscious Coach Hedge over to Nico, who was furiously strapping himself into the harness. Aurum stood guard, lunging at any earth ghosts who broke through the line.

Reyna fought shoulder to shoulder with the dead legionnaires, sending her strength into their ranks. She knew it wouldn't be enough. The earthen ghosts fell easily, but more kept rising from the ground in swirls of ash. Each time their stone fists connected, another zombie went down.

Meanwhile, the Athena Parthenos towered over the battle—regal, haughty, and unconcerned.

A little help would be nice, Reyna thought. Maybe a destructo-ray? Or some good old-fashioned smiting.

The statue did nothing except radiate hatred, which seemed directed equally at Reyna and the attacking ghosts.

*You want to lug me to Long Island?* the statue seemed to say. *Good luck with that, Roman scum.*

Reyna's destiny: to die defending a passive-aggressive goddess.

She kept fighting, extending more of her will into the undead troops. In return, they bombarded her with their despair and resentment.

*You fight for nothing*, the zombie legionnaires whispered in her mind. *The empire is gone.*

"For Rome!" Reyna cried hoarsely. She slashed her *gladius* through one earthen ghost and stabbed her dagger in another's chest. "Twelfth Legion Fulminata!"

All around her, zombies fell. Some were crushed in battle. Others disintegrated on their own as the residual power of Diocletian's scepter finally failed.

The earthen ghosts closed in—a sea of misshapen faces with hollow eyes.

"Reyna, now!" Nico yelled. "We're leaving!"

She glanced back. Nico had harnessed himself to the Athena Parthenos. He held the unconscious Gleeson Hedge in his arms like a damsel in distress. Aurum and Argentum had disappeared—perhaps too badly damaged to continue fighting.

Reyna stumbled.

A rock fist gave her a glancing blow to the rib cage, and her side erupted in pain. Her head swam. She tried to breathe, but it was like inhaling knives.

"Reyna!" Nico shouted again.

The Athena Parthenos flickered, about to disappear.

An earthen ghost swung at Reyna's head. She managed to dodge, but the pain in her ribs almost made her black out.

*Give up,* said the voices in her head. *The legacy of Rome is dead and buried, just like Pompeii.*

"No," she murmured to herself. "Not while I'm still alive."

Nico stretched out his hand as he slipped into the shadows. With the last of her strength, Reyna leaped toward him.

# LEO

**LEO DIDN'T WANT TO COME OUT OF THE WALL.**

He had three more braces to attach, and nobody else was skinny enough to fit in the crawl space. (One of the many advantages of being scrawny.)

Wedged between the layers of the hull with the plumbing and wiring, Leo could be alone with his thoughts. When he got frustrated, which happened about every five seconds, he could hit stuff with his mallet, and the other crew members would figure he was working, not throwing a tantrum.

One problem with his sanctuary: he only fit up to his waist. His butt and legs were still on view to the general public, which made it hard for him to hide.

"Leo!" Piper's voice came from somewhere behind him. "We need you."

The Celestial bronze O-ring slipped out of Leo's pliers and slid into the depths of the crawl space.

Leo sighed. "Talk to the pants, Piper! 'Cause the hands are busy!"

"I am *not* talking to the pants. Meeting in the mess hall. We're almost to Olympia."

"Yeah, fine. I'll be there in a sec."

"What are you doing, anyway? You've been poking around inside the hull for days."

Leo swept his flashlight across the Celestial bronze plates and pistons he'd been installing slowly but surely. "Routine maintenance."

Silence. Piper was a little too good at knowing when he was lying. "Leo—"

"Hey, while you're out there, do me a favor. I got this itch right below my—"

"Fine, I'm leaving!"

Leo allowed himself a couple more minutes to fasten the brace. His work wasn't done. Not by a long shot. But he was making progress.

Of course, he'd laid the groundwork for his secret project when he first built the *Argo II*, but he hadn't told anyone about it. He had barely been honest with himself about what he was doing.

*Nothing lasts forever,* his dad once told him. *Not even the best machines.*

Yeah, okay, maybe that was true. But Hephaestus had also said: *Everything can be reused.* Leo intended to test that theory.

It was a dangerous risk. If he failed, it would crush him. Not just emotionally. It would *physically* crush him.

The thought made him claustrophobic.

He wriggled out of the crawl space and went back into his cabin.

Well . . . *technically* it was his cabin, but he didn't sleep there. The mattress was littered with wires, nails, and the guts of several disassembled bronze machines. His three massive rolling tool cabinets—Chico, Harpo, and Groucho—took up most of the room. Dozens of power tools hung on the walls. The worktable was piled with photocopied blueprints from *On Spheres*, the forgotten Archimedes text Leo had liberated from an underground workshop in Rome.

Even if he wanted to sleep in his cabin, it would've been too cramped and dangerous. He preferred to bed down in the engine room, where the constant hum of machinery helped him fall asleep. Besides, ever since his time on the island of Ogygia, he had become fond of camping out. A bedroll on the floor was all he needed.

His cabin was only for storage . . . and for working on his most difficult projects.

He pulled his keys from his tool belt. He didn't really have time, but he unlocked Groucho's middle drawer and stared at the two precious objects inside: a bronze astrolabe he'd picked up in Bologna, and a fist-sized chunk of crystal from Ogygia. Leo hadn't figured out how to put the two things together yet, and it was driving him crazy.

He'd been hoping to get some answers when they visited Ithaca. After all, it was the home of Odysseus, the dude who had constructed the astrolabe. But judging from what Jason had said, those ruins hadn't held any answers for him—just a bunch of ill-tempered ghouls and ghosts.

Anyway, Odysseus never got the astrolabe to work. He hadn't had a crystal to use as a homing beacon. Leo did. He would have to succeed where the cleverest demigod of all time had failed.

Just Leo's luck. A super-hot immortal girl was waiting for him on Ogygia, but he couldn't figure out how to wire a stupid chunk of rock into the three-thousand-year-old navigation device. Some problems even duct tape couldn't solve.

Leo closed the drawer and locked it.

His eyes drifted to the bulletin board above his worktable, where two pictures hung side by side. The first was the old crayon drawing he'd made when he was seven years old—a diagram of a flying ship he'd seen his dreams. The second was a charcoal sketch Hazel had recently made for him.

Hazel Levesque . . . that girl was something. As soon as Leo rejoined the crew in Malta, she'd known right away that Leo was hurting inside. The first chance she got, after all that mess in the House of Hades, she'd marched into Leo's cabin and said, "Spill."

Hazel was a good listener. Leo told her the whole story. Later that evening, Hazel came back with her sketch pad and her charcoal pencils. "Describe her," she insisted. "Every detail."

It felt a little weird, helping Hazel make a portrait of Calypso—as if he were talking to a police artist: *Yes, officer, that's the girl who stole my heart!* Sounded like a freaking country song.

But describing Calypso had been easy. Leo couldn't close his eyes without seeing her.

Now her likeness gazed back at him from the bulletin board—her almond-shaped eyes, her pouty lips, her long straight hair swept over one shoulder of her sleeveless dress. He could almost smell her cinnamon fragrance. Her knit brow and the downward turn of her mouth seemed to say: *Leo Valdez, you are so full of it.*

Dang, he loved that woman!

Leo had pinned her portrait next to the drawing of the *Argo II* to remind himself that sometimes visions *do* come true. As a little kid, he'd dreamed about a flying ship. Eventually he built it. Now he would build a way to get back to Calypso.

The hum of the ship's engines changed to a lower pitch. Over the cabin loudspeaker, Festus's voice creaked and squeaked.

"Yeah, thanks, buddy," Leo said. "On my way."

The ship was descending, which meant Leo's projects would have to wait.

"Sit tight, Sunshine," he told Calypso's picture. "I'll get back to you, just like I promised."

Leo could imagine her response: *I am not waiting for you, Leo Valdez. I am not in love with you. And I certainly don't believe your foolish promises!*

The thought made him smile. He slipped his keys back into his tool belt and headed for the mess hall.

The other six demigods were eating breakfast.

Once upon a time, Leo would have worried about all of them being together belowdecks with nobody at the helm, but ever since Piper had permanently woken up Festus with her charmspeak—a feat Leo *still* did not understand—the dragon figurehead had been more than capable of running the *Argo II* by himself. Festus could navigate, check the radar, make a blueberry smoothie, and spew white-hot jets of fire at invaders—simultaneously—without even blowing a circuit.

Besides, they had Buford the Wonder Table as backup.

After Coach Hedge left on his shadow-travel expedition, Leo had decided that his three-legged table could do just as good a job as their "adult chaperone." He had laminated Buford's tabletop with a magic scroll that projected a pint-sized holographic simulation of Coach Hedge. Mini-Hedge would stomp around on Buford's top, randomly saying things like "CUT THAT OUT!" "I'M GONNA KILL YOU!" and the ever-popular "PUT SOME CLOTHES ON!"

Today, Buford was manning the helm. If Festus's flames didn't scare away the monsters, Buford's holographic Hedge definitely would.

Leo stood in the doorway of the mess hall, taking in the scene around the dining table. It wasn't often he got to see all his friends together.

Percy was eating a huge stack of blue pancakes (what was his deal with blue food?) while Annabeth chided him for pouring on too much syrup.

"You're drowning them!" she complained.

"Hey, I'm a Poseidon kid," he said. "I can't drown. And neither can my pancakes."

To their left, Frank and Hazel used their cereal bowls to flatten out a map of Greece. They looked over it, their heads close together. Every once in a while Frank's hand would cover Hazel's, just sweet and natural like they were an old married couple, and Hazel didn't even look flustered, which was real progress for a girl from the 1940s. Until recently, if somebody said *gosh darn*, she would nearly faint.

At the head of the table, Jason sat uncomfortably with his T-shirt rolled up to his rib cage as Nurse Piper changed his bandages.

"Hold still," she said. "I know it hurts."

"It's just cold," he said.

Leo could hear the pain in his voice. That stupid *gladius* blade had pierced him all the way through. The entrance wound on his back was an ugly shade of purple, and it steamed. Probably not a good sign.

Piper tried to stay positive, but privately she had told Leo how worried she was. Ambrosia, nectar, and mortal medicine could only help so much. A deep cut from Celestial bronze or Imperial gold could literally dissolve a demigod's essence from the inside out. Jason might get better. He *claimed* he felt better. But Piper wasn't so sure.

Too bad Jason wasn't a metal automaton. At least then Leo would have some idea of how to help his best friend. But with humans . . . Leo felt helpless. They broke *way* too easily.

He loved his friends. He'd do anything for them. But as he looked at the six of them—three couples, all focused on each other—he thought about the warning from Nemesis, the revenge goddess: *You will not find a place among your brethren. You will always be the seventh wheel.*

He was starting to think Nemesis was right. Assuming

Leo lived long enough, assuming his crazy secret plan worked, his destiny was with somebody else, on an island that no man ever found twice.

But for now, the best he could do was to follow his old rule: *Keep moving.* Don't get bogged down. Don't think about the bad stuff. Smile and joke even when you don't feel like it. *Especially* when you don't feel like it.

"What's up, guys?" He strolled into the mess hall. "Aw, *yes* to brownies!"

He grabbed the last one—from a special sea salt recipe they'd picked up from Aphros the fish centaur at the bottom of the Atlantic.

The intercom crackled. Buford's Mini-Hedge yelled over the speakers, "PUT SOME CLOTHES ON!"

Everyone jumped. Hazel ended up five feet away from Frank. Percy spilled syrup in his orange juice. Jason awkwardly wriggled back into his T-shirt, and Frank turned into a bulldog.

Piper glared at Leo. "I thought you were getting rid of that stupid hologram."

"Hey, Buford's just saying good morning. He loves his hologram! Besides, we all miss the coach. And Frank makes a cute bulldog."

Frank morphed back into a burly, grumpy Chinese Canadian dude. "Just sit down, Leo. We've got stuff to talk about."

Leo squeezed in between Jason and Hazel. He figured they were the least likely to smack him if he made bad jokes. He took a bite of his brownie and grabbed a pack of Italian junk food—Fonzies—to round out his balanced breakfast. He'd become kind of addicted to the things since buying some in Bologna. They were cheesy and corny—two of his favorite qualities.

"So . . ." Jason winced as he leaned forward. "We're going to stay airborne and drop anchor as close as we can to Olympia. It's farther inland than I'd like—about five miles—but we don't have much choice. According to Juno, we have to find the goddess of victory and, um . . . subdue her."

Uncomfortable silence around the table.

With the new drapes covering the holographic walls, the mess hall was darker and gloomier than it should've been, but that couldn't be helped. Ever since the Kerkopes dwarf twins had short-circuited the walls, the real-time video feed from Camp Half-Blood often fuzzed out, changing into playback of extreme dwarf close-ups—red whiskers, nostrils, and bad dental work. It wasn't helpful when you were trying to eat or have a serious conversation about the fate of the world.

Percy sipped his syrup-flavored orange juice. He seemed to find it okay. "I'm cool with fighting the occasional goddess, but isn't Nike one of the *good* ones? I mean, personally, I *like* victory. I can't get enough of it."

Annabeth drummed her fingers on the table. "It does seem strange. I understand why Nike would be in Olympia—home of the Olympics and all that. The contestants sacrificed to her. Greeks and Romans worshipped her there for, like, twelve hundred years, right?"

"Almost to the end of the Roman Empire," Frank agreed. "Romans called her *Victoria*, but same difference. Everybody loved her. Who doesn't like to win? Not sure why we would have to subdue her."

Jason frowned. A wisp of steam curled from the wound under his shirt. "All I know . . . the ghoul Antinous said *Victory runs rampant in Olympia.* Juno warned us that we could never heal the rift between the Greeks and Romans unless we defeated victory."

"How do we defeat victory?" Piper wondered. "Sounds like one of those impossible riddles."

"Like making stones fly," Leo said, "or eating only one Fonzie."

He popped a handful into his mouth.

Hazel wrinkled her nose. "That stuff is going to kill you."

"You kidding? So many preservatives in these things, I'll live forever. But, hey, about this victory goddess being popular and great— Don't you guys remember what her kids are like at Camp Half-Blood?"

Hazel and Frank had never been to Camp Half-Blood, but the others nodded gravely.

"He's got a point," Percy said. "Those kids in Cabin Seventeen—they're *super*-competitive. When it comes to capture the flag, they're almost worse than the Ares kids. Uh, no offense, Frank."

Frank shrugged. "You're saying Nike has a dark side?"

"Her *kids* sure do," Annabeth said. "They never turn down a challenge. They *have* to be number one at everything. If their mom is that intense . . ."

"Whoa." Piper put her hands on the table like the ship was

rocking. "Guys, all the gods are split between their Greek and Roman aspects, right? If Nike's that way, and she's the goddess of *victory*—"

"She'd be *really* conflicted," Annabeth said. "She'd want one side or the other to win so she could declare a victor. She'd literally be fighting with herself."

Hazel nudged her cereal bowl across the map of Greece. "But we don't *want* one side or the other to win. We've got to get the Greeks and Romans on the same team."

"Maybe that's the problem," Jason said. "If the goddess of victory is running rampant, torn between Greek and Roman, she might make it impossible to bring the two camps together."

"How?" Leo asked. "Start a flame war on Twitter?"

Percy stabbed at his pancakes. "Maybe she's like Ares. That guy can spark a fight just by walking into a crowded room. If Nike radiates competitive vibes or something, she could aggravate the whole Greek-Roman rivalry big-time."

Frank pointed at Percy. "You remember that old sea god in Atlanta—Phorcys? He said that Gaea's plans always have lots of layers. This could be part of the giants' strategy—keep the two camps divided; keep the gods divided. If that's the case, we can't let Nike play us against each other. We should send a landing party of *four*—two Greeks, two Romans. The balance might help keep *her* balanced."

Listening to Zhang, Leo had one of those double-take moments. He couldn't believe how much the guy had changed in the last few weeks.

Frank wasn't just taller and buffer. He was more confident

now, more willing to take charge. Maybe that was because his magic firewood lifeline was safely stashed away in a flame-proof pouch, or maybe it was because he'd commanded a zombie legion and gotten promoted to praetor. Whatever the case, Leo had trouble seeing him as the same klutzy dude who'd once *iguanaed* his way out of Chinese handcuffs.

"I think Frank is right," Annabeth said. "A party of four. We'll have to be careful who goes. We don't want to do anything that might make the goddess, um, more unstable."

"I'll go," Piper said. "I can try charmspeaking."

Worry lines deepened around Annabeth's eyes. "Not this time, Piper. Nike is all about competition. Aphrodite . . . well, she is too, in her own way. I think Nike might see you as a threat."

Once, Leo might have made a joke about that. *Piper a threat?* The girl was like a sister to him, but if he needed help beating up a gang of thugs or subduing a victory goddess, Piper was not the first person he'd turn to.

Recently, though . . . well, Piper may not have changed as obviously as Frank, but she *had* changed. She had stabbed Khione the snow goddess in the chest. She had defeated the Boreads. She'd slashed up a flock of wild harpies singlehandedly. As for her charmspeak, she'd gotten so powerful it made Leo nervous. If she told him to eat his vegetables, he might actually *do* it.

Annabeth's words didn't seem to upset her. Piper just nodded and scanned the group. "Who should go, then?"

"Jason and Percy shouldn't go together," Annabeth said.

"Jupiter and Poseidon—bad combination. Nike could start you two fighting easily."

Percy gave her a sideways smile. "Yeah, we can't have another incident like in Kansas. I might kill my bro Jason."

"Or I might kill my bro Percy," Jason said amiably.

"Which proves my point," Annabeth said. "We also shouldn't send Frank and me together. Mars and Athena—that would be just as bad."

"Okay," Leo broke in. "So Percy and me for the Greeks. Frank and Hazel for the Romans. Is that the ultimate non-competitive dream team or what?"

Annabeth and Frank exchanged war-godly looks.

"It could work," Frank decided. "I mean, *no* combination is going to be perfect, but Poseidon, Hephaestus, Pluto, Mars . . . I don't see any huge antagonism there."

Hazel traced her finger along the map of Greece. "I still wish we could've gone through the Gulf of Corinth. I was hoping we could visit Delphi, maybe get some advice. Plus it's such a long way around the Peloponnese."

"Yeah." Leo's heart sank when he looked at how much coastline they still had to navigate. "It's July twenty-second already. Counting today, only ten days until—"

"I know," Jason said. "But Juno was clear. The shorter way would have been suicide."

"And as for Delphi . . ." Piper leaned toward the map. The blue harpy feather in her hair swung like a pendulum. "What's going on there? If Apollo doesn't have his Oracle anymore . . ."

Percy grunted. "Probably something to do with that creep Octavian. Maybe he was *so* bad at telling the future, he broke Apollo's powers."

Jason managed a smile, though his eyes were cloudy from pain. "Hopefully we can find Apollo and Artemis. Then you can ask him yourself. Juno said the twins might be willing to help us."

"A lot of unanswered questions," Frank muttered. "A lot of miles to cover before we get to Athens."

"First things first," Annabeth said. "You guys have to find Nike and figure out how to subdue her . . . whatever Juno meant by that. I still don't understand how you defeat a goddess who controls victory. Seems impossible."

Leo started to grin. He couldn't help it. Sure, they only had ten days to stop the giants from waking Gaea. Sure, he could die before dinnertime. But he loved being told that something was impossible. It was like someone handing him a lemon meringue pie and telling him not to throw it. He just couldn't resist the challenge.

"We'll see about that." He rose to his feet. "Let me get my collection of grenades and I'll meet you guys on deck!"

# X

# LEO

"Smart call back there," Percy said, "choosing the air-conditioning."

He and Leo had just searched the museum. Now they were sitting on a bridge that spanned the Kladeos River, their feet dangling over the water as they waited for Frank and Hazel to finish scouting the ruins.

To their left, the Olympic valley shimmered in the afternoon heat. To their right, the visitors' lot was crammed with tour buses. Good thing the *Argo II* was moored a hundred feet in the air, because they never would've found parking.

Leo skipped a stone across the river. He wished Hazel and Frank would get back. He felt awkward hanging out with Percy.

For one thing, he wasn't sure what kind of small talk to make with a guy who'd recently come back from Tartarus. *Catch that last episode of* Doctor Who? *Oh, right. You were trudging through the Pit of Eternal Damnation!*

Percy had been intimidating enough *before*—summoning hurricanes, dueling pirates, killing giants in the Colosseum. . . .

Now . . . well, after what happened in Tartarus, it seemed like Percy had graduated to a totally different level of butt-kickery.

Leo had trouble even thinking of him as part of the same *camp*. The two of them had never been at Camp Half-Blood at the same time. Percy's leather necklace had four beads for four completed summers. Leo's leather necklace had exactly *none*.

The only thing they had in common was Calypso, and every time Leo thought about *that*, he wanted to punch Percy in the face.

Leo kept thinking he should bring it up, just to clear the air, but the timing never seemed right. And as the days went by, the subject got harder and harder to broach.

"What?" Percy asked.

Leo stirred. "What, what?"

"You were staring at me, like, *angry*."

"Was I?" Leo tried to muster a joke, or at least a smile, but he couldn't. "Um, sorry."

Percy gazed at the river. "I suppose we need to talk." He opened his hand and the stone Leo had skipped flew out of the stream, right into Percy's palm.

Oh, Leo thought, we're showing off now?

He considered shooting a column of fire at the nearest tour bus and blowing up the gas tank, but he decided that might be a tad dramatic. "Maybe we *should* talk. But not—"

"Guys!" Frank stood at the far end of the parking lot,

waving at them to come over. Next to him, Hazel sat astride her horse Arion, who had appeared unannounced as soon as they'd landed.

Saved by the Zhang, Leo thought.

He and Percy jogged over to meet their friends.

"This place is huge," Frank reported. "The ruins stretch from the river to the base of that mountain over there, about half a kilometer."

"How far is that in regular measurements?" Percy asked.

Frank rolled his eyes. "That *is* a regular measurement in Canada and the *rest* of the world. Only you Americans—"

"About five or six football fields," Hazel interceded, feeding Arion a big chunk of gold.

Percy spread his hands. "That's all you needed to say."

"Anyway," Frank continued, "from overhead, I didn't see anything suspicious."

"Neither did I," Hazel said. "Arion took me on a complete loop around the perimeter. A lot of tourists, but no crazy goddess."

The big stallion nickered and tossed his head, his neck muscles rippling under his butterscotch coat.

"Man, your horse can cuss." Percy shook his head. "He doesn't think much of Olympia."

For once, Leo agreed with the horse. He didn't like the idea of tromping through fields full of ruins under a blazing sun, shoving his way through hordes of sweaty tourists while searching for a split-personality victory goddess. Besides, Frank had already flown over the whole valley as an eagle. If his sharp eyes hadn't seen anything, maybe there was nothing to see.

On the other hand, Leo's tool belt pockets were full of dangerous toys. He would hate to go home without blowing anything up.

"So we blunder around together," he said, "and let trouble find us. It's always worked before."

They poked around for a while, avoiding tour groups and ducking from one patch of shade to the next. Not for the first time, Leo was struck by how similar Greece was to his home state of Texas—the low hills, the scrubby trees, the drone of cicadas, and the oppressive summer heat. Switch out the ancient columns and ruined temples for cows and barbed wire, and Leo would've felt right at home.

Frank found a tourist pamphlet (seriously, that dude would read the ingredients on a soup can) and gave them a running commentary on what was what.

"This is the Propylon." He waved toward a stone path lined with crumbling columns. "One of the main gates into the Olympic valley."

"Rubble!" said Leo.

"And over there"—Frank pointed to a square foundation that looked like the patio for a Mexican restaurant—"is the Temple of Hera, one of the oldest structures here."

"More rubble!" Leo said.

"And that round bandstand-looking thing—that's the Philipeon, dedicated to Philip of Macedonia."

"Even *more* rubble! First-rate rubble!"

Hazel, who was still riding Arion, kicked Leo in the arm. "Doesn't *anything* impress you?"

Leo glanced up. Her curly gold-brown hair and golden eyes matched her helmet and sword so well she might've been engineered from Imperial gold. Leo doubted Hazel would consider that a compliment, but as far as humans went, Hazel was first-rate craftsmanship.

Leo remembered their trip together through the House of Hades. Hazel had led him through that creepy maze of illusions. She'd made the sorceress Pasiphaë disappear through an imaginary hole in the floor. She'd battled the giant Clytius while Leo choked in the giant's cloud of darkness. She'd cut the chains binding the Doors of Death. Meanwhile Leo had done . . . well, pretty much nothing.

He wasn't infatuated with Hazel anymore. His heart was far away on the island of Ogygia. Still, Hazel Levesque impressed him—even when she *wasn't* sitting atop a scary immortal supersonic horse who cussed like a sailor.

He didn't say any of this, but Hazel must have picked up on his thoughts. She looked away, flustered.

Happily oblivious, Frank continued his guided tour. "And over there . . . oh." He glanced at Percy. "Uh, that semicircular depression in the hill, with the niches . . . that's a nymphaeum, built in Roman times."

Percy's face turned the color of limeade. "Here's an idea: let's not go there."

Leo had heard all about his near-death experience in the nymphaeum in Rome with Jason and Piper. "I love that idea."

They kept walking.

Once in a while, Leo's hands drifted to his tool belt. Ever since the Kerkopes had stolen it in Bologna, he was scared he might get belt-jacked again, though he doubted any monster was as good at thievery as those dwarfs. He wondered how the little crud monkeys were doing in New York. He hoped they were still having fun harassing Romans, stealing lots of shiny zippers and causing legionnaires' pants to fall down.

"This is the Pelopion," Frank said, pointing to another fascinating pile of stones.

"Come on, Zhang," Leo said. "*Pelopion* isn't even a word. What was it—a sacred spot for *plopping?*"

Frank looked offended. "It's the burial site of Pelops. This whole part of Greece, the Peloponnese, was named after him."

Leo resisted the urge to throw a grenade in Frank's face. "I suppose I should know who Pelops was?"

"He was a prince, won his wife in a chariot race. Supposedly he started the Olympic games in honor of that."

Hazel sniffed. "How romantic. 'Nice wife you have, Prince Pelops.' 'Thanks. I won her in a chariot race.'"

Leo didn't see how any of this was helping them find the victory goddess. At the moment, the only victory he wanted was to vanquish an ice-cold drink and maybe some nachos.

Still . . . the farther they got into the ruins, the more uneasy he felt. He flashed back to one of his earliest memories—his babysitter Tía Callida, a.k.a. Hera, encouraging him to prod a poisonous snake with a stick when he was four years old. The psycho goddess told him it was good training for being a hero, and maybe she'd been right. These days Leo spent most of his time poking around until he found trouble.

He scanned the crowds of tourists, wondering if they were regular mortals or monsters in disguise, like those *eidolons* who'd chased them in Rome. Every so often he thought he saw a familiar face—his bully cousin, Raphael; his mean third grade teacher, Mr. Borquin; his abusive foster mom, Teresa— all kinds of people who had treated Leo like dirt.

Probably he just imagined their faces, but it made him edgy. He remembered how the goddess Nemesis had appeared as his Aunt Rosa, the person Leo most resented and wanted revenge on. He wondered if Nemesis was around here some- where, watching to see what Leo would do. He still wasn't sure he'd paid his debt to that goddess. He suspected she wanted more suffering from him. Maybe today was the day.

They stopped at some wide steps leading to another ruined building—the Temple of Zeus, according to Frank.

"Used to be a huge gold-and-ivory statue of Zeus inside," Zhang said. "One of the seven wonders of the ancient world. Made by the same dude who did the Athena Parthenos."

"Please tell me we don't have to find it," Percy said. "I've had enough huge magic statues for one trip."

"Agreed." Hazel patted Arion's flank, as the stallion was acting skittish.

Leo felt like whinnying and stomping his hooves too. He was hot and agitated and hungry. He felt like they'd prodded the poisonous snake about as much as they could, and the snake was about strike back. He wanted to call it a day and return to the ship before that happened.

Unfortunately, when Frank mentioned *Temple of Zeus* and *statue*, Leo's brain had made a connection. Against his better judgment, he shared it.

"Hey, Percy," he said, "remember that statue of Nike in the museum? The one that was all in pieces?"

"Yeah?"

"Didn't it used to stand *here*, at the Temple of Zeus? Feel free to tell me I'm wrong. I'd love to be wrong."

Percy's hand went to his pocket. He slipped out his pen Riptide. "You're right. So if Nike was anywhere . . . this would be a good spot."

Frank scanned their surroundings. "I don't see anything."

"What if we promoted, like, Adidas shoes?" Percy wondered. "Would that make Nike mad enough to show up?"

Leo smiled nervously. Maybe he and Percy did share something else—a stupid sense of humor. "Yeah, I bet that would *totally* be against her sponsorship deal. THOSE ARE NOT THE OFFICIAL SHOES OF THE OLYMPICS! YOU WILL DIE NOW!"

Hazel rolled her eyes. "You're both impossible."

Behind Leo, a thunderous voice shook the ruins: "YOU WILL DIE NOW!"

Leo almost jumped out of his tool belt. He turned . . . and mentally kicked himself. He just *had* to invoke Adidas, the goddess of off-brand shoes.

Towering over him in a golden chariot, with a spear aimed at his heart, was the goddess Nike.

# LEO

THE GOLD WINGS WERE OVERKILL.

Leo could dig the chariot and the two white horses. He was okay with Nike's glittering sleeveless dress (Calypso totally rocked that style, but that wasn't relevant) and Nike's piled-up braids of dark hair circled with a gilded laurel wreath.

Her expression was wide-eyed and a little crazy, like she'd just had twenty espressos and ridden a roller coaster, but that didn't bother Leo. He could even deal with the gold-tipped spear pointed at his chest.

But those *wings*—they were polished gold, right down to the last feather. Leo could admire the intricate workmanship, but it was too much, too bright, too flashy. If her wings had been solar panels, Nike would've produced enough energy to power Miami.

"Lady," he said, "could you fold your flappers, please? You're giving me a sunburn."

"What?" Nike's head jerked toward him like a startled chicken's. "Oh . . . my brilliant plumage. Very well. I suppose you can't die in glory if you are blinded and burned."

She tucked in her wings. The temperature dropped to a normal hundred-and-twenty-degree summer afternoon.

Leo glanced at his friends. Frank stood very still, sizing up the goddess. His backpack hadn't yet morphed into a bow and quiver, which was probably prudent. He couldn't have been too freaked out, because he'd avoided turning into a giant goldfish.

Hazel was having trouble with Arion. The roan stallion nickered and bucked, avoiding eye contact with the white horses pulling Nike's chariot.

As for Percy, he held his magic ballpoint pen like he was trying to decide whether to bust out some sword moves or autograph Nike's chariot.

Nobody stepped forward to talk. Leo kind of missed having Piper and Annabeth with them. They were good at the whole *talking* thing.

He decided somebody had better say something before they all died in glory.

"So!" He pointed his index fingers at Nike. "I didn't get the briefing, and I'm pretty sure the information wasn't covered in Frank's pamphlet. Could you tell me what's going on here?"

Nike's wide-eyed stare unnerved him. Was Leo's nose on fire? That happened sometimes when he got stressed.

"We must have victory!" the goddess shrieked. "The contest must be decided! You have come here to determine the winner, yes?"

Frank cleared his throat. "Are you Nike or Victoria?"

"Argghh!" The goddess clutched the side of her head. Her horses reared, causing Arion to do the same.

The goddess shuddered and split into two separate images, which reminded Leo—ridiculously—of when he used to lie on the floor in his apartment as a kid and play with the coiled doorstop on the baseboard. He would pull it back and let it fly: *Sproing!* The stopper would shudder back and forth so fast it looked like it was splitting into two separate coils.

That's what Nike looked like: a divine doorstop, splitting in two.

On the left was the first version: glittery sleeveless dress, dark hair circled with laurels, golden wings folded behind her. On the right was a different version, dressed for war in a Roman breastplate and greaves. Short auburn hair peeked out from the rim of a tall helmet. Her wings were feathery white, her dress purple, and the shaft of her spear was fixed with a plate-sized Roman insignia—a golden SPQR in a laurel wreath.

"I am Nike!" cried the image on the left.

"I am Victoria!" cried the one on the right.

For the first time, Leo understood the old saying his *abuelo* used to use: *talking out of the side of your mouth.* This goddess was literally saying two different things at once. She kept shuddering and splitting, making Leo dizzy. He was tempted to get out his tools and adjust the idle on her carburetor, because that much vibration would make her engine fly apart.

"I am the decider of victory!" Nike screamed. "Once I stood here at the corner of Zeus's temple, venerated by all!

I oversaw the games of Olympia. Offerings from every city-state were piled at my feet!"

"Games are irrelevant!" yelled Victoria. "I am the goddess of success in battle! Roman generals worshipped me! Augustus himself erected my altar in the Senate House!"

"Ahhhh!" both voices screamed in agony. "We must decide! We must have victory!"

Arion bucked so violently that Hazel had to slide off his back to avoid getting thrown. Before she could calm him down, the horse disappeared, leaving a vapor trail through the ruins.

"Nike," Hazel said, stepping forward slowly, "you're confused, like all the gods. The Greeks and Romans are on the verge of war. It's causing your two aspects to clash."

"I know that!" The goddess shook her spear, the tip rubber-banding into two points. "I cannot abide unresolved conflict! Who is stronger? Who is the winner?"

"Lady, nobody's the winner," Leo said. "If that war happens, everybody loses."

*"No winner?"* Nike looked so shocked, Leo was pretty sure his nose *must* be on fire. "There is always a winner! *One* winner. Everyone else is a loser! Otherwise victory is meaningless. I suppose you want me to give certificates to all the contestants? Little plastic trophies to every single athlete or soldier for *participation*? Should we all line up and shake hands and tell each other, *Good game*? No! Victory must be real. It must be earned. That means it must be rare and difficult, against steep odds, and defeat *must* be the other possibility."

The goddess's two horses nipped at each other, as if getting into the spirit.

"Uh . . . okay," Leo said. "I can tell you've got strong feelings about that. But the real war is against Gaea."

"He's right," Hazel said. "Nike, you were Zeus's charioteer in the last war with the giants, weren't you?"

"Of course!"

"Then you know Gaea is the real enemy. We need your help to defeat her. The war isn't between the Greeks and Romans."

Victoria roared, "The Greeks must perish!"

"Victory or death!" Nike wailed. "One side must prevail!"

Frank grunted. "I get enough of this from my dad screaming in my head."

Victoria glared down at him. "A child of Mars, are you? A praetor of Rome? No true Roman would spare the Greeks. I cannot abide to be split and confused—I cannot think straight! Kill them! Win!"

"Not happening," Frank said, though Leo noticed Zhang's right eye was twitching.

Leo was struggling too. Nike was sending off waves of tension, setting his nerves on fire. He felt like he was crouched at the starting line, waiting for someone to yell "Go!" He had the irrational desire to wrap his hands around Frank's neck, which was stupid, since his hands wouldn't even *fit* around Frank's neck.

"Look, Miss Victory . . ." Percy tried for a smile. "We don't want to interrupt your crazy time. Maybe you can just finish this conversation with yourself and we'll come back later, with, um, some bigger weapons, and possibly some sedatives."

The goddess brandished her spear. "You will determine the matter once and for all! Today, *now*, you will decide the victor! Four of you? Excellent! We will have teams. Perhaps girls versus boys!"

Hazel said, "Uh . . . no."

"Shirts versus skins!"

"Definitely no," said Hazel.

"Greeks versus Romans!" Nike cried. "Yes, of course! Two and two. The last demigod standing wins. The others will die gloriously."

A competitive urge pulsed through Leo's body. It took all of his effort not to reach in his tool belt, grab a mallet, and whop Hazel and Frank upside their heads.

He realized how right Annabeth had been not to send anyone whose parents had natural rivalries. If Jason were here, he and Percy would probably already be on the ground, bashing each other's brains out.

He forced his fists to unclench. "Look, lady, we're not going to go all *Hunger Games* on each other. Isn't going to happen."

"But you will win a fabulous honor!" Nike reached into a basket at her side and produced a wreath of thick green laurels. "This crown of leaves could be yours! You can wear it on your head! Think of the glory!"

"Leo's right," Frank said, though his eyes were fixed on the wreath. His expression was a little too greedy for Leo's taste. "We don't fight each other. We fight the giants. You should help us."

"Very well!" The goddess raised the laurel wreath in one hand and her spear in the other.

Percy and Leo exchanged looks.

"Uh . . . does that mean you'll join us?" Percy asked. "You'll help us fight the giants?"

"That will be part of the prize," Nike said. "Whoever wins, I will consider you an ally. We will fight the giants together, and I will bestow victory upon you. But there can only be one winner. The others must be defeated, killed, destroyed utterly. So what will it be, demigods? Will you succeed in your quest, or will you cling to your namby-pamby ideas of friendship and *everybody wins* participation awards?"

Percy uncapped his pen. Riptide grew into a Celestial bronze sword. Leo was worried he might turn it on them. Nike's aura was *that* hard to resist.

Instead, Percy pointed his blade at Nike. "What if we fight you instead?"

"Ha!" Nike's eyes gleamed. "If you refuse to fight each other, you shall be persuaded!"

Nike spread her golden wings. Four metal feathers fluttered down, two on either side of the chariot. The feathers twirled like gymnasts, growing larger, sprouting arms and legs, until they touched the ground as four metallic, human-sized replicas of the goddess, each armed with a golden spear and a Celestial bronze laurel wreath that looked suspiciously like a barbed wire Frisbee.

"To the stadium!" the goddess cried. "You have five minutes to prepare. Then blood shall be spilled!"

Leo was about to say, *What if we refuse to go to the stadium?*

He got his answer before asking the question.

"Run!" Nike bellowed. "To the stadium with you, or my Nikai will kill you where you stand!"

The metal ladies unhinged their jaws and blasted out a sound like a Super Bowl crowd mixed with feedback. They shook their spears and charged the demigods.

It wasn't Leo's finest moment. Panic seized him, and he took off. His only comfort was that his friends did too—and they weren't the cowardly type.

The four metal women swept behind them in a loose semicircle, herding them to the northeast. All the tourists had vanished. Perhaps they'd fled to the air-conditioned comfort of the museum, or maybe Nike had somehow forced them to leave.

The demigods ran, tripping over stones, leaping over crumbled walls, dodging around columns and informational placards. Behind them, Nike's chariot wheels rumbled and her horses whinnied.

Every time Leo thought about slowing down, the metal ladies screamed again—what had Nike called them: Nikai? Nikettes?—filling Leo with terror.

He hated being filled with terror. It was embarrassing.

"There!" Frank sprinted toward a kind of trench between two earthen walls with a stone archway above. It reminded

Leo of those tunnels that football teams run through when they enter the field. "That's the entrance to the old Olympic stadium. It's called the crypt!"

"Not a good name!" Leo yelled.

"Why are we going there?" Percy gasped. "If that's where she wants us—"

The Nikettes screamed again and all rational thought abandoned Leo. He ran for the tunnel.

When they reached the arch, Hazel yelled, "Hold it!"

They stumbled to a stop. Percy doubled over, wheezing. Leo had noticed that Percy seemed to get winded more easily these days—probably because of that nasty acid air he'd been forced to breathe in Tartarus.

Frank peered back the way they'd come. "I don't see them anymore. They disappeared."

"Did they give up?" Percy asked hopefully.

Leo scanned the ruins. "Nah. They just herded us where they wanted us. What were those things, anyway? The Nikettes, I mean."

"Nikettes?" Frank scratched his head. "I think it was *Nikai*, plural, like *victories*."

"Yes." Hazel looked deep in thought, running her hands along the stone archway. "In some legends, Nike had an army of little victories she could send all over the world to do her bidding."

"Like Santa's elves," Percy said. "Except evil. And metal. And really loud."

Hazel pressed her fingers against the arch, as if taking its pulse. Beyond the narrow tunnel, the earthen walls opened into a long field with gently rising slopes on either side, like seating for spectators.

Leo guessed it would have been an open-air stadium back in the day—big enough for discus-throwing, javelin-catching, naked shot-put, or whatever else those crazy Greeks used to do to win a bunch of leaves.

"Ghosts linger in this place," Hazel murmured. "A lot of pain is embedded in these stones."

"Please tell me you have a plan," Leo said. "Preferably one that doesn't involve embedding my pain in the stones."

Hazel's eyes were stormy and distant, the way they'd been in the House of Hades—like she was peering into a different layer of reality. "This was the players' entrance. Nike said we have five minutes to prepare. Then she'll expect us to pass under this archway and begin the games. We won't be allowed to leave that field until three of us are dead."

Percy leaned on his sword. "I'm pretty sure death matches weren't an Olympic sport."

"Well, they are today," Hazel warned. "But I might be able to give us an edge. When we pass through, I could raise some obstacles on the field—hiding places to buy us some time."

Frank frowned. "You mean like on the Field of Mars—trenches, tunnels, that kind of thing? You can do that with the Mist?"

"I think so," Hazel said. "Nike would probably *like* to see an obstacle course. I can play her expectations against her. But it would be more than that. I can use any subterranean gateway—even this arch—to access the Labyrinth. I can raise part of the Labyrinth to the surface."

"Whoa, whoa, whoa." Percy made a time-out sign. "The Labyrinth is *bad*. We discussed this."

"Hazel, he's right." Leo remembered all too well how she'd led him through the illusionary maze in the House of Hades. They'd almost died about every six feet. "I mean, I know you're good with magic. But we've already got four screaming Nikettes to worry about—"

"You'll have to trust me," she said. "We've only got a couple of minutes now. When we pass through the arch, I can at least manipulate the playing field to our advantage."

Percy exhaled through his nose. "Twice now, I've been forced to fight in stadiums—once in Rome, and before that *in* the Labyrinth. I hate playing games for people's amusement."

"We all do," Hazel said. "But we have to put Nike off guard. We'll pretend to fight until we can neutralize those Nikettes—ugh, that's an awful name. Then we subdue Nike, like Juno said."

"Makes sense," Frank agreed. "You felt how powerful Nike was, trying to put us at each other's throats. If she's sending out those vibes to all the Greeks and Romans, there's no way we'll be able to prevent a war. We've got to get her under control."

"And how do we do that?" Percy asked. "Bonk her on the head and stuff her in a sack?"

Leo's mental gears started to turn.

"Actually," he said, "you're not far off. Uncle Leo brought some toys for all you good little demigods."

# XII

# LEO

TWO MINUTES WASN'T NEARLY ENOUGH TIME.

Leo hoped he'd given everybody the right gadgets and adequately explained what all the buttons did. Otherwise things would get ugly.

While he was lecturing Frank and Percy on Archimedean mechanics, Hazel stared at the stone archway and muttered under her breath.

Nothing seemed to change in the big grassy field beyond, but Leo was sure Hazel had some Mistalicious tricks up her sleeve.

He was just explaining to Frank how to avoid getting decapitated by his own Archimedes sphere when the sound of trumpets echoed through the stadium. Nike's chariot appeared on the field, the Nikettes arrayed in front of her with their spears and laurels raised.

"Begin!" the goddess bellowed.

Percy and Leo sprinted through the archway. Immediately, the field shimmered and became a maze of brick walls and trenches. They ducked behind the nearest wall and ran to the left. Back at the archway, Frank yelled, "Uh, die, *Graecus* scum!" A poorly aimed arrow sailed over Leo's head.

"More vicious!" Nike yelled. "Kill like you mean it!"

Leo glanced at Percy. "Ready?"

Percy hefted a bronze grenade. "I hope you labeled these right." He yelled, "Die, Romans!" and lobbed the grenade over the wall.

BOOM! Leo couldn't see the explosion, but the smell of buttery popcorn filled the air.

"Oh, no!" Hazel wailed. "Popcorn! Our fatal weakness!"

Frank shot another arrow over their heads. Leo and Percy scrambled to the left, ducking through a maze of walls that seemed to shift and turn on their own. Leo could still see open sky above him, but claustrophobia started to set in, making it hard for him to breathe.

Somewhere behind them, Nike yelled, "Try harder! That popcorn was not fatal!"

From the rumble of her chariot wheels, Leo guessed she was circling the perimeter of the field—Victory taking a victory lap.

Another grenade exploded over Percy's and Leo's heads. They dove into a trench as the green starburst of Greek fire singed Leo's hair. Fortunately, Frank had aimed high enough that the blast only *looked* impressive.

"Better," Nike called out, "but where is your aim? Don't you *want* this circlet of leaves?"

"I wish the river was closer," Percy muttered. "I want to drown her."

"Be patient, water boy."

"Don't call me *water boy*."

Leo pointed across the field. The walls had shifted, revealing one of the Nikettes about thirty yards away, standing with her back to them. Hazel must be doing her thing—manipulating the maze to isolate their targets.

"I distract," Leo said, "you attack. Ready?"

Percy nodded. "Go."

He dashed to the left as Leo pulled a ball-peen hammer from his tool belt and yelled, "Hey, Bronze Butt!"

The Nikette turned as Leo threw. His hammer clanged harmlessly off the metal lady's chest, but she must have been annoyed. She marched toward him, raising her barbed wire laurel wreath.

"Oops." Leo ducked as the metal circlet spun over his head. The wreath hit a wall behind him, punching a hole straight through the bricks, then arced backward through the air like a boomerang. As the Nikette raised her hand to catch it, Percy emerged from the trench behind her and slashed with Riptide, cutting the Nikette in half at the waist. The metal wreath shot past him and embedded in a marble column.

"Foul!" the victory goddess cried. The walls shifted and Leo saw her barreling toward them in her chariot. "You don't attack the Nikai unless you wish to die!"

A trench appeared in the goddess's path, causing her horses to balk. Leo and Percy ran for cover. Out of the corner of his eye, maybe fifty feet away, Leo saw Frank the grizzly bear jump from the top of a wall and flatten another Nikette. Two Bronze Butts down, two more to go.

"No!" Nike screamed in outrage. "No, no, no! Your lives are forfeit! Nikai, attack!"

Leo and Percy leaped behind a wall. They lay there for a second, trying to catch their breath.

Leo had trouble getting his bearings, but he guessed that was part of Hazel's plan. She was causing the terrain to shift around them—opening new trenches, changing the slope of the land, throwing up new walls and columns. With luck, she would make it harder for the Nikettes to find them. Traveling just twenty feet might take them several minutes.

Still, Leo hated being disoriented. It reminded him of his helplessness in the House of Hades—the way Clytius had smothered him in darkness, snuffing out his fire, possessing his voice. It reminded him of Khione, plucking him off the deck of the *Argo II* with a gust of wind and shooting him halfway across the Mediterranean.

It was bad enough being scrawny and weak. If Leo couldn't control his own senses, his own voice, his own body . . . that didn't leave him much to rely on.

"Hey," Percy said, "if we don't make it out of this—"

"Shut up, man. We're going to make it."

"If we don't, I want you to know—I feel bad about Calypso. I failed her."

Leo stared at him, dumbfounded. "You know about me and—"

"The *Argo II* is a small ship." Percy grimaced. "Word got around. I just . . . well, when I was in Tartarus, I was reminded that I hadn't followed through on my promise to Calypso. I asked the gods to free her and then . . . I just assumed they *would*. With me getting amnesia and getting sent to Camp Jupiter and all, I didn't think about Calypso much after that. I'm not making excuses. I should have made sure the gods kept their promise. Anyway, I'm glad you found her. You promised to find a way back to her, and I just wanted to say if we *do* survive all this, I'll do anything I can to help you. That's a promise I *will* keep."

Leo was speechless. Here they were, hiding behind a wall in the middle of a magical war zone, with grenades and grizzly bears and Bronze Butt Nikettes to worry about, and Percy pulls *this* on him.

"Man, what is your *problem*?" Leo grumbled.

Percy blinked. "So . . . I guess we're not cool?"

"Of course we're not cool! You're as bad as Jason! I'm trying to resent you for being all perfect and hero-y and whatnot. Then you go and act like a standup guy. How am I supposed to hate you if you apologize and promise to help and stuff?"

A smile tugged at the corner of Percy's mouth. "Sorry about that."

The ground rumbled as another grenade exploded, sending spirals of whipped cream into the sky. "That's Hazel's signal," Leo said. "They've taken down another Nikette."

Percy peeked around the corner of the wall.

Until this moment, Leo hadn't realized how much he'd resented Percy. The dude had always intimidated him. Knowing Calypso had had a crush on Percy made the feeling ten times worse. But now the knot of anger in his gut started to unravel. Leo just couldn't dislike the guy. Percy seemed sincere about being sorry and wanting to help.

Besides, Leo finally had confirmation that Percy Jackson was out of the picture with Calypso. The air was cleared. All Leo had to do was to find his way back to Ogygia. And he *would*, assuming he survived the next ten days.

"One Nikette left," Percy said. "I wonder—"

Somewhere close by, Hazel cried out in pain.

Instantly, Leo was on his feet.

"Dude, wait!" Percy called, but Leo plunged through the maze, his heart pounding.

The walls fell away on either side. Leo found himself in an open stretch of field. Frank stood at the far end of the stadium, shooting flaming arrows at Nike's chariot as the goddess bellowed insults and tried to find a path to him across the shifting network of trenches.

Hazel was closer—maybe sixty feet away. The fourth Nikette had obviously sneaked up on her. Hazel was limping away from her attacker, her jeans ripped, her left leg bleeding. She parried the metal lady's spear with her huge cavalry sword, but she was about to be overpowered. All around her, the Mist flickered like a dying strobe light. She was losing control of the magic maze.

"I'll help her," Percy said. "You stick to the plan. Get Nike's chariot."

"But the plan was to eliminate all four Nikettes first!"

"So change the plan and *then* stick to it!"

"That doesn't even make sense, but go! Help her!"

Percy rushed to Hazel's defense. Leo darted toward Nike, yelling, "Hey! I want a participation award!"

"Gah!" The goddess pulled the reins and turned her chariot in his direction. "I will destroy you!"

"Good!" Leo yelled. "Losing is way better than winning!"

*"WHAT?"* Nike threw her mighty spear, but her aim was off with the rocking of the chariot. Her weapon skittered into the grass. Sadly, a new one appeared in her hands.

She urged her horses to a full gallop. The trenches disappeared, leaving an open field, perfect for running down small Latino demigods.

"Hey!" Frank yelled from across the stadium. "I want a participation award too! Everybody wins!"

He shot a well-aimed arrow that landed in the back of Nike's chariot and began to burn. Nike ignored it. Her eyes were fixed on Leo.

"Percy . . . ?" Leo's voice sounded like a hamster's squeak. From his tool belt, he fished out an Archimedes sphere and set the concentric circles to arm the device.

Percy was still sparring with the last metal lady. Leo couldn't wait.

He threw the sphere in the chariot's path. It hit the ground and burrowed in, but he needed Percy to spring the trap. If Nike sensed any threat, she apparently didn't think much of it. She kept charging at Leo.

The chariot was twenty feet from the grenade. Fifteen feet.

"Percy!" Leo yelled. "Operation Water Balloon!"

Unfortunately, Percy was a little busy getting smacked around. The Nikette thumped him backward with the butt of her spear. She threw her wreath with such force it knocked Percy's sword from his grip. Percy stumbled. The metallic lady moved in for the kill.

Leo howled. He knew the distance was too far. He knew that if he didn't jump out of the way now, Nike would run him over. But that didn't matter. His friends were about to be skewered. He thrust out his hand and shot a white-hot bolt of fire straight at the Nikette.

It literally melted her face. The Nikette staggered, her spear still raised. Before she could regain her balance, Hazel thrust her *spatha* and impaled the metal lady through the chest. The Nikette crashed into the grass.

Percy turned toward the victory goddess's chariot. Just as those huge white horses were about to turn Leo into road-kill, the carriage passed over Leo's sunken grenade, which exploded in a high-pressure geyser. Water blasted upward, flipping the chariot—horses, carriage, goddess, and all.

Back in Houston, Leo used to live with his mom in an apartment right off the Gulf Freeway. He heard car crashes at least once a week, but this sound was worse—Celestial bronze crumpling, wood splintering, stallions screaming, and a goddess wailing in two distinct voices, both of them very surprised.

Hazel collapsed. Percy caught her. Frank ran toward them from across the field.

Leo was on his own as the goddess Nike disentangled herself from the wreckage and rose to face him. Her braided hairdo now resembled a stepped-on cow pie. A laurel wreath was stuck around her left ankle. Her horses got to their hooves and galloped away in a panic, dragging the soaked, half-burning wreckage of the chariot behind them.

*"YOU!"* Nike glared at Leo, her eyes hotter and brighter than her metal wings. "You *dare?*"

Leo didn't feel very courageous, but he forced a smile. "I know, right? I'm awesome! Do I win a leaf hat now?"

"You will die!" The goddess raised her spear.

"Hold that thought!" Leo dug around in his tool belt. "You haven't seen my best trick yet. I have a weapon guaranteed to win *any* contest!"

Nike hesitated. "What weapon? What do you mean?"

"My ultimate zap-o-matic!" He pulled out a second Archimedes sphere—the one he'd spent a whole thirty seconds modifying before they entered the stadium. "How many laurel wreaths have you got? Because I'm gonna win them all."

He fiddled with dials, hoping he'd done his calculations right.

Leo had gotten better at making spheres, but they still weren't completely reliable. More like twenty percent reliable.

It would've been nice to have Calypso's help weaving the Celestial bronze filaments. She was an *ace* at weaving. Or Annabeth: she was no slouch. But Leo had done his best, rewiring the sphere to carry out two completely different functions.

"Behold!" Leo clicked the final dial. The sphere opened. One side elongated into a gun handle. The other side unfolded into a miniature radar dish made of Celestial bronze mirrors.

Nike frowned. "What is that supposed to be?"

"An Archimedes death ray!" Leo said. "I finally perfected it. Now give me all the prizes."

"Those things don't work!" Nike yelled. "They proved it on television! Besides, I'm an immortal goddess. You can't destroy me!"

"Watch closely," Leo said. "Are you watching?"

Nike could've zapped him into a grease spot or speared him like a cheese wedge, but her curiosity got the best of her. She stared straight into the dish as Leo flipped the switch. Leo knew to look away. Even so, the blazing beam of light left him seeing spots.

"Gah!" The goddess staggered. She dropped her spear and clutched at her eyes. "I'm blind! I'm blind!"

Leo hit another button on his death ray. It collapsed back into a sphere and began to hum. Leo counted silently to three, then tossed the sphere at the goddess's feet.

*FOOM!* Metal filaments shot upward, wrapping Nike in a bronze net. She wailed, falling sideways as the net constricted, forcing her two forms—Greek and Roman—into a quivering, out-of-focus whole.

"Trickery!" Her doubled voices buzzed like muffled alarm clocks. "Your death ray did not even kill me!"

"I don't need to kill you," Leo said. "I vanquished you just fine."

"I will simply change form!" she cried. "I will rip apart your silly net! I will destroy you!"

"Yeah, see, you can't." Leo hoped he was right. "That's high quality Celestial bronze netting, and I'm a son of Hephaestus. He's kind of an expert on catching goddesses in nets."

"No. Nooooo!"

Leo left her thrashing and cursing, and went to check on his friends. Percy looked all right, just sore and bruised. Frank had propped Hazel up and was feeding her ambrosia. The cut on her leg had stopped bleeding, though her jeans were pretty much ruined.

"I'm okay," she said. "Just too much magic."

"You were awesome, Levesque." Leo did his best Hazel imitation: *"Popcorn! Our fatal weakness!"*

She smiled wanly. Together the four of them walked over to Nike, who was still writhing and flapping her wings in the net, like a golden chicken.

"What do we do with her?" Percy asked.

"Take her aboard the *Argo II*," Leo said. "Chuck her in one of the horse stalls."

Hazel's eyes widened. "You're going to keep the goddess of victory in the stable?"

"Why not? Once we sort things out between Greeks and Romans, the gods should go back to their normal selves. Then we can free her and she can . . . you know . . . grant us victory."

"Grant *you* victory?" the goddess cried. "Never! You will suffer for this outrage! Your blood shall be spilled! One of you here—one of you four—is fated to die battling Gaea!"

Leo's intestines tied themselves into a slipknot. "How do you know that?"

"I can foresee victories!" Nike yelled. "You will have no success without death! Release me and fight each other! It is better you die here than face what is to come!"

Hazel stuck the point of her *spatha* under Nike's chin. "Explain." Her voice was harder than Leo had ever heard. "Which of us will die? How do we stop it?"

"Ah, child of Pluto! Your magic helped you cheat in this contest, but you cannot cheat destiny. One of you will die. One of you *must* die!"

"No," Hazel insisted. "There's another way. There is *always* another path."

"Hecate taught you this?" Nike laughed. "You would hope for the physician's cure, perhaps? But that is impossible. Too much stands in your way: the poison of Pylos, the chained god's heartbeat in Sparta, the curse of Delos! No, you cannot cheat death."

Frank knelt. He gathered up the net under Nike's chin and raised her face to his. "What are you talking about? How do we find this cure?"

"I will not help you," Nike growled. "I will curse you with my power, net or no!"

She began to mutter in Ancient Greek.

Frank looked up, scowling. "Can she really cast magic through this net?"

"Heck if I know," Leo said.

Frank let go of the goddess. He took off one of his shoes, peeled off his sock, and stuffed it in the goddess's mouth.

"Dude," Percy said, "that is disgusting."

"Mpppphhh!" Nike complained. "Mppppphhh!"

"Leo," Frank said grimly, "you got duct tape?"

"Never leave home without it." He fished a roll from his tool belt, and in no time Frank had wrapped it around Nike's head, securing the gag in her mouth.

"Well, it's not a laurel wreath," Frank said, "but it's a new kind of victory circle: the gag of duct tape."

"Zhang," Leo said, "you got style."

Nike thrashed and grunted until Percy nudged her with his toe. "Hey, shut up. You behave or we'll get Arion back here and let him nibble your wings. He loves gold."

Nike shrieked once, then became still and quiet.

"So . . ." Hazel sounded a little nervous. "We have one tied-up goddess. Now what?"

Frank folded his arms. "We go looking for this physician's cure . . . whatever that is. Because personally, I like cheating death."

Leo grinned. "Poison in Pylos? A chained god's heartbeat in Sparta? A curse in Delos? Oh, yeah. This is gonna be fun!"

# XIII

# NICO

THE LAST THING NICO HEARD was Coach Hedge grumbling, "Well, *this* isn't good."

He wondered what he'd done wrong this time. Maybe he'd teleported them into a den of Cyclopes, or a thousand feet above another volcano. There was nothing he could do about it. His vision was gone. His other senses were shutting down. His knees buckled and he passed out.

He tried to make the most of his unconsciousness.

Dreams and death were old friends of his. He knew how to navigate their dark borderland. He sent out his thoughts, searching for Thalia Grace.

He rushed past the usual fragments of painful memories— his mother smiling down at him, her face illuminated by the sunlight rippling off the Venetian Grand Canal; his sister Bianca laughing as she pulled him across the Mall in Washington, D.C., her green floppy hat shading her eyes and the splash of freckles across her nose. He saw Percy Jackson on a snowy cliff outside Westover Hall, shielding Nico and Bianca from the manticore as Nico clutched a Mythomagic figurine and whispered, *I'm scared.* He saw Minos, his old ghostly mentor, leading him through the Labyrinth. Minos's smile was cold and cruel. *Don't worry, son of Hades. You will have your revenge.*

Nico couldn't stop the memories. They cluttered his dreams like the ghosts of Asphodel—an aimless, sorrowful mob pleading for attention. *Save me,* they seemed to whisper. *Remember me. Help me. Comfort me.*

He didn't dare stop to dwell on them. They would only crush him with wants and regrets. The best he could do was to stay focused and push through.

I am the son of Hades, he thought. I go where I wish. The darkness is my birthright.

He forged ahead through a gray-and-black terrain, looking for the dreams of Thalia Grace, daughter of Zeus. Instead, the ground dissolved at his feet and he fell into a familiar backwater—the Hypnos cabin at Camp Half-Blood.

Buried under piles of feather comforters, snoring demigods nestled in their bunks. Above the mantel, a dark tree branch dripped milky water from the River Lethe into a bowl. A cheerful fire crackled in the fireplace. In front of it, in a leather armchair, dozed the head counselor for Cabin Fifteen—a pot-bellied guy with unruly blond hair and a gentle bovine face.

"Clovis," Nico growled, "for the gods' sake, stop *dreaming* so powerfully!"

Clovis's eyes fluttered open. He turned and stared at

Nico, though Nico knew this was simply part of Clovis's own dreamscape. The actual Clovis would still be snoring in his armchair back at camp.

"Oh, hi . . ." Clovis yawned wide enough to swallow a minor god. "Sorry. Did I pull you off course again?"

Nico gritted his teeth. There was no point getting upset. The Hypnos cabin was like Grand Central Station for dream activity. You couldn't travel *anywhere* without going through it once in a while.

"As long as I'm here," Nico said, "pass along a message. Tell Chiron I'm on my way with a couple of friends. We're bringing the Athena Parthenos."

Clovis rubbed his eyes. "So it's true? How are you bringing it? Did you rent a van or something?"

Nico explained as concisely as possible. Messages sent through dreams tended to get fuzzy around the edges, especially when you were dealing with Clovis. The simpler, the better.

"We're being followed by a hunter," Nico said. "One of Gaea's giants, I think. Can you get that message to Thalia Grace? You're better at finding people in dreams than I am. I need her advice."

"I'll try." Clovis fumbled for a cup of hot chocolate on the side table. "Uh, before you go, do you have a second?"

"Clovis, this is a dream," Nico reminded him. "Time is fluid."

Even as he said it, Nico worried about what was happening in the real world. His physical self might be plummeting to his death, or surrounded by monsters. Still, he couldn't force himself to wake up—not after the amount of energy he'd expended on shadow-travel.

Clovis nodded. "Right . . . I was thinking you should probably see what happened today at the council of war. I slept through some of it, but—"

"Show me," Nico said.

The scene changed. Nico found himself in the rec room of the Big House, all the senior camp leaders gathered around the Ping-Pong table.

At one end sat Chiron the centaur, his equine posterior collapsed into his magic wheelchair so he looked like a regular human. His curly brown hair and beard had more gray streaks than a few months ago. Deep lines etched his face.

"—things we can't control," he was saying. "Now let's review our defenses. Where do we stand?"

Clarisse from the Ares cabin sat forward. She was the only one in full armor, which was typical. Clarisse probably slept in her combat gear. As she spoke, she gestured with her dagger, which made the other counselors lean away from her.

"Our defensive line is mostly solid," she said. "The campers are as ready to fight as they'll ever be. We control the beach. Our triremes are unchallenged on Long Island Sound, but those stupid giant eagles dominate our airspace. Inland, in all three directions, the barbarians have us completely cut off."

"They're Romans," said Rachel Dare, doodling with a marker on the knee of her jeans. "Not barbarians."

Clarisse pointed her dagger at Rachel. "What about their

allies, huh? Did you see that tribe of two-headed men that arrived yesterday? Or the glowing red dog-headed guys with the big poleaxes? They look pretty barbaric to me. It would've been nice if you'd *foreseen* any of that, if your Oracle power didn't break down when we needed it most!"

Rachel's face turned as red as her hair. "That's hardly my fault. Something is wrong with Apollo's gifts of prophecy. If I knew how to fix it—"

"She's right." Will Solace, head counselor for the Apollo cabin, put his hand gently on Clarisse's wrist. Not many campers could've done that without getting stabbed, but Will had a way of defusing people's anger. He got her to lower her dagger. "Everyone in our cabin has been affected. It's not just Rachel."

Will's shaggy blond hair and pale blue eyes reminded Nico of Jason Grace, but the similarities ended there.

Jason was a fighter. You could tell from the intensity of his stare, his constant alertness, the coiled-up energy in his frame. Will Solace was more like a lanky cat stretched out in the sunshine. His movements were relaxed and nonthreatening, his gaze soft and far away. In his faded SURF BARBADOS T-shirt, his cutoff shorts and flip-flops, he looked about as unaggressive as a demigod could get, but Nico knew he was brave under fire. During the Battle of Manhattan, Nico had seen him in action—the camp's best combat medic, risking his life to save wounded campers.

"We don't know what's going on at Delphi," Will continued. "My dad hasn't answered any prayers, or appeared in any dreams . . . I mean, *all* the gods have been silent, but this isn't like Apollo. Something's wrong."

Across the table, Jake Mason grunted. "Probably this Roman dirt-wipe who's leading the attack—Octavian what's-his-name. If I was Apollo and my descendant was acting that way, I'd go into hiding out of shame."

"I agree," Will said. "I wish I was a better archer . . . I wouldn't mind shooting my Roman relative off his high horse. Actually, I wish I could use *any* of my father's gifts to stop this war." He looked down at his own hands with distaste. "Unfortunately, I'm just a healer."

"Your talents are essential," Chiron said. "I fear we'll need them soon enough. As for seeing the future . . . what about the harpy Ella? Has she offered any advice from the Sibylline Books?"

Rachel shook her head. "The poor thing is scared out of her wits. Harpies hate being imprisoned. Ever since the Romans surrounded us . . . well, she feels trapped. She knows Octavian means to capture her. It's all Tyson and I can do to keep her from flying away."

"Which would be suicide." Butch Walker, son of Iris, crossed his burly arms. "With those Roman eagles in the air, flying isn't safe. I've already lost two pegasi."

"At least Tyson brought some of his Cyclops friends to help out," Rachel said. "That's a little good news."

Over by the refreshment table, Connor Stoll laughed. He had a fistful of Ritz crackers in one hand and a can of Easy Cheese in the other. "A dozen full-grown Cyclopes? That's a *lot* of good news! Plus, Lou Ellen and the Hecate kids have been putting up magic barriers, and the whole Hermes cabin has been lining the hills with traps and snares and all kinds of nice surprises for the Romans!"

Jake Mason frowned. "Most of which you stole from Bunker Nine and the Hephaestus cabin."

Clarisse grumbled in agreement. "They even stole the land mines from around the Ares cabin. How do you steal *live* land mines?"

"We *commandeered* them for the war effort." Connor sprayed a glob of Easy Cheese into his mouth. "Besides, you guys have plenty of toys. You can share!"

Chiron turned to his left, where the satyr Grover Underwood sat in silence, fingering his reed pipes. "Grover? What news from the nature spirits?"

Grover heaved a sigh. "Even on a good day, it's hard to organize nymphs and dryads. With Gaea stirring, they're almost as disoriented as the gods. Katie and Miranda from the Demeter cabin are out there right now, trying to help, but if the Earth Mother wakes . . ." He looked around the table nervously. "Well, I can't promise the woods will be safe. Or the hills. Or the strawberry fields. Or—"

"Great." Jake Mason elbowed Clovis, who was starting to nod off. "So what do we do?"

"Attack." Clarisse pounded the Ping-Pong table, which made everyone flinch. "The Romans are getting more rein-forcements by the day. We know they plan to invade on August first. Why should we let *them* set the timetable? I can only guess they're waiting to gather more forces. They already outnumber us. We should attack now, before they get any stronger; take the fight to them!"

Malcolm, the acting head counselor for Athena, coughed into his fist. "Clarisse, I get your point. But have you studied Roman engineering? Their *temporary* camp is better defended than Camp Half-Blood. Attack them at their base, and we'd be massacred."

"So we just *wait?*" Clarisse demanded. "Let them get all their forces prepared while Gaea gets closer to waking? I have Coach Hedge's pregnant wife under my protection. I am *not* going to let anything happen to her. I owe Hedge my life. Besides, I've been training the campers more than you have, Malcolm. Their morale is low. Everybody is scared. If we're under siege another nine days—"

"We should stick to Annabeth's plan." Connor Stoll looked about as serious as he ever did, despite the Easy Cheese around his mouth. "We have to hold out until she gets that magic Athena statue back here."

Clarisse rolled her eyes. "You mean if that *Roman praetor* gets the statue back here. I don't understand what Annabeth was thinking, collaborating with the enemy. Even *if* the Roman manages to bring us the statue—which is impossible—we're supposed to trust that will bring peace? The statue arrives, and suddenly the Romans lay down their weapons and start dancing around, throwing flowers?"

Rachel set down her marking pen. "Annabeth knows what she's doing. We have to try for peace. Unless we can unite the Greeks and Romans, the gods won't be healed. Unless the gods are healed, there's no way we can kill the giants. And unless we kill the giants—"

"Gaea wakes," Connor said. "Game over. Look, Clarisse, Annabeth sent me a message from Tartarus. From *fricking* Tartarus. Anybody who can do that . . . hey, I listen to them."

Clarisse opened her mouth to reply, but when she spoke it was Coach Hedge's voice: "Nico, wake up. We've got problems."

# XIV

# NICO

Nico sat up so quickly he head-butted the satyr in the nose.

"OW! Jeez, kid, you got a hard noggin!"

"S-sorry, Coach." Nico blinked, trying to get his bearings. "What's going on?"

He didn't see any immediate threat. They were camped on a sunny lawn in the middle of a public square. Beds of orange marigolds bloomed all around them. Reyna was sleeping curled up, with her two metal dogs at her feet. A stone's throw away, little kids played tag around a white marble fountain. At a nearby sidewalk café, half a dozen people sipped coffee in the shade of patio umbrellas. A few delivery vans were parked along the edges of the square, but there was no traffic. The only pedestrians were a few families, probably locals, enjoying a warm afternoon.

The square itself was cobblestone pavement, edged with white stucco buildings and lemon trees. In the center stood the well-preserved shell of a Roman temple. Its square base stretched maybe fifty feet wide and ten feet tall, with an intact facade of Corinthian columns rising another twenty-five feet. And at the top of the colonnade . . .

Nico's mouth went dry. "Oh, Styx."

The Athena Parthenos lay sideways along the tops of the columns like a nightclub singer sprawled across a piano. Lengthwise, she fit almost perfectly, but with Nike in her extended hand she was a bit too wide. She looked like she might topple forward at any moment.

"What is she *doing* up there?" Nico asked.

"You tell me." Hedge rubbed his bruised nose. "That's where we appeared. Almost fell to our deaths, but luckily I've got nimble hooves. You were unconscious, hanging in your harness like a tangled paratrooper until we managed to get you down."

Nico tried to picture that, then decided he'd rather not. "Is this Spain?"

"Portugal," Hedge said. "You overshot. By the way, Reyna speaks *Spanish*; she does not speak Portuguese. Anyway, while you were asleep, we figured out this city is Évora. Good news: it's a sleepy little place. Nobody's bothered us. Nobody seems to notice the giant Athena sleeping on top of the Roman temple, which is called the Temple of Diana, in case you were wondering. And people here appreciate my street performances! I've made about sixteen euros."

He picked up his baseball cap, which jangled with coins.

Nico felt ill. "Street performances?"

"A little singing," the coach said. "A little martial arts. Some interpretive dance."

"Wow."

"I know! The Portuguese have taste. Anyway, I supposed this was a decent place to lie low for a couple of days."

Nico stared at him. "A couple of *days?*"

"Hey, kid, we didn't have much choice. In case you haven't noticed, you've been working yourself to death with all that shadow-jumping. We tried to wake you up last night. No dice."

"So I've been asleep for—"

"About thirty-six hours. You needed it."

Nico was glad he was sitting down. Otherwise he would've fallen down. He could've sworn he'd only slept a few minutes, but as his drowsiness faded, he realized he felt more clearheaded and rested than he had in weeks, maybe since before he went looking for the Doors of Death.

His stomach growled. Coach Hedge raised his eyebrows.

"You must be hungry," said the satyr. "Either that, or your stomach speaks hedgehog. That was *quite* a statement in hedgehog."

"Food would be good," Nico agreed. "But first, what's the bad news . . . I mean, aside from the statue being sideways? You said we had trouble."

"Oh, right." The coach pointed to a gated archway at the corner of the square. Standing in the shadows was a glowing, vaguely human figure outlined in gray flames. The spirit's features were indistinct, but it seemed to be beckoning to Nico.

"Burning Man showed up a few minutes ago," said Coach Hedge. "He doesn't get any closer. When I tried to go over there, he disappeared. Not sure if he's a threat, but he seems to be asking for you."

Nico assumed it was a trap. Most things were.

But Coach Hedge promised he could guard Reyna for a little longer, and on the off chance the spirit had something useful to say, Nico decided it was worth the risk.

He unsheathed his Stygian iron blade and approached the archway.

Normally ghosts didn't scare him. (Assuming, of course, Gaea hadn't encased them in shells of stone and turned them into killing machines. That had been a new one for him.)

After his experience with Minos, Nico realized that most specters held only as much power as you allowed them to have. They pried into your mind, using fear or anger or longing to influence you. Nico had learned to shield himself. Sometimes he could even turn the tables and bend ghosts to his will.

As he approached the fiery gray apparition, he was fairly sure it was a garden-variety wraith—a lost soul who had died in pain. Shouldn't be a problem.

Still, Nico took nothing for granted. He remembered Croatia all too well. He'd gone into that situation smug and confident, only to have his feet swept out from under him, lit-erally and emotionally. First Jason Grace had grabbed him and flown him over a wall. Then the god Favonius had dissolved him into wind. And as for that arrogant thug, Cupid . . .

Nico clenched his sword. Sharing his secret crush hadn't been the worst of it. Eventually he might have done that, in his own time, in his own way. But being *forced* to talk about Percy, being bullied and harassed and strong-armed simply for Cupid's amusement . . .

Tendrils of darkness were now spreading out from his feet, killing all the weeds between the cobblestones. Nico tried to rein in his anger.

When he reached the ghost, he saw it wore a monk's habit—sandals, woolen robes, and a wooden cross around his neck. Gray flames swirled around him—burning his sleeves, blistering his face, turning his eyebrows to ashes. He seemed to be stuck in the moment of his immolation, like a black-and-white video on a permanent loop.

"You were burned alive," Nico sensed. "Probably in the Middle Ages?"

The ghost's face distorted in a silent scream of agony, but his eyes looked bored, even a little annoyed, as if the scream was just an automatic reflex he couldn't control.

"What do you want of me?" Nico asked.

The ghost gestured for Nico to follow. It turned and walked through the open gateway. Nico glanced back at Coach Hedge. The satyr just made a shooing gesture like, *Go. Do your Underworld thing.*

Nico trailed the ghost through the streets of Évora.

They zigzagged through narrow cobblestone walkways, past courtyards with potted hibiscus trees, and white stucco buildings with butterscotch trim and wrought iron balconies. No one noticed the ghost, but the locals looked askance at Nico. A young girl with a fox terrier crossed the street to avoid him.

Her dog growled, the hair on its back standing straight up like a dorsal fin.

The ghost led Nico to another public plaza, anchored at one end by a large square church with whitewashed walls and limestone arches. The ghost passed through the portico and disappeared inside.

Nico hesitated. He had nothing against churches, but this one radiated death. Inside would be tombs, or perhaps something less pleasant . . .

He ducked through the doorway. His eyes were drawn to a side chapel, lit from within by eerie golden light. Carved over the door was a Portuguese inscription. Nico didn't speak the language, but he remembered his childhood Italian well enough to glean the general meaning: *We, the bones that are here, await yours.*

"Cheery," he muttered.

He entered the chapel. At the far end stood an altar, where the fiery wraith knelt in prayer, but Nico was more interested in the room itself. The walls were constructed of bones and skulls—thousands upon thousands, cemented together. Columns of bones held up a vaulted ceiling decorated with images of death. On one wall, like coats on a coatrack, hung the desiccated, skeletal remains of two people—an adult and a small child.

"A beautiful room, isn't it?"

Nico turned. A year ago, he would've jumped out of his skin if his father suddenly appeared next to him. Now, Nico was able to control his heart rate, along with his desire to knee his father in the groin and run away.

Like the wraith, Hades was dressed in the habit of a Franciscan monk, which Nico found vaguely disturbing. His black robes were tied at the waist with a simple white cord. His cowl was pushed back, revealing dark hair shorn close to the scalp and eyes that glittered like frozen tar. The god's expression was calm and content, as if he'd just come home from a lovely evening strolling through the Fields of Punishment, enjoying the screams of the damned.

"Getting some redecorating ideas?" Nico asked. "Maybe you could do your dining room in medieval monk skulls."

Hades arched an eyebrow. "I can never tell when you're joking."

"Why are you here, Father? *How* are you here?"

Hades traced his fingers along the nearest column, leaving bleached white marks on the old bones. "You're a hard mortal to find, my son. For several days I've been searching. When the scepter of Diocletian exploded . . . well, that got my attention."

Nico felt a flush of shame. Then he felt angry for feeling ashamed. "Breaking the scepter wasn't my fault. We were about to be overrun—"

"Oh, the scepter isn't important. A relic that old, I'm surprised you got two uses out of it. The explosion simply gave me some clarity. It allowed me to pinpoint your location. I was hoping to speak to you in Pompeii, but it is so . . . well, *Roman*. This chapel was the first place where my presence was strong enough that I could appear to you as myself—by which I mean *Hades*, god of the dead, not split with that *other* manifestation."

Hades breathed in the stale dank air. "I am very drawn to this place. The remains of five thousand monks were used to build the Chapel of Bones. It serves as a reminder that life is short and death is eternal. I feel *focused* here. Even so, I only have a few moments."

Story of our relationship, Nico thought. You only have a few moments.

"So tell me, Father. What do you want?"

Hades clasped his hands together in the sleeves of his robe. "Can you entertain the notion that I might be here to help you, not simply because I want something?"

Nico almost laughed, but his chest felt too hollow. "I can entertain the notion that you might be here for multiple reasons."

The god frowned. "I suppose that's fair enough. You seek information about Gaea's hunter. His name is Orion."

Nico hesitated. He wasn't used to getting a direct answer, without games or riddles or quests. "Orion. Like the constellation. Wasn't he . . . a friend of Artemis?"

"He was," Hades said. "A giant, born to oppose the twins, Apollo and Artemis, but much like Artemis, Orion rejected his destiny. He sought to live on his own terms. First he tried to live among mortals as a huntsman for the king of Khios. He, ah, ran into some trouble with the king's daughter. The king had Orion blinded and exiled."

Nico thought back to what Reyna had told him. "My friend dreamed of a hunter with glowing eyes. If Orion is blind—"

"He *was* blind," Hades corrected. "Shortly after his exile, Orion met Hephaestus, who took pity on the giant and

crafted him new mechanical eyes even better than the origi-
nals. Orion became friends with Artemis. He was the first
male ever allowed to join her Hunt. But . . . things went
wrong between them. How exactly, I do not know. Orion
was slain. Now he has returned as a loyal son of Gaea, ready
to do her bidding. He is driven by bitterness and anger. You
can understand that."

Nico wanted to yell: *Like you know what I feel?*

Instead he asked, "How do we stop him?"

"You cannot," Hades said. "Your only hope is to outrun
him, accomplish your quest before he reaches you. Apollo or
Artemis *might* be able to slay him, arrows against arrows, but
the twins are in no condition to aid you. Even now, Orion has
your scent. His hunting pack is almost upon you. You won't
have the luxury of more rest from here to Camp Half-Blood."

A belt seemed to tighten around Nico's ribs. He'd left
Coach Hedge on guard duty with Reyna asleep. "I need to
get back to my companions."

"Indeed," Hades said. "But there is more. Your sister . . ."
Hades faltered. As always, the subject of Bianca lay between
them like a loaded gun—deadly, easy to reach, impossible to
ignore. "I mean your *other* sister, Hazel . . . she has discovered
that one of the Seven will die. She may try to prevent this. In
doing so, she may lose sight of her priorities."

Nico didn't trust himself to speak.

To his surprise, his thoughts didn't leap first to Percy.
His primary concern was for Hazel, then for Jason, then for
Percy and the others aboard the *Argo II*. They'd saved him
in Rome. They'd welcomed him aboard their ship. Nico had

never allowed himself the luxury of friends, but the crew of the *Argo II* was as close as he'd ever come. The idea of any of them dying made him feel empty—like he was back in the giants' bronze jar, alone in the dark, subsisting only on sour pomegranate seeds.

Finally he asked, "Is Hazel all right?"

"For the moment."

"And the others? Who will die?"

Hades shook his head. "Even if I were certain, I could not say. I tell you this because you are my son. You know that some deaths cannot be prevented. Some deaths *should* not be prevented. When the time comes, you may need to act."

Nico didn't know what that meant. He didn't *want* to know.

"My son." Hades's tone was almost gentle. "Whatever happens, you have earned my respect. You brought honor to our house when we stood together against Kronos in Manhattan. You risked my wrath to help the Jackson boy—guiding him to the River Styx, freeing him from my prison, pleading with me to raise the armies of Erebos to assist him. Never before have I been so *harassed* by one of my sons. *Percy this* and *Percy that.* I nearly blasted you to cinders."

Nico took a shallow breath. The walls of the room began to tremble, dust trickling from the cracks between the bones. "I didn't do all that just for him. I did it because the whole world was in danger."

Hades allowed himself the faintest smile, but there was nothing cruel in his eyes. "I can entertain the possibility that you acted for *multiple* reasons. My point is this: you and I rose to the aid of Olympus because you convinced me to let go of my anger. I would encourage you to do likewise. My children are so rarely happy. I . . . I would like to see you be an exception."

Nico stared at his father. He didn't know what to do with that statement. He could accept many unreal things—hordes of ghosts, magical labyrinths, travel through shadows, chapels made of bones. But tender words from the Lord of the Underworld? No. That made no sense.

Over at the altar, the fiery ghost rose. He approached, burning and screaming silently, his eyes conveying some urgent message.

"Ah," Hades said. "This is Brother Paloan. He's one of hundreds who were burned alive in the square near the old Roman temple. The Inquisition had its headquarters there, you know. At any rate, he suggests you leave now. You have very little time before the wolves arrive."

"Wolves? You mean Orion's pack?"

Hades flicked his hand. The ghost of Brother Paloan disappeared. "My son, what you are attempting—shadow-travel across the world, carrying the statue of Athena—it may well destroy you."

"Thanks for the encouragement."

Hades placed his hands briefly on Nico's shoulders.

Nico didn't like to be touched, but somehow this brief contact with his father felt reassuring—the same way the Chapel of Bones was reassuring. Like death, his father's presence was cold and often callous, but it was *real*—brutally honest, inescapably dependable. Nico found a sort of freedom in knowing that eventually, no matter what happened, he would end up at the foot of his father's throne.

"I will see you again," Hades promised. "I will prepare a room for you at the palace in case you do not survive. Perhaps your chambers would look good decorated with the skulls of monks."

"Now I can't tell if *you're* joking."

Hades's eyes glittered as his form began to fade. "Then perhaps we are alike in some important ways."

The god vanished.

Suddenly the chapel felt oppressive—thousands of hollow eye sockets staring at Nico. *We, the bones that are here, await yours.*

He hurried out of the church, hoping he remembered the way back to his friends.

# NICO

"WOLVES?" REYNA ASKED.

They were eating dinner from the nearby sidewalk café.

Despite Hades's warning to hurry back, Nico had found nothing much changed at the camp. Reyna had just awoken. The Athena Parthenos still lay sideways across the top of the temple. Coach Hedge was entertaining a few locals with tap dancing and martial arts, occasionally singing into his megaphone, though nobody seemed to understand what he was saying.

Nico wished the coach hadn't brought the megaphone. Not only was it loud and obnoxious, but also, for no reason Nico understood, it occasionally blurted out random Darth Vader lines from *Star Wars* or yelled, "THE COW GOES MOO!"

As the three of them sat on the lawn to eat, Reyna seemed alert and rested. She and Coach Hedge listened as Nico described his dreams, then his meeting with Hades at the

Chapel of Bones. Nico held back a few personal details from his talk with his father, though he sensed that Reyna knew plenty about wrestling with one's feelings.

When he mentioned Orion and the wolves that were supposedly on their way, Reyna frowned.

"Most wolves are friendly to Romans," she said. "I've never heard stories about Orion hunting with a pack."

Nico finished his ham sandwich. He eyed the plate of pastries and was surprised to find he still had an appetite. "It could have been a figure of speech: *very little time before the wolves arrive.* Perhaps Hades didn't literally mean wolves. At any rate, we should leave as soon as it's dark enough for shadows."

Coach Hedge stuffed an issue of *Guns & Ammo* into his bag. "Only problem, the Athena Parthenos is still thirty feet in the air. Gonna be fun hauling you guys and your gear to the top of that temple."

Nico tried a pastry. The lady at the café had called them *farturas.* They looked like spiral donuts and tasted great—just the right combination of crispy, sugary, and buttery, but when Nico first heard *fartura*, he knew Percy would have made a joke out of the name.

*America has do-nuts,* Percy would have said. *Portugal has fart-nuts.*

The older Nico got, the more juvenile Percy seemed to him, though Percy was three years older. Nico found his sense of humor equal parts endearing and annoying. He decided to concentrate on the *annoying.*

Then there were the times Percy was deadly serious: looking up at Nico from that chasm in Rome: *The other side, Nico! Lead them there. Promise me!*

And Nico had promised. It didn't seem to matter how much he resented Percy Jackson. Nico would do anything for him. He hated himself for that.

"So . . ." Reyna's voice jarred him from his thoughts. "Will Camp Half-Blood wait for August first, or will they attack?"

"We have to hope they wait," Nico said. "We can't . . . *I* can't get the statue back any faster."

*Even at this rate, my dad thinks I might die.* Nico kept that thought private.

He wished Hazel was with him. Together they had shadow-traveled the entire crew of the *Argo II* out of the House of Hades. When they shared their power, Nico felt like anything was possible. The trip to Camp Half-Blood could've been done in half the time.

Besides, Hades's words about one of the crew dying had sent a chill through him. He couldn't lose Hazel. Not another sister. Not again.

Coach Hedge looked up from counting the change in his baseball cap. "And you're sure Clarisse said Mellie was okay?"

"Yes, Coach. Clarisse is taking good care of her."

"That's a relief. I don't like what Grover said about Gaea whispering to the nymphs and dryads. If the nature spirits turn evil . . . that's not going to be pretty."

Nico had never heard of such a thing happening. Then again, Gaea hadn't been awake since the dawn of humanity.

Reyna took a bite of her pastry. Her chain mail glittered

in the afternoon sun. "I wonder about these wolves . . . Is it possible we've misunderstood the message? The goddess Lupa has been very quiet. Perhaps she is sending us aid. The wolves could be from her—to *defend* us from Orion and his pack."

The hopefulness in her voice was as thin as gauze. Nico decided not to rip through it.

"Maybe," he said. "But wouldn't Lupa be busy with the war between the camps? I thought she'd be sending wolves to help your legion."

Reyna shook her head. "Wolves are not front-line fighters. I don't think she would help Octavian. Her wolves might be patrolling Camp Jupiter, defending it in the legion's absence, but I just don't know . . ."

She crossed her legs at the ankles, and the iron tips of her combat boots glinted. Nico made a mental note not to get into any kicking contests with Roman legionnaires.

"There's something else," she said. "I haven't had any luck contacting my sister, Hylla. It makes me uneasy that both the wolves *and* the Amazons have gone silent. If something has happened on the West Coast . . . I fear the only hope for either camp lies with us. We *must* return the statue soon. That means the greatest burden is on you, son of Hades."

Nico tried to swallow his bile. He wasn't mad at Reyna. He kind of liked Reyna. But so often he'd been called on to do the impossible. Normally, as soon as he accomplished it, he was forgotten.

He remembered how nice the kids at Camp Half-Blood had been to him after the war with Kronos. *Great job, Nico! Thanks for bringing the armies of the Underworld to save us!*

Everybody smiled. They all invited him to sit at their table.

After about a week, his welcome wore thin. Campers would jump when he walked up behind them. He would emerge from the shadows at the campfire, startle somebody, and see the discomfort in their eyes: *Are you still here? Why are you here?*

It didn't help that immediately after the war with Kronos, Annabeth and Percy had started dating . . .

Nico set down his *fartura*. Suddenly it didn't taste so good.

He recalled his talk with Annabeth at Epirus, just before he'd left with the Athena Parthenos.

She'd pulled him aside and said, "Hey, I have to talk to you."

Panic had seized him. *She knows.*

"I want to thank you," she continued. "Bob . . . the Titan . . . he only helped us in Tartarus because you were kind to him. You told him we were worth saving. That's the only reason we're alive."

She said *we* so easily, as if she and Percy were interchangeable, inseparable.

Nico had once read a story from Plato, who claimed that in the ancient times, all humans had been a combination of male and female. Each person had two heads, four arms, four legs. Supposedly, these combo-humans had been so powerful they made the gods uneasy, so Zeus split them in half—man and woman. Ever since, humans had felt incomplete. They spent their lives searching for their other halves.

*And where does that leave me?* Nico wondered.

It wasn't his favorite story.

He wanted to hate Annabeth, but he just couldn't. She'd gone out of her way to thank him at Epirus. She was genuine and sincere. She never overlooked him or avoided him like most people did. Why couldn't she be a horrible person? That would've made it easier.

The wind god Favonius had warned him in Croatia: *If you let your anger rule you . . . your fate will be even sadder than mine.*

But how could his fate be anything *but* sad? Even if he lived through this quest, he would have to leave both camps forever. That was the only way he would find peace. He wished there was another option—a choice that didn't hurt like the waters of the Phlegethon—but he couldn't see one.

Reyna was studying him, probably trying to read his thoughts. She glanced down at his hands, and Nico realized he was twisting his silver skull ring—the last gift Bianca had given him.

"Nico, how can we help you?" Reyna asked.

Another question he wasn't used to hearing.

"I'm not sure," he admitted. "You've already let me rest as much as possible. That's important. Perhaps you can lend me your strength again. This next jump will be the longest. I'll have to muster enough energy to get us across the Atlantic."

"You'll succeed," Reyna promised. "Once we're back in the U.S., we should encounter fewer monsters. I might even be able to get help from retired legionnaires along the eastern seaboard. They are obliged to aid any Roman demigod who calls on them."

Hedge grunted. "If Octavian hasn't already won them over. In which case, you might find yourself arrested for treason."

"Coach," Reyna scolded, "not helping."

"Hey, just sayin'. Personally, I wish we could stay in Évora longer. Good food, good money, and so far no sign of these figurative *wolves*—"

Reyna's dogs sprang to their feet.

In the distance, howls pierced the air. Before Nico could stand, wolves appeared from every direction—huge black beasts leaping from the roofs, surrounding their encampment.

The largest of them padded forward. The alpha wolf stood on his haunches and began to change. His forelegs grew into arms. His snout shrank into a pointy nose. His gray fur morphed into a cloak of woven animal pelts. He became a tall, wiry man with a haggard face and glowing red eyes. A crown of finger bones circled his greasy black hair.

"Ah, little satyr . . ." The man grinned, revealing pointed fangs. "Your wish is granted! You will stay in Évora forever, because sadly for you, my figurative wolves are *literally* wolves."

# XVI

# NICO

"You're not Orion," Nico blurted.

A stupid comment, but it was the first thing that came to his mind.

The man before him clearly was not a hunter giant. He wasn't tall enough. He didn't have dragon legs. He didn't carry a bow or quiver, and he didn't have the headlamp eyes Reyna had described from her dream.

The gray man laughed. "Indeed not. Orion has merely employed me to assist him in his hunt. I am—"

"Lycaon," Reyna interrupted. "The first werewolf."

The man gave her a mock bow. "Reyna Ramírez-Arellano, Praetor of Rome. One of Lupa's whelps! I'm pleased you recognize me. No doubt, I am the stuff of your nightmares."

"The stuff of my indigestion, perhaps." From her belt pouch, Reyna produced a foldable camping knife. She flicked it open and the wolves snarled, backing away. "I never travel without a silver weapon."

Lycaon bared his teeth. "Would you keep a dozen wolves and their king at bay with a pocketknife? I heard you were brave, *filia Romana*. I did not realize you were foolhardy."

Reyna's dogs crouched, ready to spring. The coach gripped his baseball bat, though for once he didn't look anxious to swing.

Nico reached for the hilt of his sword.

"Don't bother," muttered Coach Hedge. "These guys are only hurt by silver or fire. I remember them from Pikes Peak. They're annoying."

"And I remember you, Gleeson Hedge." The werewolf's eyes glowed lava red. "My pack will be delighted to have goat meat for dinner."

Hedge snorted. "Bring it on, mangy boy. The Hunters of Artemis are on their way right now, just like last time! That's a temple of *Diana* over there, you idiot. You're on their home turf!"

Again the wolves snarled and widened their circle. Some glanced nervously toward the rooftops.

Lycaon only glared at the coach. "A nice try, but I'm afraid that temple has been misnamed. I passed through here during Roman times. It was actually dedicated to the Emperor Augustus. Typical demigod vanity. Regardless, I've been much more careful since our last encounter. If the Hunters were anywhere close by, I would know."

Nico tried to think of an escape plan. They were surrounded and outnumbered. Their only effective weapon was a pocketknife. The scepter of Diocletian was gone. The Athena Parthenos was thirty feet above them at the top of the temple, and even if they could reach it, they couldn't shadow-travel until they actually had *shadows*. The sun wouldn't set for hours.

He hardly felt brave, but he stepped forward. "So you've got us. What are you waiting for?"

Lycaon studied him like a new type of meat in a butcher's display case. "Nico di Angelo . . . son of Hades. I've heard of you. I'm sorry I can't kill you promptly, but I promised my employer Orion that I would detain you until he arrives. No worries. He should be here in a few moments. Once he's done with you, I shall spill your blood and mark this place as my territory for ages to come!"

Nico grit his teeth. "Demigod blood. The blood of Olympus."

"Of course!" Lycaon said. "Spilled upon the ground, especially *sacred* ground, demigod blood has many uses. With the proper incantations, it can awaken monsters or even gods. It can cause new life to spring up or make a place barren for generations. Alas, *your* blood will not wake Gaea herself. That honor is reserved for your friends aboard the *Argo II*. But fear not. Your death will be almost as painful as theirs."

The grass started dying around Nico's feet. The marigold beds withered. Barren ground, he thought. Sacred ground.

He remembered the thousands of skeletons in the Chapel of Bones. He recalled what Hades had said about this public square, where the Inquisition had burned hundreds of people alive.

This was an ancient city. How many dead lay in the ground beneath his feet?

"Coach," he said, "you can climb?"

Hedge scoffed. "I'm half *goat.* Of course I can climb!"

"Get up to the statue and secure the rigging. Make a rope ladder and drop it down for us."

"Uh, but the pack of wolves—"

"Reyna," Nico said, "you and your dogs will have to cover our retreat."

The praetor nodded grimly. "Understood."

Lycaon howled with laughter. "Retreat to where, son of Hades? There is no escape. You cannot kill us!"

"Maybe not," Nico said. "But I can slow you down."

He spread his hands and the ground erupted.

Nico hadn't expected it to work so well. He had pulled bone fragments from the earth before. He'd animated rat skeletons and unearthed the odd human skull. Nothing prepared him for the wall of bones that burst skyward—hundreds of femurs, ribs, and fibulas entangling the wolves, forming a spiky briar of human remains.

Most of the wolves were hopelessly trapped. Some writhed and gnashed their teeth, trying to free themselves from their haphazard cages. Lycaon himself was immobilized in a cocoon of rib bones, but that didn't stop him from screaming curses.

"You worthless child!" he roared. "I will rip the flesh from your limbs!"

"Coach, go!" Nico said.

The satyr sprinted toward the temple. He made the top of the podium in a single leap and scrambled up the left pillar.

Two wolves broke free from the thicket of bones. Reyna

threw her knife and impaled one in the neck. Her dogs pounced on the other. Aurum's fangs and claws slipped harmlessly off the wolf's hide, but Argentum brought the beast down.

Argentum's head was still bent sideways from the fight in Pompeii. His left ruby eye was still missing, but he managed to sink his fangs into the wolf's scruff. The wolf dissolved into a puddle of shadow.

Thank goodness for silver dogs, Nico thought.

Reyna drew her sword. She scooped a handful of silver coins from Hedge's baseball cap, grabbed duct tape from the coach's supply bag, and began taping coins around her blade. The girl was nothing if not inventive.

"Go!" she told Nico. "I'll cover you!"

The wolves struggled, causing the bone thicket to crack and crumble. Lycaon freed his right arm and began smashing through his prison of rib cages.

"I will flay you alive!" he promised. "I will add your pelt to my cloak!"

Nico ran, pausing just long enough to grab Reyna's silver pocketknife from the ground.

He wasn't a mountain goat, but he found a set of stairs at the back of the temple and raced to the top. He reached the base of the columns and squinted up at Coach Hedge, who was precariously perched at the feet of the Athena Parthenos, unraveling ropes and knotting a ladder.

"Hurry!" Nico yelled.

"Oh, really?" the coach called down. "I thought we had tons of time!"

The last thing Nico needed was satyr sarcasm. Down in the square, more wolves broke free of their bone restraints. Reyna swatted them aside with her modified duct-tape-coin-sword, but a handful of change wasn't going to hold back a pack of werewolves for long. Aurum snarled and snapped in frustration, unable to hurt the enemy. Argentum did his best, sinking his claws into the throat of another wolf, but the silver dog was already damaged. Soon he'd be hopelessly outnumbered.

Lycaon freed both his arms. He started pulling his legs from their rib cage restraints. There were only a few seconds until he would be loose.

Nico was out of tricks. Summoning that wall of bones had drained him. It would take all his remaining energy to shadow-travel—assuming he could even find a shadow to travel into.

*A shadow.*

He looked at the silver pocketknife in his hand. An idea came to him—possibly the stupidest, craziest idea he'd had since he thought: *Hey, I'll get Percy to swim in the River Styx! He'll love me for that!*

"Reyna, get up here!" he yelled.

She slammed another wolf in the head and ran. In mid-stride, she flicked her sword, which elongated into a javelin, then used it to launch herself up like a pole-vaulter. She landed next to Nico.

"What's the plan?" she asked, not even out of breath.

"Show-off," he grumbled.

A knotted rope fell from above.

"Climb, ya silly non-goats!" Hedge yelled.

"Go," Nico told her. "Once you're up there, hang on tight to the rope."

"Nico—"

"Do it!"

Her javelin shrank back into a sword. Reyna sheathed it and began to climb, scaling the column despite her armor and her supplies.

Down in the plaza, Aurum and Argentum were nowhere to be seen. Either they'd retreated or they'd been destroyed.

Lycaon broke free of his bone cage with a triumphant howl. "You will suffer, son of Hades!"

*What else is new?* Nico thought.

He palmed the pocketknife. "Come get me, you mutt! Or do you have to *stay* like a good dog until your master shows up?"

Lycaon sprang through the air, his claws extended, his fangs bared. Nico wrapped his free hand around the rope and concentrated, a bead of sweat trickling down his neck.

As the wolf king fell on him, Nico thrust the silver knife into Lycaon's chest. All around the temple, wolves howled as one.

The wolf king sank his claws into Nico's arms. His fangs stopped less than an inch from Nico's face. Nico ignored his own pain and jabbed the pocketknife to the hilt between Lycaon's ribs.

"Be useful, dog," he snarled. "Back to the shadows."

Lycaon's eyes rolled up in his head. He dissolved into a pool of inky darkness.

Then several things happened at once. The outraged pack of wolves surged forward. From a nearby rooftop, a booming voice yelled, "STOP THEM!"

Nico heard the unmistakable sound of a large bow being drawn taut.

Then he melted into the pool of Lycaon's shadow, taking his friends and the Athena Parthenos with him—slipping into cold ether with no idea where he would emerge.

# XVII

# PIPER

PIPER COULDN'T BELIEVE how hard it was to find deadly poison.

All morning she and Frank had scoured the port of Pylos. Frank allowed only Piper to come with him, thinking her charmspeak might be useful if they ran into his shape-shifting relatives.

As it turned out, her sword was more in demand. So far, they'd slain a Laistrygonian ogre in the bakery, battled a giant warthog in the public square, and defeated a flock of Stymphalian birds with some well-aimed vegetables from Piper's cornucopia.

She was glad for the work. It kept her from dwelling on her conversation with her mother the night before—that bleak glimpse of the future Aphrodite had made her promise not to share . . .

Meanwhile, Piper's biggest challenge in Pylos was the ads plastered all over town for her dad's new movie. The posters were in Greek, but Piper knew what they said: TRISTAN MCLEAN IS JAKE STEEL: *SIGNED IN BLOOD.*

Gods, what a horrible title. She wished her father had never taken on the Jake Steel franchise, but it had become one of his most popular roles. There he was on the poster, his shirt ripped open to reveal perfect abs (gross, Dad!), an AK-47 in each hand, a rakish smile on his chiseled face.

Halfway across the world, in the smallest, most out-of-the-way town imaginable, there was her dad. It made Piper feel sad, disoriented, homesick, and annoyed all at once. Life went on. So did Hollywood. While her dad pretended to save the world, Piper and her friends actually *had* to. In eight more days, unless Piper could pull off the plan Aphrodite had explained . . . well, there wouldn't be any more movies, or theaters, or people.

Around one in the afternoon, Piper finally put her charmspeak to work. She spoke with an Ancient Greek ghost in a Laundromat (on a one-to-ten scale for weird conversations, definitely an eleven) and got directions to an ancient stronghold where the shape-shifting descendants of Periclymenus supposedly hung out.

After trudging across the island in the afternoon heat, they found the cave perched halfway up a beachside cliff. Frank insisted that Piper wait for him at the bottom while he checked it out.

Piper wasn't happy about that, but she stood obediently on the beach, squinting up at the cave entrance and hoping she hadn't guided Frank into a death trap.

Behind her, a stretch of white sand hugged the foot of the

hills. Sunbathers sprawled on blankets. Little kids splashed in the waves. The blue sea glittered invitingly.

Piper wished she could surf those waters. She'd promised to teach Hazel and Annabeth someday, if they ever came out to Malibu . . . if Malibu still existed after August 1.

She glanced up at the cliff's summit. The ruins of an old castle clung to the ridge. Piper wasn't sure if that was part of the shape-changers' hideout or not. Nothing moved on the parapets. The entrance of the cave sat about seventy feet down the cliff face—a circle of black in the chalky yellow rock like the hole of a giant pencil sharpener.

*Nestor's Cave*, the Laundromat ghost had called it. Supposedly the ancient king of Pylos had stashed his treasure there in times of crisis. The ghost also claimed that Hermes had once hidden the stolen cattle of Apollo in that cave.

*Cows.*

Piper shuddered. When she was little, her dad had driven her past a meat processing plant in Chino. The smell had been enough to turn her into a vegetarian. Ever since, just the thought of cows made her ill. Her experiences with Hera the cow queen, the *katoblepones* of Venice, and the pictures of creepy death cows in the House of Hades hadn't helped.

Piper was just starting to think *Frank's been gone too long*—when he appeared at the cave entrance. Next to him stood a tall gray-haired man in a white linen suit and a pale yellow tie. The older man pressed a small shiny object—like a stone or a piece of glass—into Frank's hands. He and Frank exchanged a few words. Frank nodded gravely. Then the man turned into a seagull and flew away.

Frank picked his way down the trail until he reached Piper.
"I found them," he said.

"I noticed. You okay?"

He stared at the seagull as it flew toward the horizon.

Frank's close-cropped hair pointed forward like an arrow, making his gaze even more intense. His Roman badges—*mural crown, centurion, praetor*—glittered on his shirt collar. On his forearm, the SPQR tattoo with the crossed spears of Mars stood out darkly in the full sunlight.

He looked good in his new outfit. The giant warthog had slimed his old clothes pretty badly, so Piper had taken him for some emergency shopping in Pylos. Now he wore new black jeans, soft leather boots, and a dark green Henley shirt that fit him snugly. He'd been self-conscious about the shirt. He was used to hiding his bulk in baggy clothes, but Piper assured him he didn't have to worry about that anymore. Since his growth spurt in Venice, he'd grown into his bulkiness just fine.

*You haven't changed, Frank,* she'd told him. *You're just more* you.

It was a good thing Frank Zhang was still so sweet and soft-spoken. Otherwise he would've been a scary guy.

"Frank?" she prompted gently.

"Yeah, sorry." He focused on her. "My, uh . . . cousins, I guess you'd call them . . . they've been living here for generations, all descended from Periclymenus the Argonaut. I told them my story, how the Zhang family had gone from Greece to Rome to China to Canada. I told them about the legionnaire ghost I saw in the House of Hades, urging me to come to Pylos. They . . . they didn't seem surprised. They said it's happened before, long-lost relatives coming home."

Piper heard the wistfulness in his voice. "You were expecting something different."

He shrugged. "A bigger welcome. Some party balloons. I'm not sure. My grandmother told me I would close the circle—bring our family honor and all that. But my cousins here . . . they acted kind of cold and distant, like they didn't want me around. I don't think they liked that I'm a son of Mars. Honestly, I don't think they liked that I'm Chinese, either."

Piper glared into the sky. The seagull was long gone, which was probably a good thing. She would have been tempted to shoot it out of the air with a glazed ham. "If your cousins feel that way, they're idiots. They don't know how great you are."

Frank shuffled from foot to foot. "They got a little more friendly when I told them I was just passing through. They gave me a going-away present."

He opened his hand. In his palm gleamed a metallic vial no bigger than an eyedropper.

Piper resisted the urge to step away. "Is that the poison?"

Frank nodded. "They call it *Pylosian mint*. Apparently the plant sprang from the blood of a nymph who died on a mountain near here, back in ancient times. I didn't ask for details."

The vial was so tiny . . . Piper worried there wouldn't be enough. Normally she didn't wish for *more* deadly poison. Nor was she sure how it would help them make the so-called *physician's cure* that Nike had mentioned. But if the cure could really cheat death, Piper wanted to brew a six-pack—one dose for each of her friends.

Frank rolled the vial around in his palm. "I wish Vitellius Reticulus were here."

Piper wasn't sure she'd heard him right. "Ridiculous who?"

A smile flickered across his mouth. "Gaius Vitellius Reticulus, although we *did* call him Ridiculous sometimes. He was one of the Lares of the Fifth Cohort. Kind of a goofball, but he was the son of Aesculapius, the healing god. If anybody knew about this physician's cure . . . he might."

"A healing god would be nice," Piper mused. "Better than having a screaming, tied-up victory goddess on board."

"Hey, you're lucky. My cabin is closest to the stables. I can hear her yelling all night: *FIRST PLACE OR DEATH! AN A MINUS IS A FAILING GRADE!* Leo really needs to design a gag that's better than my old sock."

Piper shuddered. She still didn't understand why it had been a good idea to take the goddess captive. The sooner they got rid of Nike, the better. "So your cousins . . . did they have any advice about what comes next? This chained god we're supposed to find in Sparta?"

Frank's expression darkened. "Yeah. I'm afraid they had some thoughts on that. Let's get back to the ship, and I'll tell you about it."

Piper's feet were killing her. She wondered if she could convince Frank to turn into a giant eagle and carry her, but before she could ask, she heard footsteps in the sand behind them.

"Hello, nice tourists!" A scraggly fisherman with a white captain's hat and a mouth full of gold teeth beamed at them. "Boat ride? Very cheap!"

He gestured to the shore, where a skiff with an outboard motor waited.

Piper returned his smile. She loved it when she could communicate with the locals.

"Yes, please," she said in her best charmspeak. "And we'd like you to take us somewhere special."

The boat captain dropped them at the *Argo II*, anchored a quarter mile out to sea. Piper pressed a wad of euros into the captain's hands.

She wasn't above using charmspeak on mortals, but she'd decided to be as fair and careful as possible. Her days of stealing BMWs from car dealerships were over.

"Thank you," she told him. "If anyone asks, you took us around the island and showed us the sights. You dropped us at the docks in Pylos. You never saw any giant warship."

"No warship," the captain agreed. "Thank you, nice American tourists!"

They climbed aboard the *Argo II* and Frank smiled at her awkwardly. "Well . . . nice killing giant warthogs with you."

Piper laughed. "You too, Mr. Zhang."

She gave him a hug, which seemed to fluster him, but Piper couldn't help liking Frank. Not only was he a kind and considerate boyfriend to Hazel, but whenever Piper saw him wearing Jason's old praetor's badge, she felt grateful to him for stepping up and accepting that job. He had taken a huge responsibility off Jason's shoulders and left him free (Piper hoped) to pursue a new path at Camp Half-Blood . . . assuming, of course, that they all lived through the next eight days.

The crew gathered for a hurried meeting on the foredeck—mostly because Percy was keeping an eye on a giant red sea serpent swimming off the port side.

"That thing is *really* red," Percy muttered. "I wonder if it's cherry-flavored."

"Why don't you swim over and find out?" Annabeth asked.

"How about no."

"Anyway," Frank said, "according to my Pylos cousins, the chained god we're looking for in Sparta is my dad . . . uh, I mean Ares, not Mars. Apparently the Spartans kept a statue of him chained up in their city so the spirit of war would never leave them."

"Oo-kay," Leo said. "The Spartans were freaks. Of course, we've got Victory tied up downstairs, so I guess we can't talk."

Jason leaned against the forward ballista. "On to Sparta, then. But how does a chained god's heartbeat help us find a cure for dying?"

From the tightness in his face, Piper could tell he was still in pain. She remembered what Aphrodite had told her: *It's not just his sword wound, my dear. It's the ugly truth he saw in Ithaca. If the poor boy doesn't stay strong, that truth will eat right through him.*

"Piper?" Hazel asked.

She stirred. "Sorry, what?"

"I was asking you about the visions," Hazel prompted. "You told me you'd seen some stuff in your dagger blade?"

"Uh . . . right." Piper reluctantly unsheathed Katoptris. Ever since she'd used it to stab the snow goddess Khione, the visions in the blade had become colder and harsher, like images etched in ice. She'd seen eagles swirling over Camp Half-Blood, a wave of earth destroying New York. She'd seen scenes from the past: her father beaten and bound at the top of Mount Diablo, Jason and Percy fighting giants in the Roman Colosseum, the river god Achelous reaching out to her, pleading for the cornucopia she'd cut from his head.

"I, um . . ." She tried to clear her thoughts. "I don't see anything right now. But one vision kept popping up. Annabeth and I are exploring some ruins—"

"Ruins!" Leo rubbed his hands. "Now we're talking. How many ruins can there be in Greece?"

"Quiet, Leo," Annabeth scolded. "Piper, do you think it was Sparta?"

"Maybe," Piper said. "Anyway . . . suddenly we're in this dark place like a cave. We're staring at this bronze warrior statue. In the vision I touch the statue's face and flames start swirling around us. That's all I saw."

"Flames." Frank scowled. "I don't like that vision."

"Me neither." Percy kept one eye on the red sea serpent, which was still slithering through the waves about a hundred yards to port. "If the statue engulfs people in fire, we should send Leo."

"I love you too, man."

"You know what I mean. You're immune. Or, heck, give me some of those nice water grenades and *I'll* go. Ares and I have tangled before."

Annabeth stared at the coastline of Pylos, now retreating in the distance. "If Piper saw the two of us going after the statue, then that's who should go. We'll be all right. There's always a way to survive."

"Not always," Hazel warned.

Since she was the only one in the group who had actually died and come back to life, her observation sort of killed the mood.

Frank held out the vial of Pylosian mint. "What about this stuff? After the House of Hades, I kind of hoped we were done drinking poison."

"Store it securely in the hold," Annabeth said. "For now, that's all we can do. Once we figure out this chained god situation, we'll head to the island of Delos."

"*The curse of Delos,*" Hazel remembered. "That sounds fun."

"Hopefully Apollo will be there," Annabeth said. "Delos was his home island. He's the god of medicine. He should be able to advise us."

Aphrodite's words came back to Piper: *You must bridge the gap between Roman and Greek, my child. Neither storm nor fire can succeed without you.*

Aphrodite had warned her of what was to come, told her what Piper would have to do to stop Gaea. Whether or not she would have the courage . . . Piper didn't know.

Off the port bow, the cherry-flavored sea serpent spewed steam.

"Yeah, it's definitely checking us out," Percy decided. "Maybe we should take to the air for a while."

"Airborne it is!" Leo said. "Festus, do the honors!"

The bronze dragon figurehead creaked and clacked. The ship's engine hummed. The oars lifted, expanding into aerial blades with a sound like ninety umbrellas opening at once, and the *Argo II* rose into the sky.

"We should reach Sparta by morning," Leo announced. "And remember to come by the mess hall tonight, folks, 'cause Chef Leo is making his famous three-alarm tofu tacos!"

XVIII

# PIPER

PIPER DIDN'T WANT TO get yelled at by a three-legged table.

When Jason visited her cabin that evening, she made sure to keep the door open, because Buford the Wonder Table took his duties as acting chaperone very seriously. If he had the slightest suspicion a girl and a boy were in the same cabin without supervision, he would steam and clatter down the hall, his holographic projection of Coach Hedge yelling, "CUT THAT OUT! GIVE ME TWENTY PUSH-UPS! PUT SOME CLOTHES ON!"

Jason sat at the foot of her bunk. "I was about to go on duty. Just wanted to check on you first."

Piper nudged his leg with her foot. "The guy who got run through with a sword wants to check on *me*? How are *you* feeling?"

He gave her a lopsided smile. His face was so tan from their time on the coast of Africa that the scar on his lip looked like a chalk mark. His blue eyes were even more startling.

His hair had grown out corn-silk white, though he still had a groove along his scalp where he'd been grazed by a bullet from the bandit Sciron's flintlock. If such a minor scrape from Celestial bronze took so long to heal, Piper wondered how he'd ever get over the Imperial gold wound in his gut.

"I've been worse," Jason assured her. "Once, in Oregon, this *dracaena* cut off my arms."

Piper blinked. Then she slapped his arm gently. "Shut up."

"I had you for a second."

They held hands in comfortable silence. For a moment, Piper could almost imagine they were normal teenagers, enjoying each other's company and learning to be together as a couple. Sure, Jason and she had had a few months at Camp Half-Blood, but the war with Gaea had always been looming. Piper wondered what it would be like if they didn't have to worry about dying a dozen times every day.

"I never thanked you." Jason's expression turned serious. "Back on Ithaca, after I saw my mom's . . . remnant, her *mania* . . . When I was wounded, you kept me from slipping away, Pipes. Part of me . . ." His voice faltered. "Part of me wanted to close my eyes and stop fighting."

Piper's heart did a slow twist. She felt her own pulse in her fingers. "Jason . . . you're a fighter. You'd never give up. When you faced your mother's spirit—that was *you* being strong. Not me."

"Maybe." His voice was dry. "I didn't mean to lay something so heavy on you, Pipes. It's just . . . I have my mom's DNA. The human part of me is all *her*. What if I make the wrong choices? What if I make a mistake I can't take back when we're fighting Gaea? I don't want to end up like my mom—reduced to a *mania*, chewing on my regrets forever."

Piper cupped her hands around his. She felt like she was back on the deck of the *Argo II*, holding the Boreads' ice grenade just before it detonated.

"You'll make the right choices," she said. "I don't know what will happen to any of us, but you could *never* end up like your mom."

"How can you be so sure?"

Piper studied the tattoo on his forearm—SPQR, the eagle of Jupiter, twelve lines for his years in the legion. "My dad used to tell me this story about making choices . . ." She shook her head. "No, never mind. I'll sound like Grandpa Tom."

"Go on," Jason said. "What's the story?"

"Well . . . these two Cherokee hunters were out in the woods, right? Each of them was under a taboo."

"A taboo—something they weren't allowed to do."

"Yeah." Piper began to relax. She wondered if this was why her dad and granddad always liked telling stories. You could make even the most terrifying topic easier to talk about by framing it as something that happened to a couple of Cherokee hunters hundreds of years ago. Take a problem; turn it into entertainment. Perhaps that's why her dad had become an actor.

"So one of the hunters," she continued, "he wasn't supposed to eat deer meat. The other guy wasn't supposed to eat squirrel meat."

"Why?"

"Hey, I don't know. Some Cherokee taboos were permanent

no-no's, like killing eagles." She tapped the symbol on Jason's arm. "*That* was bad luck for almost everybody. But sometimes, individual Cherokee took on temporary taboos—maybe to cleanse their spirit, or because they *knew*, from listening to the spirit world or whatever, that the taboo was important. They went with their instincts."

"Okay." Jason sounded unsure. "So back to these two hunters."

"They were out hunting in the woods all day. The only things they caught were squirrels. At night they made camp, and the guy who *could* eat squirrel meat started cooking it over the fire."

"Yum."

"Another reason I'm a vegetarian. Anyway, the second hunter, who wasn't allowed squirrel meat—*he* was starving. He just sat there clutching his stomach while his friend ate. Finally the first hunter started feeling guilty. 'Ah, go ahead,' he said. 'Eat some.' But the second hunter resisted. 'It's taboo for me. I'll get in serious trouble. I'll probably turn into a snake or something.' The first hunter laughed. 'Where did you get that crazy idea? Nothing will happen to you. You can go back to avoiding squirrel meat tomorrow.' The second hunter knew he shouldn't, but he ate."

Jason traced his finger across her knuckles, which made it hard to concentrate. "What happened?"

"In the middle of the night, the second hunter woke up screaming in pain. The first hunter ran over to see what was wrong. He threw off his friend's covers and saw that his friend's legs had fused together in a leathery tail. As he watched, snakeskin crept up his friend's body. The poor hunter wept and apologized to the spirits and cried in fear, but there was nothing to be done. The first hunter stayed by his side and tried to comfort him until the unfortunate guy fully transformed into a giant snake and slithered away. The end."

"I love these Cherokee stories," Jason said. "They're so cheerful."

"Yeah, well."

"So the guy turned into a snake. The moral is: Frank has been eating squirrels?"

She laughed, which felt good. "No, stupid. The point is, trust your instincts. Squirrel meat might be just fine for one person, but taboo for another. The second hunter *knew* he had a serpent spirit inside him, waiting to take over. He *knew* he shouldn't feed that bad spirit by eating squirrel meat, but he did it anyway."

"So . . . *I* shouldn't eat squirrels."

Piper was relieved to see the gleam in his eyes. She thought about something Hazel had confided to her a few nights ago: *I think Jason is the linchpin to Hera's whole scheme. He was her first play; he's going to be her last.*

"My point," Piper said, poking his chest, "is that you, Jason Grace, are very familiar with your own bad spirits, and you try your best not to feed them. You have solid instincts, and you know how to follow them. Whatever annoying qualities you have, you are a genuinely good person who always tries to make the right choice. So no more talk about giving up."

Jason frowned. "Wait. I have annoying qualities?"

She rolled her eyes. "Come here."

She was about to kiss him when there was a knock on the door.

Leo leaned inside. "A party? Am I invited?"

Jason cleared his throat. "Hey, Leo. What's going on?"

"Oh, not much." He pointed upstairs. "The usual obnoxious *venti* trying to destroy the ship. You ready for guard duty?"

"Yeah." Jason leaned forward and kissed Piper. "Thanks. And don't worry. I'm good."

"That," she told him, "was kind of my point."

After the boys left, Piper lay on her pegasus-down pillows and watched the constellations her lamp projected on the ceiling. She didn't think she could sleep, but a full day of fighting monsters in the summer heat had taken its toll. At last she closed her eyes and drifted into a nightmare.

The Acropolis.

Piper had never been there, but she recognized it from pictures—an ancient stronghold perched on a hill almost as impressive as Gibraltar. Rising four hundred feet over the nighttime sprawl of modern Athens, the sheer cliffs were topped with a crown of limestone walls. On the clifftop, a collection of ruined temples and modern cranes gleamed silver in the moonlight.

In her dream, Piper flew above the Parthenon—the ancient temple of Athena, the left side of its hollow shell encased in metal scaffolding.

The Acropolis seemed devoid of mortals, perhaps because of the financial problems in Greece. Or perhaps Gaea's forces had arranged some pretext to keep the tourists and construction workers away.

Piper's view zoomed to the center of the temple. So many giants had gathered there it looked like a cocktail party for redwood trees. A few Piper recognized: those horrible twins from Rome, Otis and Ephialtes, dressed in matching construction worker outfits; Polybotes, looking just as Percy had described him, with poison dripping from his dreadlocks and a breastplate sculpted to resemble hungry mouths; worst of all, Enceladus, the giant who had kidnapped Piper's dad. His armor was etched with flame designs, his hair braided with bones. His flagpole-sized spear burned with purple fire.

Piper had heard that each giant was born to oppose a particular god, but there were *way* more than twelve giants gathered in the Parthenon. She counted at least twenty, and if that wasn't intimidating enough, around the giants' feet milled a horde of smaller monsters—Cyclopes, ogres, six-armed Earthborn, and serpent-legged *dracaenae*.

In the center of the crowd stood an empty, makeshift throne of twisted scaffolding and stone blocks apparently yanked at random from the ruins.

As Piper watched, a new giant lumbered up the steps at the far end of the Acropolis. He wore a massive velour tracksuit with gold chains around his neck and greased-back hair, so he looked like a thirty-foot-tall mobster—if mobsters had dragon feet and burnt-orange skin. The mafia giant ran toward the Parthenon and stumbled inside, flattening several Earthborn under his feet. He stopped, gasping for breath at the foot of the throne.

"Where is Porphyrion?" he demanded. "I have news!"

Piper's old enemy Enceladus stepped forward. "Tardy as usual, Hippolytos. I hope your news is worth the wait. King Porphyrion should be . . ."

The ground between them split. An even larger giant leaped from the earth like a breaching whale.

"King Porphyrion is here," announced the king.

He looked just as Piper remembered from the Wolf House in Sonoma. Forty feet tall, he towered over his brethren. In fact, Piper realized queasily, he was the same size as the Athena Parthenos that had once dominated the temple. In his seaweed-colored braids, captured demigod weapons glittered. His face was cruel and pale green, his eyes as white as the Mist. His body radiated its own sort of gravity, causing the other monsters to lean toward him. Dirt and pebbles skittered across the ground, pulled toward his massive dragon feet.

The mobster giant Hippolytos kneeled. "My king, I bring word of the enemy!"

Porphyrion took his throne. "Speak."

"The demigod ship sails around the Peloponnese. Already they have destroyed the ghosts at Ithaca and captured the goddess Nike in Olympia!"

The crowd of monsters stirred uneasily. A Cyclops chewed his fingernails. Two *dracaenae* exchanged coins like they were taking bets for the End-of-the-World office pool.

Porphyrion just laughed. "Hippolytos, do you wish to kill your enemy Hermes and become the messenger of the giants?"

"Yes, my king!"

"Then you will have to bring fresher news. I know all this

already. None of it matters! The demigods have taken the route we *expected* them to take. They would have been fools to go any other way."

"But, sire, they will arrive at Sparta by morning! If they manage to unleash the *makhai*—"

"Idiot!" Porphyrion's voice shook the ruins. "Our brother Mimas awaits them at Sparta. You need not worry. The demigods cannot change their fate. One way or another, their blood shall be spilled upon these stones and wake the Earth Mother!"

The crowd roared approval and brandished their weapons. Hippolytos bowed and retreated, but another giant approached the throne.

With a start, Piper realized this one was *female*. Not that it was easy to tell. The giantess had the same dragon-like legs and the same long braided hair. She was just as tall and burly as the males, but her breastplate was definitely fashioned for a woman. Her voice was higher and reedier.

"Father!" she cried. "I ask again: Why here, in this place? Why not on the slopes of Mount Olympus itself? Surely—"

"Periboia," the king growled, "the matter is settled. The original Mount Olympus is now a barren peak. It offers us no glory. Here, in the center of the Greek world, the roots of the gods truly run deep. There may be older temples, but this *Parthenon* holds their memory best. In the minds of mortals, it is the most powerful symbol of the Olympians. When the blood of the last heroes is spilled here, the Acropolis shall be razed. This hill shall crumble, and the entire city shall be consumed by the Earth Mother. We will be the masters of Creation!"

The crowd hollered and howled, but the giantess Periboia didn't look convinced.

"You tempt fate, Father," she said. "The demigods have friends here as well as enemies. It is not wise—"

"WISE?" Porphyrion rose from his throne. All the giants took a step back. "Enceladus, my counselor, explain to my daughter what wisdom is!"

The fiery giant came forward. His eyes glowed like diamonds. Piper loathed his face. She'd seen it too many times in her dreams when her father was held captive.

"You need not worry, princess," Enceladus said. "We have taken Delphi. Apollo was driven out of Olympus in shame. The future is closed to the gods. They stumble forward blindly. As for tempting fate . . ." He gestured to his left, and a smaller giant shuffled forward. He had ratty gray hair, a wrinkled face, and eyes that were milky with cataracts. Instead of armor, he wore a tattered sackcloth tunic. His dragon-scale legs were as white as frost.

He didn't look like much, but Piper noticed that the other monsters kept their distance. Even Porphyrion leaned away from the old giant.

"This is Thoon," Enceladus said. "Just as many of us were born to kill certain gods, Thoon was born to kill the Three Fates. He will strangle the old ladies with his bare hands. He will shred their yarn and destroy their loom. He will destroy Fate itself!"

King Porphyrion rose and spread his arms in triumph. "No more prophecies, my friends! No more futures foretold! The time of Gaea shall be our era, and we will make our own destiny!"

The crowd cheered so loudly, Piper felt as if she were crumbling to pieces.

Then she realized someone was shaking her awake.

"Hey," Annabeth said. "We made it to Sparta. Can you get ready?"

Piper sat up groggily, her heart still pounding.

"Yeah . . ." She gripped Annabeth's arm. "But first, there's something you need to hear."

# XIX

# PIPER

WHEN SHE RECOUNTED her dream for Percy, the ship's toilets exploded.

"No way are you two going down there alone," Percy said.

Leo ran down the hall waving a wrench. "Man, did you *have* to destroy the plumbing?"

Percy ignored him. Water ran down the gangway. The hull rumbled as more pipes burst and sinks overflowed. Piper guessed that Percy hadn't meant to cause so much damage, but his glowering expression made her want to leave the ship as soon as possible.

"We'll be all right," Annabeth told him. "Piper foresaw the two of us going down there, so that's what needs to happen."

Percy glared at Piper like it was all her fault. "And this Mimas dude? I'm guessing he's a giant?"

"Probably," she said. "Porphyrion called him *our brother*."

"And a bronze statue surrounded by fire," Percy said. "And those . . . other things you mentioned. Mackies?"

"*Makhai,*" Piper said. "I think the word means *battles* in Greek, but I don't know how that applies, exactly."

"That's my point!" Percy said. "We don't know what's down there. I'm going with you."

"No." Annabeth put her hand on his arm. "If the giants want our blood, the *last* thing we need is a boy and a girl going down there together. Remember? They want one of each for their big sacrifice."

"Then I'll get Jason," Percy said. "And the two of us—"

"Seaweed Brain, are you implying that two boys can handle this better than two girls?"

"No. I mean . . . no. But—"

Annabeth kissed him. "We'll be back before you know it."

Piper followed her upstairs before the whole lower deck could flood with toilet water.

An hour later, the two of them stood on a hill overlooking the ruins of Ancient Sparta. They'd already scouted the modern city, which, strangely, reminded Piper of Albuquerque—a bunch of low, boxy, whitewashed buildings sprawled across a plain at the foot of some purplish mountains. Annabeth had insisted on checking the archaeology museum, then the giant metal statue of the Spartan warrior in the public square, then the National Museum of Olives and Olive Oil (yes, that was a real thing). Piper had learned more about olive oil than she ever wanted to know, but no giants attacked them. They found no statues of chained gods.

Annabeth seemed reluctant to check the ruins on the edge of town, but finally they ran out of other places to look.

There wasn't much to see. According to Annabeth, the hill they stood on had once been Sparta's acropolis—its highest point and main fortress—but it was nothing like the massive Athenian acropolis Piper had seen in her dreams.

The weathered slope was covered with dead grass, rocks, and stunted olive trees. Below, ruins stretched out for maybe a quarter mile: limestone blocks, a few broken walls, and some tiled holes in the ground like wells.

Piper thought about her dad's most famous movie, *King of Sparta*, and how the Spartans were portrayed as invincible supermen. She found it sad that their legacy had been reduced to a field of rubble and a small modern town with an olive oil museum.

She wiped the sweat from her forehead. "You'd think if there was a thirty-foot-tall giant around, we'd see him."

Annabeth stared at the distant shape of the *Argo II* floating above downtown Sparta. She fingered the red coral pendant on her necklace—a gift from Percy when they started dating.

"You're thinking about Percy," Piper guessed.

Annabeth nodded.

Since she'd come back from Tartarus, Annabeth had told Piper a lot of scary things that had happened down there. At the top of her list: Percy controlling a tide of poison and suffocating the goddess Akhlys.

"He seems to be adjusting," Piper said. "He's smiling more often. You know he cares about you more than ever."

Annabeth sat, her face suddenly pale. "I don't know why

it's hitting me so hard all of a sudden. I can't quite get that memory out of my head . . . how Percy looked when he was standing at the edge of Chaos."

Maybe Piper was just picking up on Annabeth's uneasiness, but she started to feel agitated as well.

She thought about what Jason had said last night: *Part of me wanted to close my eyes and stop fighting.*

She had tried her best to reassure him, but still she worried. Like that Cherokee hunter who changed into a serpent, *all* demigods had their share of bad spirits inside. Fatal flaws. Some crises brought them out. Some lines shouldn't be crossed.

If that was true for Jason, how could it not be true for Percy? The guy had literally been through hell and back. Even when he wasn't trying, he made the toilets explode. What would Percy be like if he *wanted* to act scary?

"Give him time." She sat next to Annabeth. "The guy is crazy about you. You've been through so much together."

"I know . . ." Annabeth's gray eyes reflected the green of the olive trees. "It's just . . . Bob the Titan, he warned me there would be more sacrifices ahead. I want to believe we can have a normal life someday. . . . But I allowed myself to hope for that last summer, after the Titan War. Then Percy disappeared for *months*. Then we fell into that pit . . ." A tear traced its way down her cheek. "Piper, if you'd seen the face of the god Tartarus, all swirling darkness, devouring monsters and vaporizing them—I've never felt so *helpless*. I try not to think about it . . ."

Piper took her friend's hands. They were trembling badly.

She remembered her first day at Camp Half-Blood, when Annabeth had given her a tour. Annabeth had been shaken up about Percy's disappearance, and though Piper was pretty disoriented and scared herself, comforting Annabeth had made her feel needed, like she might actually have a place among these crazy-powerful demigods.

Annabeth Chase was the bravest person she knew. If even *she* needed a shoulder to cry on once in a while . . . well, Piper was glad to offer hers.

"Hey," she said gently. "Don't try to shut out the feelings. You won't be able to. Just let them wash over you and drain out again. You're scared."

"Gods, yes, I'm scared."

"You're angry."

"At Percy for frightening me," she said. "At my mom for sending me on that horrible quest in Rome. At . . . well, pretty much everybody. Gaea. The giants. The gods for being jerks."

"At me?" Piper asked.

Annabeth managed a shaky laugh. "Yes, for being so annoyingly calm."

"It's all a lie."

"And for being a good friend."

"Ha!"

"And for having your head on straight about guys and relationships and—"

"I'm sorry. Have you *met* me?"

Annabeth punched her arm, but there was no force to it. "I'm stupid, sitting here talking about my feelings when we have a quest to finish."

"The chained god's heartbeat can wait." Piper tried for a smile, but her own fears welled up inside her—for Jason and her friends on the *Argo II*, for herself, if she wasn't able to do what Aphrodite had advised. *In the end, you will only have the power for one word. It must be the right word, or you will lose everything.*

"Whatever happens," she told Annabeth, "I'm your friend. Just . . . remember that, okay?"

Especially if I'm not around to remind you, Piper thought.

Annabeth started to say something. Suddenly a roaring sound came from the ruins. One of the stone-lined pits, which Piper had mistaken for wells, spewed out a three-story geyser of flames and shut off just as quickly.

"What the heck?" Piper asked.

Annabeth sighed. "I don't know, but I have a feeling it's something we should check out."

Three pits lay side by side like finger holes on a recorder. Each one was perfectly round, two feet in diameter, tiled around the rim with limestone; each one plunged straight into darkness. Every few seconds, seemingly at random, one of the three pits shot a column of fire into the sky. Each time, the color and intensity of the flames were different.

"They weren't doing this before." Annabeth walked a wide arc around the pits. She still looked shaky and pale, but her mind was now obviously engaged in the problem at hand. "There doesn't seem to be any pattern. The timing, the color, the height of the fire . . . I don't get it."

"Did we activate them somehow?" Piper wondered.

"Maybe that surge of fear you felt on the hill . . . Uh, I mean we *both* felt."

Annabeth didn't seem to hear her. "There must be some kind of mechanism . . . a pressure plate, a proximity alarm."

Flames shot from the middle pit. Annabeth counted silently. The next time, a geyser erupted on the left. She frowned. "That's not right. It's inconsistent. It has to follow some kind of logic."

Piper's ears started to ring. Something about these pits . . .

Each time one ignited, a horrible thrill went through her—fear, panic, but also a strong desire to get closer to the flames.

"It isn't rational," she said. "It's emotional."

"How can fire pits be emotional?"

Piper held her hand over the pit on the right. Instantly, flames leaped up. Piper barely had time to withdraw her fingers. Her nails steamed.

"Piper!" Annabeth ran over. "What were you *thinking*?"

"I wasn't. I was feeling. What we want is down there. These pits are the way in. I'll have to jump."

"Are you *crazy*? Even if you don't get stuck in the tube, you have no idea how deep it is."

"You're right."

"You'll be burned alive!"

"Possibly." Piper unbuckled her sword and tossed it into the pit on the right. "I'll let you know if it's safe. Wait for my word."

"Don't you dare," Annabeth warned.

Piper jumped.

For a moment she was weightless in the dark, the sides of the hot stone pit burning her arms. Then the space opened up around her. Instinctively she tucked and rolled, absorbing most of the impact as she hit the stone floor.

Flames shot up in front of her, singeing her eyebrows, but Piper snatched up her sword, unsheathed it, and swung before she'd even stopped rolling. A bronze dragonhead, neatly decapitated, wobbled across the floor.

Piper stood, trying to get her bearings. She looked down at the fallen dragonhead and felt a moment of guilt, as if she'd killed Festus. But this wasn't Festus.

Three bronze dragon statues stood in a row, aligned with the holes in the roof. Piper had decapitated the middle one. The two intact dragons were each three feet tall, their snouts pointed upward and their steaming mouths open. They were clearly the source of the flames, but they didn't seem to be automatons. They didn't move or try to attack her. Piper calmly sliced off the heads of the other two.

She waited. No more flames shot upward.

"Piper?" Annabeth's voice echoed from far above like she was yelling down a chimney.

"Yeah!" Piper shouted.

"Thank the gods! You okay?"

"Yeah. Hold on a sec."

Her eyesight adjusted to the dark. She scanned the chamber. The only light came from her glowing blade and the openings above. The ceiling was about thirty feet high. By all rights, Piper should've broken both legs in the fall, but she wasn't going to complain.

The chamber itself was round, about the size of a helicopter pad. The walls were made of rough-hewn stone blocks chiseled with Greek inscriptions—thousands and thousands of them, like graffiti.

At the far end of the room, on a stone dais, stood the human-sized bronze statue of a warrior—the god Ares, Piper guessed—with heavy bronze chains wrapped around his body, anchoring him to the floor.

On either side of the statue loomed two dark doorways, each ten feet high, with a gruesome stone face carved over the archway. The faces reminded Piper of gorgons, except they had lions' manes instead of snakes for hair.

Piper suddenly felt very much alone.

"Annabeth!" she called. "It's a long drop, but it's safe to come down. Maybe . . . uh, you have a rope you could fasten so we can get back up?"

"On it!"

A few minutes later a rope dropped from the center pit. Annabeth shinnied down.

"Piper McLean," she grumbled, "that was without a doubt the *dumbest* risk I've ever seen anyone take, and I *date* a dumb risk-taker."

"Thank you." Piper nudged the nearest decapitated dragonhead with her foot. "I'm guessing these are the dragons of Ares. That's one of his sacred animals, right?"

"And there's the chained god himself. Where do you think those doorways—"

Piper held up her hand. "Do you hear that?"

The sound was like a drumbeat . . . with a metallic echo.

"It's coming from inside the statue," Piper decided. "The heartbeat of the chained god."

Annabeth unsheathed her drakon-bone sword. In the dim light, her face was ghostly pale, her eyes colorless. "I—I don't like this, Piper. We need to leave."

The rational part of Piper agreed. Her skin crawled. Her legs ached to run. But something about this room felt strangely familiar . . .

"The shrine is ramping up our emotions," she said. "It's like being around my mom, except this place radiates fear, not love. That's why you started feeling overwhelmed on the hill. Down here, it's a thousand times stronger."

Annabeth scanned the walls. "Okay . . . we need a plan to get the statue out. Maybe haul it up with the rope, but—"

"Wait." Piper glanced at the snarling stone faces above the doorways. "A shrine that radiates fear. Ares had two divine sons, didn't he?"

"Ph-phobos and Deimos." Annabeth shivered. "Panic and Fear. Percy met them once in Staten Island."

Piper decided not to ask what the twin gods of panic and fear had been doing in Staten Island. "I think those are their faces above the doors. This place isn't just a shrine to Ares. It's a temple of fear."

Deep laughter echoed through the chamber.

On Piper's right, a giant appeared. He didn't come through either doorway. He simply emerged from the darkness as if he'd been camouflaged against the wall.

He was small for a giant—perhaps twenty-five feet tall, which would give him enough room to swing the massive sledgehammer in his hands. His armor, his skin, and his dragon-scale legs were all the color of charcoal. Copper wires and smashed circuit boards glittered in the braids of his oil-black hair.

"Very good, child of Aphrodite." The giant smiled. "This is indeed the Temple of Fear. And I am here to make you believers."

# PIPER

PIPER KNEW FEAR, BUT THIS WAS DIFFERENT.

Waves of terror crashed over her. Her joints turned to jelly. Her heart refused to beat.

Her worst memories crowded her mind—her father tied up and beaten on Mount Diablo; Percy and Jason fighting to the death in Kansas; the three of them drowning in the nymphaeum in Rome; herself standing alone against Khione and the Boreads. Worst of all, she relived her conversation with her mother about what was to come.

Paralyzed, she watched as the giant raised his sledgehammer to smash them flat. At the last moment, she leaped to one side, tackling Annabeth.

The hammer cracked the floor, peppering Piper's back with stone shrapnel.

The giant chuckled. "Oh, that wasn't fair!" He hefted his sledgehammer again.

"Annabeth, get up!" Piper helped her to her feet. She

pulled her toward the far end of the room, but Annabeth moved sluggishly, her eyes wide and unfocused.

Piper understood why. The temple was amplifying their personal fears. Piper had seen some horrible things, but it was *nothing* compared to what Annabeth had experienced. If she was having flashbacks of Tartarus, enhanced and compounded with all her other bad memories, her mind wouldn't be able to cope. She might literally go insane.

"I'm here," Piper promised, filling her voice with reassurance. "We *will* get out of this."

The giant laughed. "A child of Aphrodite leading a child of Athena! Now I've seen everything. How would you defeat me, girl? With makeup and fashion tips?"

A few months ago that comment might've stung, but Piper was way past that. The giant lumbered toward them. Fortunately, he was slow and carrying a heavy hammer.

"Annabeth, trust me," Piper said.

"A—a plan," she stammered. "I go left. You go right. If we—"

"Annabeth, no plans."

"W-what?"

"*No* plans. Just follow me!"

The giant swung his hammer, but they dodged it easily. Piper leaped forward and slashed her sword across the back of the giant's knee. As the giant bellowed in outrage, Piper pulled Annabeth into the nearest tunnel. Immediately they were engulfed in total darkness.

"Fools!" the giant roared somewhere behind them. "That is the wrong way!"

"Keep moving." Piper held tight to Annabeth's hand. "It's fine. Come on."

She couldn't see anything. Even the glow of her sword was snuffed out. She barreled ahead anyway, trusting her emotions. From the echo of their footfalls, the space around them must have been a vast cavern, but she couldn't be sure. She simply went the direction that made her fear the sharpest.

"Piper, it's like the House of Night," Annabeth said. "We should close our eyes."

"No!" Piper said. "Keep them open. We can't try to hide."

The giant's voice came from somewhere in front of them. "Lost forever. Swallowed by the darkness."

Annabeth froze, forcing Piper to stop too.

"Why did we just plunge in?" Annabeth demanded. "We're lost. We did what he *wanted* us to! We should have bided our time, talked to the enemy, figured out a plan. That *always* works!"

"Annabeth, I *never* ignore your advice." Piper kept her voice soothing. "But this time I have to. We can't defeat this place with reason. You can't *think* your way out of your emotions."

The giant's laughter echoed like a detonating depth charge. "Despair, Annabeth Chase! I am Mimas, born to slay Hephaestus. I am the breaker of plans, the destroyer of the well-oiled machines. Nothing goes right in my presence. Maps are misread. Devices break. Data is lost. The finest minds turn to mush!"

"I—I've faced worse than you!" Annabeth cried.

"Oh, I see!" The giant sounded much closer now. "Are you not afraid?"

"Never!"

"Of course we're afraid," Piper corrected. "Terrified!"

The air moved. Just in time, Piper pushed Annabeth to one side.

*CRASH!*

Suddenly they were back in the circular room, the dim light almost blinding now. The giant stood close by, trying to yank his hammer out of the floor where he'd embedded it. Piper lunged and drove her blade into the giant's thigh.

"AROOO!" Mimas let go of the hammer and arched his back.

Piper and Annabeth scrambled behind the chained statue of Ares, which still pulsed with a metallic heartbeat: *thump, thump, thump.*

The giant Mimas turned toward them. The wound on his leg was already closing.

"You cannot defeat me," he growled. "In the last war, it took *two* gods to bring me down. I was born to kill Hephaestus, and would have done so if Ares hadn't ganged up on me as well! You should have stayed paralyzed in your fear. Your death would've been quicker."

Days ago, when she faced Khione on the *Argo II*, Piper had started talking without thinking, following her heart no matter what her brain said. Now she did the same thing. She moved in front of the statue and faced the giant, though the rational part of her screamed: *RUN, YOU IDIOT!*

"This temple," she said. "The Spartans didn't chain Ares because they wanted his spirit to stay in their city."

"You think not?" The giant's eyes glittered with amusement. He wrapped his hands around his sledgehammer and pulled it from the floor.

"This is the temple of my brothers, Deimos and Phobos." Piper's voice shook, but she didn't try to hide it. "The Spartans came here to prepare for battle, to face their fears. Ares was chained to remind them that war has consequences. His power—the spirits of battle, the *makhai*—should never be unleashed unless you understand how terrible they are, unless you've *felt* fear."

Mimas laughed. "A child of the love goddess lectures me about war. What do you know of the *makhai*?"

"We'll see." Piper ran straight at the giant, unbalancing his stance. At the sight of her jagged blade coming at him, his eyes widened and he stumbled backward, cracking his head against the wall. A jagged fissure snaked upward in the stones. Dust rained from the ceiling.

"Piper, this place is unstable!" Annabeth warned. "If we don't leave—"

"Don't think about escape!" Piper ran toward their rope, which dangled from the ceiling. She leaped as high as she could and cut it.

"Piper, have you lost your mind?"

*Probably,* she thought. But Piper knew this was the only way to survive. She had to go against reason, follow emotion instead, keep the giant off balance.

"That hurt!" Mimas rubbed his head. "You *realize* you

cannot kill me without the help of a god, and Ares is not here! The next time I face that blustering idiot, I will smash him to bits. I wouldn't have had to fight him in the *first* place if that cowardly fool Damasen had done his job—"

Annabeth let loose a guttural cry. "Do *not* insult Damasen!"

She ran at Mimas, who barely managed to parry her dragon-blade with the handle of his hammer. He tried to grab Annabeth and Piper lunged, slashing her blade across the side of the giant's face.

"GAHHH!" Mimas staggered.

A severed pile of dreadlocks fell to the floor along with something else—a large fleshy *thing* lying in a pool of golden ichor.

"My ear!" Mimas wailed. Before he could recover his wits, Piper grabbed Annabeth's arm and together they plunged through the second doorway.

"I will bring down this chamber!" the giant thundered. "The Earth Mother shall deliver me, but you shall be crushed!"

The floor shook. The sound of breaking stone echoed all around them.

"Piper, stop," Annabeth begged. "How—how are you dealing with this? The fear, the anger—"

"Don't try to control it. That's what the temple is about. You have to accept the fear, adapt to it, ride it like the rapids on a river."

"How do you *know* that?"

"I don't know it. I just feel it."

Somewhere nearby, a wall crumbled with a sound like an artillery blast.

"You cut the rope," Annabeth said. "We're going to die down here!"

Piper cupped her friend's face. She pulled Annabeth forward until their foreheads touched. Through her fingertips, she could feel Annabeth's rapid pulse. "Fear can't be reasoned with. Neither can hate. They're like love. They're almost *identical* emotions. That's why Ares and Aphrodite like each other. Their twin sons—Fear and Panic—were spawned from both war and love."

"But I don't . . . this doesn't make sense."

"No," Piper agreed. "Stop thinking about it. Just *feel.*"

"I *hate* that."

"I know. You can't plan for feelings. Like with Percy, and your future—you can't control every contingency. You have to accept that. *Let* it scare you. Trust that it'll be okay anyway."

Annabeth shook her head. "I don't know if I can."

"Then for right now, concentrate on revenge for Damasen. Revenge for Bob."

A moment of silence. "I'm good now."

"Great, because I need your help. We're going to run out there together."

"Then what?"

"I have no idea."

"Gods, I hate it when you lead."

Piper laughed, which surprised even her. Fear and love really *were* related. At that moment she clung to the love she had for her friend. "Come on!"

They ran in no particular direction and found themselves

back in the shrine room, right behind the giant Mimas. They each slashed one of his legs and brought him to his knees.

The giant howled. More chunks of stone tumbled from the ceiling.

"Weak mortals!" Mimas struggled to stand. "No plan of yours can defeat me!"

"That's good," Piper said. "Because I don't have a plan."

She ran toward the statue of Ares. "Annabeth, keep our friend occupied!"

"Oh, he's occupied!"

"GAHHHHH!"

Piper stared at the cruel bronze face of the war god. The statue thrummed with a low metallic pulse.

*The spirits of battle,* she thought. *They're inside, waiting to be freed.*

But they weren't hers to unleash—not until she'd proven herself.

The chamber shook again. More cracks appeared in the walls. Piper glanced at the stone carvings above the doorways: the scowling twin faces of Fear and Panic.

"My brothers," Piper said, "sons of Aphrodite . . . I give you a sacrifice."

At the feet of Ares, she set her cornucopia. The magic horn had become so attuned to her emotions it could amplify her anger, love, or grief and spew forth its bounty accordingly. She hoped that would appeal to the gods of fear. Or maybe they would just appreciate some fresh fruits and vegetables in their diets.

"I'm terrified," she confessed. "I hate doing this. But I accept that it's necessary."

She swung her blade and took off the bronze statue's head.

"No!" Mimas yelled.

Flames roared up from the statue's severed neck. They swirled around Piper, filling the room with a firestorm of emotions: hatred, bloodlust, and fear, but also love—because no one could face battle without caring for *something*: comrades, family, home.

Piper held out her arms and the *makhai* made her the center of their whirlwind.

*We will answer your call,* they whispered in her mind. *Once only, when you need us, destruction, waste, carnage shall answer. We shall complete your cure.*

The flames vanished along with the cornucopia, and the chained statue of Ares crumbled into dust.

"Foolish girl!" Mimas charged her, Annabeth at his heels. "The *makhai* have abandoned you!"

"Or maybe they've abandoned *you*," Piper said.

Mimas raised his hammer, but he'd forgotten about Annabeth. She jabbed him in the thigh and the giant staggered forward, off balance. Piper stepped in calmly and stabbed him in the gut.

Mimas crashed face-first into the nearest doorway. He turned over just as the stone face of Panic cracked off the wall above him and toppled down for a one-ton kiss.

The giant's cry was cut short. His body went still. Then he disintegrated into a twenty-foot pile of ash.

Annabeth stared at Piper. "What just happened?"

"I'm not sure."

"Piper, you were amazing, but those fiery spirits you released—"

"The *makhai*."

"How does that help us find the cure we're looking for?"

"I don't know. They said I could summon them when the time comes. Maybe Artemis and Apollo can explain—"

A section of the wall calved like a glacier.

Annabeth stumbled and almost slipped on the giant's severed ear. "We need to get out of here."

"I'm working on it," Piper said.

"And, uh, I think this ear is your spoil of war."

"Gross."

"Would make a lovely shield."

"Shut up, Chase." Piper stared at the second doorway, which still had the face of Fear above it. "Thank you, brothers, for helping to kill the giant. I need one more favor—an escape. And believe me, I am properly terrified. I offer you this, uh, lovely ear as a sacrifice."

The stone face made no answer. Another section of the wall peeled away. A starburst of cracks appeared in the ceiling.

Piper grabbed Annabeth's hand. "We're going through that doorway. If this works, we might find ourselves back on the surface."

"And if it doesn't?"

Piper looked up at the face of Fear. "Let's find out."

The room collapsed around them as they plunged into the dark.

# REYNA

**At least they didn't end up on another cruise ship.**

The jump from Portugal had landed them in the middle of the Atlantic, where Reyna had spent her whole day on the lido deck of the *Azores Queen*, shooing little kids off the Athena Parthenos, which they seemed to think was a waterslide.

Unfortunately, the next jump brought Reyna home.

They appeared ten feet in the air, hovering over a restaurant courtyard that Reyna recognized. She and Nico dropped onto a large birdcage, which promptly broke, dumping them into a cluster of potted ferns along with three very alarmed parrots. Coach Hedge hit the canopy over a bar. The Athena Parthenos landed on her feet with a *THUMP*, flattening a patio table and flipping a dark green umbrella, which settled onto the Nike statue in Athena's hand, so the goddess of wisdom looked like she was holding a tropical drink.

"Gah!" Coach Hedge yelled. The canopy ripped and he fell behind the bar with a crash of bottles and glasses. He recovered well. He popped up with a dozen miniature plastic swords in his hair, grabbed the soda gun, and served himself a drink.

"I like it!" He tossed a wedge of pineapple into his mouth. "But next time, kid, can we land on the floor and not ten feet *above* it?"

Nico dragged himself out of the ferns. He collapsed into the nearest chair and waved off a blue parrot that was trying to land on his head. After the fight with Lycaon, Nico had discarded his shredded aviator jacket. His black skull-pattern T-shirt wasn't in much better shape. Reyna had stitched up the gashes on his biceps, which gave Nico a slightly creepy Frankenstein look, but the cuts were still swollen and red. Unlike bites, werewolf claw marks wouldn't transmit lycanthropy, but Reyna knew firsthand that they healed slowly and burned like acid.

"I've gotta sleep." Nico looked up in a daze. "Are we safe?"

Reyna scanned the courtyard. The place seemed deserted, though she didn't understand why. This time of night, it should've been packed. Above them, the evening sky glowed a murky terracotta, the same color as the building's walls. Ringing the atrium, the second-story balconies were empty except for potted azaleas hanging from the white metal railings. Behind a wall of glass doors, the restaurant's interior was dark. The only sound was the fountain gurgling forlornly and the occasional squawk of a disgruntled parrot.

"This is Barrachina," Reyna said.

"What kind of bear?" Hedge opened a jar of maraschino cherries and chugged them down.

"It's a famous restaurant," Reyna said, "in the middle of Old San Juan. They invented the piña colada here, back in the 1960s, I think."

Nico pitched out of his chair, curled up on the floor, and started snoring.

Coach Hedge belched. "Well, it looks like we're staying for a while. If they haven't invented any new drinks since the sixties, they're overdue. I'll get to work!"

While Hedge rummaged behind the bar, Reyna whistled for Aurum and Argentum. After their fight with the werewolves, the dogs looked a little worse for wear, but Reyna placed them on guard duty. She checked the street entrance to the atrium. The decorative ironwork gates were locked. A sign in Spanish and English announced that the restaurant was closed for a private party. That seemed odd, since the place was deserted. At the bottom of the sign were embossed initials: HTK. These bothered Reyna, though she wasn't sure why.

She peered through the gates. Calle Fortaleza was unusually quiet. The blue cobblestone pavement was free of traffic and pedestrians. The pastel-colored shop fronts were closed and dark. Was it Sunday? Or some sort of holiday? Reyna's unease grew.

Behind her, Coach Hedge whistled happily as he set up a row of blenders. The parrots roosted on the shoulders of the Athena Parthenos. Reyna wondered whether the Greeks would be offended if their sacred statue arrived covered in tropical bird poop.

Of all the places Reyna could have ended up . . . San Juan.

Maybe it was a coincidence, but she feared not. Puerto Rico wasn't really on the way from Europe to New York. It was much too far south.

Besides, Reyna had been lending Nico her strength for days now. Perhaps she'd influenced him subconsciously. He was drawn to painful thoughts, fear, darkness. And Reyna's darkest, most painful memory was San Juan. Her biggest fear? Coming back here.

Her dogs picked up on her agitation. They prowled the courtyard, snarling at shadows. Poor Argentum turned in circles, trying to aim his sideways head so he could see out of his one ruby eye.

Reyna tried to concentrate on positive memories. She'd missed the sound of the little *coquí* frogs, singing around the neighborhood like a chorus of popping bottle caps. She'd missed the smell of the ocean, the blossoming magnolias and citrus trees, the fresh-baked bread from the local *panaderías*. Even the humidity felt comfortable and familiar—like the scented air from a dryer vent.

Part of her wanted to open the gates and explore the city. She wanted to visit the Plaza de Armas, where the old men played dominos and the coffee kiosk sold espresso so strong it made your ears pop. She wanted to stroll down her old street, Calle San Jose, counting and naming the stray cats, making up a story for each one, the way she used to do with her sister. She wanted to break into Barrachina's kitchen and cook up some real *mofongo* with fried plantains and bacon and garlic—a taste that would always remind her of Sunday afternoons, when she and Hylla could briefly escape the house and, if they were lucky, eat here in the kitchen, where the staff knew them and took pity on them.

On the other hand, Reyna wanted to leave immediately. She wanted to wake up Nico, no matter how tired he was, and force him to shadow-travel out of here—*anywhere* but San Juan.

Being so close to her old house made Reyna feel ratcheted tight like a catapult winch.

She glanced at Nico. Despite the warm night, he shivered on the tile floor. She pulled a blanket out of her pack and covered him up.

Reyna no longer felt self-conscious about wanting to protect him. For better or worse, they shared a connection now. Each time they shadow-traveled, his exhaustion and torment washed over her, and she understood him a little better.

Nico was devastatingly alone. He'd lost his big sister Bianca. He'd pushed away all other demigods who'd tried to get close to him. His experiences at Camp Half-Blood, in the Labyrinth, and in Tartarus had left him scarred, afraid to trust anyone.

Reyna doubted she could change his feelings, but she wanted Nico to have support. All heroes deserved that. It was the whole point of the Twelfth Legion. You joined forces to fight for a higher cause. You weren't alone. You made friends and earned respect. Even when you mustered out, you had a place in the community. No demigod should have to suffer alone the way Nico did.

Tonight was July 25. Seven more days until August 1. In theory, that was plenty of time to reach Long Island. Once they completed their mission, *if* they completed their mission, Reyna would make sure Nico was recognized for his bravery.

She slipped off her backpack. She tried to place it under Nico's head as a makeshift pillow, but her fingers passed right through him as if he were a shadow. She recoiled her hand.

Cold with dread, she tried again. This time, she was able to lift his neck and slide the pillow under. His skin felt cool, but otherwise normal.

Had she been hallucinating?

Nico had expended so much energy traveling through shadows . . . perhaps he was starting to fade permanently. If he kept pushing himself to the limit for seven more days . . .

The sound of a blender startled her out of her thoughts.

"You want a smoothie?" asked the coach. "This one is pineapple, mango, orange, and banana, buried under a mound of shaved coconut. I call it the Hercules!"

"I—I'm all right, thanks." She glanced up at the balconies ringing the atrium. It still didn't seem right to her that the restaurant was empty. A private party. HTK. "Coach, I think I'll scout the second floor. I don't like—"

A wisp of movement caught her eye. The balcony on the right—a dark shape. Above that, at the edge of the roof, several more silhouettes appeared against the orange clouds.

Reyna drew her sword, but it was too late.

A flash of silver, a faint *whoosh*, and the point of a needle buried itself in her neck. Her vision blurred. Her limbs turned to spaghetti. She collapsed next to Nico.

As her eyes dimmed, she saw her dogs running toward her, but they froze in mid-bark and toppled over.

At the bar, the coach yelled, "Hey!"

Another *whoosh.* The coach collapsed with a silver dart in his neck.

Reyna tried to say, *Nico, wake up.* Her voice wouldn't work. Her body had been deactivated as completely as her metal dogs had.

Dark figures lined the rooftop. Half a dozen leaped into the courtyard, silent and graceful.

One leaned over Reyna. She could only make out a hazy smudge of gray.

A muffled voice said, "Take her."

A cloth sack was wrestled over her head. Reyna wondered dimly if this was how she would die—without even a fight.

Then it didn't matter. Several pairs of rough hands lifted her like an unwieldy piece of furniture and she drifted into unconsciousness.

# XXII

# REYNA

THE ANSWER CAME TO HER before she was fully conscious.

The initials on the sign at Barrachina: HTK.

"Not funny," Reyna muttered to herself. "Not *remotely* funny."

Years ago, Lupa had taught her how to sleep lightly, wake up alert, and be ready to attack. Now, as her senses returned, she took stock of her situation.

The cloth sack still covered her head, but it didn't seem to be cinched around her neck. She was tied to a hard chair—wood, by the feel of it. Cords were tight against the ribs. Her hands were bound behind her, but her legs were free at the ankles.

Either her captors were sloppy, or they hadn't expected her to wake up so quickly.

Reyna wriggled her fingers and toes. Whatever tranquilizer they'd used, the effects had worn off.

Somewhere in front of her, footsteps echoed down a

corridor. The sound got closer. Reyna let her muscles go slack. She rested her chin against her chest.

A lock clicked. A door creaked open. Judging from the acoustics, Reyna was in a small room with brick or concrete walls: maybe a basement or a cell. One person entered the room.

Reyna calculated the distance. No more than five feet.

She surged upward, spinning so the chair legs smashed against her captor's body. The force broke the chair. Her captor fell with a pained grunt.

Shouts from the corridor. More footsteps.

Reyna shook the cloth sack off her head. She dropped into a backward roll, pulling her bound hands under her legs so her arms were in front of her. Her captor—a teen girl in gray camouflage—lay dazed on the floor, a knife at her belt.

Reyna grabbed the knife and straddled her, pressing the blade against her captor's throat.

Three more girls crowded the doorway. Two drew knives. The third nocked an arrow in her bow.

For a moment, everyone froze.

Her hostage's carotid artery pulsed under the blade. Wisely, the girl made no attempt to move.

Reyna ran scenarios on how she could overcome the three in the doorway. All of them wore gray camouflage T-shirts, faded black jeans, black athletic shoes, and utility belts like they were going camping or hiking . . . or hunting.

"You're the Hunters of Artemis," Reyna realized.

"Take it easy," said the girl with the bow. Her ginger hair

was shaved on the sides, long on top. She had the build of a professional wrestler. "You've got the wrong impression."

The girl on the floor exhaled, but Reyna knew that trick—trying to loosen an enemy's hold. Reyna pressed the knife tighter against the girl's throat.

"*You've* got the wrong impression," Reyna said, "if you think you can attack me and take me captive. Where are my friends?"

"Unharmed, right where you left them," the ginger girl promised. "Look, it's three to one and your hands are tied."

"You're right," Reyna growled. "Get another six of you in here, and it might be a fair fight. I demand to see your lieutenant, Thalia Grace."

The ginger girl blinked. Her comrades gripped their knives uneasily.

On the floor, Reyna's hostage began to shake. Reyna thought she might be having a fit. Then she realized the girl was laughing.

"Something funny?" Reyna asked.

The girl's voice was a gravelly whisper. "Jason told me you were good. He didn't say *how* good."

Reyna focused more carefully on her hostage. The girl looked about sixteen, with choppy black hair and startling blue eyes. Across her forehead glinted a circlet of silver.

"*You're* Thalia?"

"And I'd be happy to explain," Thalia said, "if you'd kindly not cut my throat."

• • •

The Hunters guided her through a maze of corridors. The walls were concrete blocks painted army green, devoid of windows. The only light came from dim fluorescents spaced every twenty feet. The passages twisted, turned, and doubled back, but the ginger-haired Hunter, Phoebe, took the lead. She seemed to know where she was going.

Thalia Grace limped along, holding her ribs where Reyna had hit her with the chair. The Hunter must've been in pain, but her eyes sparkled with amusement.

"Again, my apologies for abducting you." Thalia didn't sound very sorry. "This lair is secret. The Amazons have certain protocols—"

"The Amazons. You work for them?"

"*With* them," Thalia corrected. "We have a mutual understanding. Sometimes the Amazons send recruits our way. Sometimes, if we come across girls who don't wish to be maidens forever, we send them to the Amazons. The Amazons do not have such vows."

One of the other Hunters snorted in disgust. "Keeping male slaves in collars and orange jumpsuits. I'd rather keep a pack of dogs any day."

"Their males aren't slaves, Celyn," Thalia chided. "Merely subservient." She glanced at Reyna. "The Amazons and Hunters don't see eye to eye on everything, but since Gaea began to stir, we have been cooperating closely. With Camp Jupiter and Camp Half-Blood at each other's throats, well . . . someone has to deal with all the monsters. Our forces are spread across the entire continent."

Reyna massaged the rope marks on her wrists. "I thought

you told Jason you knew nothing of Camp Jupiter."

"That was true *then*. But those days are over, thanks to Hera's scheming." Thalia's expression turned serious. "How is my brother?"

"When I left him in Epirus, he was fine." Reyna told her what she knew.

She found Thalia's eyes distracting: electric blue, intense, and alert, so much like Jason's. Otherwise the siblings looked nothing alike. Thalia's hair was choppy and dark. Her jeans were tattered, held together with safety pins. She wore metal chains around her neck and wrists, and her gray camo shirt sported a button that read PUNK IS NOT DEAD. YOU ARE.

Reyna had always thought of Jason Grace as the all-American boy. Thalia looked more like the girl who robbed all-American boys at knifepoint in an alley.

"I hope he's still well," Thalia mused. "A few nights ago I dreamed about our mother. It . . . wasn't pleasant. Then I got Nico's message in my dreams—about Orion hunting you. That was even *less* pleasant."

"That's why you're here. You got Nico's message."

"Well, we didn't rush to Puerto Rico for a vacation. This is one of the Amazons' most secure strongholds. We took a gamble that we'd be able to intercept you."

"Intercept us . . . how? And why?"

In front of them, Phoebe stopped. The corridor dead-ended at a set of metal doors. Phoebe tapped on them with the butt of her knife—a complicated series of knocks like Morse code.

Thalia rubbed her bruised ribs. "I'll have to leave you here.

The Hunters are patrolling the old city, keeping a lookout for Orion. I need to get back to the front lines." She held out her hand expectantly. "My knife, please?"

Reyna handed it back. "What about my own weapons?"

"They'll be returned when you leave. I know it seems silly—the kidnapping and blindfolding and whatnot—but the Amazons take their security seriously. Last month they had an incident at their main center in Seattle. Maybe you heard about it. A girl named Hazel Levesque stole a horse."

The Hunter Celyn grinned. "Naomi and I saw the security footage. Legendary."

"Epic," agreed the third Hunter.

"At any rate," Thalia said, "we're keeping an eye on Nico and the satyr. Unauthorized males aren't allowed anywhere *near* this place, but we left them a note so they wouldn't worry."

From her belt, Thalia unfolded a piece of paper. She handed it to Reyna. It was a photocopy of a handwritten note:

*IOU one Roman praetor.*
*She will be returned safely.*
*Sit tight.*
*Otherwise you'll be killed.*
*XOX, the Hunters of Artemis*

Reyna handed back the letter. "Right. That won't worry them at all."

Phoebe grinned. "It's cool. I covered your Athena Parthenos with this new camouflage netting I designed. It should keep monsters—even Orion—from finding it. Besides, if my guess is right, Orion isn't tracking the statue as much as he's tracking *you*."

Reyna felt like she'd been punched between the eyes. "How could you know that?"

"Phoebe is my best tracker," Thalia said. "And my best healer. And . . . well, she's generally right about most things."

"*Most* things?" Phoebe protested.

Thalia raised her hands in an *I-give-up* gesture. "As for why we intercepted you, I'll let the Amazons explain. Phoebe, Celyn, Naomi—accompany Reyna inside. I have to see to our defenses."

"You're expecting a fight," Reyna noted. "But you said this place was secret and secure."

Thalia sheathed her knife. "You don't know Orion. I wish we had more time, Praetor. I'd like to hear about your camp and how you ended up there. You remind me so much of your sister, and yet—"

"You know Hylla?" Reyna asked. "Is she safe?"

Thalia tilted her head. "None of us are safe these days, Praetor, so I really must go. Good hunting!"

Thalia disappeared down the corridor.

The metal doors creaked open. The three Hunters led Reyna through.

After the claustrophobic tunnels, the size of the warehouse took Reyna's breath away. An aerie of giant eagles could've done maneuvers under the vast ceiling. Three-story-tall rows of shelves stretched into the distance. Robotic forklifts zipped through the aisles, retrieving boxes. Half a dozen young women in black pantsuits stood nearby, comparing notes on their tablet computers. In front of them were crates labeled: EXPLOSIVE ARROWS AND GREEK FIRE (16 OZ. EZ-OPEN PACK) and GRYPHON FILLETS (FREE-RANGE ORGANIC).

Directly in front of Reyna, behind a conference table piled high with reports and bladed weapons, sat a familiar figure.

"Baby sister." Hylla rose. "Here we are, home again. Facing certain death again. We have to stop meeting like this."

# XXIII

# REYNA

REYNA'S FEELINGS WEREN'T SO MUCH *MIXED.*

They were thrown into a blender with gravel and ice.

Every time she saw her sister, she didn't know whether to hug her, cry, or walk away. Of course she loved Hylla. Reyna would have been dead many times over if not for her sister.

But their past together was beyond complicated.

Hylla walked around the table. She looked good in her black leather pants and black tank top. Around her waist glittered a cord of gold Labyrinthine links—the belt of the Amazon queen. She was twenty-two now, but she could've been mistaken for Reyna's twin. They had the same long dark hair, the same brown eyes. They even wore the same silver ring with the torch-and-spear emblem of their mother, Bellona. The most obvious difference between them was the long white scar on Hylla's forehead. It had faded over the last four years. Anyone who didn't know better might've mistaken it for a worry line. But Reyna remembered the day Hylla got that scar in a duel on board the pirate ship.

"Well?" Hylla prompted. "No warm words for your sister?"

"Thank you for having me abducted," Reyna said. "For shooting me with a tranquilizer dart, putting a bag over my head, and tying me to a chair."

Hylla rolled her eyes. "Rules are rules. As a praetor, you should understand that. This distribution center is one of our most important bases. We have to control access. I can't make exceptions, especially not for my family."

"I think you just enjoyed it."

"That too."

Reyna wondered if her sister was as cool and collected as she seemed. She found it amazing, and a little scary, how quickly Hylla had adapted to her new identity.

Six years ago, she'd been a scared big sister, doing her best to shield Reyna from their father's rage. Her main skills had been running and finding them places to hide.

Then on Circe's island, Hylla had worked hard to be noticed. She wore flashy clothes and makeup. She smiled and laughed and always stayed perky, as if acting happy would *make* her happy. She'd become one of Circe's favorite attendants.

After their island sanctuary burned, they were taken prisoner aboard the pirates' ship. Again Hylla changed. She'd dueled for their freedom, out-pirated the pirates, gained the crew's respect so well that Blackbeard finally put them ashore lest Hylla take over his ship.

Now she'd reinvented herself again as queen of the Amazons.

Of course, Reyna understood why her sister was such a chameleon. If she kept changing, she could never fossilize into the thing their father had become. . . .

"Those initials on the reservation sign at Barrachina," Reyna said. "HTK. Hylla Twice-Kill, your new nickname. A little joke?"

"Just checking to see if you were paying attention."

"You knew we would land in that courtyard. How?"

Hylla shrugged. "Shadow-travel is magic. Several of my followers are daughters of Hecate. It was a simple enough matter for them to pull you off course, especially since you and I share a connection."

Reyna tried to keep her anger in check. Hylla, of all people, should know how she would feel about being dragged back to Puerto Rico.

"You went to a lot of trouble," Reyna noted. "The queen of the Amazons and the lieutenant of Artemis both rushing to Puerto Rico on a moment's notice to intercept us—I'm guessing that's not because you missed me."

Phoebe the ginger-haired Hunter chuckled. "She's smart."

"Of course," Hylla said. "I taught her everything she knows."

Other Amazons started to gather around, probably sensing a potential fight. Amazons loved violent entertainment almost as much as pirates did.

"Orion," Reyna guessed. "That's what brought you here. His name got your attention."

"I couldn't let him kill you," Hylla said.

"It's more than that."

"Your mission to escort the Athena Parthenos—"

"—is important. But it's more than that too. This is personal for you. And for the Hunters. What's your game?"

Hylla ran her thumbs along her golden belt. "Orion is a problem. Unlike the other giants, Orion has been walking the earth for centuries. He takes a special interest in killing Amazons, or Hunters, or *any* female who dares to be strong."

"Why would he want that?"

A ripple of dread seemed to pass through the girls around her.

Hylla looked at Phoebe. "Do you want to explain? You were there."

The Hunter's smile faded. "In the ancient times, Orion joined the Hunters. He was Lady Artemis's best friend. He had no rivals at the bow—except for the goddess herself, and perhaps her brother, Apollo."

Reyna shivered. Phoebe looked no more than fourteen. To think that she knew Orion three or four thousand years ago . . .

"What went wrong?" she asked.

Phoebe's ears reddened. "Orion crossed the line. He fell in love with Artemis."

Hylla sniffed. "Always happens with men. They promise friendship. They promise to treat you as an equal. In the end, all they want is to possess you."

Phoebe picked at her thumbnail. Behind her, the other two Hunters, Naomi and Celyn, shifted uneasily.

"Lady Artemis rebuffed him, of course," Phoebe said. "Orion became bitter. He started going on longer and longer trips by himself in the wilderness. Finally . . . I'm not sure what happened. One day Artemis came back to camp and told us Orion had been killed. She refused to speak of it."

Hylla frowned, which accentuated the white scar across her brow. "Whatever the case, when Orion rose again from Tartarus, he was Artemis's bitterest enemy. No one can hate you with more intensity than someone who used to love you."

Reyna understood that. She thought back to a conversation she'd had with the goddess Aphrodite two years ago in Charleston . . .

"If he's such a problem," Reyna said, "why doesn't Artemis simply slay him again?"

Phoebe grimaced. "Easier said than done. Orion is sneaky. Whenever Artemis is with us, he stays far away. Whenever we Hunters are on our own, like we are now . . . he strikes without warning and disappears again. Our last lieutenant, Zoë Nightshade, spent centuries trying to track him down and kill him."

"The Amazons have also tried," Hylla said. "Orion doesn't distinguish between us and the Hunters. I think we *all* remind him too much of Artemis. He sabotages our warehouses, disrupts our distribution centers, kills our warriors—"

"In other words," Reyna said dryly, "he's getting in the way of your plans for world domination."

Hylla shrugged. "Exactly."

"That's why you rushed here to intercept me," Reyna said.

"You knew Orion would be right behind me. You're setting up an ambush. I'm the bait."

The other girls all found somewhere else to look besides Reyna's face.

"Oh, please," Reyna chided, "don't develop a guilty conscience now. It's a good plan. How do we proceed?"

Hylla gave her comrades a lopsided smile. "I told you my sister was tough. Phoebe, you want to explain the details?"

The Hunter shouldered her bow. "Like I said, I believe Orion is tracking *you*, not the Athena Parthenos. He seems especially good at sensing the presence of female demigods. I guess you'd say we're his natural prey."

"Charming," Reyna said. "So my friends, Nico and Gleeson Hedge—are they safe?"

"I still don't see why you travel with *males*," Phoebe grumbled, "but my guess is that they are safer without you around. I did my best to camouflage your statue. With luck, Orion will follow you here, straight into our line of defenses."

"And then?" Reyna asked.

Hylla gave her the sort of cold smile that used to make Blackbeard's pirates nervous. "Thalia and most of her Hunters are scouting the perimeter of Viejo San Juan. As soon as Orion gets close, we'll know. We've set traps at every approach. I have my best fighters on alert. We'll snare the giant. Then, one way or another, we'll send him back to Tartarus."

"*Can* he be killed?" Reyna asked. "I thought most giants could only be destroyed by a god and demigod working together."

"We intend to find out," Hylla said. "Once Orion is taken

down, your quest will be much easier. We'll send you on your way with our blessings."

"We could use more than your blessings," Reyna said. "Amazons ship things all around the world. Why not provide safe transport for the Athena Parthenos? Get us to Camp Half-Blood before August first—"

"I can't," Hylla said. "If I could, sister, I would, but surely you've felt the anger radiating from the statue. We Amazons are honorary daughters of Ares. The Athena Parthenos would never tolerate our interference. Besides, you know how the Fates operate. For your quest to succeed, *you* have to deliver the statue personally."

Reyna must've looked crestfallen.

Phoebe shoulder-bumped her like an over-friendly cat. "Hey, not so glum. We'll help you as much as we can. The Amazon service department has repaired those metal dogs of yours. And we have some cool parting gifts!"

Celyn handed Phoebe a leather satchel.

Phoebe rummaged inside. "Let's see . . . healing potions. Tranquilizer darts like the ones we used on you. Hmm, what else? Oh, yeah!" Phoebe triumphantly produced a rectangle of folded silvery cloth.

"A handkerchief?" Reyna asked.

"Better. Back up a little." Phoebe tossed the cloth on the floor. Instantly it expanded into a ten-by-ten camping tent.

"It's air-conditioned," Phoebe said. "Sleeps four. It has a buffet table and sleeping bags inside. Whatever extra gear you put in it will collapse with the tent. Um, within reason . . . don't try to stick your giant statue in there."

Celyn snickered. "If your male traveling companions get annoying, you could always leave them inside."

Naomi frowned. "That wouldn't work . . . would it?"

"*Anyway,*" Phoebe said, "these tents are great. I have one just like it; use it all the time. When you're ready to close it up, the command word is *actaeon.*"

The tent collapsed into a tiny rectangle. Phoebe picked it up, stuffed it into the satchel, and handed the bag to Reyna.

"I . . . I don't know what to say," Reyna stammered. "Thank you."

"Aww . . ." Phoebe shrugged. "It's the least I can do for—"

Fifty feet away, a side door banged open. An Amazon ran straight toward Hylla. The newcomer wore a black pantsuit, her long auburn hair pulled back in a ponytail.

Reyna recognized her from the battle at Camp Jupiter. "Kinzie, isn't it?"

The girl gave her a distracted nod. "Praetor." She whispered something in Hylla's ear.

Hylla's expression hardened. "I see." She glanced at Reyna. "Something is wrong. We've lost contact with the outer defenses. I'm afraid Orion—"

Behind Reyna, the metal doors exploded.

# XXIV

# REYNA

REYNA REACHED FOR HER SWORD—then realized she didn't have one.

"Get out of here!" Phoebe readied her bow.

Celyn and Naomi ran to the smoking doorway, only to be cut down by black arrows.

Phoebe screamed in rage. She returned fire as Amazons rushed forward with shields and swords.

"Reyna!" Hylla pulled her arm. "We must leave!"

"We can't just—"

"My guards will buy you time!" Hylla shouted. "Your quest *must* succeed!"

Reyna hated it, but she ran after Hylla.

They reached the side door and Reyna glanced back. Dozens of wolves—gray wolves like the ones in Portugal—surged into the warehouse. Amazons hurried to intercept them. The smoke-filled doorway was piled with bodies of the fallen: Celyn, Naomi, Phoebe. The ginger-haired Hunter who'd lived for thousands of years now sprawled unmoving, her eyes wide with shock, an oversized black-and-red arrow buried in her gut. The Amazon Kinzie charged forward, long knives flashing. She leaped over the bodies and into the smoke.

Hylla pulled Reyna into the passageway. Together they ran.

"They'll all die!" Reyna yelled. "There must be something—"

"Don't be stupid, sister!" Hylla's eyes were bright with tears. "Orion outfoxed us. He's turned the ambush into a massacre. All we can do now is hold him back while you escape. You *must* get that statue to the Greeks and defeat Gaea!"

She led Reyna up a flight of stairs. They navigated a maze of corridors, then rounded a corner into a locker room. They found themselves face to face with a large gray wolf, but before the beast could even snarl, Hylla punched it between the eyes. The wolf crumpled.

"Over here." Hylla ran to the nearest row of lockers. "Your weapons are inside. Hurry."

Reyna grabbed her knife, her sword, and her pack. Then she followed her sister up a circular metal stairwell.

The top dead-ended at the ceiling. Hylla turned and gave her a stern look. "I won't have time to explain this, all right? Stay strong. Stay close."

Reyna wondered what could be worse than the scene they'd just left. Hylla pushed open the trapdoor and they climbed through . . . into their old home.

The great room was just as Reyna remembered. Opaque skylights glowed on the twenty-foot ceilings. The stark white walls were devoid of decoration. The furniture was oak, steel, and white leather—impersonal and masculine. Both sides of the room were overhung with terraces, which had always made Reyna feel like she was being watched (because often, she *was*).

Their father had done everything he could to make the centuries-old hacienda feel like a modern home. He'd added the skylights, painted everything white to make it brighter and airier. But he'd only succeeded in making the place look like a well-groomed corpse in a new suit.

The trapdoor had opened into the massive fireplace. Why they even *had* a fireplace in Puerto Rico, Reyna had never understood, but she and Hylla used to pretend the hearth was a secret hideout where their father couldn't find them. They used to imagine they could step inside and go to other places.

Now, Hylla had made that true. She had linked her underground lair to their childhood home.

"Hylla—"

"I told you, we don't have time."

"But—"

"I own the building now. I put the deed in my name."

"You did *what*?"

"I was tired of running from the past, Reyna. I decided to reclaim it."

Reyna stared at her, dumbfounded. You could reclaim a lost phone or a bag at the airport. You could even reclaim a hazardous waste dump. But this house, and what had happened here? There was *no* reclaiming that.

"Sister," Hylla said, "we're wasting time. Are you coming or not?"

Reyna eyed the balconies, half expecting luminous shapes to flicker at the railing. "Have you seen them?"

"Some of them."

"Papa?"

"Of course not," Hylla snapped. "You know he's gone for good."

"I don't know anything of the sort. How *could* you come back? Why?"

"To understand!" Hylla shouted. "Don't you want to know how it happened to him?"

"No! You can't learn anything from ghosts, Hylla. You of all people should realize—"

"I'm leaving," Hylla said. "Your friends are a few blocks away. Are you coming with me, or should I tell them you died because you got lost in the past?"

"*I'm* not the one who took possession of this place!"

Hylla turned on her heel and marched out the front door.

Reyna looked around one more time. She remembered her last day here, when she was ten years old. She could almost hear her father's angry roar echoing through the great room, the chorus of wailing ghosts on the balconies.

She ran for the exit. She burst into warm afternoon sunlight and found that the street hadn't changed—the crumbling pastel houses, the blue cobblestones, dozens of cats sleeping under cars or in the shade of banana trees.

Reyna might have felt nostalgic . . . except that her sister stood a few feet away, facing Orion.

"Well, now." The giant smiled. "Both daughters of Bellona together. Excellent!"

Reyna felt personally offended.

She had worked up an image of Orion as a towering ugly demon, even worse than Polybotes, the giant who had attacked Camp Jupiter.

Instead, Orion could have passed for human—a tall, muscular, *handsome* human. His skin was the color of wheat toast. His dark hair was undercut, swept into spikes on top. With his black leather breeches and jerkin, his hunting knife, and his bow and quiver, he might have been Robin Hood's evil, better-looking brother.

Only his eyes ruined the image. At first glance, he appeared to be wearing military night vision goggles. Then Reyna realized they weren't goggles. They were the work of Hephaestus—bronze mechanical eyes embedded in the giant's sockets. Focusing rings spun and clicked as he regarded Reyna. Targeting lasers flashed red to green. Reyna got the uncomfortable impression he was seeing much more than her form—her heat signature, her heart rate, her level of fear.

At his side he held a black composite bow almost as fancy as his eyes. Multiple strings ran through a series of pulleys that looked like miniature steam train wheels. The grip was polished bronze, studded with dials and buttons.

He had no arrow nocked. He made no threatening moves.

He smiled so dazzlingly it was hard to remember he was an enemy—someone who'd killed at least half a dozen Hunters and Amazons to get here.

Hylla drew her knives. "Reyna, go. I will deal with this monster."

Orion chuckled. "Hylla Twice-Kill, you have courage. So did your lieutenants. They are dead."

Hylla took a step forward.

Reyna grabbed her arm. "Orion!" she said. "You have enough Amazon blood on your hands. Perhaps it's time you try a Roman."

The giant's eyes clicked and dilated. Red laser dots floated across Reyna's breastplate. "Ah, the young praetor. I admit, I've been curious. Before I slay you, perhaps you'll enlighten me. Why would a child of Rome go to such lengths to help the Greeks? You have forfeited your rank, abandoned your legion, made yourself an outlaw—and for what? Jason Grace scorned you. Percy Jackson refused you. Haven't you been . . . what's the word . . . *dumped* enough?"

Reyna's ears buzzed. She recalled Aphrodite's warning, two years ago in Charleston: *You will not find love where you wish or where you hope. No demigod shall heal your heart.*

She forced herself to meet the giant's gaze. "I don't define myself by the boys who may or may not like me."

"Brave words." The giant's smile was infuriating. "But you are no different from the Amazons, or the Hunters, or Artemis herself. You speak of strength and independence. As soon as you face a man of *true* prowess, your confidence crumbles. You feel threatened by my dominance, and how it *attracts* you. So you run, or you surrender, or you die."

Hylla shrugged off Reyna's hand. "I will kill you, giant. I will chop you into pieces so small—"

"Hylla," Reyna interrupted. Whatever else happened here, she could *not* watch her sister die. Reyna had to keep the giant focused on her. "Orion, you claim to be strong. Yet you couldn't keep the vows of the Hunt. You died rejected. And now you're running errands for your mother. So tell me again, how exactly are you threatening?"

Orion's jaw muscles clenched. His smile became thinner and colder.

"A good try," he admitted. "You're hoping to unbalance me. You think, perhaps, if you keep me talking, reinforcements will save you. Alas, Praetor, there *are* no reinforcements. I burned your sister's underground lair with her own Greek fire. No one survived."

Hylla roared and attacked. Orion hit her with the butt of his bow. She flew backward into the street. Orion pulled an arrow from his quiver.

"Stop!" Reyna yelled.

Her heart hammered in her rib cage. She needed to find the giant's weakness.

Barrachina was only a few blocks away. If they could make it that far, Nico might be able to shadow-travel them away. And the Hunters couldn't *all* be dead . . . They'd been patrolling the entire perimeter of the old city. Surely some of them were still out there. . . .

"Orion, you asked what motivates me." She kept her voice level. "Don't you want your answer before you kill us? Surely it must puzzle you, why women keep rejecting a big handsome guy like you."

The giant nocked his arrow. "Now you have mistaken me for Narcissus. I cannot be flattered."

"Of course not," Reyna said. Hylla rose with a murderous look on her face, but Reyna reached out with her senses, trying to share with her sister the most difficult kind of strength—restraint. "Still . . . it must infuriate you. First you were dumped by a mortal princess—"

"Merope." Orion sneered. "A beautiful girl, but stupid. If she'd had any sense, she would have understood I was flirting with her."

"Let me guess," Reyna said. "She screamed and called for the guards instead."

"I was without my weapons at the time. You don't bring your bow and knives when you're courting a princess. The guards took me easily. Her father the king had me blinded and exiled."

Just above Reyna's head, a pebble skittered across a clay-tiled roof. It might have been her imagination, but she remembered that sound from the many nights Hylla would sneak out of her own locked room and creep across the roof to check on her.

It took all of Reyna's willpower not to glance up.

"But you got new eyes," she said to the giant. "Hephaestus took pity on you."

"Yes . . ." Orion's gaze became unfocused. Reyna could

tell, because the laser targets disappeared from her chest. "I ended up on Delos, where I met Artemis. Do you know how strange it is to meet your mortal enemy and end up being attracted to her?" He laughed. "Praetor, what am I saying? Of *course* you know. Perhaps you feel for the Greeks as I felt for Artemis—a guilty fascination, an admiration that turns to love. But too much love is poison, especially when that love is not returned. If you do not understand that already, Reyna Ramírez-Arellano, you soon will."

Hylla limped forward, her knives still in hand. "Sister, why do you let this beast talk? Let's put him down."

"Can you?" Orion mused. "Many have tried. Even Artemis's own brother, Apollo, was not able to kill me back in the ancient times. He had to use trickery to get rid of me."

"He didn't like you hanging out with his sister?" Reyna listened for more sounds from the roofs, but heard nothing.

"Apollo was jealous." The giant's fingers curled around his bowstring. He drew it back, setting the bow's wheels and pulleys spinning. "He feared I might charm Artemis into forgetting her vows of maidenhood. And who knows? Without Apollo's interference, perhaps I would have. She would have been happier."

"As your servant?" Hylla growled. "Your meek little housewife?"

"It hardly matters now," Orion said. "At any rate, Apollo inflicted me with madness—a bloodlust to kill all the beasts of the earth. I slaughtered thousands before my mother, Gaea, finally put a stop to my rampage. She summoned a giant scorpion from the earth. It stabbed me in the back and its poison killed me. I owe her for that."

"You owe Gaea," Reyna said, "for killing you."

Orion's mechanical pupils spiraled into tiny, glowing points. "My mother showed me the truth. I was fighting against my own nature, and it brought me nothing but misery. Giants are not *meant* to love mortals or gods. Gaea helped me accept what I am. Eventually we all must return home, Praetor. We must embrace our past, no matter how bitter and dark." He nodded his chin toward the villa behind her. "Just as you have done. You have your own share of ghosts, eh?"

Reyna drew her sword. *You can't learn anything from ghosts,* she had told her sister. Perhaps she couldn't learn anything from giants, either.

"This is not my home," she said. "And we are not alike."

"I have seen the truth." The giant sounded truly sympathetic. "You cling to the fantasy that you can make your enemies love you. You cannot, Reyna. There is no love for you at Camp Half-Blood."

Aphrodite's words echoed in her head: *No demigod shall heal your heart.*

Reyna studied the giant's handsome, cruel face, his glowing mechanical eyes. For a terrible moment, she could understand how even a goddess, even an eternal maiden like Artemis, might fall for Orion's honeyed words.

"I could have killed you twenty times by now," the giant said. "You realize that, don't you? Let me spare you. A simple show of faith is all I need. Tell me where the statue is."

Reyna almost dropped her sword. *Where the statue is . . .*

Orion hadn't located the Athena Parthenos. The Hunters' camouflage had worked. All this time, the giant had been tracking Reyna, which meant that even if she died right now, Nico and Coach Hedge might stay safe. The quest was not doomed.

She felt as if she'd shed a hundred pounds of armor. She laughed. The sound echoed down the cobblestone street.

"Phoebe outsmarted you," she said. "By tracking me, you lost the statue. Now my friends are free to continue their mission."

Orion curled his lip. "Oh, I will find them, Praetor. After I deal with you."

"Then I suppose," Reyna said, "we will have to deal with you first."

"*That* is my sister," Hylla said proudly.

Together they charged.

The giant's first shot would have skewered Reyna, but Hylla was fast. She sliced the arrow out of the air and lunged at Orion. Reyna stabbed at his chest. The giant intercepted both of their attacks with his bow.

He kicked Hylla backward into the hood of an old Chevy. Half a dozen cats scattered from underneath it. The giant spun, a dagger suddenly in his hand, and Reyna just managed to dodge the blade.

She stabbed again, ripping through his leather jerkin, but only managed to graze his chest.

"You fight well, Praetor," he admitted. "But not well enough to live."

Reyna willed her blade to extend into a *pilum*. "My death means nothing."

If her friends could continue their quest in peace, she was fully prepared to go down fighting. But first she intended to hurt this giant so badly he would never forget her name.

"What about your sister's death?" Orion asked. "Does that mean something?"

Faster than Reyna could blink, he sent an arrow flying toward Hylla's chest. A scream built in Reyna's throat, but somehow Hylla *caught* the arrow.

Hylla slid off the hood of the car and snapped the arrow with one hand. "I am the queen of the Amazons, you idiot. I wear the royal belt. With the strength it gives me, I will avenge the Amazons you killed today."

Hylla grabbed the front fender of the Chevy and flipped the entire car toward Orion, as easily as if she were splashing him with water in a swimming pool.

The Chevy sandwiched Orion against the wall of the nearest house. Stucco cracked. A banana tree toppled. More cats fled.

Reyna ran toward the wreckage, but the giant bellowed and shoved away the car.

"You will die together!" he promised. Two arrows appeared nocked in his bow, the string fully drawn back.

Then the rooftops exploded with noise.

"DIE!" Gleeson Hedge dropped directly behind Orion, smacking his baseball bat over the giant's head so hard the Louisville Slugger cracked in half.

At the same time, Nico di Angelo dropped in front. He

slashed his Stygian sword across the giant's bowstring, causing pulleys and gears to zip and creak, the string recoiling with hundreds of pounds of force until it whacked Orion in the nose like a hydraulic bullwhip.

"OOOOOOOOW!!" Orion staggered backward, dropping his bow.

Hunters of Artemis appeared along the rooftops, shooting Orion full of silver arrows until he resembled a glowing hedgehog. He staggered blindly, holding his nose, his face streaming with golden ichor.

Someone grabbed Reyna's arm. "Come on!" Thalia Grace had returned.

"Go with her!" Hylla ordered.

Reyna's heart felt like it was shattering. "Sister—"

"You have to leave! NOW!" It was exactly what Hylla had said to her six years ago, the night they escaped their father's house. "I'll delay Orion as long as possible."

Hylla grabbed one of the giant's legs. She yanked him off balance and tossed him several blocks down the Calle San Jose, to the general consternation of several dozen more cats. The Hunters ran after him along the rooftops, shooting arrows that exploded in Greek fire, wreathing the giant in flames.

"Your sister's right," Thalia said. "You need to go."

Nico and Hedge fell in alongside her, both looking very pleased with themselves. They had apparently gone shopping at the Barrachina souvenir shop, where they'd replaced their dirty tattered shirts with loud tropical numbers.

"Nico," Reyna said, "you look—"

"Not a word about the shirt," he warned. "Not one word."

"Why did you come looking for me?" she demanded. "You could have gotten away free. The giant has been tracking *me*. If you had just left—"

"You're welcome, cupcake," the coach grumbled. "We weren't about to leave without you. Now let's get out of . . ."

He glanced over Reyna's shoulder and his voice faltered.

Reyna turned.

Behind her, the second-story balconies of her family house were crowded with glowing figures: a man with a forked beard and rusted conquistador armor; another bearded man in eighteenth-century pirate clothes, his shirt peppered with gunshot holes; a lady in a bloody nightgown; a U.S. Navy captain in his dress whites; and a dozen more Reyna knew from her childhood—all of them glaring at her accusingly, their voices whispering in her mind: *Traitor. Murderer.*

"No . . ." Reyna felt like she was ten years old again. She wanted to curl up in the corner of her room and press her hands over her ears to stop the whispering.

Nico took her arm. "Reyna, who are they? What do they—?"

"I can't," she pleaded. "I—I can't."

She'd spent so many years building a dam inside her to hold back the fear. Now, it broke. Her strength washed away.

"It's all right." Nico gazed up at the balconies. The ghosts disappeared, but Reyna knew they weren't really gone. They were *never* really gone. "We'll get you out of here," Nico promised. "Let's move."

Thalia took Reyna's other arm. The four of them ran for the restaurant and the Athena Parthenos. Behind them, Reyna heard Orion roaring in pain, Greek fire exploding.

And in her mind, the voices still whispered: *Murderer. Traitor. You can never flee your crime.*

# XXV

# JASON

JASON ROSE FROM HIS DEATHBED so he could drown with the rest of the crew.

The ship was tilting so violently he had to climb the floor to get out of sickbay. The hull creaked. The engine groaned like a dying water buffalo. Cutting through the roar of the wind, the goddess Nike screamed from the stables: "YOU CAN DO BETTER, STORM! GIVE ME A HUNDRED AND TEN PERCENT!"

Jason climbed the stairs to the middle deck. His legs shook. His head spun. The ship pitched to port, knocking him against the opposite wall.

Hazel stumbled out of her cabin, hugging her stomach. "I *hate* the ocean!"

When she saw him, her eyes widened. "What are you doing out of bed?"

"I'm going up there!" he insisted. "I can help!"

Hazel looked like she wanted to argue. Then the ship

tilted to starboard and she staggered toward the bathroom, her hand over her mouth.

Jason fought his way to the stairs. He hadn't been out of bed in a day and a half, ever since the girls got back from Sparta and he'd unexpectedly collapsed. His muscles rebelled at the effort. His gut felt like Michael Varus was standing behind him, repeatedly stabbing him and yelling: *Die like a Roman! Die like a Roman!*

Jason forced down the pain. He was tired of people taking care of him, whispering how worried they were. He was tired of dreaming about being a shish kabob. He'd spent enough time nursing the wound in his gut. Either it would kill him or it wouldn't. He wasn't going to wait around for the wound to decide. He had to help his friends.

Somehow he made it above deck.

What he saw there made him almost as nauseous as Hazel. A wave the size of a skyscraper crashed over the forward deck, washing the front crossbows and half the port railing out to sea. The sails were ripped to shreds. Lightning flashed all around, hitting the sea like spotlights. Horizontal rain blasted Jason's face. The clouds were so dark he honestly couldn't tell if it was day or night.

The crew was doing what they could . . . which wasn't much.

Leo had lashed himself to the console with a bungee cord harness. That might have seemed like a good idea when he rigged it up, but every time a wave hit he was washed away, then smacked back into his control board like a human paddleball.

Piper and Annabeth were trying to save the rigging. Since Sparta they'd become quite a team—able to work together without even talking, which was just as well, since they couldn't have heard each other over the storm.

Frank—at least Jason *assumed* it was Frank—had turned into a gorilla. He was swinging upside down off the starboard rail, using his massive strength and his flexible feet to hang on while he untangled some broken oars. Apparently the crew was trying to get the ship airborne, but even if they managed to take off, Jason wasn't sure the sky would be any safer.

Even Festus the figurehead was trying to help. He spewed fire at the rain, though that didn't seem to discourage the storm.

Only Percy was having much luck. He stood by the center mast, his hands extended like he was on a tightrope. Every time the ship tilted, he pushed in the opposite direction and the hull stabilized. He summoned giant fists of water from the ocean to slam into the larger waves before they could reach the deck, so it looked like the ocean was hitting itself repeatedly in the face.

With the storm as bad as it was, Jason realized the ship would've already capsized or been smashed to bits if Percy wasn't on the job.

Jason staggered toward the mast. Leo yelled something— probably *Go downstairs!*—but Jason only waved back. He made it to Percy's side and grabbed his shoulder.

Percy nodded like *'sup*. He didn't look shocked, or demand that Jason go back to sickbay, which Jason appreciated.

Percy could stay dry if he concentrated, but obviously he

had bigger things to worry about right now. His dark hair was plastered to his face. His clothes were soaked and ripped.

He shouted something in Jason's ear, but Jason could only make out a few words: "THING . . . DOWN . . . STOP IT!"

Percy pointed over the side.

"Something is causing the storm?" Jason asked.

Percy grinned and tapped his ears. Clearly, he couldn't hear a word. He made a gesture with his hand like diving overboard. Then he tapped Jason on the chest.

"You want me to go?" Jason felt kind of honored. Everybody else had been treating him like a glass vase, but Percy . . . well, he seemed to figure that if Jason was on deck, he was ready for action.

"Happy to!" Jason shouted. "But I can't breathe underwater!"

Percy shrugged. *Sorry, can't hear you.*

Then Percy ran to the starboard rail, pushed another massive wave away from the ship, and jumped overboard.

Jason glanced at Piper and Annabeth. They both clung to the rigging, staring at him in shock. Piper's expression said *Are you out of your mind?*

He gave her an *okay* sign, partly to assure her that he would be fine (which he wasn't sure about), partly to agree that he was in fact crazy (which he *was* sure about).

He staggered to the railing and looked up at the storm.

Winds raged. Clouds churned. Jason sensed an entire army of *venti* swirling above him, too angry and agitated to take physical form, but hungry for destruction.

He raised his arm and summoned a lasso of wind. Jason had learned long ago that the best way to control a crowd of bullies was to pick the meanest, biggest kid and force him into submission. Then the others would fall in line. He lashed out with his wind rope, searching for strongest, most ornery *ventus* in the storm.

He lassoed a nasty patch of storm cloud and pulled it in. "You're serving me today."

Howling in protest, the *ventus* encircled him. The storm above the ship seemed to lessen just a bit, as if the other *venti* were thinking *Oh, crud. That guy means business.*

Jason levitated off the deck, encased in his own miniature tornado. Spinning like a corkscrew, he plunged into the water.

Jason assumed things would be calmer underwater.

Not so much.

Of course, that could've been due to his mode of travel. Riding a cyclone to the bottom of the ocean definitely gave him some unexpected turbulence. He dropped and swerved with no apparent logic, his ears popping, his stomach pressed against his ribs.

Finally he drifted to a stop next to Percy, who stood on a ledge jutting over a deeper abyss.

"Hey," Percy said.

Jason could hear him perfectly, though he wasn't sure how. "What's going on?"

In his *ventus* air cocoon, his own voice sounded like he was talking through a vacuum cleaner.

Percy pointed into the void. "Wait for it."

Three seconds later, a shaft of green light swept through the darkness like a spotlight, then disappeared.

"Something's down there," Percy said, "stirring up this storm." He turned and sized up Jason's tornado. "Nice outfit. Can you hold it together if we go deeper?"

"I have no idea how I'm doing this," Jason said.

"Okay," Percy said. "Well, just don't get knocked unconscious."

"Shut up, Jackson."

Percy grinned. "Let's see what's down there."

They sank so deep that Jason couldn't see anything except Percy swimming next to him in the dim light of their gold and bronze blades.

Every so often the green searchlight shot upward. Percy swam straight toward it. Jason's *ventus* crackled and roared, straining to escape. The smell of ozone made him light-headed, but he kept his shell of air intact.

At last, the darkness lessened below them. Soft white luminous patches, like schools of jellyfish, floated before Jason's eyes. As he approached the seafloor, he realized the patches were glowing fields of algae surrounding the ruins of a palace. Silt swirled through empty courtyards with abalone floors. Barnacle-covered Greek columns marched into the gloom. In the center of the complex rose a citadel larger than Grand Central Station, its walls encrusted with pearls, its domed golden roof cracked open like an egg.

"Atlantis?" Jason asked.

"That's a myth," Percy said.

"Uh . . . don't we deal in myths?"

"No, I mean it's a *made-up* myth. Not, like, an actual true myth."

"So this is why Annabeth is the brains of the operation, then?"

"Shut up, Grace."

They floated through the broken dome and down into shadows.

"This place seems familiar." Percy's voice became edgy. "Almost like I've been here—"

The green spotlight flashed directly below them, blinding Jason.

He dropped like a stone, touching down on the smooth marble floor. When his vision cleared, he saw that they weren't alone.

Standing before them was a twenty-foot-tall woman in a flowing green dress, cinched at the waist with a belt of abalone shells. Her skin was as luminous white as the fields of algae. Her hair swayed and glowed like jellyfish tendrils.

Her face was beautiful but unearthly—her eyes too bright, her features too delicate, her smile too cold, as if she'd been studying human smiles and hadn't quite mastered the art.

Her hands rested on a disk of polished green metal about six feet in diameter, sitting on a bronze tripod. It reminded Jason of a steel drum he'd once seen a street performer play at the Embarcadero in San Francisco.

The woman turned the metal disk like a steering wheel. A shaft of green light shot upward, churning the water, shaking the walls of the old palace. Shards from the domed ceiling broke and tumbled down in slow motion.

"You're making the storm," Jason said.

"Indeed I am." The woman's voice was melodic—yet it had a strange resonance, as if it extended past the human range of hearing. Pressure built between Jason's eyes. His sinuses felt like they might explode.

"Okay, I'll bite," Percy said. "Who are you, and what do you want?"

The woman turned toward him. "Why, I am your sister, Perseus Jackson. And I wanted to meet you before you die."

# XXVI

# JASON

JASON SAW TWO OPTIONS: FIGHT OR TALK.

Usually, when faced with a creepy twenty-foot-tall lady with jellyfish hair, he would've gone with *fight*.

But since she called Percy *brother*—that made him hesitate.

"Percy, do you know this . . . individual?"

Percy shook his head. "Doesn't look like my mom, so I'm gonna guess we're related on the godly side. You a daughter of Poseidon, Miss . . . uh . . . ?"

The pale lady raked her fingernails against the metal disk, making a screeching sound like a tortured whale. "No one knows me," she sighed. "Why would I assume my *own brother* would recognize me? I am Kymopoleia!"

Percy and Jason exchanged looks.

"So . . ." Percy said. "We're going to call you Kym. And you'd be a, hmm, Nereid, then? Minor goddess?"

*"Minor?"*

"By which," Jason said quickly, "he means under the drinking age! Because obviously you're so young and beautiful."

Percy flashed him a look: *Nice save.*

The goddess turned her full attention to Jason. She pointed her index finger and traced his outline in the water. Jason could feel his captured air spirit rippling around him, as if it were being tickled.

"Jason Grace," said the goddess. "Son of Jupiter."

"Yeah. I'm a friend of Percy's."

Kym's narrowed. "So it's true . . . these times make for strange friends and unexpected enemies. The Romans never worshipped me. To them, I was a nameless fear—a sign of Neptune's greatest wrath. They never worshipped Kymopoleia, the goddess of violent sea storms!"

She spun her disk. Another beam of green light flashed upward, churning the water and making the ruins rumble.

"Uh, yeah," Percy said. "The Romans aren't big on navies. They had, like, one rowboat. Which I sank. Speaking of violent storms, you're doing a first-rate job upstairs."

"Thank you," said Kym.

"Thing is, our ship is caught in it, and it's kind of being ripped apart. I'm sure you didn't mean to—"

"Oh, yes, I did."

"You did." Percy grimaced. "Well . . . that sucks. I don't suppose you'd cut it out, then, if we asked nicely?"

"No," the goddess agreed. "Even now, the ship is close to sinking. I'm rather amazed it's held together this long. Excellent workmanship."

Sparks flew from Jason's arms into the tornado. He thought about Piper and the rest of the crew frantically trying to keep the ship in one piece. By coming down here, he and Percy had left the others defenseless. They had to act soon.

Besides, Jason's air was getting stale. He wasn't sure if it was possible to use up a *ventus* by inhaling it, but if he was going to have to fight, he'd better take on Kym before he ran out of oxygen.

The thing was . . . fighting a goddess on her home court wouldn't be easy. Even if they managed to take her down, there was no guarantee the storm would stop.

"So . . . Kym," he said, "what could we do to make you change your mind and let our ship go?"

Kym gave him that creepy alien smile. "Son of Jupiter, do you know where you are?"

Jason was tempted to answer *underwater*. "You mean these ruins. An ancient palace?"

"Indeed," Kym said. "The original palace of my father, Poseidon."

Percy snapped his fingers, which sounded like a muffled explosion. "That's why I recognized it. Dad's new crib in the Atlantic is kind of like this."

"I wouldn't know," Kym said. "I am never invited to see my parents. I can only wander the ruins of their *old* domains. They find my presence . . . disruptive."

She spun her wheel again. The entire back wall of the building collapsed, sending a cloud of silt and algae through the chamber. Fortunately the *ventus* acted like a fan, blowing the debris out of Jason's face.

"Disruptive?" Jason said. "You?"

"My father does not welcome me in his court," Kym said. "He restricts my powers. This storm above? I haven't had this much fun in ages, yet it is only a small *taste* of what I can do!"

"A little goes a long way," Percy said. "Anyway, to Jason's question about changing your mind—"

"My father even married me off," Kym said, "without my permission. He gave me away like a trophy to Briares, a Hundred-Handed One, as a reward for supporting the gods in the war with Kronos eons ago."

Percy's face brightened. "Hey, I *know* Briares. He's a friend of mine! I freed him from Alcatraz."

"Yes, I know." Kym's eyes glinted coldly. "I *hate* my husband. I was not *at all* pleased to have him back."

"Oh. So . . . is Briares around?" Percy asked hopefully.

Kym's laugh sounded like dolphin chatter. "He's off at Mount Olympus in New York, shoring up the gods' defenses. Not that it will matter. My point, dear brother, is that Poseidon has never treated me fairly. I like to come here, to his old palace, because it pleases me to see his works in ruins. Someday soon, his *new* palace will look like this one, and the seas will rage unchecked."

Percy looked at Jason. "This is the part where she tells us she's working for Gaea."

"Yeah," Jason said. "And the Earth Mother promised her a better deal once the gods are destroyed, blah, blah, blah." He turned to Kym. "You understand that Gaea won't keep her promises, right? She's using you, just like she's using the giants."

"I am touched by your concern," said the goddess. "The Olympian gods, on the other hand, have *never* used me, eh?"

Percy spread his hands. "At least the Olympians are trying. After the last Titan war, they started paying more attention to the other gods. A lot of them have cabins now at Camp Half-Blood: Hecate, Hades, Hebe, Hypnos . . . uh, and probably some that don't begin with *H* too. We give them offerings at every meal, cool banners, special recognition in the end-of-summer program—"

"And have *I* gotten such offerings?" Kym asked.

"Well . . . no. We didn't know you existed. But—"

"Then save your words, brother." Kym's jellyfish tentacle hair floated toward him, as if anxious to paralyze new prey. "I have heard so much about the great Percy Jackson. The giants are quite obsessed with capturing you. I must say . . . I don't see what the fuss is about."

"Thanks, sis. But if you're going to try to kill me, I gotta warn you it's been tried before. I've faced a lot of goddesses recently—Nike, Akhlys, even Nyx herself. Compared to them, you're not scaring me. Also, you laugh like a dolphin."

Kym's delicate nostrils flared. Jason got his sword ready.

"Oh, I won't kill you," Kym said. "My part of the bargain was simply to get your attention. Someone else is here, though, who very much wants to kill you."

Above them, at the edge of the broken roof, a dark shape appeared—a figure even taller than Kymopoleia.

"The son of Neptune," boomed a deep voice.

The giant floated down. Clouds of dark viscous fluid—poison, perhaps—curled from his blue skin. His green breastplate was fashioned to resemble a cluster of open hungry mouths. In his hands were the weapons of a *retiarius*—a trident and a weighted net.

Jason had never met this particular giant, but he'd heard stories. "Polybotes," he said, "the anti-Poseidon."

The giant shook his dreadlocks. A dozen serpents swam free—each one lime green with a frilled crown around its head. *Basilisks.*

"Indeed, son of Rome," the giant said. "But if you'll excuse me, my immediate business is with Perseus Jackson. I tracked him all the way across Tartarus. Now, here in his father's ruins, I mean to crush him once and for all."

# XXVII

# JASON

JASON HATED BASILISKS.

The little scum-suckers loved to burrow under the temples in New Rome. Back when Jason was a centurion, his cohort always got the unpopular chore of clearing out their nests.

A basilisk didn't look like much—just an arm-length serpent with yellow eyes and a white frill collar—but it moved fast and could kill anything it touched. Jason had never faced more than two at a time. Now a dozen were swimming around the giant's legs. The only good thing: underwater, basilisks wouldn't be able to breathe fire, but that didn't make them any less deadly.

Two of the serpents shot toward Percy. He sliced them in half. The other ten swirled around him, just out of blade's reach. They writhed back and forth in a hypnotic pattern, looking for an opening. One bite, one touch was all it would take.

"Hey!" Jason yelled. "How about some love over here?"

The snakes ignored him.

So did the giant, who stood back and watched with a smug smile, apparently happy for his pets to do the killing.

"Kymopoleia." Jason tried his best to pronounce her name right. "You have to stop this."

She regarded him with her glowing white eyes. "Why would I do that? The Earth Mother has promised me unrestricted power. Could you make me a better offer?"

*A better offer . . .*

He sensed the possibility of an opening—room to negotiate. But what did he have that a storm goddess would want?

The basilisks closed in on Percy. He blasted them away with currents of water, but they just kept circling.

"Hey, basilisks!" Jason yelled.

Still no reaction. He could charge in and help, but even together he and Percy couldn't possibly fight off ten basilisks at once. He needed a better solution.

He glanced up. A thunderstorm raged above, but they were hundreds of feet down. He couldn't possibly summon lightning at the bottom of the sea, could he? Even if he could, water conducted electricity a little too well. He might fry Percy.

But he couldn't think of a better option. He thrust up his sword. Immediately the blade glowed red-hot.

A diffuse cloud of yellow light billowed through the depths, like someone had poured liquid neon into the water. The light hit Jason's sword and sprayed outward in ten separate tendrils, zapping the basilisks.

Their eyes went dark. Their frills disintegrated. All ten serpents turned belly-up and floated dead in the water.

"Next time," Jason said, "*look* at me when I'm talking to you."

Polybotes's smile curdled. "Are you so anxious to die, Roman?"

Percy raised his sword. He hurled himself at the giant, but Polybotes swept his hand through the water, leaving an arc of black oily poison. Percy charged straight into it faster than Jason could yell *Dude, what are you thinking?*

Percy dropped Riptide. He gasped, clawing at his throat. The giant threw his weighted net and Percy collapsed to the floor, hopelessly entangled as the poison thickened around him.

"Let him go!" Jason's voice cracked with panic.

The giant chuckled. "Don't worry, son of Jupiter. Your friend will take a *long* time to die. After all the trouble he's caused me, I wouldn't dream of killing him quickly."

Noxious clouds expanded around the giant, filling the ruins like thick cigar smoke. Jason scrambled backward, not fast enough, but his *ventus* proved a useful filter. As the poison engulfed him, the miniature tornado spun faster, repelling the clouds. Kymopoleia wrinkled her nose and waved away the darkness, but otherwise it didn't seem to affect her.

Percy writhed in the net, his face turning green. Jason charged to help him, but the giant blocked him with his huge trident.

"Oh, I can't let you ruin my fun," Polybotes chided. "The poison will kill him eventually, but first come the paralysis and hours of excruciating pain. I want him to have the full experience! He can watch as I destroy you, Jason Grace!"

Polybotes advanced slowly, giving Jason plenty of time to contemplate the three-story-tall tower of armor and muscle bearing down on him.

He dodged the trident and, using his *ventus* to shoot forward, jabbed his sword into the giant's reptilian leg. Polybotes roared and stumbled, golden ichor pluming from the wound.

"Kym!" Jason yelled. "Is this really what you want?"

The storm goddess looked rather bored, idly spinning her metal disk. "Unlimited power? Why not?"

"But is it any fun?" Jason asked. "So you destroy our ship. You destroy the entire coastline of the world. Once Gaea wipes out human civilization, who's left to fear you? You'll still be unknown."

Polybotes turned. "You are a pest, son of Jupiter. You will be crushed!"

Jason tried to summon more lightning. Nothing happened. If he ever met his dad, he'd have to petition for an increased daily allowance of bolts.

Jason managed to avoid the prongs of the trident again, but the giant swung the other end around and smacked him in the chest.

Jason reeled back, stunned and in pain. Polybotes came in for the kill. Just before the trident would have perforated him, Jason's *ventus* acted on its own. It spiraled sideways, whisking Jason thirty feet across the courtyard.

Thanks, buddy, Jason thought. I owe you some air freshener.

If the *ventus* liked that idea, Jason couldn't tell.

"Actually, Jason Grace," Kym said, studying her fingernails, "now that you mention it, I *do* enjoy being feared by mortals. I am not feared enough."

"I can help with that!" Jason dodged another swipe of the trident. He extended his *gladius* into a javelin and poked Polybotes in the eye.

"AUGH!" The giant staggered.

Percy writhed in the net, but his movements were getting sluggish. Jason needed to hurry. He had to get Percy to sickbay, and if the storm kept raging above them, there wouldn't be any sickbay to get him to.

He flew to Kym's side. "You know gods depend on mortals. The more we honor you, the more powerful you get."

"I wouldn't know. I've never been honored!"

She ignored Polybotes, who was now stampeding around her, trying to swat Jason out of his whirlwind. Jason did his best to keep the goddess between them.

"I can change that," he promised. "I will *personally* arrange a shrine for you on Temple Hill in New Rome. Your first *ever* Roman shrine! I'll raise one at Camp Half-Blood as well, right on the shore of Long Island Sound. Imagine, being honored—"

"And feared."

"—and feared by both Greeks and Romans. You'll be famous!"

"STOP TALKING!" Polybotes swung his trident like a baseball bat.

Jason ducked. Kym did not. The giant slammed her in the rib cage so hard that strands of her jellyfish hair came loose and drifted through the poisoned water.

Polybotes's eyes widened. "I'm sorry, Kymopoleia. You shouldn't have been in the way!"

"IN THE WAY?" The goddess straightened. "I am *in the way?*"

"You heard him," Jason said. "You're nothing but a tool for the giants. They'll cast you aside as soon as they're through destroying the mortals. Then no demigods, no shrines, no fear, no respect."

"LIES!" Polybotes tried to stab him, but Jason hid behind the goddess's dress. "Kymopoleia, when Gaea rules, you will rage and storm without restraint!"

"Will there be mortals to terrorize?" Kym asked.

"Well . . . no."

"Ships to destroy? Demigods to cower in awe?"

"Um . . ."

"Help me," Jason urged. "Together, a goddess and a demigod can kill a giant."

"No!" Polybotes suddenly looked very nervous. "No, that's a terrible idea. Gaea will be most displeased!"

"*If* Gaea wakes," Jason said. "The mighty Kymopoleia can help us make sure that never happens. Then all demigods will honor you *big*-time!"

"Will they cower?" Kym asked.

"Tons of cowering! Plus your name in the summer program. A custom-designed banner. A cabin at Camp Half-Blood. Two shrines. I'll even throw in a Kymopoleia action figure."

"No!" Polybotes wailed. "Not merchandising rights!"

Kymopoleia turned on the giant. "I'm afraid that deal beats what Gaea has offered."

"Unacceptable!" the giant bellowed. "You cannot trust this vile Roman!"

"If I don't honor the bargain," Jason said, "Kym can always kill me. With Gaea, she has no guarantee at all."

"That," Kym said, "is difficult to argue with."

As Polybotes struggled to answer, Jason charged forward and stabbed his javelin in the giant's gut.

Kym lifted her bronze disk from its pedestal. "Say good-bye, Polybotes."

She spun the disk at the giant's neck. Turned out, the rim was sharp.

Polybotes found it difficult to say good-bye, since he no longer had a head.

# XXVIII

# JASON

"**POISON IS A NASTY HABIT.**" Kymopoleia waved her hand and the murky clouds dissipated. "Secondhand poison can kill a person, you know."

Jason wasn't too fond of firsthand poison either, but he decided not to mention that. He cut Percy out of the net and propped him against the temple wall, enveloping him in the airy shell of the *ventus*. The oxygen was getting thin, but Jason hoped it might help expel the poison from his friend's lungs.

It seemed to work. Percy doubled over and began to retch. "Ugh. Thanks."

Jason exhaled with relief. "You had me worried there, bro."

Percy blinked, cross-eyed. "I'm still a little fuzzy. But did you . . . promise Kym an action figure?"

The goddess loomed over them. "Indeed he did. And I expect him to deliver."

"I will," Jason said. "When we win this war, I'm going to make sure *all* the gods get recognized." He put a hand on Percy's shoulder. "My friend here started that process last summer. He made the Olympians promise to pay you guys more attention."

Kym sniffed. "We know what an Olympian promise is worth."

"Which is why I'm going to finish the job." Jason didn't know where these words were coming from, but the idea felt absolutely right. "I'll make sure none of the gods are forgotten at either camp. Maybe they'll get temples, or cabins, or at least shrines—"

"Or collectible trading cards," Kym suggested.

"Sure." Jason smiled. "I'll go back and forth between the camps until the job is done."

Percy whistled. "You're talking about dozens of gods."

"Hundreds," Kym corrected.

"Well, then," Jason said, "it might take a while. But you'll be first on the list, Kymopoleia . . . the storm goddess who beheaded a giant and saved our quest."

Kym stroked her jellyfish hair. "That will do nicely." She regarded Percy. "Though I am still sorry I won't see you die."

"I get that comment a lot," Percy said. "Now about our ship—?"

"Still in one piece," said the goddess. "Not in very good shape, but you should be able to make it to Delos."

"Thank you," Jason said.

"Yeah," Percy said. "And, really, your husband Briares is a good dude. You should give him a chance."

The goddess picked up her bronze disk. "Don't push your luck, brother. Briares has fifty faces; all of them are ugly. He's got a hundred hands, and he's *still* all thumbs around the house."

"Okay," Percy relented. "Not pushing my luck."

Kym turned over the disk, revealing straps on the bottom side like a shield. She slipped it over her shoulders, Captain America style. "I will be watching your progress. Polybotes was not boasting when he warned that your blood would awaken the Earth Mother. The giants are very confident of this."

"My blood, personally?" Percy asked.

Kym's smile was even creepier than usual. "I am not an Oracle. But I heard what the seer Phineas told you in the city of Portland. You will face a sacrifice that you may not be able to make, and it will cost you the world. You have yet to face your fatal flaw, my brother. Look around. All works of gods and men eventually turn to ruins. Would it not be easier to flee into the depths with that girlfriend of yours?"

Percy put his hand on Jason's shoulder and struggled to his feet. "Juno offered me a choice like that, back when I found Camp Jupiter. I'll give you the same answer. I don't run when my friends need me."

Kym turned up her palms. "And there is your flaw, being unable to step away. I will retreat to the depths and watch this battle unfold. You should know that the forces of the ocean are also at war. Your friend Hazel Levesque made quite an impression on the merpeople, and on their mentors, Aphros and Bythos."

"The fish pony dudes," Percy muttered. "They didn't want to meet me."

"Even now they are waging war for your sake," Kym said, "trying to keep Gaea's allies away from Long Island. Whether or not they will survive . . . that remains to be seen. As for you, Jason Grace, your path will be no easier than your friend's. You will be tricked. You will face unbearable sorrow."

Jason tried to keep from sparking. He wasn't sure Percy's heart could take the shock. "Kym, you said you're not an Oracle? They should give you the job. You're definitely depressing enough."

The goddess let loose her dolphin laugh. "You amuse me, son of Jupiter. I hope you live to defeat Gaea."

"Thanks," he said. "Any pointers on defeating a goddess who can't be defeated?"

Kymopoleia tilted her head. "Oh, but you know the answer. You are a child of the sky, with storms in your blood. A primordial god has been defeated once before. You know of whom I speak."

Jason's insides started swirling faster than the *ventus.* "Ouranos, the first god of the sky. But that means—"

"Yes." Kym's alien features took on an expression that almost resembled sympathy. "Let us hope it does not come to that. If Gaea *does* wake . . . well, your task will not be easy. But if you win, remember your promise, Pontifex."

Jason took a moment to process her words. "I'm not a priest."

"No?" Kym's white eyes gleamed. "By the way, your *ventus* servant says he wishes to be freed. Since he has helped you, he hopes you will let him go when you reach the surface. He promises he will not bother you a third time."

"A *third* time?"

Kym paused, as if listening. "He says he joined the storm above to take revenge on you, but had he known how strong you've become since the Grand Canyon, he never would've approached your ship."

"The Grand Canyon . . ." Jason recalled that day on the Skywalk, when one of his jerk classmates turned out to be a wind spirit. "Dylan? Are you kidding me? I'm breathing *Dylan?*"

"Yes," Kym said. "That seems to be his name."

Jason shuddered. "I'll let him go as soon as I reach the surface. No worries."

"Farewell, then," said the goddess. "And may the Fates smile upon you . . . assuming the Fates survive."

They needed to leave.

Jason was running out of air (Dylan air—gross) and everyone on the *Argo II* would be worried about them.

But Percy was still woozy from the poison, so they sat on the edge of the ruined golden dome for a few minutes to let Percy catch his breath . . . or catch his water, whatever a son of Poseidon catches when he's at the bottom of the ocean.

"Thanks, man," Percy said. "You saved my life."

"Hey, that's what we do for our friends."

"But, uh, the Jupiter guy saving the Poseidon guy at the bottom of the ocean . . . maybe we can keep the details to ourselves? Otherwise I'll never hear the end of it."

Jason grinned. "You got it. How you feeling?"

"Better. I . . . I have to admit, when I was choking on that poison, I kept thinking about Akhlys, the misery goddess in Tartarus. I almost destroyed her with poison." He shivered. "It felt *good*, but in a bad way. If Annabeth hadn't stopped me—"

"But she did," Jason said. "That's another thing friends have to do for each other."

"Yeah . . . Thing is, as I was choking just now, I kept thinking: this is payback for Akhlys. The Fates are letting me die the same way I tried to kill that goddess. And . . . honestly, a part of me felt I deserved it. That's why I didn't try to control the giant's poison and move it away from me. That probably sounds crazy."

Jason thought back to Ithaca, when he was despairing over the visit from his mom's spirit. "No. I think I get it."

Percy studied his face. When Jason didn't say any more, Percy changed the subject. "What did Kym mean about defeating Gaea? You mentioned Ouranos . . ."

Jason stared at the silt swirling between the columns of the old palace. "The sky god . . . the Titans defeated him by calling him down to the earth. They got him away from his home territory, ambushed him, held him down, and cut him up."

Percy looked like his nausea was coming back. "How would we do that with Gaea?"

Jason recalled a line from the prophecy: *To storm or fire the world must fall.* He had an idea what that meant now . . . but if he was right, Percy wouldn't be able to help. In fact, he might unintentionally make things harder.

*I don't run when my friends need me,* Percy had said.

*And there is your flaw,* Kym had warned, *being unable to step away.*

Today was July 27. In five days, Jason would know if he was right.

"Let's get to Delos first," he said. "Apollo and Artemis might have some advice."

Percy nodded, though he didn't seem satisfied with that answer. "Why did Kymopoleia call you a *Pontiac?*"

Jason's laugh literally cleared the air. "*Pontifex.* It means priest."

"Oh." Percy frowned. "Still sounds like a kind of car. 'The new Pontifex XLS.' Will you have to wear a collar and bless people?"

"Nah. Romans used to have a *pontifex maximus,* who oversaw all the proper sacrifices and whatnot, to make sure none of the gods got mad. Which I offered to do . . . I guess it does sound like a *pontifex's* job."

"So you meant it?" Percy asked. "You're really going to try building shrines for all the minor gods?"

"Yeah. I never really thought about it before, but I like the idea of going back and forth between the two camps—assuming, you know, we make it through next week and the two camps still exist. What you did last year on Olympus, turning down immortality and asking the gods to play nice instead—that was noble, man."

Percy grunted. "Believe me, some days I regret the choice. *Oh, you want to turn down our offer? Okay, fine! ZAP! Lose your memory! Go to Tartarus!*"

"You did what a hero should do. I admire you for that. The least I can do, if we survive, is continue that work—make sure all the gods get some recognition. Who knows? If the gods get along better, maybe we can stop more of these wars from breaking out."

"That would most definitely be good," Percy agreed. "You know, you look different . . . *better* different. Does your wound still hurt?"

"My wound . . ." Jason had been so busy with the giant and the goddess, he'd forgotten about the sword wound in his gut, even though he'd been dying from it in sickbay only an hour ago.

He lifted his shirt and pulled away the bandages. No smoke. No bleeding. No scar. No pain.

"It's . . . gone," he said, stunned. "I feel completely normal. What the heck?"

"You beat it, man!" Percy laughed. "You found your own cure."

Jason considered that. He guessed it must be true. Maybe putting aside his pain to help his friends had done the trick.

Or maybe his decision to honor the gods at both camps had healed him, giving him a clear path to the future. Roman or Greek . . . the difference didn't matter. Like he'd told the ghosts at Ithaca, his family had just gotten bigger. Now he saw his place in it. He would keep his promise to the storm goddess. And because of that, Michael Varus's sword meant nothing.

*Die a Roman.*

No. If he had to die, he would die a son of Jupiter, a child of the gods—the blood of Olympus. But he wasn't about to let himself get sacrificed—at least not without a fight.

"Come on." Jason clapped his friend on the back. "Let's go check on our ship."

# XXIX

# NICO

GIVEN A CHOICE between death and the Buford Zippy Mart, Nico would've had a tough time deciding. At least he knew his way around the Land of the Dead. Plus the food was fresher.

"I still don't get it," Coach Hedge muttered as they roamed the center aisle. "They named a whole town after Leo's table?"

"I think the town was here first, Coach," Nico said.

"Huh." The coach picked up a box of powdered donuts. "Maybe you're right. These look at least a hundred years old. I miss those Portuguese *farturas*."

Nico couldn't think about Portugal without his arms hurting. Across his biceps, the werewolf claw marks were still swollen and red. The store clerk had asked Nico if he'd picked a fight with a bobcat.

They bought a first-aid kit, a pad of paper (so Coach Hedge could write more paper airplane messages to his wife), some junk food and soda (since the banquet table in Reyna's new magic tent only provided healthy food and fresh water), and some miscellaneous camping supplies for Coach Hedge's useless but impressively complicated monster traps.

Nico had been hoping to find some fresh clothes. Two days since they'd fled San Juan, he was tired of walking around in his tropical ISLA DEL ENCANTORICO shirt, especially since Coach Hedge had a matching one. Unfortunately, the Zippy Mart only carried T-shirts with Confederate flags and corny sayings like KEEP CALM AND FOLLOW THE REDNECK. Nico decided he'd stick with parrots and palm trees.

They walked back to the campsite down a two-lane road under the blazing sun. This part of South Carolina seemed to consist mostly of overgrown fields, punctuated by telephone poles and trees covered in kudzu vines. The town of Buford itself was a collection of portable metal sheds—six or seven, which was probably also the town's population.

Nico wasn't exactly a sunshine person, but for once he welcomed the warmth. It made him feel more substantial—anchored to the mortal world. With every shadow-jump, coming back got harder and harder. Even in broad daylight his hand passed through solid objects. His belt and sword kept falling around his ankles for no apparent reason. Once, when he wasn't looking where he was going, he walked straight through a tree.

Nico remembered something Jason Grace had told him in the palace of Notus: *Maybe it's time you come out of the shadows.*

If only I could, he thought. For the first time in his life, he had begun to fear the dark, because he might melt into it permanently.

Nico and Hedge had no trouble finding their way back to

camp. The Athena Parthenos was the tallest landmark for miles around. In its new camouflage netting, it glittered silver like an extremely flashy forty-foot-tall ghost.

Apparently, the Athena Parthenos had wanted them to visit a place with educational value, because she'd landed right next to a historical marker that read MASSACRE OF BUFORD, on a gravel turnout at the intersection of Nowhere and Nothing.

Reyna's tent sat in a grove of trees about thirty yards back from the road. Nearby lay a rectangular cairn—hundreds of stones piled in the shape of an oversized grave with a granite obelisk for a headstone. Scattered around it were faded wreathes and crushed bouquets of plastic flowers, which made the place seem even sadder.

Aurum and Argentum were playing keep-away in the woods with one of the coach's handballs. Ever since getting repaired by the Amazons, the metal dogs had been frisky and full of energy—unlike their owner.

Reyna sat cross-legged at the entrance of the tent, staring at the memorial obelisk. She hadn't said much since they fled San Juan two days ago. They'd also encountered no monsters, which made Nico uneasy. They'd had no further word from the Hunters or the Amazons. They didn't know what had happened to Hylla, or Thalia, or the giant Orion.

Nico didn't like the Hunters of Artemis. Tragedy followed them as surely as their dogs and birds of prey. His sister Bianca had died after joining the Hunters. Then Thalia Grace became their leader and started recruiting even more young women to their cause, which grated on Nico—as if Bianca's death could be forgotten. As if she could be replaced.

When Nico had woken up at Barrachina and found the Hunters' note about kidnapping Reyna, he'd torn apart the courtyard in rage. He didn't want the Hunters stealing another important person from him.

Fortunately, he'd gotten Reyna back, but he didn't like how brooding she had become. Every time he tried to ask her about the incident on the Calle San Jose—those ghosts on the balcony, all staring at her, whispering accusations—Reyna shut him down.

Nico knew something about ghosts. Letting them get inside your head was dangerous. He wanted to help Reyna, but since his own strategy was to deal with his problems alone, spurning anyone who tried to get close, he couldn't exactly criticize Reyna for doing the same thing.

She glanced up as they approached. "I figured it out."

"What historical site this is?" Hedge asked. "Good, 'cause it's been driving me crazy."

"The Battle of Waxhaws," she said.

"Ah, right . . ." Hedge nodded sagely. "That was a vicious little smackdown."

Nico tried to sense any restless spirits in the area, but he felt nothing. Unusual for a battleground. "Are you sure?"

"In 1780," Reyna said. "The American Revolution. Most of the Colonial leaders were Greek demigods. The British generals were Roman demigods."

"Because England was like Rome back then," Nico guessed. "A rising empire."

Reyna picked up a crushed bouquet. "I think I know why we landed here. It's my fault."

"Ah, come on," Hedge scoffed. "The Buford Zippy Mart isn't anybody's fault. Those things just happen."

Reyna picked at the faded plastic flowers. "During the Revolution, four hundred Americans got overtaken here by British cavalry. The Colonial troops tried to surrender, but the British were out for blood. They massacred the Americans even after they threw down their weapons. Only a few survived."

Nico supposed he should have been shocked. But after traveling through the Underworld, hearing so many stories of evil and death, a wartime massacre hardly seemed newsworthy. "Reyna, how is that your fault?"

"The British commander was Banastre Tarleton."

Hedge snorted. "I've heard of him. Crazy dude. They called him Benny the Butcher."

"Yes . . ." Reyna took a shaky breath. "He was a son of Bellona."

"Oh." Nico stared at the oversized grave. It still bothered him that he couldn't sense any spirits. Hundreds of soldiers massacred at this spot . . . that should've sent out *some* kind of death vibe.

He sat next to Reyna, and decided to take a risk. "So you think we were drawn here because you have some sort of connection to the ghosts. Like what happened in San Juan?"

For a ten count she said nothing, turning the plastic bouquet in her hand. "I don't want to talk about San Juan."

"You should." Nico felt like a stranger in his own body. Why was he encouraging Reyna to share? It wasn't his style or his business. Nevertheless, he kept talking. "The main thing about ghosts—most of them have lost their voices. In Asphodel, millions of them wander around aimlessly, trying to remember who they were. You know why they end up like that? Because in life they never took a stand one way or another. They never spoke out, so they were never heard. Your voice is your identity. If you don't use it," he said with a shrug, "you're halfway to Asphodel already."

Reyna scowled. "Is that your idea of a pep talk?"

Coach Hedge cleared his throat. "This is getting too psychological for me. I'm going to write some letters."

He took his notepad and headed into the woods. The last day or so, he'd been writing a lot—apparently not just to Mellie. The coach wouldn't share details, but he hinted that he was calling in some favors to help with the quest. For all Nico knew, he was writing to Jackie Chan.

Nico opened his shopping bag. He pulled out a box of Little Debbie Oatmeal Creme Pies and offered one to Reyna.

She wrinkled her nose. "Those look like they went stale in dinosaur times."

"Maybe. But I've got a big appetite these days. *Any* kind of food tastes good . . . except maybe pomegranate seeds. I'm done with those."

Reyna picked out a creme pie and took a bite. "The ghosts in San Juan . . . they were my ancestors."

Nico waited. The breeze ruffled the camouflage netting over the Athena Parthenos.

"The Ramírez-Arellano family goes back a long way," Reyna continued. "I don't know the whole story. My ancestors lived in Spain when it was a Roman province. My

great-great-something-something-grandfather was a conquistador. He came over to Puerto Rico with Ponce de León."

"One of the ghosts on the balcony was wearing conquistador armor," Nico recalled.

"That's him."

"So . . . is your whole family descended from Bellona? I
thought you and Hylla were her daughters, not legacies."

Too late, Nico realized he shouldn't have brought up Hylla.
A look of despair passed over Reyna's face, though she managed to hide it quickly.

"We *are* her daughters," Reyna said. "We're the first actual
children of Bellona in the Ramírez-Arellano family. And
Bellona has always favored our clan. Millennia ago, she
decreed that we would play pivotal roles in many battles."

"Like you're doing now," Nico said.

Reyna brushed crumbs from her chin. "Perhaps. Some of
my ancestors have been heroes. Some have been villains. You
saw the ghost with the gunshot wounds in the chest?"

Nico nodded. "A pirate?"

"The most famous in Puerto Rican history. He was known
as the Pirate Cofresí, but his family name was Ramírez de
Arellano. Our house, the family villa, was built with money
from treasure that he buried."

For a moment, Nico felt like a little kid again. He was
tempted to blurt out: *That's so cool!* Even before he got into
Mythomagic, he'd been obsessed with pirates. Probably that
was one reason he'd been so smitten with Percy, a son of the
sea god.

"And the other ghosts?" he asked.

Reyna took another bite of creme pie. "The guy in the U.S. Navy uniform . . . he's my great-great-uncle from World War II, the first Latino submarine commander. You get the idea. A lot of warriors. Bellona was our patron goddess for generations."

"But she never had demigod children in your family—until you."

"The goddess . . . she fell in love with my father, Julian. He was a soldier in Iraq. He was—" Reyna's voice broke. She tossed aside the plastic bouquet of flowers. "I can't do this. I can't talk about him."

A cloud passed overhead, blanketing the woods in shadows. Nico didn't want to push Reyna. What right did he have?

He set down his oatmeal creme pie . . . and noticed that his fingertips were turning to smoke. The sunlight returned. His hands became solid again, but Nico's nerves jangled. He felt as if he'd been pulled back from the edge of a high balcony.

*Your voice is your identity,* he'd told Reyna. *If you don't use it, you're halfway to Asphodel already.*

He hated when his own advice applied to himself.

"My dad gave me a present once," Nico said. "It was a zombie."

Reyna stared at him. "What?"

"His name is Jules-Albert. He's French."

"A . . . French zombie?"

"Hades isn't the greatest dad, but occasionally he has these *want-to-know-my-son* moments. I guess he thought the zombie was a peace offering. He said Jules-Albert could be my chauffeur."

The corner of Reyna's mouth twitched. "A French zombie chauffeur."

Nico realized how ridiculous it sounded. He'd never told anyone about Jules-Albert—not even Hazel. But he kept talking.

"Hades had this idea that I should, you know, try to act like a modern teenager. Make friends. Get to know the twenty-first century. He vaguely understood that mortal parents drive their kids around a lot. He couldn't do that. So his solution was a zombie."

"To take you to the mall," Reyna said. "Or the drive-through at In-N-Out Burger."

"I suppose." Nico's nerves began to settle. "Because nothing helps you make friends faster than a rotting corpse with a French accent."

Reyna laughed. "I'm sorry . . . I shouldn't make fun."

"It's okay. Point is . . . I don't like talking about my dad either. But sometimes," he said, looking her in the eyes, "you have to."

Reyna's expression turned serious. "I never knew my father in his better days. Hylla said he used to be gentler when she was very small, before I was born. He was a good soldier—fearless, disciplined, cool under fire. He was handsome. He could be very charming. Bellona blessed him, as she had with so many of my ancestors, but that wasn't enough for my dad. He wanted her for his wife."

Over in the woods, Coach Hedge muttered to himself as he wrote. Three paper airplanes were already spiraling upward in the breeze, heading to gods knew where.

"My father dedicated himself completely to Bellona," Reyna continued. "It's one thing to respect the power of war. It's another thing to fall in love with it. I don't know how he did it, but he managed to win Bellona's heart. My sister was born just before he went to Iraq for his last tour of duty. He was honorably discharged, came home a hero. If . . . if he'd been able to adjust to civilian life, everything might have been all right."

"But he couldn't," Nico guessed.

Reyna shook her head. "Shortly after he got back, he had one last encounter with the goddess . . . that's the, um, reason I was born. Bellona gave him a glimpse of the future. She explained why our family was so important to her. She said the legacy of Rome would never fail as long as one of our bloodline remained, fighting to defend our homeland. Those words . . . I think she meant them to be reassuring, but my father became fixated on them."

"War can be hard to get over," Nico said, remembering Pietro, one of his neighbors from his childhood in Italy. Pietro had come back from Mussolini's African campaign in one piece, but after shelling Ethiopian civilians with mustard gas, his mind was never the same.

Despite the heat, Reyna drew her cloak around her. "Part of the problem was post-traumatic stress. He couldn't stop thinking about the war. And then there was the constant pain—a roadside bomb had left shrapnel in his shoulder and chest. But it was more than that. Over the years, as I was growing up, he . . . he changed."

Nico didn't respond. He'd never had anyone talk to him

this openly before, except maybe for Hazel. He felt like he was watching a flock of birds settle on a field. One loud sound might startle them away.

"He became paranoid," Reyna said. "He thought Bellona's words were a warning that our bloodline would be exterminated and the legacy of Rome would fail. He saw enemies everywhere. He collected weapons. He turned our house into a fortress. At night, he would lock Hylla and me in our rooms. If we sneaked out, he would yell at us and throw furniture and . . . well, he terrified us. At times, he even thought *we* were the enemies. He became convinced we were spying on him, trying to undermine him. Then the ghosts started appearing. I guess they'd always been there, but they picked up on my father's agitation and began to manifest. They whispered to him, feeding his suspicions. Finally one day . . . I can't tell you for sure when, I realized he had ceased to be my father. He had become one of the ghosts."

A cold tide rose in Nico's chest. "A *mania*," he speculated. "I've seen it before. A human withers away until he's not human anymore. Only his worst qualities remain. His insanity . . ."

It was clear from Reyna's expression that his explanation wasn't helping.

"Whatever he was," Reyna said, "he became impossible to live with. Hylla and I escaped the house as often as we could, but eventually we'd come . . . back . . . and face his rage. We didn't know what else to do. He was our only family. The last time we returned, he—he was so angry he was literally glowing. He couldn't physically touch things anymore, but he could move them . . . like a poltergeist, I guess. He tore up the floor tiles. He ripped open the sofa. Finally he tossed a chair and it hit Hylla. She collapsed. She was only knocked unconscious, but I thought she was dead. She'd spent so many years protecting me . . . I just lost it. I grabbed the nearest weapon I could find—a family heirloom, the Pirate Cofresí's saber. I—I didn't know it was Imperial gold. I ran at my father's spirit and . . ."

"You vaporized him," Nico guessed.

Reyna's eyes brimmed with tears. "I killed my own father."

"No. Reyna, no. That wasn't him. That was a ghost. Even worse: a *mania.* You were protecting your sister."

She twisted the silver ring on her finger. "You don't understand. Patricide is the worst crime a Roman can commit. It's unforgivable."

"You didn't kill your father. The man was already dead," Nico insisted. "You dispelled a ghost."

"It doesn't matter!" Reyna sobbed. "If word of this got out at Camp Jupiter—"

"You'd be executed," said a new voice.

At the edge of the woods stood a Roman legionnaire in full armor, holding a *pilum.* A mop of brown hair hung in his eyes. His nose had obviously been broken at least once, which made his smile look even more sinister. "Thank you for your confession, *former* Praetor. You've made my job much easier."

# NICO

COACH HEDGE CHOSE THAT MOMENT to burst into the clearing, waving a paper airplane and yelling, "Good news, everyone!"

He froze when he saw the Roman. "Oh . . . never mind."

He quickly crumpled the airplane and ate it.

Reyna and Nico got to their feet. Aurum and Argentum scampered to Reyna's side and growled at the intruder.

How this guy had gotten so close with *none* of them noticing, Nico didn't understand.

"Bryce Lawrence," Reyna said. "Octavian's newest attack dog."

The Roman inclined his head. His eyes were green, but not sea green like Percy's . . . more like pond scum green.

"The augur has many attack dogs," Bryce said. "I'm just the lucky one who found you. Your *Graecus* friend here"—he pointed his chin at Nico—"he was easy to track. He stinks of the Underworld."

Nico unsheathed his sword. "You know the Underworld? Would you like me to arrange a visit?"

Bryce laughed. His front teeth were two different shades of yellow. "Do you think you can frighten me? I'm a descendant of Orcus, the god of broken vows and eternal punishment. I've heard the screams in the Fields of Punishment firsthand. They're music to my ears. Soon, I'll be adding one more damned soul to the chorus."

He grinned at Reyna. "Patricide, eh? Octavian will love this news. You are under arrest for multiple violations of Roman law."

"You *being* here is against Roman law," Reyna said. "Romans don't quest alone. A mission has to be led by someone of centurion rank or higher. You're *in probatio*, and even giving you *that* rank was a mistake. You have no right to arrest me."

Bryce shrugged. "In times of war, some rules have to be flexible. But don't worry. Once I bring you in for trial, I'll be rewarded with full membership in the legion. I imagine I'll be promoted to centurion too. Doubtless there will be vacancies after the coming battle. Some officers won't survive, especially if their loyalties aren't in the right place."

Coach Hedge hefted his bat. "I don't know the proper Roman etiquette, but can I bash this kid now?"

"A faun," Bryce said. "Interesting. I heard the Greeks actually *trusted* their goat men."

Hedge bleated. "I'm a satyr. And you can trust I'm going to put this bat upside your head, you little punk."

The coach advanced, but as soon as his foot touched the

cairn, the stones rumbled like they were coming to a boil. Out of the gravesite, skeletal warriors erupted—*spartoi* in the tattered remains of British redcoat uniforms.

Hedge scrambled away, but the first two skeletons grabbed his arms and lifted him off the ground. The coach dropped his bat and kicked his hooves.

"Lemme go, ya stupid boneheads!" he bellowed.

Nico watched, paralyzed, as the grave spewed forth more dead British soldiers—five, ten, twenty, multiplying so quickly that Reyna and her metal dogs were surrounded before Nico even thought to raise his sword.

How could he *not* have sensed so many dead, so close at hand?

"I forgot to mention," Bryce said, "I'm actually not alone on this quest. As you can see, I have backup. These redcoats promised quarter to the colonials. Then they butchered them. Personally, I like a good massacre, but because they broke their oaths, their spirits were damned, and they are perpetually under the power of Orcus. Which means they are also under *my* control." He pointed to Reyna. "Seize the girl."

The *spartoi* surged forward. Aurum and Argentum took down the first few, but they were quickly wrestled to the ground, skeletal hands clamped over their muzzles. The redcoats grabbed Reyna's arms. For undead creatures, they were surprisingly quick.

Finally, Nico came to his senses. He slashed at the *spartoi*, but his sword passed harmlessly through them. He exerted his will, ordering the skeletons to dissolve. They acted as if he didn't exist.

"What's wrong, son of Hades?" Bryce's voice was filled with fake sympathy. "Losing your grip?"

Nico tried to push his way through the skeletons. There were too many. Bryce, Reyna, and Coach Hedge might as well have been behind a metal wall.

"Nico, get out of here!" Reyna said. "Get to the statue and leave."

"Yes, off you go!" Bryce agreed. "Of course, you realize that your next shadow-jump will be your last. You know you don't have the strength to survive another. But by all means, take the Athena Parthenos."

Nico glanced down. He still held his Stygian sword, but his hands were dark and transparent like smoky glass. Even in the direct sunlight, he was dissolving.

"Stop this!" he said.

"Oh, I'm not doing a thing," Bryce said. "But I am curious to see what will happen. If you take the statue, you'll disappear with it forever, right into oblivion. If you *don't* take it . . . well, I have orders to bring Reyna in alive to stand trial for treason. I have no orders to bring *you* in alive, or the faun."

"Satyr!" the coach yelled. He kicked a skeleton in its bony crotch, which seemed to hurt Hedge more than the redcoat. "Ow! Stupid British dead guys!"

Bryce lowered his javelin and poked the coach in the belly. "I wonder what this one's pain tolerance would be. I've experimented on all kinds of animals. I even killed my own centurion once. I've never tried a faun . . . excuse me, *a satyr.* You reincarnate, don't you? How much pain can you take before you turn into a patch of daisies?"

Nico's anger turned as cold and dark as his blade. He'd been morphed into a few plants himself, and he didn't appreciate it. He hated people like Bryce Lawrence, who inflicted pain just for fun.

"Leave him alone," Nico warned.

Bryce raised an eyebrow. "Or what? By all means, try something Underworld-y, Nico. I'd love to see it. I have a feeling anything major will make you fade out permanently. Go ahead."

Reyna struggled. "Bryce, forget about them. If you want me as your prisoner, fine. I'll go willingly and face Octavian's stupid trial."

"A fine offer." Bryce turned his javelin, letting the tip hover a few inches from Reyna's eyes. "You really don't know what Octavian has planned, do you? He's been busy pulling in favors, spending the legion's money."

Reyna clenched her fists. "Octavian has no right—"

"He has the right of *power*," Bryce said. "You forfeited your authority when you ran off to the ancient lands. On August first, your Greek friends at Camp Half-Blood will find out what a powerful enemy Octavian is. I've seen the designs for his machines. . . . Even *I'm* impressed."

Nico's bones felt like they were changing into helium, the way they'd felt when the god Favonius turned him into a breeze.

Then he locked eyes with Reyna. Her strength surged through him—a wave of courage and resilience that made him feel substantial again, anchored to the mortal world.

Even surrounded by the dead and facing execution, Reyna Ramírez-Arellano had a huge reservoir of bravery to share.

"Nico," she said, "do what you need to do. I've got your back."

Bryce chuckled, clearly enjoying himself. "Oh, Reyna. *You've got his back?* It's going to be so fun dragging you before a tribunal, forcing you to confess that you killed your father. I hope they'll execute you in the ancient way—sewn into a sack with a rabid dog, then thrown into a river. I've always wanted to see that. I can't wait until your little secret comes out."

*Until your little secret comes out.*

Bryce flicked the point of his *pilum* across Reyna's face, leaving a line of blood.

And Nico's rage exploded.

# XXXI

# NICO

**LATER, THEY TOLD HIM WHAT HAPPENED.** All he remembered was the screaming.

According to Reyna, the air around him dropped to freezing. The ground blackened. In one horrible cry, he unleashed a flood of pain and anger on everyone in the clearing. Reyna and the coach experienced his journey through Tartarus, his capture by the giants, his days wasting away inside that bronze jar. They felt Nico's anguish from his days on the *Argo II*, and his encounter with Cupid in the ruins of Salona.

They heard his unspoken challenge to Bryce Lawrence, loud and clear: *You want secrets? Here.*

The *spartoi* disintegrated into ashes. The rocks of the cairn turned white with frost. Bryce Lawrence stumbled, clutching his head, both nostrils bleeding.

Nico marched toward him. He grabbed Bryce's *probatio* tablet and ripped it off his neck.

"You aren't worthy of this," Nico growled.

The earth split under Bryce's feet. He sank up to his waist. "Stop!" Bryce clawed at the dirt and the plastic bouquets, but his body kept sinking.

"You took an oath to the legion." Nico's breath steamed in the cold. "You broke its rules. You inflicted pain. You killed your own centurion."

"I—I didn't! I—"

"You should've died for your crimes," Nico continued. "That was the punishment. Instead you got exile. You should have stayed away. Your father Orcus may not approve of broken oaths. But my father Hades *really* doesn't approve of those who escape punishment."

"Please!"

That word didn't make sense to Nico. The Underworld had no mercy. It only had justice.

"You're already dead," Nico said. "You're a ghost with no tongue, no memory. You won't be sharing any secrets."

"No!" Bryce's body turned dark and smoky. He slipped into the earth, up to his chest. "No, I am Bryce Lawrence! I'm alive!"

"Who are you?" Nico asked.

The next sound from Bryce's mouth was a chattering whisper. His face became indistinct. He could have been anyone—just another nameless spirit among millions.

"Begone," Nico said.

The spirit dissipated. The earth closed.

Nico looked back and saw that his friends were safe.

Reyna and the coach stared at him in horror. Reyna's face was bleeding. Aurum and Argentum turned in circles, as if their mechanical brains had short-circuited.

Nico collapsed.

His dreams made no sense, which was almost a relief.

A flock of ravens circled in a dark sky. Then the ravens turned into horses galloping through the surf.

He saw his sister Bianca sitting in the dining pavilion at Camp Half-Blood with the Hunters of Artemis. She smiled and laughed with her new group of friends. Then Bianca changed into Hazel, who kissed Nico on the cheek and said, "I want you to be an exception."

He saw the harpy Ella with her shaggy red hair and red feathers, her eyes like dark coffee. She perched on the couch of the Big House's living room. Propped next to her was the magical stuffed leopard head Seymour. Ella rocked back and forth, feeding the leopard Cheetos.

"Cheese is not good for harpies," she muttered. Then she scrunched up her face and chanted one of her memorized lines of prophecy: *"The fall of the sun, the final verse."* She fed Seymour more Cheetos. "Cheese is good for leopard heads."

Seymour roared in agreement.

Ella changed into a dark-haired, extremely pregnant cloud nymph, writhing in pain in a camp bunk bed. Clarisse La Rue sat next to her, wiping the nymph's head with a cool cloth. "Mellie, you'll be fine," Clarisse said, though she sounded worried.

"No, nothing is fine!" Mellie wailed. "Gaea is rising!"

The scene shifted. Nico stood with Hades in the Berkeley Hills on the day Hades first led him to Camp Jupiter. "Go to them," said the god. "Introduce yourself as a child of Pluto. It is important you make this connection."

"Why?" Nico asked.

Hades dissolved. Nico found himself back in Tartarus, standing before Akhlys, the goddess of misery. Blood streaked her cheeks. Tears streamed from her eyes, dripped on the shield of Hercules in her lap. "Child of Hades, what more could I do to you? You are perfect! So much sorrow and pain!"

Nico gasped.

His eyes flew open.

He was flat on his back, staring at the sunlight in the tree branches.

"Thank the gods." Reyna leaned over him, her hand cool on his forehead. The bleeding cut on her face was completely gone.

Next to her, Coach Hedge scowled. Sadly, Nico had a great view right up the coach's nostrils.

"Good," said Coach Hedge. "Just a few more applications."

He held up a large square bandage coated with sticky brown gunk and plastered it over Nico's nose.

"What is . . . ? Ugh."

The gunk smelled like potting soil, cedar chips, grape juice, and just a hint of fertilizer. Nico didn't have the strength to remove it.

His senses started to work again. He realized he was lying on a sleeping bag outside the tent. He was wearing nothing but his boxer shorts and a thousand gross, brown-plastered bandages all over his body. His arms, legs, and chest were itchy from the drying mud.

"Are—are you trying to plant me?" he murmured.

"It's sports medicine with a little nature magic," said the coach. "Kind of a hobby of mine."

Nico tried to focus on Reyna's face. "You approved this?"

She looked like she was about to pass out from exhaustion, but she managed a smile. "Coach Hedge brought you back from the brink. The unicorn draught, ambrosia, nectar . . . we couldn't use any of it. You were fading so badly."

"Fading . . . ?"

"Don't worry about that now, kid." Hedge put a drinking straw next to Nico's mouth. "Have some Gatorade."

"I—I don't want—"

"You'll have some Gatorade," the coach insisted.

Nico had some Gatorade. He was surprised at how thirsty he was.

"What happened to me?" he asked. "To Bryce . . . to those skeletons . . . ?"

Reyna and the coach exchanged an uneasy look.

"There's good news and bad news," Reyna said. "But first, eat something. You'll need your strength back before you hear the bad news."

# XXXII

# NICO

"*Three days?*"

Nico wasn't sure he'd heard her right the first dozen times.

"We couldn't move you," Reyna said. "I mean . . . *literally*, you couldn't be moved. You had almost no substance. If it weren't for Coach Hedge—"

"No biggie," the coach assured him. "One time in the middle of a play-off game I had to splint a quarterback's leg with nothing but tree branches and strapping tape."

Despite his nonchalance, the satyr had bags under his eyes. His cheeks were sunken. He looked almost as bad as Nico felt.

Nico couldn't believe he'd been unconscious for so long. He recounted his weird dreams—the mutterings of Ella the harpy, the glimpse of Mellie the cloud nymph (which worried the coach)—but Nico felt as if those visions had lasted only seconds. According to Reyna, it was the afternoon of July 30. He'd been in a shadow coma for *days*.

"The Romans will attack Camp Half-Blood the day after

tomorrow." Nico sipped more Gatorade, which was nice and cold, but without flavor. His taste buds seemed to have phased into the shadow world permanently. "We have to hurry. I have to get ready."

"No." Reyna pressed her hand against his forearm, making the bandages crinkle. "Any more shadow-travel would kill you."

He gritted his teeth. "If it kills me, it kills me. We *have* to get the statue to Camp Half-Blood."

"Hey, kid," said the coach, "I appreciate your dedication, but if you zap us all into eternal darkness along with the Athena Parthenos, it's not going to help anybody. Bryce Lawrence was right about that."

At the mention of Bryce, Reyna's metallic dogs pricked up their ears and snarled.

Reyna stared at the cairn of rocks, her eyes full of torment, as if more unwelcome spirits might emerge from the grave.

Nico took a breath, getting a nose full of Hedge's fragrant home remedy. "Reyna, I . . . I didn't think. What I did to Bryce—"

"You destroyed him," Reyna said. "You turned him into a ghost. And, yes, it reminded me of what happened to my father."

"I didn't mean to scare you," Nico said bitterly. "I didn't mean to . . . to poison another friendship. I'm sorry."

Reyna studied his face. "Nico, I have to admit, the first day you were unconscious, I didn't know what to think or feel. What you did was hard to watch . . . hard to process."

Coach Hedge chewed on a stick. "I gotta agree with the

girl on this one, kid. Smashing somebody's head in with a baseball bat, that's one thing. But ghostifying that creep? That was some *dark* stuff."

Nico expected to feel angry—to shout at them for trying to judge him. That's what he normally did.

But his anger wouldn't materialize. He still felt plenty of rage toward Bryce Lawrence, and Gaea, and the giants. He wanted to find the augur Octavian and strangle him with his chain belt. But he wasn't mad at Reyna or the coach.

"Why did you bring me back?" he asked. "You knew I couldn't help you anymore. You should've found another way to keep going with the statue. But you wasted three days watching over me. Why?"

Coach Hedge snorted. "You're part of the team, you idiot. We're not going to leave you behind."

"It's more than that." Reyna rested her hand on Nico's. "While you were asleep, I did a lot of thinking. What I told you about my father . . . I'd never shared that with anyone. I guess I knew you were the right person to confide in. You lifted some of my burden. I trust you, Nico."

Nico stared at her, mystified. "How can you trust me? You both felt my anger, saw my worst feelings . . ."

"Hey, kid," said Coach Hedge, his tone softer. "We all get angry. Even a sweetheart like me."

Reyna smirked. She squeezed Nico's hand. "Coach is right, Nico. You're not the only one who lets out the darkness once in a while. I told you what happened with my dad, and you supported me. You shared your painful experiences; how can we not support you? We're friends."

Nico wasn't sure what to say. They'd seen his deepest secrets. They knew who he was, what he was.

But they didn't seem to care. No . . . they cared *more*.

They weren't judging him. They were concerned. None of it made sense to him.

"But Bryce. I . . ." Nico couldn't continue.

"You did what had to be done. I see that now," Reyna said. "Just promise me, no more turning people into ghosts if we can avoid it."

"Yeah," Coach said. "Unless you let me whale on them *first*. Besides, it's not all bad news."

Reyna nodded. "We've seen no sign of other Romans, so it appears Bryce didn't notify anyone else where he was. Also, no sign of Orion. Hopefully that means he was taken down by the Hunters."

"And Hylla?" Nico asked. "Thalia?"

The lines tightened around Reyna's mouth. "No word. But I have to believe they're still alive."

"You didn't tell him the best news," the coach prompted.

Reyna frowned. "Maybe because it's so hard to believe. Coach Hedge thinks he's found another way to transport the statue. It's all he's talked about for the past three days. But so far we've seen no sign of—"

"Hey, it'll happen!" Coach grinned at Nico. "You remember that paper airplane I got right before Creepmeister Lawrence showed up? It was a message from one of Mellie's contacts in the palace of Aeolus. This harpy, Nuggets—she and Mellie go way back. Anyway . . . she knows a guy who knows a guy who knows a horse who knows a goat who knows another horse—"

"Coach," Reyna chided, "you'll make him sorry he came out of his coma."

"Fine," the satyr huffed. "Long story short, I pulled in a lot of favors. I got word to the right wind-type spirits that we needed help. The letter I ate? Confirmation that the cavalry is coming. They said it would take a while to organize, but he should be here soon—any minute, in fact."

"Who's *he*?" Nico asked. "What cavalry?"

Reyna stood abruptly. She stared toward the north, her face slack with awe. "*That* cavalry. . . ."

Nico followed her gaze. A flock of birds was approaching— *large* birds.

They got closer, and Nico realized they were horses with wings—at least half a dozen in V formation, without riders.

Flying on point was a massive stallion with a golden coat and multicolored plumage like an eagle's, his wingspan twice as wide as the other horses'.

"*Pegasi,*" Nico said. "You summoned enough to carry the statue."

Coach laughed with delight. "Not just any pegasi, kid. You're in for a real treat."

"The stallion in front . . ." Reyna shook her head in disbelief. "That's *the* Pegasus, the immortal lord of horses."

# LEO

TYPICAL.

Just as Leo finished his modifications, a big storm goddess came along and smacked the grommets right out of his ship.

After their encounter with Kymopo-what's-her-name, the *Argo II* limped through the Aegean, too damaged to fly, too slow to outrun monsters. They fought hungry sea serpents about every hour. They attracted schools of curious fish. At one point they got stuck on a rock, and Percy and Jason had to get out and push.

The wheezing sound of the engine made Leo want to cry. Over the course of three long days, he finally got the ship more or less back to working order just as they made port at the island of Mykonos, which probably meant it was time for them to get bashed to pieces again.

Percy and Annabeth went ashore to scout while Leo stayed on the quarterdeck, fine-tuning the control console. He was so engrossed in the wiring, he didn't notice the landing party was back until Percy said, "Hey, man. Gelato."

Instantly, Leo's day got better. The whole crew sat on deck, without a storm or a monster attack to worry about for the first time in days, and ate ice cream. Well, except for Frank, who was lactose intolerant. He got an apple.

The day was hot and windy. The sea glittered with chop, but Leo had fixed the stabilizers well enough that Hazel didn't look too seasick.

Curving off to their starboard side was the town of Mykonos—a collection of white stucco buildings with blue roofs, blue windows, and blue doors.

"We saw these pelicans walking around town," Percy reported. "Like, just going through the shops, stopping at the bars."

Hazel frowned. "Monsters in disguise?"

"No," Annabeth said, laughing, "just regular old pelicans. They're the town mascots or something. And there's a 'Little Italy' section of town. That's why the gelato is so good."

"Europe is messed up." Leo shook his head. "First we go to Rome for Spanish steps. Then we go to Greece for Italian ice cream."

But he couldn't argue with the gelato. He ate his double chocolate delight and tried to imagine that he and his friends were just chilling on a vacation. Which made him wish Calypso was with him, which made him wish the war was over and everybody was alive . . . which made him sad. It was July 30. Less than forty-eight hours until G-Day, when

Gaea the Princess of Potty Sludge would awaken in all her dirt-faced glory.

The strange thing was, the closer they got to August 1, the more upbeat his friends acted. Or maybe *upbeat* wasn't the right word. They seemed to be pulling together for the final lap—aware that the next two days would make or break them. There was no point moping around when you faced imminent death. The end of the world made gelato taste a lot better.

Of course, the rest of the crew hadn't been down in the stables with Leo, talking with the victory goddess Nike over the past three days. . . .

Piper set down her ice cream cup. "So, the island of Delos is right across the harbor. Artemis and Apollo's home turf. Who's going?"

"Me," Leo said immediately.

Everybody stared at him.

"What?" Leo demanded. "I'm diplomatic and stuff. Frank and Hazel volunteered to back me up."

"We did?" Frank lowered his half-eaten apple. "I mean . . . sure we did."

Hazel's gold eyes flashed in the sunlight. "Leo, did you have a dream about this or something?"

"Yes," Leo blurted. "Well . . . no. Not exactly. But . . . you got to trust me on this, guys. I need to talk to Apollo and Artemis. I've got an idea I need to bounce off them."

Annabeth frowned. She looked like she might object, but Jason spoke up.

"If Leo has an idea," he said, "we need to trust him."

Leo felt guilty about that, especially considering what his idea was, but he mustered a smile. "Thanks, man."

Percy shrugged. "Okay. But a word of advice: when you see Apollo, don't mention haiku."

Hazel knit her eyebrows. "Why not? Isn't he the god of poetry?"

"Just trust me."

"Got it." Leo rose to his feet. "And guys, if they have a souvenir shop on Delos, I'm totally bringing you back some Apollo and Artemis bobbleheads!"

Apollo didn't seem to be in the mood for haiku. He wasn't selling bobbleheads, either.

Frank had turned into a giant eagle to fly to Delos, but Leo hitched a ride with Hazel on Arion's back. No offense to Frank, but after the fiasco at Fort Sumter, Leo had become a conscientious objector to riding giant eagles. He had a one hundred percent failure rate.

They found the island deserted, maybe because the seas were too choppy for the tourist boats. The windswept hills were barren except for rocks, grass, and wildflowers—and, of course, a bunch of crumbling temples. The rubble was probably very impressive, but ever since Olympia, Leo had been on ancient ruins overload. He was *so* done with white marble columns. He wanted to get back to the U.S., where the oldest buildings were the public schools and Ye Olde McDonald's.

They walked down an avenue lined with white stone lions, the faces weathered almost featureless.

"It's eerie," Hazel said.

"You sense any ghosts?" Frank asked.

She shook her head. "The *lack* of ghosts is eerie. Back in ancient times, Delos was sacred ground. No mortal was allowed to be born here or die here. There are literally *no* mortal spirits on this whole island."

"Cool with me," Leo said. "Does that mean nobody's allowed to kill us here?"

"I didn't say that." Hazel stopped at the summit of a low hill. "Look. Down there."

Below them, the hillside had been carved into an amphitheater. Scrubby plants sprouted between the rows of stone benches, so it looked like a concert for thorn bushes. Down at the bottom, sitting on a block of stone in the middle of the stage, the god Apollo hunched over a ukulele, plucking out a mournful tune.

At least, Leo assumed it was Apollo. The dude looked about seventeen, with curly blond hair and a perfect tan. He wore tattered jeans, a black T-shirt, and a white linen jacket with glittering rhinestone lapels, like he was trying for an Elvis/Ramones/Beach Boys hybrid look.

Leo didn't usually think of the ukulele as a sad instrument. (Pathetic, sure. But not sad.) Yet the tune Apollo strummed was so melancholy, it broke Leo's feels.

Sitting in the front row was a young girl of about thirteen, wearing black leggings and a silver tunic, her dark hair pulled back in a ponytail. She was whittling on a long piece of wood—making a bow.

"Those are the gods?" Frank asked. "They don't look like twins."

"Well, think about it," Hazel said. "If you're a god, you can look like whatever you want. If you had a twin—"

"I'd choose to look like anything *but* my sibling," Frank agreed. "So what's the plan?"

"Don't shoot!" yelled Leo. It seemed like a good opening line, facing two archery gods. He raised his arms and headed down to the stage.

Neither god looked surprised to see them.

Apollo sighed and went back to playing his ukulele.

When they got to the front row, Artemis muttered, "There you are. We were beginning to wonder."

That took the pressure out of Leo's pistons. He'd been ready to introduce himself, explain how they'd come in peace, maybe tell a few jokes, and offer breath mints.

"So you were expecting us, then," Leo said. "I can tell, because you're both so excited."

Apollo plucked a tune that sounded like the funeral version of "Camptown Races." "We were expecting to be found, bothered, and tormented. We didn't know by whom. Can you not leave us to our misery?"

"You know they can't, brother," Artemis chided. "They require our help with their quest, even if the odds are hopeless."

"You two are full of good cheer," Leo said. "Why are you hiding out here anyway? Shouldn't you be . . . I dunno, fighting giants or something?"

Artemis's pale eyes made Leo feel like he was a deer carcass about to be gutted.

"Delos is our birthplace," said the goddess. "Here, we are unaffected by the Greek-Roman schism. Believe me, Leo Valdez, if I could, I would be with my Hunters, facing our old enemy Orion. Unfortunately, if I stepped off this island, I would become incapacitated with pain. All I can do is watch helplessly while Orion slaughters my followers. Many gave their lives to protect your friends and that accursed Athena statue."

Hazel made a strangled sound. "You mean Nico? Is he all right?"

"*All right?*" Apollo sobbed over his ukulele. "*None* of us are all right, girl! Gaea is rising!"

Artemis glared at Apollo. "Hazel Levesque, your brother is still alive. He is a brave fighter, like you. I wish I could say the same for *my* brother."

"You wrong me!" Apollo wailed. "I was misled by Gaea and that horrible Roman child!"

Frank cleared his throat. "Uh, Lord Apollo, you mean Octavian?"

"Do not speak his name!" Apollo strummed a minor chord. "Oh, Frank Zhang, if only you were my child. I heard your prayers, you know, all those weeks you wanted to be claimed. But alas! Mars gets all the good ones. I get . . . *that creature* as my descendant. He filled my head with compliments. He told me of the great temples he would build in my honor."

Artemis snorted. "You are easily flattered, brother."

"Because I have so many amazing qualities to praise!

Octavian said he wanted to make the Romans strong again. I said fine! I gave him my blessing."

"As I recall," said Artemis, "he also promised to make you the most important god of the legion, above even Zeus."

"Well, who was I to argue with an offer like that? Does Zeus have a perfect tan? Can *he* play the ukulele? I think not! But I *never* thought Octavian would start a war! Gaea must have been clouding my thoughts, whispering in my ear."

Leo remembered the crazy wind dude Aeolus, who'd gone homicidal after hearing Gaea's voice.

"So fix it," he said. "Tell Octavian to stand down. Or, you know, shoot him with one of your arrows. That would be fine too."

"I cannot!" Apollo wailed. "Look!"

His ukulele turned into a bow. He aimed at the sky and shot. The golden arrow sailed about two hundred feet, then disintegrated into smoke.

"To shoot my bow, I would have to step off Delos," Apollo cried. "Then I would be incapacitated, or Zeus would strike me down. Father never liked me. He hasn't trusted me for millennia!"

"Well," Artemis said, "to be fair, there was that time you conspired with Hera to overthrow him."

"That was a misunderstanding!"

"And you killed some of Zeus's Cyclopes."

"I had a good reason for that! At any rate, now Zeus blames me for *everything*—Octavian's schemes, the fall of Delphi—"

"Wait." Hazel made a time-out sign. "The fall of Delphi?"

Apollo's bow turned back into a ukulele. He plucked a

dramatic chord. "When the schism began between Greek and Roman, while I struggled with confusion, Gaea took advantage! She raised my old enemy Python, the great serpent, to repossess the Delphic Oracle. That horrible creature is now coiled in the ancient caverns, blocking the magic of prophecy. I am stuck here, so I can't even fight him."

"Bummer," Leo said, though secretly he thought that no more prophecies might be a good thing. His to-do list was already pretty full.

"Bummer indeed!" Apollo sighed. "Zeus was *already* angry with me for appointing that new girl, Rachel Dare, as my Oracle. Zeus seems to think I *hastened* the war with Gaea by doing so, since Rachel issued the Prophecy of Seven as soon as I blessed her. But prophecy doesn't work that way! Father just needed someone to blame. So of course he picked the handsomest, most talented, hopelessly awesome god."

Artemis made a gagging gesture.

"Oh, stop it, sister!" Apollo said. "You're in trouble too!"

"Only because I stayed in touch with my Hunters against Zeus's wishes," Artemis said. "But I can always charm Father into forgiving me. He's never been able to stay mad at me. It's *you* I'm worried about."

"I'm worried about me too!" Apollo agreed. "We have to do something. We can't kill Octavian. Hmm. Perhaps we should kill *these* demigods."

"Whoa there, Music Man." Leo resisted the urge to hide behind Frank and yell, *Take the big Canadian dude!* "We're on your side, remember? Why would you kill us?"

"It might make me feel better!" Apollo said. "I have to do something!"

"Or," Leo said quickly, "you could help us. See, we've got this plan. . . ."

He told them how Hera had directed them to Delos, and how Nike had described the ingredients for the physician's cure.

"The physician's cure?" Apollo stood and smashed his ukulele on the stones. "That's your plan?"

Leo raised his hands. "Hey, um, usually I'm all for smashing ukuleles, but—"

"I cannot help you!" Apollo cried. "If I told you the secret of the physician's cure, Zeus would *never* forgive me!"

"You're already in trouble," Leo pointed out. "How could it get worse?"

Apollo glared at him. "If you knew what my father is capable of, mortal, you would not ask. It would be simpler if I just smote you all. That might please Zeus—"

"Brother . . ." Artemis said.

The twins locked eyes and had a silent argument. Apparently Artemis won. Apollo heaved a sigh and kicked his broken ukulele across the stage.

Artemis rose. "Hazel Levesque, Frank Zhang, come with me. There are things you should know about the Twelfth Legion. As for you, Leo Valdez—" The goddess turned those cold silver eyes on him. "Apollo will hear you out. See if you can strike a deal. My brother always likes a good bargain."

Frank and Hazel both glanced at him like *Please don't die.*

Then they followed Artemis up the steps of the amphitheater and over the crest of the hill.

"Well, Leo Valdez?" Apollo folded his arms. His eyes glowed with golden light. "Let us bargain, then. What can you offer that would convince me to help you rather than kill you?"

# XXXIV

# LEO

"A BARGAIN." Leo's fingers twitched. "Yeah. Absolutely."

His hands went to work before his mind knew what he was doing. He started pulling things out of the pockets of his magic tool belt—copper wire, some bolts, a brass funnel. For months he'd been stashing away bits and pieces of machinery, because he never knew what he might need. And the longer he used the belt, the more intuitive it became. He'd reach in and the right items would simply appear.

"So the thing is," Leo said as his hands twisted wire, "Zeus is already P.O.'ed at you, right? If you help us defeat Gaea, you could make it up to him."

Apollo wrinkled his nose. "I suppose that's possible. But it would be easier to smite you."

"What kind of ballad would *that* make?" Leo's hands worked furiously, attaching levers, fastening the metal funnel to an old gear shaft. "You're the god of music, right? Would you listen to a song called 'Apollo Smites a Runty

Little Demigod'? I wouldn't. But 'Apollo Defeats the Earth Mother and Saves the Freaking Universe' . . . *that* sounds like a Billboard chart-topper!"

Apollo gazed into the air, as if envisioning his name on a marquee. "What do you want exactly? And what do I get out of it?"

"First thing I need: advice." Leo strung some wires across the mouth of the funnel. "I want to know if a plan of mine will work."

Leo explained what he had in mind. He'd been chewing on the idea for days, ever since Jason came back from the bottom of the sea and Leo started talking with Nike.

*A primordial god has been defeated once before,* Kymopoleia had told Jason. *You know of whom I speak.*

Leo's conversations with Nike had helped him fine-tune the plan, but he still wanted a second opinion from another god. Because once Leo committed himself, there would be no going back.

He half hoped Apollo would laugh and tell him to forget it.

Instead, the god nodded thoughtfully. "I will give you this advice for free. You *might* be able to defeat Gaea in the way you describe, similar to the way Ouranos was defeated eons ago. However, any mortal close by would be utterly . . ." Apollo's voice faltered. "What is that you have made?"

Leo looked down at the contraption in his hands. Layers of copper wires, like multiple sets of guitar strings, crisscrossed inside the funnel. Rows of striking pins were controlled by levers on the outside of the cone, which was fixed to a square metal base with a bunch of crank handles.

"Oh, this . . . ?" Leo's mind raced furiously. The thing looked like a music box fused with an old-fashioned phonograph, but what *was* it?

*A bargaining chip.*

Artemis had told him to make a deal with Apollo.

Leo remembered a story the kids in Cabin Eleven used to brag about: how their father Hermes had avoided punishment for stealing Apollo's sacred cows. When Hermes got caught, he made a musical instrument—the first lyre—and traded it to Apollo, who immediately forgave him.

A few days ago, Piper mentioned seeing the cave on Pylos where Hermes hid those cows. That must've triggered Leo's subconscious. Without even meaning to, he'd built a musical instrument, which kind of surprised him, since he knew nothing about music.

"Um, well," Leo said, "this is quite simply the most amazing instrument ever!"

"How does it work?" asked the god.

Good question, Leo thought.

He turned the crank handles, hoping the thing wouldn't explode in his face. A few clear tones rang out—metallic yet warm. Leo manipulated the levers and gears. He recognized the song that sprang forth—the same wistful melody Calypso sang for him on Ogygia about homesickness and longing. But through the strings of the brass cone, the tune sounded even sadder, like a machine with a broken heart—the way Festus might sound if he could sing.

Leo forgot Apollo was there. He played the song all the way through. When he was done, his eyes stung. He could almost smell the fresh-baked bread from Calypso's kitchen. He could taste the only kiss she'd ever given him.

Apollo stared in awe at the instrument. "I must have it. What is it called? What do you want for it?"

Leo had a sudden instinct to hide the instrument and keep it for himself. But he swallowed his melancholy. He had a task to complete.

Calypso . . . Calypso needed him to succeed.

"This is the Valdezinator, of course!" He puffed out his chest. "It works by, um, translating your feelings into music as you manipulate the gears. It's really meant for me, a child of Hephaestus, to use, though. I don't know if you could—"

"I am the god of music!" Apollo cried. "I can *certainly* master the Valdezinator. I must! It is my duty!"

"So let's wheel and deal, Music Man," Leo said. "I give you this; you give me the physician's cure."

"Oh . . ." Apollo bit his godly lip. "Well, I don't actually *have* the physician's cure."

"I thought you were the god of medicine."

"Yes, but I'm the god of *many* things! Poetry, music, the Delphic Oracle—" He broke into a sob and covered his mouth with his fist. "Sorry. I'm fine, I'm fine. As I was saying, I have many spheres of influence. Then, of course, I have the whole 'sun god' gig, which I inherited from Helios. The point is, I'm rather like a general practitioner. For the physician's cure, you would need to see a specialist—the only one who has ever successfully cured death: my son Asclepius, the god of healers."

Leo's heart sank into his socks. The *last* thing they needed was another quest to find another god who would probably demand his own commemorative T-shirt or Valdezinator.

"That's a shame, Apollo. I was hoping we could make a deal." Leo turned the levers on his Valdezinator, coaxing out an even sadder tune.

"Stop!" Apollo wailed. "It's too beautiful! I'll give you directions to Asclepius. He's really very close!"

"How do we know he'll help us? We've only got two days until Gaea wakes."

"He'll help!" Apollo promised. "My son is *very* helpful. Just plead with him in my name. You'll find him at his old temple in Epidaurus."

"What's the catch?"

"Ah . . . well, nothing. Except, of course, he's guarded."

"Guarded by what?"

"I don't know!" Apollo spread his hands helplessly. "I only know Zeus is keeping Asclepius under guard so he doesn't go running around the world resurrecting people. The first time Asclepius raised the dead . . . well, he caused quite an uproar. It's a long story. But I'm *sure* you can convince him to help."

"This isn't sounding like much of a deal," Leo said. "What about the last ingredient—the curse of Delos. What is it?"

Apollo eyed the Valdezinator greedily. Leo worried the god might just take it, and how could Leo stop him? Blasting the sun god with fire probably wouldn't do much good.

"I can give the last ingredient to you," Apollo said. "Then you'll have everything you need for Asclepius to brew the potion."

Leo played another verse. "I dunno. Trading this beautiful Valdezinator for some Delos curse—"

"It's not actually a curse! Look . . ." Apollo sprinted to the nearest patch of wildflowers and picked a yellow one from a crack between the stones. "*This* is the curse of Delos."

Leo stared at it. "A cursed daisy?"

Apollo sighed in exasperation. "That's just a nickname. When my mother, Leto, was ready to give birth to Artemis and me, Hera was angry, because Zeus had cheated on her again. So she went around to every single landmass on earth. She made the nature spirits in each place promise to turn my mother away so she couldn't give birth anywhere."

"Sounds like something Hera would do."

"I know, right? Anyway, Hera exacted promises from every land that was rooted on the earth—but *not* from Delos, because back then Delos was a floating island. The nature spirits of Delos welcomed my mother. She gave birth to my sister and me, and the island was so happy to be our new sacred home it covered itself in these little yellow flowers. The flowers are a blessing, because we're awesome. But they also symbolize a curse, because once we were born, Delos got rooted in place and wasn't able to drift around the sea anymore. That's why yellow daisies are called the curse of Delos."

"So I could have just picked a daisy myself and walked away."

"No, no! Not for the potion you have in mind. The flower would have to be picked by either my sister or me. So what do you say, demigod? Directions to Asclepius and your last magical ingredient in exchange for that new musical instrument—do we have a deal?"

Leo hated to give away a perfectly good Valdezinator for a wildflower, but he saw no other choice. "You drive a hard bargain, Music Man."

They made the trade.

"Excellent!" Apollo turned the levers of the Valdezinator, which made a sound like a car engine on a cold morning. "Hmm . . . perhaps it'll take some practice, but I'll get it! Now let us find your friends. The sooner you leave the better!"

Hazel and Frank waited at the Delos docks. Artemis was nowhere in sight.

When Leo turned to tell Apollo good-bye, the god was gone too.

"Man," Leo muttered, "he was really anxious to practice his Valdezinator."

"His *what*?" Hazel asked.

Leo told them about his new hobby as a genius inventor of musical funnels.

Frank scratched his head. "And in exchange you got a daisy?"

"It's the final ingredient to cure death, Zhang. It's a super daisy! How about you guys? Learn anything from Artemis?"

"Unfortunately, yes." Hazel gazed across the water, where the *Argo II* bobbed at anchor. "Artemis knows a lot about missile weapons. She told us Octavian has ordered some . . . *surprises* for Camp Half-Blood. He's used most of the legion's treasure to purchase Cyclopes-built onagers."

"Oh, no, not onagers!" Leo said. "Also, what's an onager?"

Frank scowled. "You build machines. How can you not know what an onager is? It's just the biggest, baddest catapult ever used by the Roman army."

"Fine," Leo said. "But *onager* is a stupid name. They should've called them Valdezapults."

Hazel rolled her eyes. "Leo, this is serious. If Artemis is right, six of these machines will be rolling into Long Island tomorrow night. That's what Octavian has been waiting for. At dawn on August first, he'll have enough firepower to completely destroy Camp Half-Blood without a single Roman casualty. He thinks that'll make him a hero."

Frank muttered a Latin curse. "Except he's also summoned so many monstrous 'allies' that the legion is completely surrounded by wild centaurs, tribes of dog-headed *cynocephali*, and who knows what else. As soon as the legion destroys Camp Half-Blood, the monsters will turn on Octavian and destroy the legion."

"And then Gaea rises," Leo said. "And bad stuff happens."

In his head, gears turned as the new information clicked into place. "All right . . . this just makes my plan even more important. Once we get this physician's cure, I'm going to need your help. Both of you."

Frank glanced nervously at the cursed yellow daisy. "What kind of help?"

Leo told them his plan. The more he talked, the more shocked they looked, but when he was done, neither of them told him he was crazy. A tear glistened on Hazel's cheek.

"It has to be this way," Leo said. "Nike confirmed it.

Apollo confirmed it. The others would never accept it, but you guys . . . you're Romans. That's why I wanted you to come to Delos with me. You get the whole sacrifice thing—doing your duty, jumping on your sword."

Frank sniffled. "I think you mean falling on your sword."

"Whatever," Leo said. "You know this *has* to be the answer."

"Leo . . ." Frank choked up.

Leo himself wanted to cry like a Valdezinator, but he kept his cool. "Hey, big guy, I'm counting on you. Remember you told me about that conversation with Mars? Your dad said you'd have to step up, right? You'd have to make the call nobody else was willing to make."

"Or the war would go sideways," Frank remembered. "But still—"

"And Hazel," Leo said. "Crazy Mist-magicky Hazel, you've got to cover for me. You're the only one who can. My great-granddad Sammy saw how special you were. He blessed me when I was a baby, because I think somehow he knew you were going to come back and help me. Our whole lives, *mi amiga*, they've been leading up to this."

"Oh, Leo . . ." She really did burst into tears then. She grabbed him and hugged him, which was sweet until Frank started crying too and wrapped them both in his arms.

That got a little weird.

"Okay, well . . ." Leo gently extricated himself. "So we're in agreement?"

"I hate this plan," Frank said.

"I despise it," Hazel said.

"Think how *I* feel," Leo said. "But you know it's our best shot."

Neither of them argued. Leo kind of wished they had.

"Let's get back to the ship," he said. "We have a healer god to find."

# XXXV

# LEO

**LEO SPOTTED THE SECRET ENTRANCE IMMEDIATELY.**

"Oh, that's beautiful." He maneuvered the ship over the ruins of Epidaurus.

The *Argo II* really wasn't in good shape to fly, but Leo had gotten her airborne after only one night of work. With the world ending tomorrow morning, he was highly motivated.

He'd primed the oar flaps. He'd injected Styx water into the samophlange. He'd treated Festus the figurehead to his favorite brew—thirty-weight motor oil and Tabasco sauce. Even Buford the Wonder Table had pitched in, rattling around belowdecks while his holographic Mini-Hedge yelled, "GIVE ME THIRTY PUSH-UPS!" to inspire the engine.

Now, at last, they hovered over the ancient temple complex of the healing god Asclepius, where they could hopefully find the physician's cure and maybe also some ambrosia, nectar, and Fonzies, because Leo's supplies were running low.

Next to him on the quarterdeck, Percy peered over the railing.

"Looks like more rubble," he noted.

His face was still green from his underwater poisoning, but at least he wasn't running to the bathroom to upchuck quite so often. Between him and Hazel's seasickness, it had been impossible to find an unoccupied toilet onboard for the past few days.

Annabeth pointed to the disk-shaped structure about fifty yards off their port side. "There."

Leo smiled. "Exactly. See, the architect knows her stuff."

The rest of the crew gathered around.

"What are we looking at?" Frank asked.

"Ah, *Señor* Zhang," Leo said, "you know how you're always saying, 'Leo, you are the only true genius among demigods'?"

"I'm pretty sure I never said that."

"Well, turns out there are other true geniuses! Because one of them must have made that work of art down there."

"It's a stone circle," Frank said. "Probably the foundation of an old shrine."

Piper shook her head. "No, it's more than that. Look at the ridges and grooves carved around the rim."

"Like the teeth of a gear," Jason offered.

"And those concentric rings." Hazel pointed to the center of the structure, where curved stones formed a sort of bull's-eye. "The pattern reminds me of Pasiphaë's pendant: the symbol of the Labyrinth."

"Huh." Leo scowled. "Well, I hadn't thought of that. But

think *mechanical.* Frank, Hazel . . . where did we see concentric circles like that before?"

"The laboratory under Rome," Frank said.

"The Archimedes lock on the door," Hazel recalled. "It had rings within rings."

Percy snorted. "You're telling me that's a massive stone lock? It's, like, fifty feet in diameter."

"Leo might be right," Annabeth said. "In ancient times, the temple of Asclepius was like the General Hospital of Greece. *Everybody* came here for the best healing. Aboveground, it was the size of a major city, but supposedly the real action happened belowground. That's where the high priests had their intensive care, super-magical-type compound, accessed by a secret passage."

Percy scratched his ear. "So if that big round thing is the lock, how do we get the key?"

"Way ahead of you, Aquaman," Leo said.

"Okay, do *not* call me *Aquaman*. That's even worse than *water boy.*"

Leo turned to Jason and Piper. "You guys remember the giant Archimedes grabber arm I told you I was building?"

Jason raised an eyebrow. "I thought you were kidding."

"Oh, my friend, I *never* kid about giant grabber arms!" Leo rubbed his hands in anticipation. "It's time to go fishing for prizes!"

Compared to the other modifications Leo had made to the ship, the grabber arm was a piece of cake. Originally,

Archimedes had designed it to pluck enemy ships out of the water. Now Leo found another use for it.

He opened the hull's forward access vent and extended the arm, guided by the console monitor and Jason, who flew outside, yelling directions.

"Left!" Jason called. "A couple of inches—yeah! Okay, down. Keep it coming. You're good."

Using his trackpad and turntable controls, Leo opened the claw. Its prongs settled around the grooves in the circular stone structure below. He checked the aerial stabilizers and the monitor's video feed.

"Okay, little buddy." Leo patted the Archimedes sphere embedded in the helm. "This is all you."

He activated the sphere.

The grabber arm began to turn like a corkscrew. It rotated the outer ring of stone, which grinded and rumbled but thankfully didn't shatter. Then the claw detached, fixed itself around the second stone ring, and turned it in the opposite direction.

Standing next to him at the monitor, Piper kissed him on the cheek. "It's working. Leo, you're amazing."

Leo grinned. He was about to make a comment about his own awesomeness, then he remembered the plan he had worked out with Hazel and Frank—and the fact that he might never see Piper again after tomorrow. The joke sort of died in his throat. "Yeah, well . . . thanks, Beauty Queen."

Below them, the last stone ring turned and settled with a deep pneumatic hiss. The entire fifty-foot pedestal telescoped downward into a spiral staircase.

Hazel exhaled. "Leo, even from up here, I'm sensing bad stuff at the bottom of those stairs. Something . . . large and dangerous. You sure you don't want me to come along?"

"Thanks, Hazel, but we'll be good." He patted Piper on the back. "Me and Piper and Jason—we're old pros at large and dangerous."

Frank held out the vial of Pylosian mint. "Don't break it."

Leo nodded gravely. "Don't break the vial of deadly poison. Man, I'm glad you said that. *Never* would have occurred to me."

"Shut up, Valdez." Frank gave him a bear hug. "And be careful."

"Ribs," Leo squeaked.

"Sorry."

Annabeth and Percy wished them good luck. Then Percy excused himself to go throw up.

Jason summoned the winds and whisked Piper and Leo down to the surface.

The stairs spiraled downward about sixty feet before opening into a chamber as large as Bunker Nine—which is to say, *ginormous.*

The polished white tiles on the walls and floor reflected the light of Jason's sword so well that Leo didn't need to make a fire. Rows of long stone benches filled the entire chamber, reminding Leo of one of those mega-churches they always advertised back in Houston. At the far end of the room, where the altar would have been, stood a ten-foot-tall statue of pure white alabaster—a young woman in a white robe, a serene smile on her face. In one hand she raised a cup, while a golden serpent coiled around her arm, its head poised over the brim as if ready to drink.

"Large and dangerous," Jason guessed.

Piper scanned the room. "This must have been the sleeping area." Her voice echoed a little too loudly for Leo's comfort. "The patients stayed here overnight. The god Asclepius was supposed to send them a dream, telling them what cure to ask for."

"How do you know that?" Leo asked. "Annabeth told you?"

Piper looked offended. "I know stuff. That statue over there is Hygeia, the daughter of Asclepius. She's the goddess of good health. That's where we get the word *hygiene*."

Jason studied the statue warily. "What's with the snake and the cup?"

"Uh, not sure," Piper admitted. "But back in the day, this place—the Asclepeion—was a medical school as well as a hospital. All the best doctor-priests trained here. They would've worshipped both Asclepius and Hygeia."

Leo wanted to say, *Okay, good tour. Let's leave.*

The silence, the gleaming white tiles, the creepy smile on Hygeia's face . . . it all made him want to crawl out of his skin. But Jason and Piper headed down the center aisle toward the statue, so Leo figured he'd better follow.

Strewn across the benches were old magazines: *Highlights for Children, Autumn, 20 B.C.E.; Hephaestus-TV Weekly—Aphrodite's Latest Baby Bump; A: The Magazine of Asclepius—Ten Simple Tips to Get the Most out of Your Leeching!*

"It's a reception area," Leo muttered. "I *hate* reception areas."

Here and there, piles of dust and scattered bones lay on the floor, which did not say encouraging things about the average wait time.

"Check it out." Jason pointed. "Were those signs here when we walked in? And that door?"

Leo didn't think so. On the wall to the right of the statue, above a closed metal door, were two electronic signboards. The top one read:

THE DOCTOR IS:
INCARCERATED.

The sign below that read:

NOW SERVING NUMBER: 0000000

Jason squinted. "I can't read it that far away. *The doctor is . . .*"

"Incarcerated," Leo said. "Apollo warned me that Asclepius was being held under guard. Zeus didn't want him sharing his medical secrets or something."

"Twenty bucks and a box of Froot Loops that statue is the guardian," Piper said.

"I'm not taking that bet." Leo glanced at the nearest pile of waiting room dust. "Well . . . I guess we take a number."

The giant statue had other ideas.

When they got within five feet, she turned her head and looked at them. Her expression remained frozen. Her mouth didn't move. But a voice issued from somewhere above, echoing through the room.

"Do you have an appointment?"

Piper didn't miss a beat. "Hello, Hygeia! Apollo sent us. We need to see Asclepius."

The alabaster statue stepped off her dais. She might have been mechanical, but Leo couldn't hear any moving parts. To be certain, he'd actually have to touch her, and he didn't want to get that close.

"I see." The statue kept smiling, though she didn't sound pleased. "May I make a copy of your insurance cards?"

"Ah, well . . ." Piper faltered. "We don't have them on us, but—"

*"No insurance cards?"* The statue shook her head. An exasperated sigh echoed through the chamber. "I suppose you haven't prepared for your visit, either. Have you washed your hands thoroughly?"

"Uh . . . yes?" Piper said.

Leo looked at his hands, which, as usual, were streaked with grease and grime. He hid them behind his back.

"Are you wearing clean underwear?" the statue asked.

"Hey, lady," Leo said, "that's getting personal."

"You should always wear clean underwear to the doctor's office," chided Hygeia. "I'm afraid you are a health hazard. You will have to be sanitized before we can proceed."

The golden snake uncurled and dropped from her arm. It reared its head and hissed, flashing saber-like fangs.

"Uh, you know," Jason said, "getting sanitized by large snakes isn't covered by our medical plan. Darn it."

"Oh, that doesn't matter," Hygeia assured him. "Sanitizing is a community service. It's complimentary!"

The snake lunged.

Leo had had a lot of practice dodging mechanical monsters, which was good, because the golden serpent was fast. Leo leaped to one side and the snake missed his head by an inch. Leo rolled and came up, hands blazing. As the snake attacked, Leo blasted it in the eyes, causing it to veer left and smash into the bench.

Piper and Jason went to work on Hygeia. They slashed through the statue's knees, felling her like an alabaster Christmas tree. Her head hit a bench. Her chalice splashed steaming acid all over the floor. Jason and Piper moved in for the kill, but before they could strike, Hygeia's legs popped back on like they were magnetic. The goddess rose, still smiling.

"Unacceptable," she said. "The doctor will not see you until you are properly sanitized."

She sloshed her cup toward Piper, who jumped out of the way as more acid splashed across the nearest benches, dissolving the stone in a hissing cloud of steam.

The snake, meanwhile, recovered its senses. Its melted metal eyes somehow repaired themselves. Its face popped back into shape like a dent-resistant car hood.

It struck at Leo, who ducked and tried to grapple its neck, but it was like trying to grab sandpaper going sixty miles an hour. The serpent shot past, its rough metal skin leaving Leo's hands scraped and bleeding.

The momentary contact did give Leo some insight,

however. The snake *was* a machine. He sensed its inner workings, and if the statue of Hygeia operated on a similar schematic, Leo might have a chance . . .

Across the room, Jason soared into the air and lopped the goddess's head off.

Sadly, the head flew right back into place.

"Unacceptable," Hygeia said calmly. "Decapitation is not a healthy lifestyle choice."

"Jason, get over here!" Leo yelled. "Piper, buy us some time!"

Piper glanced over like *Easier said than done.*

"Hygeia!" she yelled. "I have insurance!"

That got the statue's attention. Even the golden snake turned toward her, as if insurance was some sort of tasty rodent.

"Insurance?" the statue said eagerly. "Who is your provider?"

"Um . . . Blue Lightning," Piper said. "I have the card right here. Just a second."

She made a big show of patting down her pockets. The snake slithered over to watch.

Jason ran to Leo's side, gasping. "What's the plan?"

"We can't destroy these things," Leo said. "They're designed for self-healing. They're immune to pretty much every kind of damage."

"Great," Jason said. "So . . . ?"

"You remember Chiron's old gaming system?" Leo asked.

Jason's eyes widened. "Leo . . . this isn't Mario Party Six."

"Same principle, though."

"Idiot mode?"

Leo grinned. "I'll need you and Piper to run interference. I'll reprogram the snake, then Big Bertha."

"Hygeia."

"Whatever. Ready?"

"No."

Leo and Jason ran for the snake.

Hygeia was assailing Piper with health care questions. "Is Blue Lightning an HMO? What is your deductible? Who is your primary care deity?"

As Piper ad-libbed answers, Leo jumped on the serpent's back. This time he knew what he was looking for, and for a moment the serpent didn't even seem to notice him. Leo pried open a service panel near the snake's head. He held on with his legs, trying to ignore the pain and sticky blood on his hands as he redid the serpent's wiring.

Jason stood by, ready to attack, but the snake seemed transfixed by Piper's problems with Blue Lightning's coverage.

"Then the advice nurse said I had to call a service center," Piper reported. "And the medications weren't covered by my plan! And—"

The snake lurched as Leo connected the last two wires. Leo jumped off and the golden serpent began shaking uncontrollably.

Hygeia whirled to face them. "What have you done? My snake requires medical assistance!"

"Does it have insurance?" Piper asked.

"WHAT?" The statue turned back to her, and Leo jumped. Jason summoned a gust of wind, which boosted Leo onto the statue's shoulders like a little kid at a parade. He popped open the back of the statue's head as she staggered around, sloshing acid.

"Get off!" she yelled. "This is not hygienic!"

"Hey!" Jason yelled, flying circles around her. "I have a question about my deductibles!"

*"What?"* the statue cried.

"Hygeia!" Piper shouted. "I need an invoice submitted to Medicare!"

"No, please!"

Leo found the statue's regulator chip. He clicked a few dials and pulled some wires, trying to pretend that Hygeia was just one large, dangerous Nintendo game system.

He reconnected her circuits and Hygeia began to spin, hollering and flailing her arms. Leo jumped away, barely avoiding an acid bath.

He and his friends backed up while Hygeia and her snake underwent a violent religious experience.

"What did you do?" Piper demanded.

"Idiot mode," Leo said.

"Excuse me?"

"Back at camp," Jason explained, "Chiron had this ancient gaming system in the rec room. Leo and I used to play it sometimes. You'd compete against, like, computer-controlled opponents, coms—"

"—and they had three difficulty options," Leo said. *"Easy, medium,* and *hard."*

"I've played video games before," Piper said. "So what did you do?"

"Well . . . I got bored with those settings." Leo shrugged. "So I invented a fourth difficulty level: *idiot mode*. It makes the coms *so* stupid it's funny. They always choose exactly the wrong thing to do."

Piper stared at the statue and snake, both of which were writhing and starting to smoke. "Are you sure you set them to *idiot mode*?"

"We'll know in a minute."

"What if you set them to *extreme* difficulty?"

"Then we'll know that, too."

The snake stopped shuddering. It coiled up and looked around as if bewildered.

Hygeia froze. A puff of smoke drifted from her right ear. She looked down at Leo. "You must die! Hello! You must die!"

She raised her cup and poured acid over her face. Then she turned and marched face-first into the nearest wall. The snake reared up and slammed its head repeatedly into the floor.

"Okay," Jason said. "I think we have achieved *idiot mode*."

"Hello! Die!" Hygeia backed up from the wall and face-slammed it again.

"Let's go." Leo ran for the metal door next to the dais. He grabbed the handle. It was still locked, but Leo sensed the mechanisms inside—wires running up the frame, connected to . . .

He stared at the two blinking signs above the door.

"Jason," he said, "give me a boost."

Another gust of wind levitated him upward. Leo went to work with his pliers, reprogramming the signs until the top one flashed:

THE DOCTOR IS:
IN DA HOUSE.

The bottom sign changed to read:

NOW SERVING:
ALL DA LADIES LUV LEO!

The metal door swung open, and Leo settled to the floor. "See, the wait wasn't so bad!" Leo grinned at his friends. "The doctor will see us now."

# XXXVI

# LEO

**AT THE END OF THE HALL** stood a walnut door with a bronze plaque:

ASCLEPIUS

MD, DMD, DME, DC, DVS, FAAN, OMG, EMT, TTYL, FRCP,

ME, IOU, OD, OT, PHARMD, BAMF, RN, PHD, INC., SMH

There may have been more acronyms in the list, but by that point Leo's brain had exploded.

Piper knocked. "Dr. Asclepius?"

The door flew open. The man inside had a kindly smile, crinkles around his eyes, short salt-and-pepper hair, and a well-trimmed beard. He wore a white lab coat over a business suit and a stethoscope around his neck—your stereotypical doctor outfit, except for one thing: Asclepius held a polished black staff with a live green python coiled around it.

Leo wasn't happy to see another snake. The python

regarded him with pale yellow eyes, and Leo had a feeling it was *not* set to *idiot mode.*

"Hello!" said Asclepius.

"Doctor." Piper's smile was so warm it would've melted a Boread. "We'd be so *grateful* for your help. We need the physician's cure."

Leo wasn't even her target, but Piper's charmspeak washed over him irresistibly. He would've done anything to help her get that cure. He would've gone to medical school, gotten twelve doctorate degrees, and bought a large green python on a stick.

Asclepius put his hand over his heart. "Oh, my dear, I would be delighted to help."

Piper's smile wavered. "You would? I mean, of course you would."

"Come in! Come in!" Asclepius ushered them into his office.

The guy was so nice, Leo figured his office would be full of torture devices, but it looked like . . . well, a doctor's office: a big maple desk, bookshelves stuffed with medical books, and some of those plastic organ models Leo loved to play with as a kid. He remembered getting in trouble one time because he had turned a cross-section kidney and some skeleton legs into a kidney monster and scared the nurse.

Life was simpler back then.

Asclepius took the big comfy doctor's chair and laid his staff and serpent across his desk. "Please, sit!"

Jason and Piper took the two chairs on the patients' side.

Leo had to remain standing, which was fine with him. He didn't want to be eye-level with the snake.

"So." Asclepius leaned back. "I can't tell you how nice it is to actually talk with patients. The last few thousand years, the paperwork has gotten out of control. Rush, rush, rush. Fill in forms. Deal with red tape. Not to mention the giant alabaster guardian who kills everyone in the waiting room. It takes all the fun out of medicine!"

"Yeah," Leo said. "Hygeia is kind of a downer."

Asclepius grinned. "My *real* daughter Hygeia isn't like that, I assure you. She's quite nice. At any rate, you did well reprogramming the statue. You have a surgeon's hands."

Jason shuddered. "Leo with a scalpel? Don't encourage him."

The doctor god chuckled. "Now, what seems to be the trouble?" He sat forward and peered at Jason. "Hmm . . . Imperial gold sword wound, but that's healed nicely. No cancer, no heart problems. Watch that mole on your left foot, but I'm sure it's benign."

Jason blanched. "How did you—"

"Oh, of course!" Asclepius said. "You're a bit nearsighted! Simple fix."

He opened his drawer, whipped out a prescription pad and an eyeglasses case. He scribbled something on the pad, then handed the glasses and the scrip to Jason. "Keep the prescription for future reference, but these lenses should work. Try them on."

"Wait," Leo said. "Jason is nearsighted?"

Jason opened the case. "I—I *have* had a little trouble seeing stuff from a distance lately," he admitted. "I thought I was just tired." He tried on the glasses, which had thin frames of Imperial gold. "Wow. Yeah. That's better."

Piper smiled. "You look very distinguished."

"I don't know, man," Leo said. "I'd go for contacts—glowing orange ones with cat's-eye pupils. Those would be cool."

"Glasses are fine," Jason decided. "Thanks, uh, Dr. Asclepius, but that's not why we came."

"No?" Asclepius steepled his fingers. "Well, let's see then . . ." He turned to Piper. "You seem fine, my dear. Broken arm when you were six. Fell off a horse?"

Piper's jaw dropped. "How could you possibly know that?"

"Vegetarian diet," he continued. "No problem, just make sure you're getting enough iron and protein. Hmm . . . a little weak in the left shoulder. I assume you got hit with something heavy about a month ago?"

"A sandbag in Rome," Piper said. "That's amazing."

"Alternate ice and a hot pack if it bothers you," Asclepius advised. "And you . . ." He faced Leo.

"Oh, my." The doctor's expression turned grim. The friendly twinkle disappeared from his eyes. "Oh, I see . . ."

The doctor's expression said *I am so, so sorry.*

Leo's heart filled with cement. If he'd harbored any last hopes of avoiding what was to come, they now sank.

"What?" Jason's new glasses flashed. "What's wrong with Leo?"

"Hey, doc." Leo shot him a *drop it* look. Hopefully they knew about patient confidentiality in Ancient Greece. "We came for the physician's cure. Can you help us? I've got some Pylosian mint here, and a very nice yellow daisy." He set the ingredients on the desk, carefully avoiding the snake's mouth.

"Hold it," Piper said. "Is there something wrong with Leo or not?"

Asclepius cleared his throat. "I . . . never mind. Forget I said anything. Now, you want the physician's cure."

Piper frowned. "But—"

"Seriously, guys," Leo said, "I'm fine, except for the fact that Gaea's destroying the world tomorrow. Let's focus."

They didn't look happy about it, but Asclepius forged ahead. "So this daisy was picked by my father, Apollo?"

"Yep," Leo said. "He sends hugs and kisses."

Asclepius picked up the flower and sniffed it. "I do hope Dad comes through this war all right. Zeus can be . . . quite unreasonable. Now, the only missing ingredient is the heartbeat of the chained god."

"I have it," Piper said. "At least . . . I can summon the *makhai.*"

"Excellent. Just a moment, dear." He looked at his python. "Spike, are you ready?"

Leo stifled a laugh. "Your snake's name is Spike?"

Spike looked at him balefully. He hissed, revealing a crown of spikes around his neck like a basilisk's.

Leo's laugh crawled back down his throat to die. "My bad," he said. "Of course your name is Spike."

"He's a little grumpy," Asclepius said. "People are always confusing *my* staff with the staff of Hermes, which has two snakes, obviously. Over the centuries, people have called Hermes's staff the symbol of medicine, when of course it should be *my* staff. Spike feels slighted. George and Martha get all the attention. Anyway . . ."

Asclepius set the daisy and poison in front of Spike. "Pylosian mint—certainty of death. The curse of Delos—anchoring that which cannot be anchored. Now the final ingredient: the heartbeat of the chained god—chaos, violence, and fear of mortality." He turned to Piper. "My dear, you may release the *makhai*."

Piper closed her eyes.

Wind swirled through the room. Angry voices wailed. Leo felt a strange desire to smack Spike with a hammer. He wanted to strangle the good doctor with his bare hands.

Then Spike unhinged his jaw and swallowed the angry wind. His neck ballooned as the spirits of battle went down his throat. He snapped up the daisy and the vial of Pylosian mint for dessert.

"Won't the poison hurt him?" Jason asked.

"No, no," Asclepius said. "Wait and see."

A moment later Spike belched out a new vial—a stoppered glass tube no bigger than Leo's finger. Dark red liquid glowed inside.

"The physician's cure." Asclepius picked up the vial and turned it in the light. His expression became serious, then bewildered. "Wait . . . why did I agree to make this?"

Piper placed her hand palm up on the desk. "Because we

need it to save the world. It's very important. You're the only one who can help us."

Her charmspeak was so potent even Spike the snake relaxed. He curled around his staff and went to sleep. Asclepius's expression softened, like he was easing himself into a hot bath.

"Of course," the god said. "I forgot. But you must be careful. Hades hates it when I raise people from the dead. The last time I gave someone this potion, the Lord of the Underworld complained to Zeus, and I was killed by a lightning bolt. BOOM!"

Leo flinched. "You look pretty good for a dead guy."

"Oh, I got better. That was part of the compromise. You see, when Zeus killed me, my father Apollo got very upset. He couldn't take out his anger on Zeus directly; the king of the gods was much too powerful. So Apollo took revenge on the makers of lightning bolts instead. He killed some of the Elder Cyclopes. For that, Zeus punished Apollo . . . quite severely. Finally, to make peace, Zeus agreed to make me a god of medicine, with the understanding that I wouldn't bring anyone else back to life." Asclepius's eyes filled with uncertainty. "And yet here I am . . . giving you the cure."

"Because you realize how important this is," Piper said, "you're willing to make an exception."

"Yes . . ." Reluctantly, Asclepius handed Piper the vial. "At any rate, the potion must be administered as soon as possible after death. It can be injected or poured into the mouth. And there is only enough for one person. Do you understand me?" He looked directly at Leo.

"We understand," Piper promised. "Are you sure you don't want to come with us, Asclepius? Your guardian is out of commission. You'd be really helpful aboard the *Argo II*."

Asclepius smiled wistfully. "The *Argo* . . . back when I was a demigod, I sailed on the original ship, you know. Ah, to be a carefree adventurer again!"

"Yeah . . ." Jason muttered. "Carefree."

"But alas, I cannot. Zeus will already be quite angry with me for helping you. Besides, the guardian will reprogram itself soon. You should leave." Asclepius rose. "Best wishes, demigods. And if you see my father again, please . . . give him my regrets."

Leo wasn't sure what that meant, but they took their leave.

As they passed through the waiting room, the statue of Hygeia was sitting on a bench, pouring acid on her face and singing "Twinkle, Twinkle, Little Star," while her golden snake gnawed at her foot. The peaceful scene was almost enough to lift Leo's spirits.

Back on the *Argo II*, they gathered in the mess hall and filled in the rest of the crew.

"I don't like it," Jason said. "The way Asclepius looked at Leo—"

"Aw, he just sensed my heartsickness." Leo tried for a smile. "You know, I'm dying to see Calypso."

"That is *so* sweet," Piper said. "But I'm not sure that's it."

Percy frowned at the glowing red vial that sat in the middle of the table. "Any of us might die, right? So we just need to keep the potion handy."

"Assuming only *one* of us dies," Jason pointed out. "There's only one dose."

Hazel and Frank stared at Leo.

He gave them a look like *Knock it off.*

The others didn't see the full picture. *To storm or fire the world must fall*—Jason or Leo. In Olympia, Nike had warned that one of the four demigods present would die: Percy, Hazel, Frank, or Leo. Only one name overlapped those two lists: Leo. And if Leo's plan was going to work, he couldn't have anybody else close by when he pulled the trigger.

His friends would never accept his decision. They would argue. They would try to save him. They would insist on finding another way.

But this time, Leo was convinced, there *was* no other way. Like Annabeth always told them, fighting against a prophecy never worked. It just created more trouble. He had to make sure this war ended, once and for all.

"We have to keep our options open," Piper suggested. "We need, like, a designated medic to carry the potion—somebody who can react quickly and heal whoever gets killed."

"Good idea, Beauty Queen," Leo lied. "I nominate you."

Piper blinked. "But . . . Annabeth is wiser. Hazel can move faster on Arion. Frank can turn into animals—"

"But you've got heart." Annabeth squeezed her friend's hand. "Leo's right. When the time comes, you'll know what to do."

"Yeah," Jason agreed. "I have a feeling you're the best choice, Pipes. You're going to be there with us at the end, whatever happens, storm or fire."

Leo picked up the vial. "Is everyone in agreement?"

No one objected.

Leo locked eyes with Hazel. *You know what needs to happen.*

He pulled a chamois cloth from his tool belt and made a big show of wrapping up the physician's cure. Then he presented the package to Piper.

"Okay, then," he said. "Athens tomorrow morning, gang. Be ready to fight some giants."

"Yeah . . ." Frank murmured. "I know *I'll* sleep well."

After dinner broke up, Jason and Piper tried to waylay Leo. They wanted to talk about what had happened with Asclepius, but Leo evaded them.

"I've got to work on the engine," he said, which was true.

Once in the engine room, with only Buford the Wonder Table for company, Leo took a deep breath. He reached into his tool belt and pulled out the actual vial of physician's cure—not the trick-of-the-Mist version he'd handed to Piper.

Buford blew steam at him.

"Hey, man, I had to," Leo said.

Buford activated his holographic Hedge. "PUT SOME CLOTHES ON!"

"Look, it's got to be this way. Otherwise we'll *all* die."

Buford made a plaintive squeal, then clattered into the corner in a sulk.

Leo stared at the engine. He'd spent so much time putting it together. He'd sacrificed months of sweat and pain and loneliness.

Now the *Argo II* was approaching the end of its voyage. Leo's whole life—his childhood with Tía Callida; his mother's death in that warehouse fire; his years as a foster kid; his months at Camp Half-Blood with Jason and Piper—all of it would culminate tomorrow morning in one final battle.

He opened the access panel.

Festus's voice creaked over the intercom.

"Yeah, buddy," Leo agreed. "It's time."

More creaking.

"I know," Leo said. "Together till the end?"

Festus squeaked affirmatively.

Leo checked the ancient bronze astrolabe, which was now fitted with the crystal from Ogygia. Leo could only hope it would work.

"I will get back to you, Calypso," he muttered. "I promised on the River Styx."

He flipped a switch and brought the navigation device online. He set the timer for twenty-four hours.

Finally he opened the engine's ventilator line and pushed inside the vial of physician's cure. It disappeared into the veins of the ship with a decisive *thunk*.

"Too late to turn back now," Leo said.

He curled on the floor and closed his eyes, determined to enjoy the familiar hum of the engine for one last night.

# XXXVII

# REYNA

**"TURN BACK!"**

Reyna wasn't keen to give orders to Pegasus, the Lord of Flying Horses, but she was even *less* keen to get shot out of the sky.

As they approached Camp Half-Blood in the predawn hours of August 1, she spotted six Roman onagers. Even in the dark, their Imperial gold plating glinted. Their massive throwing arms bent back like ship masts listing in a storm. Crews of artillerists scurried around the machines, loading the slings, checking the torsion of the ropes.

"What are those?" Nico called.

He flew about twenty feet to her left on the dark pegasus Blackjack.

"Siege weapons," Reyna said. "If we get any closer, they can shoot us out of the sky."

"From this high up?"

On her right, Coach Hedge shouted from the back of his

steed, Guido, "Those are onagers, kid! Those things can kick higher than Bruce Lee!"

"Lord Pegasus," Reyna said, resting her hand on the stallion's neck, "we need a safe place to land."

Pegasus seemed to understand. He wheeled to the left. The other flying horses followed—Blackjack, Guido, and six others who were towing the Athena Parthenos beneath them on cables.

As they skirted the western edge of the camp, Reyna took in the scene. The legion lined the base of the eastern hills, ready for a dawn attack. The onagers were arrayed behind them in a loose semicircle at three-hundred-yard intervals. Judging from the size of the weapons, Reyna calculated that Octavian had enough firepower to destroy every living thing in the valley.

But that was only part of the threat. Encamped along the legion's flanks were hundreds of *auxilia* forces. Reyna couldn't see well in the dark, but she spotted at least one tribe of wild centaurs and an army of *cynocephali*, the dog-headed men who'd made an uneasy truce with the legion centuries ago. The Romans were badly outnumbered, surrounded by a sea of unreliable allies.

"There." Nico pointed toward Long Island Sound, where the lights of a large yacht gleamed a quarter mile offshore. "We could land on the deck of that ship. The Greeks control the sea."

Reyna wasn't sure the Greeks would be any friendlier than the Romans, but Pegasus seemed to like the idea. He banked toward the dark waters of the Sound.

The ship was a white pleasure craft a hundred feet long, with sleek lines and dark tinted portals. Painted on the bow in red letters was the name MI AMOR. On the forward deck was a helipad big enough for the Athena Parthenos.

Reyna saw no crew. She guessed the ship was a regular mortal vessel anchored for the night, but if she was wrong and the ship was a trap . . .

"It's our best shot," Nico said. "The horses are tired. We need to set down."

She nodded reluctantly. "Let's do it."

Pegasus landed on the forward deck with Guido and Blackjack. The six other horses gently set the Athena Parthenos on the helipad and then settled around it. With their cables and harnesses, they looked like carousel animals.

Reyna dismounted. As she had two days ago, when she first met Pegasus, she knelt before the horse.

"Thank you, great one."

Pegasus spread his wings and inclined his head.

Even now, after flying halfway up the East Coast together, Reyna could scarcely believe the immortal horse had allowed her to ride.

Reyna had always pictured him as a solid white with dove-like wings, but Pegasus's coat was rich brown, mottled with red and gold around the muzzle—which Hedge claimed were the marks where the stallion had emerged from the blood and ichor of his beheaded mother, Medusa. Pegasus's wings were the colors of an eagle's—gold, white, brown, and rust—which made him look much more handsome and regal than plain white. He was the color of *all* horses, representing all his offspring.

Lord Pegasus nickered.

Hedge trotted over to translate. "Pegasus says he should leave before the shooting starts. His life force connects *all* pegasi, see, so if he gets injured, *all* winged horses feel his pain. That's why he doesn't get out much. *He's* immortal, but his offspring aren't. He doesn't want them to suffer on his account. He's asked the other horses to stay with us, to help us complete our mission."

"I understand," Reyna said. "Thank you."

Pegasus whinnied.

Hedge's eyes widened. He choked back a sob, then fished a handkerchief out of his backpack and dabbed his eyes.

"Coach?" Nico frowned with concern. "What did Pegasus say?"

"He—he says he didn't come to us in person because of my message." Hedge turned to Reyna. "He did it because of *you*. He experiences the feelings of all winged horses. He followed your friendship with Scipio. Pegasus says he's never been more touched by a demigod's compassion for a winged horse. He gives you the title Horse Friend. This is a great honor."

Reyna's eyes stung. She bowed her head. "Thank you, lord."

Pegasus pawed the deck. The other winged horses whinnied in salute. Then their sire launched himself upward and spiraled into the night.

Hedge stared at the clouds in amazement. "Pegasus hasn't

shown himself in hundreds of years." He patted Reyna on the back. "You did good, Roman."

Reyna didn't feel like she deserved credit for putting Scipio through so much suffering, but she forced down her feelings of guilt.

"Nico, we should check the ship," she said. "If there's anyone aboard—"

"Way ahead of you." He stroked Blackjack's muzzle. "I sense two mortals asleep in the main cabin. Nobody else. I'm no child of Hypnos, but I've sent some deep dreams their way. Should be enough to keep them snoozing until well after sunrise."

Reyna tried not to stare at him. In the last few days he'd gotten so much stronger. Hedge's nature magic had brought him back from the brink. She'd seen Nico do some impressive things, but manipulating dreams . . . had he always been able to do that?

Coach Hedge rubbed his hands eagerly. "So when can we go ashore? My wife is waiting!"

Reyna scanned the horizon. A Greek trireme patrolled just offshore, but it didn't seem to have noticed their arrival. No alarms sounded. No signs of movement along the beach.

She caught a glimpse of silver wake in the moonlight, a half-mile to the west. A black motorboat was speeding toward them with no running lights. Reyna hoped it was a mortal vessel. Then it got closer, and Reyna's hand tightened on the hilt of her sword. Glinting on the boat's prow was a laurel wreath design with the letters SPQR.

"The legion has sent a welcoming committee."

Nico followed her gaze. "I thought the Romans didn't have a navy."

"We didn't," she said. "Apparently Octavian has been busier than I realized."

"So we attack!" Hedge said. "'Cause nobody's standing in my way when I'm this close."

Reyna counted three people in the speedboat. The two in back wore helmets, but Reyna recognized the driver's wedge-shaped face and stocky shoulders: Michael Kahale.

"We'll try to parlay," Reyna decided. "That's one of Octavian's right-hand men, but he's a good legionnaire. I may be able to reason with him."

The wind swept Nico's dark hair across his face. "But if you're wrong . . ."

The black boat slowed and pulled alongside. Michael called up: "Reyna! I've got orders to arrest you and confiscate that statue. I'm coming aboard with two other centurions. I'd prefer to do this without bloodshed."

Reyna tried to control her trembling legs. "Come aboard, Michael!"

She turned to Nico and Coach Hedge. "If I'm wrong, be ready. Michael Kahale won't be easy to fight."

Michael wasn't dressed for combat. He wore only his purple camp shirt, jeans, and running shoes. He carried no visible weapon, but that didn't make Reyna feel any better. His arms were as thick as bridge cables, his expression as welcoming as a brick wall. The dove tattoo on his forearm looked more like a bird of prey.

His eyes glittered darkly as he took in the scene—the Athena Parthenos harnessed to its team of pegasi, Nico with his Stygian sword drawn, Coach Hedge with his baseball bat.

Michael's backup centurions were Leila from the Fourth Cohort and Dakota from the Fifth. Strange choices . . . Leila, daughter of Ceres, wasn't known for her aggressiveness. She was usually quite levelheaded. And Dakota . . . Reyna couldn't believe the son of Bacchus, the most good-natured of officers, would side with Octavian.

"Reyna Ramírez-Arellano," Michael said, like he was reading a scroll, "former praetor—"

"I *am* praetor," Reyna corrected. "Unless I have been removed by a vote of the full senate. Is that the case?"

Michael sighed heavily. His heart didn't seem to be in his task. "I have orders to arrest you and hold you for trial."

"On whose authority?"

"You know whose—"

"On what charges?"

"Listen, Reyna"—Michael rubbed his palm across his forehead, like it might wipe away his headache—"I don't like this any more than you do. But I have my orders."

"Illegal orders."

"It's too late for argument. Octavian has assumed emergency powers. The legion is behind him."

"Is that true?" She looked pointedly at Dakota and Leila.

Leila wouldn't meet her eyes. Dakota winked like he was trying to convey a message, but it was hard to tell with him. He might've been twitching simply from too much sugary Kool-Aid.

"We're at war," Michael said. "We have to pull together. Dakota and Leila have not been the most enthusiastic supporters. Octavian gave them this one last chance to prove themselves. If they help me bring you in—preferably alive, but dead if necessary—then they keep their rank and prove their loyalty."

"To Octavian," Reyna noted. "Not the legion."

Michael spread his hands, which were only slightly smaller than baseball mitts. "You can't blame the officers for falling into line. Octavian has a plan to win, and it's a good plan. At dawn those onagers will destroy the Greek camp without a single loss of Roman life. The gods should be healed."

Nico stepped in. "You'd wipe out half the demigods in the world, half the gods' legacy, to *heal* them? You'll tear apart Olympus before Gaea even wakes up. And she *is* waking, Centurion."

Michael scowled. "Ambassador of Pluto, son of Hades . . . whatever you call yourself, you've been named an enemy spy. I've got orders to take you in for execution."

"You can try," Nico said coldly.

The face-off was so absurd it should have been humorous. Nico was several years younger, half a foot shorter, and fifty pounds lighter. But Michael didn't make a move. The veins in his neck pulsed.

Dakota coughed. "Um, Reyna . . . just come with us peacefully. Please. We can work this out." He was definitely winking at her.

"All right, enough talk." Coach Hedge sized up Michael Kahale. "Let me take this joker down. I've handled bigger."

Michael smirked at that. "I'm sure you're a brave faun, but—"

"Satyr!"

Coach Hedge leaped at the centurion. He brought his baseball bat down with full force, but Michael simply caught it and yanked it away from the coach. Michael broke the bat over his knee. Then he pushed the coach back, though Reyna could tell Michael wasn't trying to hurt him.

"That's it!" Hedge growled. "Now I'm really mad!"

"Coach," Reyna warned, "Michael is *very* strong. You'd need to be an ogre or a—"

From somewhere off the port side, down at the waterline, a voice yelled, "Kahale! What's taking so long?"

Michael flinched. "Octavian?"

"Of course it's me!" yelled the voice from the dark. "I got tired of waiting for you to carry out my orders! I'm coming aboard. Everyone on both sides, drop your weapons!"

Michael frowned. "Uh . . . sir? Everyone? Even us?"

"You don't solve every problem with a sword or a fist, you big dolt! I can handle these *Graecus* scum!"

Michael looked unsure about that, but he motioned to Leila and Dakota, who set their swords on the deck.

Reyna glanced at Nico. Obviously, something was wrong. She couldn't think of any reason Octavian would be here, putting himself in harm's way. He definitely wouldn't order his own officers to get rid of their weapons. But Reyna's instincts told her to play along. She dropped her blade. Nico did the same.

"Everyone is disarmed, sir," Michael called.

"Good!" yelled Octavian.

A dark silhouette appeared at the top of the ladder, but he was much too big to be Octavian. A smaller shape with wings fluttered up behind him—a harpy? By the time Reyna realized what was happening, the Cyclops had crossed the deck in two large strides. He bopped Michael Kahale on the head. The centurion fell like a sack of rocks. Dakota and Leila backed up in alarm.

The harpy fluttered to the deckhouse roof. In the moonlight, her feathers were the color of dried blood.

"Strong," said Ella, preening her wings. "Ella's boyfriend is stronger than Romans."

"Friends!" boomed Tyson the Cyclops. He scooped up Reyna in one arm and Hedge and Nico in the other. "We have come to save you. Hooray for us!"

## XXXVIII

# REYNA

Reyna had never been so glad to see a Cyclops, at least until Tyson set them down and wheeled on Leila and Dakota. "Bad Romans!"

"Tyson, wait!" Reyna said. "Don't hurt them!"

Tyson frowned. He was small for a Cyclops, still a child, really—a little over six feet tall, his messy brown hair crusted with saltwater, his big single eye the color of maple syrup. He wore only a swimsuit and a flannel pajama shirt, like he couldn't decide whether to go swimming or go to sleep. He exuded a strong smell of peanut butter.

"They are not bad?" he asked.

"No," Reyna said. "They were following bad orders. I think they're sorry for that. *Aren't* you, Dakota?"

Dakota put his arms up so fast he looked like Superman about to take off. "Reyna, I was trying to clue you in! Leila and I planned to switch sides and help you take down Michael."

"That's right!" Leila almost fell backward over the railing. "But before we could, the Cyclops did it for us!"

Coach Hedge snorted. "A likely story!"

Tyson sneezed. "Sorry. Goat fur. Itchy nose. Do we trust Romans?"

"I do," Reyna said. "Dakota, Leila, you understand what our mission is?"

Leila nodded. "You want to return that statue to the Greeks as a peace offering. Let us help."

"Yeah." Dakota nodded vigorously. "The legion's not nearly as united as Michael claimed. We don't trust all the *auxilia* forces Octavian has gathered."

Nico laughed bitterly. "A little late for doubts. You're surrounded. As soon as Camp Half-Blood is destroyed, those *allies* will turn on you."

"So what do we do?" asked Dakota. "We have an hour at most until sunrise."

"Five fifty-two A.M.," said Ella, still perched on the boathouse. "Sunrise, Eastern seaboard, August first. *Timetables for Naval Meteorology.* One hour and twelve minutes is more than one hour."

Dakota's eye ticked. "I stand corrected."

Coach Hedge looked at Tyson. "Can we get into Camp Half-Blood safely? Is Mellie all right?"

Tyson scratched his chin thoughtfully. "She is very round."

"But she's okay?" Hedge persisted. "She hasn't given birth yet?"

"'Delivery occurs at the end of the third trimester,'" Ella advised. "Page forty-three, *The New Mother's Guide to—*"

"I gotta get over there!" Hedge looked like he was ready to jump overboard and swim.

Reyna put her hand on his shoulder. "Coach, we'll get you to your wife, but let's do it right. Tyson, how did you and Ella get out to this ship?"

"Rainbow!"

"You . . . took a rainbow?"

"He is my fish pony friend."

"A hippocampus," Nico advised.

"I see." Reyna thought for a moment. "Could you and Ella escort the coach back to Camp Half-Blood safely?"

"Yes!" Tyson said. "We can do that!"

"Good. Coach, go see your wife. Tell the campers I plan to fly the Athena Parthenos to Half-Blood Hill at sunrise. It's a gift from Rome to Greece, to heal our divisions. If they could refrain from shooting me out of the sky, I'd be grateful."

"You got it," Hedge said. "But what about the Roman legion?"

"That's a problem," Leila said gravely. "Those onagers *will* blast you out of the sky."

"We'll need a distraction," Reyna said. "Something to delay the attack on Camp Half-Blood and preferably put those weapons out of commission. Dakota, Leila, will your cohorts follow you?"

"I—I think so, yes," Dakota said. "But if we ask them to commit treason—"

"It isn't treason," Leila said. "Not if we're acting on direct orders from our praetor. And Reyna *is* still praetor."

Reyna turned to Nico. "I need you to go with Dakota

and Leila. While they're stirring trouble in the ranks, trying to delay the attack, you have to find a way to sabotage those onagers."

Nico's smile made Reyna glad he was on *her* side. "My pleasure. We'll buy you time to deliver the Athena Parthenos."

"Um . . ." Dakota shuffled his feet. "Even if you get the statue to the hill, what's to stop Octavian from destroying it once it's in place? He's got lots of firepower, even without the onagers."

Reyna peered up at the ivory face of Athena, veiled beneath camouflage netting. "Once the statue is returned to the Greeks . . . I think it will be difficult to destroy. It has great magic. It has simply chosen not to use it yet."

Leila bent down slowly and retrieved her sword, keeping her eyes on the Athena Parthenos. "I'll take your word for it. What do we do with Michael?"

Reyna regarded the snoring mountain of Hawaiian demigod. "Put him in your boat. Don't hurt him or bind him. I have a feeling Michael's heart is in the right place. He just had the bad luck of being sponsored by the wrong person."

Nico sheathed his black sword. "You sure about this, Reyna? I don't like leaving you alone."

Blackjack whinnied and licked the side of Nico's face.

"Gah! Okay, I'm sorry." Nico wiped off the horse spit. "Reyna's not alone. She's got a herd of excellent pegasi."

Reyna couldn't help but smile. "I'll be fine. With luck, we'll all meet again soon enough. We'll fight side by side against Gaea's forces. Be careful, and *Ave Romae!*"

Dakota and Leila repeated the cheer.

Tyson furrowed his single eyebrow. "Who is Ave?"

"It means *Go, Romans.*" Reyna clapped the Cyclops's forearm. "But by all means, *Go, Greeks,* too." The words sounded strange in her mouth.

She faced Nico. She wanted to hug him but wasn't sure the gesture would be welcome. She extended her hand. "It's been an honor questing with you, son of Hades."

Nico's grip was strong. "You're the most courageous demigod I've ever met, Reyna. I—" He faltered, perhaps realizing he had a large audience. "I won't let you down. See you on Half-Blood Hill."

The sky began to lighten in the east as the group dispersed. Soon Reyna stood on the deck of the *Mi Amor* . . . alone except for eight pegasi and a forty-foot-tall Athena.

She tried to steady her nerves. Until Nico, Dakota, and Leila had time to disrupt the legion's attack, she couldn't do anything, but she hated standing around and waiting.

Just over that dark line of hills, her comrades in the Twelfth Legion were preparing for a needless attack. If Reyna had stayed with them, she could've guided them better. She could've kept Octavian in check. Perhaps the giant Orion was correct: she'd failed in her duties.

She remembered the ghosts on the balcony in San Juan—pointing at her, whispering accusations: *Murderer. Traitor.* She remembered the feel of the golden saber in her hand as she slashed down her father's specter—his face full of outrage and betrayal.

*You are a Ramírez-Arellano!* her father used to rant. *Never abandon your post. Never let anyone in. Above all, never betray your own!*

By helping the Greeks, Reyna had done all of those things. A Roman was supposed to destroy her enemies. Instead, Reyna had joined forces with them. She'd left her legion in the hands of a madman.

What would her mother say? Bellona, the war goddess . . .

Blackjack must have sensed her agitation. He clopped over and nuzzled her.

She stroked his muzzle. "I don't have any treats for you, boy."

He bumped her affectionately. Nico had told her that Blackjack was Percy's usual ride, but he seemed friendly to everyone. He'd carried the son of Hades without protest. Now he was comforting a Roman.

She wrapped her arms around his powerful neck. His coat smelled just like Scipio's—a mixture of fresh-cut grass and warm bread. She let loose a sob that had been building in her chest. As praetor, she couldn't show weakness or fear to her comrades. She had to stay strong. But the horse didn't seem to mind.

He nickered gently. Reyna couldn't understand Horse, but he seemed to say: *It's all right. You've done well.*

She looked up at the fading stars.

"Mother," she said, "I haven't prayed to you enough. I've never met you. I've never asked for your help. But please . . . this morning, give me the strength to do what is right."

As if on cue, something flashed on the eastern horizon—a

light across the Sound, approaching fast like another speedboat.

For one elated moment, Reyna thought it was a sign from Bellona.

The dark shape got closer. Reyna's hope turned to dread. She waited too long, paralyzed with disbelief, as the figure resolved into a large humanoid, running toward her across the surface of the water.

The first arrow struck Blackjack's flank. The horse collapsed with a shriek of pain.

Reyna screamed, but before she could move, a second arrow hit the deck between her feet. Attached to its shaft was a glowing LED readout the size of a wristwatch, counting down from 5:00.

4:59.

4:58.

# XXXIX

# REYNA

"I WOULDN'T MOVE, PRAETOR!"

Orion stood on the surface of the water, fifty feet to starboard, an arrow nocked in his bow.

Through Reyna's haze of rage and grief, she noticed the giant's new scars. His fight with the Hunters had left him with mottled gray and pink scar tissue on his arms and face, so he looked like a bruised peach in the process of rotting. The mechanical eye on his left side was dark. His hair had burned away, leaving only ragged patches. His nose was swollen and red from the bowstring that Nico had snapped in his face. All of this gave Reyna a twinge of dark satisfaction.

Regrettably, the giant still had his smug smile.

At Reyna's feet, the timer on the arrow read: 4:42.

"Explosive arrows are *very* touchy," said Orion. "Once they're embedded, even the slightest motion can set them off. I wouldn't want you to miss the last four minutes of your life."

Reyna's senses sharpened. The pegasi clopped nervously around the Athena Parthenos. Dawn began to break. The wind from the shore brought a faint scent of strawberries. Lying next to her on the deck, Blackjack wheezed and shuddered—still alive, but badly wounded.

Her heart pounded so hard she thought her eardrums might burst. She extended her strength to Blackjack, trying to keep him alive. She would *not* see him die.

She wanted to shout insults at the giant, but her first words were surprisingly calm. "What of my sister?"

Orion's white teeth flashed in his ruined face. "I would love to tell you she is dead. I would love to see the pain on your face. Alas, as far as I know, your sister still lives. So do Thalia Grace and her annoying Hunters. They surprised me, I'll admit. I was forced into the sea to escape them. For the past few days I have been wounded and in pain, healing slowly, building a new bow. But don't worry, Praetor. You will die first. Your precious statue will be burned in a great conflagration. After Gaea has risen, when the mortal world is ending, I will find your sister. I will tell her you died painfully. Then I will kill her." He grinned. "So all is well!"

4:04.

Hylla was alive. Thalia and the Hunters were still out there somewhere. But none of that would matter if Reyna's mission failed. The sun was rising on the last day of the world. . . .

Blackjack's breathing became more labored.

Reyna mustered her courage. The winged horse needed her. Lord Pegasus had named her Horse Friend, and she would not let him down. She couldn't think about the entire world right now. She had to concentrate on what was right next to her.

3:54.

"So." She glared at Orion. "You're damaged and ugly, but not dead. I suppose that means I'll need the help of a god to kill you."

Orion chuckled. "Sadly, you Romans have never been very good at summoning gods to your aid. I guess they don't think much of you, eh?"

Reyna was tempted to agree. She had prayed to her mother . . . and been blessed with the arrival of a homicidal giant. Not exactly a ringing endorsement.

And yet . . .

Reyna laughed. "Ah, Orion."

The giant's smile wavered. "You have a strange sense of humor, girl. What are you laughing about?"

"Bellona *has* answered my prayer. She doesn't fight my battles for me. She doesn't guarantee me easy victory. She grants me opportunities to prove myself. She gives me strong enemies and potential allies."

Orion's left eye sparked. "You speak nonsense. A column of fire is about to destroy you and your precious Greek statue. No ally can help you. Your mother has abandoned you as you abandoned your legion."

"But she hasn't," Reyna said. "Bellona wasn't just a war goddess. She wasn't like the Greek *Enyo*, who was simply an embodiment of carnage. Bellona's Temple was where Romans greeted foreign ambassadors. Wars were declared there, but *peace* treaties were also negotiated—lasting peace, based on strength."

3:01.

Reyna drew her knife. "Bellona gave me the chance to make peace with the Greeks and increase the strength of Rome. I took it. If I die, I will die defending that cause. So I say my mother *is* with me today. She will add her strength to mine. Shoot your arrow, Orion. It won't matter. When I throw this blade and pierce your heart, you *will* die."

Orion stood motionless on the waves. His face was a mask of concentration. His one good eye blinked amber.

"A bluff," he growled. "I've killed hundreds like you: girls playing at war, pretending they are the equal to giants! I will not grant you a quick death, Praetor. I will watch you burn, the way the Hunters burned me."

2:31.

Blackjack wheezed, kicking his legs against the deck. The sky was turning pink. A wind from the shore caught the camouflage netting on the Athena Parthenos and stripped it away, sending the silvery cloth rippling across the Sound. The Athena Parthenos gleamed in the early light, and Reyna thought how beautiful the goddess would look on the hill above the Greek camp.

It must happen, she thought, hoping the pegasi could sense her intentions. You must complete the journey without me.

She inclined her head to the Athena Parthenos. "My lady, it has been my honor to escort you."

Orion scoffed. "Talking to enemy statues now? Futile. You have roughly two minutes of life."

"Oh, but I don't abide by *your* time frame, giant," Reyna said. "A Roman does not wait for death. She seeks it out, and meets it on her own terms."

She threw her knife. It hit true—right in the middle of the giant's chest.

Orion bellowed in agony, and Reyna thought what a pleasing last sound that was to hear.

She flung her cloak in front of her and fell on the explosive arrow, determined to shield Blackjack and the other pegasi, and hopefully protect the mortals sleeping belowdecks. She had no idea whether her body would contain the explosion, whether her cloak could smother the flames, but it was her best chance to save her friends and her mission.

She tensed, waiting to die. She felt the pressure as the arrow detonated . . . but it wasn't what she expected. Against her ribs, the explosion made only the smallest *pop*, like an overinflated balloon. Her cloak became uncomfortably warm. No flames burst forth.

Why was she still alive?

*Rise*, said a voice in her head.

In a trance, Reyna got to her feet. Smoke curled from the edges of her cloak. She realized something was different about the purple fabric. It glittered as if woven through with filaments of Imperial gold. At her feet, a section of the deck had been reduced to a circle of charcoal, but her cloak wasn't even singed.

*Accept my aegis, Reyna Ramírez-Arellano,* said the voice. *For today, you have proven yourself a hero of Olympus.*

Reyna stared in amazement at the Athena Parthenos, glowing with a faint golden aura.

The *aegis*... From Reyna's years of study, she recalled that the term *aegis* didn't apply only to Athena's shield. It also meant the goddess's cloak. According to legend, Athena sometimes cut pieces off her mantle and draped them over statues in her temples, or over her chosen heroes, to shield them.

Reyna's cloak, which she'd worn for years, had suddenly changed. It had absorbed the explosion.

She tried to say something, to thank the goddess, but her voice wouldn't work. The statue's glowing aura faded. The ringing in Reyna's ears cleared. She became aware of Orion, still roaring in pain as he staggered across the surface of the water.

"You have failed!" He clawed her knife from his chest and tossed it into the waves. "I still live!"

He drew his bow and fired, but it seemed to happen in slow motion. Reyna swept her cloak in front of her. The arrow shattered against the cloth. She charged to the railing and leaped at the giant.

The jump should have been impossibly far, but Reyna felt a surge of power in her limbs, as if her mother, Bellona, was lending her strength—a return for all the strength Reyna had lent others over the years.

Reyna grabbed the giant's bow and swung around on it like a gymnast, landing on the giant's back. She locked her legs around his waist, then twisted her cloak into a rope and pulled it across Orion's neck with all her might.

He instinctively dropped his bow. He clutched at the glimmering fabric, but his fingers steamed and blistered when he touched it. Sour, acrid smoke rose from his neck.

Reyna pulled tighter.

"This is for Phoebe," she snarled in his ear. "For Kinzie. For all those you killed. You will die at the hands of a *girl*."

Orion thrashed and fought, but Reyna's will was unshakable. The power of Athena infused her cloak. Bellona blessed her with strength and resolve. Not one but *two* powerful goddesses aided her, yet the kill was for Reyna to complete.

Complete it she did.

The giant crumpled to his knees and sank in the water. Reyna didn't let go until he ceased to thrash and his body dissolved into sea foam. His mechanical eye disappeared beneath the waves. His bow began to sink.

Reyna let it. She had no interest in spoils of war—no desire to let any part of the giant survive. Like her father's *mania*—and all the other angry ghosts of her past—Orion could teach her nothing. He deserved to be forgotten.

Besides, dawn was breaking.

Reyna swam for the yacht.

# X L

# REYNA

No time for enjoying her victory over Orion.

Blackjack's muzzle was foaming. His legs spasmed. Blood trickled from the arrow wound in his flank.

Reyna ripped through the supply bag that Phoebe had given her. She swabbed the wound with healing potion. She poured unicorn draught over the blade of her silver pocketknife.

"Please, please," she murmured to herself.

In truth, she had no idea what she was doing, but she cleaned the wound as best she could and gripped the shaft of the arrow. If it had a barbed tip, pulling it out might cause more damage. But if it was poisoned, she couldn't leave it in. Nor could she push it through, since it was embedded in the middle of his body. She would have to choose the lesser evil.

"This will hurt, my friend," she told Blackjack.

He huffed, as if to say *Tell me something I don't know.*

With her knife, she cut a slit on either side of the wound.

She pulled out the arrow. Blackjack shrieked, but the arrow came out cleanly. The point wasn't barbed. It could have been poisoned, but there was no way to be sure. One problem at a time.

Reyna poured more healing potion over the wound and bandaged it. She applied pressure, counting under her breath. The oozing seemed to lessen.

She trickled unicorn draught into Blackjack's mouth.

She lost track of time. The horse's pulse became stronger and steadier. His eyes cleared of pain. His breathing eased.

By the time Reyna stood up, she was shaking with fear and exhaustion, but Blackjack was still alive.

"You're going to be fine," she promised. "I'll get you help from Camp Half-Blood."

Blackjack made a grumbling sound. Reyna could've sworn he tried to say *donuts*. She must have been going delirious.

Belatedly, she realized how much the sky had lightened. The Athena Parthenos gleamed in the sun. Guido and the other winged horses pawed the deck impatiently.

"The battle . . ." Reyna turned toward the shore but saw no signs of combat. A Greek trireme bobbed lazily in the morning tide. The hills looked green and peaceful.

For a moment, she wondered if the Romans had decided not to attack.

Perhaps Octavian had come to his senses. Perhaps Nico and the others had managed to win over the legion.

Then an orange glow illuminated the hilltops. Multiple streaks of fire climbed skyward like burning fingers.

The onagers had shot their first volley.

# XLI

# PIPER

PIPER WASN'T SURPRISED when the snake people arrived.

All week, she'd been thinking about her encounter with Sciron the bandit, when she'd stood on the deck of the *Argo II* after escaping a gigantic Destructo-Turtle and made the mistake of saying, "We're safe."

Instantly an arrow had hit the mainmast, an inch in front of her nose.

Piper learned a valuable lesson from that: Never assume you're safe, and never, ever tempt the Fates by *announcing* that you think you're safe.

So when the ship docked at the harbor in Piraeus, on the outskirts of Athens, Piper resisted the urge to breathe a sigh of relief. Sure, they had finally reached their destination. Somewhere nearby—past those rows of cruise ships, past those hills crowded with buildings—they would find the Acropolis. Today, one way or another, their journey would end.

But that didn't mean she could relax. Any moment, a nasty surprise might come flying out of nowhere.

As it turned out, the surprise was three dudes with snake tails instead of legs.

Piper was on watch while her friends geared up for combat—checking their weapons and armor, loading the ballistae and catapults. She spotted the snake guys slithering along the docks, winding through crowds of mortal tourists who paid them no attention.

"Um . . . Annabeth?" Piper called.

Annabeth and Percy came to her side.

"Oh, great," Percy said. *"Dracaenae."*

Annabeth narrowed her eyes. "I don't think so. At least not like any *I've* seen. *Dracaenae* have two serpent trunks for legs. These guys just have one."

"You're right," Percy said. "These look more human on top too. Not all scaly and green and stuff. So do we talk or fight?"

Piper was tempted to say *fight*. She couldn't help thinking of the story she'd told Jason—about the Cherokee hunter who broke his taboo and turned into a snake. These three looked like they'd been eating a lot of squirrel meat.

Weirdly, the one in the lead reminded Piper of her dad when he'd grown a beard for his role in *King of Sparta*. The snake man held his head high. His face was chiseled and bronze, his eyes black as basalt, his curly dark hair glistening with oil. His upper body rippled with muscles, covered only by a Greek *chlamys*—a white wool cloak loosely wrapped and pinned at the shoulder. From the waist down, his body was one giant serpent trunk—about eight feet of green tail undulating behind him as he moved.

In one hand he carried a staff topped with a glowing green jewel. In his other, he carried a platter covered with a silver dome, like an entrée for a fancy dinner.

The two guys behind him appeared to be guards. They wore bronze breastplates and elaborate helmets topped with horsehair bristles. Their spears were tipped with green stone points. Their oval shields were emblazoned with a large Greek letter K—*kappa.*

They stopped a few yards from the *Argo II.* The leader looked up and studied the demigods. His expression was intense but inscrutable. He might have been angry or worried or terribly in need of a restroom.

"Permission to come aboard." His rasping voice made Piper think of a straight razor being wiped across a strop—like in her grandfather's barbershop back in Oklahoma.

"Who are you?" she asked.

He fixed his dark eyes on her. "I am Kekrops, the first and eternal king of Athens. I would welcome you to my city." He held up the covered platter. "Also, I brought a Bundt cake."

Piper glanced at her friends. "A trick?"

"Probably," Annabeth said.

"At least he brought dessert." Percy smiled down at the snake guys. "Welcome aboard!"

Kekrops agreed to leave his guards above deck with Buford the table, who ordered them to drop and give him twenty push-ups. The guards seemed to take this as a challenge.

Meanwhile, the king of Athens was invited to the mess hall for a "get to know you" meeting.

"Please take a seat," Jason offered.

Kekrops wrinkled his nose. "Snake people do not sit."

"Please remain standing," Leo said. He cut the cake and stuffed a piece in his mouth before Piper could warn him it might be poisoned, or inedible for mortals, or just plain bad.

"Dang!" He grinned. "Snake people know how to make Bundt cake. Kind of orangey, with a hint of honey. Needs a glass of milk."

"Snake people do not drink milk," Kekrops said. "We are lactose intolerant reptiles."

"Me too!" Frank said. "I mean . . . lactose intolerant. Not a reptile. Though I *can* be a reptile sometimes—"

"Anyway," Hazel interrupted, "King Kekrops, what brings you here? How did you know we'd arrived?"

"I know everything that happens in Athens," Kekrops said. "I was the city's founder, its first king, born of the earth. I am the one who judged the dispute between Athena and Poseidon, and chose Athena to be the patron of the city."

"No hard feelings, though," Percy muttered.

Annabeth elbowed him. "I've heard of you, Kekrops. You were the first to offer sacrifices to Athena. You built her first shrine on the Acropolis."

"Correct." Kekrops sounded bitter, like he regretted his decision. "My people were the *original* Athenians—the *gemini.*"

"Like your zodiac sign?" Percy asked. "I'm a Leo."

"No, stupid," Leo said. "I'm a Leo. You're a Percy."

"Will you two stop it?" Hazel chided. "I think he means *gemini* like *doubled*—half man, half snake. That's what his people are called. He's a *geminus*, singular."

"Yes . . ." Kekrops leaned away from Hazel as if she somehow offended him. "Millennia ago, we were driven underground by the two-legged humans, but I know the ways of the city better than any. I came to warn you. If you try to approach the Acropolis aboveground, you will be destroyed."

Jason stopped nibbling his cake. "You mean . . . by you?"

"By Porphyrion's armies," said the snake king. "The Acropolis is ringed with great siege weapons—onagers."

"*More* onagers?" Frank protested. "Did they have a sale on them or something?"

"The Cyclopes," Hazel guessed. "They're supplying both Octavian and the giants."

Percy grunted. "Like we needed more proof that Octavian is on the wrong side."

"That is not the only threat," Kekrops warned. "The air is filled with storm spirits and gryphons. All roads to the Acropolis are patrolled by the Earthborn."

Frank drummed his fingers on the Bundt cake cover. "So, what, we should just give up? We've come too far for that."

"I offer you an alternative," said Kekrops. "Underground passage to the Acropolis. For the sake of Athena, for the sake of the gods, I will help you."

The back of Piper's neck tingled. She remembered what the giantess Periboia had said in her dream: that the demigods would find friends in Athens as well as enemies. Perhaps the giantess had meant Kekrops and his snake people. But there was something in Kekrops's voice that Piper didn't like—that razor-against-strop tone, as if he were preparing to make a sharp cut.

"What's the catch?" she asked.

Kekrops turned those inscrutable dark eyes on her. "Only a small party of demigods—no more than three—could pass undetected by the giants. Otherwise your scent would give you away. But our underground passages could lead you straight into the ruins of the Acropolis. Once there, you could disable the siege weapons by stealth and allow the rest of your crew to approach. With luck, you could take the giants by surprise. You might be able to disrupt their ceremony."

"Ceremony?" Leo asked. "Oh . . . like to wake Gaea."

"Even now it has begun," Kekrops warned. "Can you not feel the earth trembling? We, the *gemini*, are your best chance."

Piper heard eagerness in his voice—almost hunger.

Percy looked around the table. "Any objections?"

"Just a few," Jason said. "We're on the enemy's doorstep. We're being asked to split up. Isn't that how people get killed in horror movies?"

"Also," Percy said, "Gaea *wants* us to reach the Parthenon. She wants our blood to water the stones and all that other psycho garbage. Won't we be playing right into her hands?"

Annabeth caught Piper's eye. She asked a silent question: *What's your feeling?*

Piper still wasn't used to that—the way Annabeth looked to her for advice now. Ever since Sparta, they'd learned that they could tackle problems together from two different sides.

Annabeth saw the logical thing, the tactical move. Piper had gut reactions that were anything but logical. Together, they either solved the problem twice as fast, or they hopelessly confused each other.

Kekrops's offer made sense. At least, it sounded like the least suicidal option. But Piper was certain the snake king was hiding his true intentions. She just didn't know how to prove it. . . .

Then she remembered something her father had told her years ago: *You were named Piper because Grandpa Tom thought you would have a powerful voice. You would learn all the Cherokee songs, even the song of the snakes.*

A myth from a totally different culture, yet here she was, facing the king of the snake people.

She began to sing: "Summertime," one of her dad's favorites.

Kekrops stared at her in wonder. He began to sway.

At first Piper was self-conscious, singing in front of all her friends and a snake guy. Her dad had always told her she had a good voice, but she didn't like to draw attention to herself. She didn't even like to participate at campfire sing-alongs. Now her words filled the mess hall. Everyone listened, transfixed.

She finished the first verse. No one spoke for a count of five.

"Pipes," Jason said, "I had no idea."

"That was beautiful," Leo agreed. "Maybe not . . . you know, *Calypso* beautiful, but still . . ."

Piper kept the snake king's gaze. "What are your real intentions?"

"To deceive you," he said in a trance, still swaying. "We hope to lead you into the tunnels and destroy you."

"Why?" Piper asked.

"The Earth Mother has promised us great rewards. If we spill your blood under the Parthenon, that will be sufficient to complete her awakening."

"But you serve Athena," Piper said. "You founded her city."

Kekrops made a low hiss. "And in return, the goddess abandoned me. Athena replaced me with a two-legged *human* king. She drove my daughters mad. They leaped to their deaths from the cliffs of the Acropolis. The original Athenians, the *gemini*, were driven underground and forgotten. Athena, the goddess of wisdom, turned her back on us, but wisdom comes from the earth as well. We are, first and last, the children of Gaea. The Earth Mother has promised us a place in the sun of the upper world."

"Gaea is lying," Piper said. "She intends to destroy the upper world, not *give* it to anyone."

Kekrops bared his fangs. "Then we will be no worse off than we were under the treacherous gods!"

He raised his staff, but Piper launched into another verse of "Summertime."

The snake king's arms went limp. His eyes glassed over.

Piper sang a few more lines, then she risked another question: "The giants' defenses, the underground passage to the Acropolis—how much of what you told us is true?"

"All of it," Kekrops said. "The Acropolis *is* heavily defended, just as I described. Any approach aboveground would be impossible."

"So you *could* guide us through your tunnels," Piper said. "That's also true?"

Kekrops frowned. "Yes . . ."

"And if you ordered your people *not* to attack us," she said, "they would obey?"

"Yes, but . . ." Kekrops shuddered. "Yes, they would obey. Three of you at most could go without attracting the attention of the giants."

Annabeth's eyes darkened. "Piper, we'd be crazy to try it. He'll kill us at the first opportunity."

"Yes," the snake king agreed. "Only this girl's music controls me. I hate it. Please, sing some more."

Piper gave him another verse.

Leo got into the act. He picked up a couple of spoons and made them do high kicks on the tabletop until Hazel slapped his arm.

"I should go," Hazel said, "if it's underground."

"Never," Kekrops said. "A child of the Underworld? My people would find your presence revolting. No charming music would keep them from slaying you."

Hazel swallowed. "Or I could stay here."

"Me and Percy," Annabeth suggested.

"Um . . ." Percy raised his hand. "Just gonna throw this out here again. That's exactly what Gaea wants—you and me, our blood watering the stones, et cetera."

"I know." Annabeth's expression was grim. "But it's the most logical choice. The oldest shrines on the Acropolis are dedicated to Poseidon and Athena. Kekrops, wouldn't that mask our approach?"

"Yes," the snake king admitted. "Your . . . your scent would be difficult to discern. The ruins always radiate the power of those two gods."

"And me," Piper said at the end of her song. "You'll need me to keep our friend here in line."

Jason squeezed her hand. "I still hate the idea of splitting up."

"But it's our best shot," Frank said. "The three of them sneak in and disable the onagers, cause a distraction. Then the rest of us fly in with ballistae blazing."

"Yes," Kekrops said, "that plan could work. If I do not kill you first."

"I've got an idea," Annabeth said. "Frank, Hazel, Leo . . . let's talk. Piper, can you keep our friend musically incapacitated?"

Piper started a different song: "Happy Trails," a silly tune her dad used to sing to her whenever they left Oklahoma to return to L.A. Annabeth, Leo, Frank, and Hazel left to talk strategy.

"Well." Percy rose and offered his hand to Jason. "Until we meet again at the Acropolis, bro. I'll be the one killing giants."

# XLII

# PIPER

**PIPER'S DAD USED TO SAY** that being in the airport didn't count as visiting a city. Piper felt the same way about sewers.

From the port to the Acropolis, she didn't see anything of Athens except dark, putrid tunnels. The snake men led them through an iron storm grate at the docks, straight into their underground lair, which smelled of rotting fish, mold, and snakeskin.

The atmosphere made it hard to sing about summertime and cotton and easy living, but Piper kept it up. If she stopped for longer than a minute or two, Kekrops and his guards started hissing and looking angry.

"I don't like this place," Annabeth murmured. "Reminds me of when I was underneath Rome."

Kekrops hissed with laughter. "Our domain is much older. *Much*, much older."

Annabeth slipped her hand into Percy's, which made Piper

feel downhearted. She wished Jason were with her. Heck, she'd even settle for Leo . . . though maybe she wouldn't have held his hand. Leo's hands tended to burst into flames when he was nervous.

Piper's voice echoed through the tunnels. As they traveled farther into the lair, more snake people gathered to hear her. Soon they had a procession following behind them—dozens of *gemini* all swaying and slithering.

Piper had lived up to her granddad's prediction. She had learned the song of the snakes—which turned out to be a George Gershwin number from 1935. So far she had even kept the snake king from biting, just like in the old Cherokee story. The only problem with that legend: the warrior who learned the snake song had to sacrifice his wife for the power. Piper didn't want to sacrifice anyone.

The vial of physician's cure was still wrapped in its chamois cloth, tucked in her belt pouch. She hadn't had time to consult with Jason and Leo before she left. She just had to hope they would all be reunited on the hilltop before anyone needed the cure. If one of them died and she couldn't reach them . . .

*Just keep singing,* she told herself.

They passed through crude stone chambers littered with bones. They climbed slopes so steep and slippery it was nearly impossible to keep their footing. At one point, they passed a warm cave the size of a gymnasium filled with snake eggs, their tops covered with a layer of silver filaments like slimy Christmas tinsel.

More and more snake people joined their procession.

Slithering behind her, they sounded like an army of football players shuffling with sandpaper on their cleats.

Piper wondered how many *gemini* lived down here. Hundreds, maybe thousands.

She thought she heard her own heartbeat echoing through the corridors, getting louder and louder the deeper they went. Then she realized the persistent *boom ba-boom* was all around them, resonating through the stone and the air.

*I wake.* A woman's voice, as clear as Piper's singing.

Annabeth froze. "Oh, that's not good."

"It's like Tartarus," Percy said, his voice edgy. "You remember . . . his heartbeat. When he appeared—"

"Don't," Annabeth said. "Just don't."

"Sorry." In the light of his sword, Percy's face was like a large firefly—a hovering, momentary smudge of brightness in the dark.

The voice of Gaea spoke again, louder: *At last.*

Piper's singing wavered.

Fear washed over her, as it had in the Spartan temple. But the gods Phobos and Deimos were old friends to her now. She let the fear burn inside her like fuel, making her voice even stronger. She sang for the snake people, for her friends' safety. Why not for Gaea too?

Finally they reached the top of a steep slope, where the path ended in a curtain of green goo.

Kekrops faced the demigods. "Beyond this camouflage is the Acropolis. You must remain here. I will check that your way is clear."

"Wait." Piper turned to address the crowd of *gemini*. "There is only death above. You will be safer in the tunnels. Hurry back. Forget you saw us. Protect yourselves."

The fear in her voice channeled perfectly with the charm-speak. The snake people, even the guards, turned and slithered into the darkness, leaving only the king.

"Kekrops," Piper said, "you're planning to betray us as soon as you step through that goo."

"Yes," he agreed. "I will alert the giants. They will destroy you." Then he hissed. "Why did I tell you that?"

"Listen to the heartbeat of Gaea," Piper urged. "You can sense her rage, can't you?"

Kekrops wavered. The end of his staff glowed dimly. "I can, yes. She is angry."

"She'll destroy everything," Piper said. "She'll reduce the Acropolis to a smoking crater. Athens—your city—will be utterly destroyed, your people along with it. You believe me, don't you?"

"I—I do."

"Whatever hatred you have for humans, for demigods, for Athena, we are the only chance to stop Gaea. So you will *not* betray us. For your own sake, and your people, you will scout the territory and make sure the way is clear. You will say nothing to the giants. Then you will return."

"That is . . . what I'll do." Kekrops disappeared through the membrane of goo.

Annabeth shook her head in amazement. "Piper, that was incredible."

"We'll see if it works." Piper sat down on the cool stone floor. She figured she might as well rest while she could.

The others squatted next to her. Percy handed her a canteen of water.

Until she took a drink, Piper hadn't realized how dry her throat was. "Thanks."

Percy nodded. "You think the charm will last?"

"I'm not sure," she admitted. "If Kekrops comes back in two minutes with an army of giants, then no."

The heartbeat of Gaea echoed through the floor. Strangely, it made Piper think of the sea—how the waves boomed along the cliffs of Santa Monica back home.

She wondered what her father was doing right now. It would be the middle of the night in California. Maybe he was asleep, or doing a late night TV interview. Piper hoped he was in his favorite spot: the porch off the living room, watching the moon over the Pacific, enjoying some quiet time. Piper wanted to think he was happy and content right now . . . in case they failed.

She thought about her friends in the Aphrodite cabin at Camp Half-Blood. She thought about her cousins in Oklahoma, which was odd, since she'd never spent much time with them. She didn't even know them very well. Now she was sorry about that.

She wished she'd taken more advantage of her life, appreciated things more. She would always be grateful for her family aboard the *Argo II*—but she had so many other friends and relatives she wished she could see one last time.

"Do you guys ever think about your families?" she asked.

It was a silly question, especially on the cusp of a battle. Piper should have been focused on their quest, not distracting her friends.

But they didn't chide her.

Percy's gaze became unfocused. His lower lip quivered. "My mom . . . I—I haven't even *seen* her since Hera made me disappear. I called her from Alaska. I gave Coach Hedge some letters to deliver to her. I . . ." His voice broke. "She's all I've got. Her and my stepdad, Paul."

"And Tyson," Annabeth reminded him. "And Grover. And—"

"Yeah, of course," Percy said. "Thanks. I feel much better."

Piper probably shouldn't have laughed, but she was too full of nervousness and melancholy to hold it in. "What about you, Annabeth?"

"My dad . . . my stepmom and stepbrothers." She turned the drakon-bone blade in her lap. "After all I've been through in the past year, it seems stupid that I resented them for so long. And my dad's relatives . . . I haven't thought about them in years. I have an uncle and cousin in Boston."

Percy looked shocked. "You, with the Yankees cap? You've got family in Red Sox country?"

Annabeth smiled weakly. "I never see them. My dad and my uncle don't get along. Some old rivalry. I don't know. It's stupid what keeps people apart."

Piper nodded. She wished she had the healing powers of Asclepius. She wished she could look at people and see what was hurting them, then whip out her prescription pad and make everything better. But she guessed there was a reason Zeus kept Asclepius locked away in his underground temple.

Some pain shouldn't be wished away so easily. It had to be dealt with, even embraced. Without the agony of the last few months, Piper never would have found her best friends, Hazel and Annabeth. She never would've discovered her own courage. She certainly wouldn't have had the guts to sing show tunes to the snake people under Athens.

At the top of the tunnel, the green membrane rippled.

Piper grabbed her sword and rose, prepared for a flood of monsters.

But Kekrops emerged alone.

"The way is clear," he said. "But hurry. The ceremony is almost complete."

Pushing through a curtain of mucus was almost as fun as Piper imagined.

She emerged feeling like she'd just rolled through a giant's nostril. Fortunately, none of the gunk stuck to her, but still her skin tingled with revulsion.

Percy, Annabeth, and she found themselves in a cool, damp pit that seemed to be the basement level of a temple. All around them, uneven ground stretched into darkness under a low ceiling of stone. Directly above their heads, a rectangular gap was open to the sky. Piper could see the edges of walls and the tops of columns, but no monsters . . . yet.

The camouflage membrane had closed behind them and

blended into the ground. Piper pressed her hand against it. The area seemed to be solid rock. They wouldn't be leaving the way they'd come.

Annabeth ran her hand along some marks on the ground—a jagged crow's-foot shape as long as a human body. The area was lumpy and white, like stone scar tissue. "This is the place," she said. "Percy, these are the trident marks of Poseidon."

Hesitantly, Percy touched the scars. "He must've been using his extra-extra-large trident."

"This is where he struck the earth," Annabeth said, "where he made a saltwater spring appear when he had the contest with my mom to sponsor Athens."

"So this is where the rivalry started," Percy said.

"Yeah."

Percy pulled Annabeth close and kissed her . . . long enough for it to get really awkward for Piper, though she said nothing. She thought about the old rule of Aphrodite's cabin: that to be recognized as a daughter of the love goddess, you had to break someone's heart. Piper had long ago decided to change that rule. Percy and Annabeth were a perfect example of why. You should have to make someone's heart *whole*. That was a much better test.

When Percy pulled away, Annabeth looked like a fish gasping for air.

"The rivalry ends here," Percy said. "I love you, Wise Girl."

Annabeth made a little sigh, like something in her rib cage had melted.

Percy glanced at Piper. "Sorry, I had to do that."

Piper grinned. "How could a daughter of Aphrodite not approve? You're a great boyfriend."

Annabeth made another grunt-whimper. "Uh . . . anyway. We're beneath the Erechtheion. It's a temple to both Athena and Poseidon. The Parthenon should be catty-corner to the southeast. We'll need to sneak around the perimeter and disable as many siege weapons as we can, make an approach path for the *Argo II.*"

"It's broad daylight," Piper said. "How will we go unnoticed?"

Annabeth scanned the sky. "That's why I made a plan with Frank and Hazel. Hopefully . . . ah. Look."

A bee zipped overhead. Dozens more followed. They swarmed around a column, then hovered over the opening of the pit.

"Say hi to Frank, everybody," Annabeth said.

Piper waved. The cloud of bees zipped away.

"How does that even work?" Percy said. "Like . . . one bee is a finger? Two bees are his eyes?"

"I don't know," Annabeth admitted. "But he's our go-between. As soon as he gives Hazel the word, she will—"

"Gah!" Percy yelped.

Annabeth clamped her hand over his mouth.

Which looked strange, because suddenly each of them had turned into a hulking, six-armed Earthborn.

"Hazel's Mist." Piper's voice sounded deep and gravelly. She looked down and realized that she, too, now had a lovely

Neanderthal body—belly hair, loincloth, stubby legs, and oversized feet. If she concentrated, she could see her normal arms, but when she moved them they rippled like mirages, separating into three different sets of muscular Earthborn arms.

Percy grimaced, which looked even worse on his newly uglified face. "Wow, Annabeth . . . I'm really glad I kissed you *before* you changed."

"Thanks a lot," she said. "We should get going. I'll move clockwise around the perimeter. Piper, you move counter-clockwise. Percy, you scout the middle—"

"Wait," Percy said. "We're walking right into the whole blood-spilling sacrifice trap we've been warned about, and you want to split up *even more?*"

"We'll cover more ground that way," Annabeth said. "We have to hurry. That chanting . . ."

Piper hadn't noticed it until then, but now she heard it: an ominous drone in the distance, like a hundred forklifts idling. She looked at the ground and noticed bits of gravel trembling, skittering southeast, as if pulled toward the Parthenon.

"Right," Piper said. "We'll meet up at the giant's throne."

At first it was easy.

Monsters were everywhere—hundreds of ogres, Earth-born, and Cyclopes milling through the ruins—but most of them were gathered at the Parthenon, watching the ceremony in progress. Piper strolled along the cliffs of the Acropolis unchallenged.

Near the first onager, three Earthborn were sunning themselves on the rocks. Piper walked right up to them and smiled. "Hello."

Before they could make a sound, she cut them down with her sword. All three melted into slag heaps. She slashed the onager's spring cord to disable the weapon, then kept moving.

She was committed now. She had to do as much damage as possible before the sabotage was discovered.

She skirted a patrol of Cyclopes. The second onager was surrounded by an encampment of tattooed Laistrygonian ogres, but Piper managed to get to the machine without raising suspicion. She dropped a vial of Greek fire in the sling. With luck, as soon as they tried to load the catapult, it would explode in their faces.

She kept moving. Gryphons roosted on the colonnade of an old temple. A group of *empousai* had retreated into a shadowy archway and appeared to be slumbering, their fiery hair flickering dimly, their brass legs glinting. Hopefully the sunlight would make them sluggish if they had to fight.

Whenever she could, Piper slew isolated monsters. She walked past larger groups. Meanwhile the crowd at the Parthenon grew larger. The chanting got louder. Piper couldn't see what was happening inside the ruins—just the heads of twenty or thirty giants standing in a circle, mumbling and swaying, maybe doing the evil monster version of "Kumbayah."

She disabled a third siege weapon by sawing through the torsion ropes, which should give the *Argo II* a clear approach from the north.

She hoped Frank was watching her progress. She wondered how long it would take for the ship to arrive.

Suddenly, the chanting stopped. A *BOOM* echoed across the hillside. In the Parthenon, the giants roared in triumph. All around Piper, monsters surged toward the sound of celebration.

That couldn't be good. Piper blended into a crowd of soursmelling Earthborn. She bounded up the main steps of the temple, then climbed a section of metal scaffolding so she could see above the heads of the ogres and Cyclopes.

The scene in the ruins almost made her cry aloud.

Before Porphyrion's throne, dozens of giants stood in a loose ring, hollering and shaking their weapons as two of their number paraded around the circle, showing off their prizes. The princess Periboia held Annabeth by the neck like a feral cat. The giant Enceladus had Percy wrapped in his massive fist.

Annabeth and Percy both struggled helplessly. Their captors displayed them to the cheering horde of monsters, then turned to face King Porphyrion, who sat in his makeshift throne, his white eyes gleaming with malice.

"Right on time!" the giant king bellowed. "The blood of Olympus to raise the Earth Mother!"

# PIPER

**PIPER WATCHED IN HORROR** as the giant king rose to his full height—almost as tall as the temple columns. His face looked just as Piper remembered—green as bile, with a twisted sneer, his seaweed-colored hair braided with swords and axes taken from dead demigods.

He loomed over the captives, watching them wriggle. "They arrived just as you foresaw, Enceladus! Well done!"

Piper's old enemy bowed his head, braided bones clattering in his dreadlocks. "It was simple, my king."

The flame designs gleamed on his armor. His spear burned with purplish fire. He only needed one hand to hold his captive. Despite all of Percy Jackson's power, despite everything he had survived, in the end he was helpless against the sheer strength of the giant—and the inevitability of the prophecy.

"I knew these two would lead the assault," Enceladus continued. "I understand how they think. Athena and Poseidon . . . they were just like these children! They both came here thinking to claim this city. Their arrogance has undone them!"

Over the roar of the crowd, Piper could barely hear herself think, but she replayed Enceladus's words: *these two would lead the assault.* Her heart raced.

The giants had expected Percy and Annabeth. They didn't expect *her.*

For once, being Piper McLean, the daughter of Aphrodite, the one nobody took seriously, might play to her advantage.

Annabeth tried to say something, but the giantess Periboia shook her by the neck. "Shut up! None of your silver-tongued trickery!"

The princess drew a hunting knife as long as Piper's sword. "Let me do the honors, Father!"

"Wait, Daughter." The king stepped back. "The sacrifice must be done properly. Thoon, destroyer of the Fates, come forward!"

The wizened gray giant shuffled into sight, holding an oversized meat cleaver. He fixed his milky eyes on Annabeth.

Percy shouted. At the other end of the Acropolis, a hundred yards away, a geyser of water shot into the sky.

King Porphyrion laughed. "You'll have to do better than that, son of Poseidon. The earth is too powerful here. Even your father wouldn't be able to summon more than a salty spring. But never fear. The only liquid we require from you is your blood!"

Piper scanned the sky desperately. Where was the *Argo II*?

Thoon knelt and touched the blade of his cleaver reverently against the earth.

"Mother Gaea . . ." His voice was impossibly deep, shaking the ruins, making the metal scaffold resonate under Piper's feet. "In ancient times, blood mixed with your soil to create life. Now, let the blood of these demigods return the favor. We bring you to full wakefulness. We greet you as our eternal mistress!"

Without thinking, Piper leaped from the scaffolding. She sailed over the heads of the Cyclopes and ogres, landed in the center of the courtyard, and pushed her way into the circle of giants. As Thoon rose to use his cleaver, Piper slashed upward with her sword. She took off Thoon's hand at the wrist.

The old giant wailed. The cleaver and severed hand lay in the dust at Piper's feet. She felt her Mist disguise burn away until she was just Piper again—one girl in the midst of an army of giants, her jagged bronze blade like a toothpick compared to their massive weapons.

"WHAT IS THIS?" Porphyrion thundered. "How dare this weak, useless creature interrupt?"

Piper followed her gut. She attacked.

Piper's advantages: she was small, she was quick, and she was absolutely insane. She drew her knife Katoptris and threw it at Enceladus, hoping she wouldn't hit Percy by accident. She veered aside without witnessing the results, but judging from the giant's painful howl, she'd aimed well.

Several giants ran at her at once. Piper dodged between their legs and let them bash their heads together.

She wove through the crowd, jabbing her sword into

dragon-scale feet at every opportunity, and yelling, "RUN! RUN AWAY!" to sow confusion.

"NO! STOP HER!" Porphyrion shouted. "KILL HER!"

A spear almost impaled her. Piper swerved and kept running. *It's just like capture the flag,* she told herself. *Only the enemy team is all thirty feet tall.*

A huge sword sliced across her path. Compared to her sparring practice with Hazel, the strike was ridiculously slow. Piper leaped over the blade and zigzagged toward Annabeth, who was still kicking and writhing in Periboia's grip. Piper *had* to free her friend.

Unfortunately, the giantess seemed to anticipate her plan.

"I think not, demigod!" Periboia yelled. "This one bleeds!"

The giantess raised her knife.

Piper screamed in charmspeak: "MISS!"

At the same time, Annabeth kicked up with her legs to make herself a smaller target.

Periboia's knife passed beneath Annabeth's legs and stabbed the giantess's own palm.

"OWWW!"

Periboia dropped Annabeth—alive, but not unscathed. The dagger had sliced a nasty gash across the back of her thigh. As Annabeth rolled away, her blood soaked into the earth.

*The blood of Olympus,* Piper thought with dread.

But she couldn't do anything about that. She had to help Annabeth.

Piper lunged at the giantess. Her jagged blade suddenly felt ice cold in her hands. The surprised giantess glanced down as the sword of the Boread pierced her gut. Frost spread across her bronze breastplate.

Piper yanked out her sword. The giantess toppled backward—steaming white and frozen solid. Periboia hit the ground with a thud.

"My daughter!" King Porphyrion leveled his spear and charged.

But Percy had other ideas.

Enceladus had dropped him . . . probably because the giant was busy staggering around with Piper's knife embedded in his forehead, ichor streaming into his eyes.

Percy had no weapon—perhaps his sword had been confiscated or lost in the fighting—but he didn't let that stop him. As the giant king ran toward Piper, Percy grabbed the tip of Porphyrion's spear and forced it down into the ground. The giant's own momentum lifted him off his feet in an unintentional pole-vault maneuver and he flipped over onto his back.

Meanwhile Annabeth dragged herself across the dirt. Piper ran to her side. She stood over her friend, sweeping her blade back and forth to keep the giants at bay. Cold blue steam now wreathed her blade.

"Who wants to be the next Popsicle?" she yelled, channeling anger into her charmspeak. "Who wants to go back to Tartarus?"

That seemed to hit a nerve. The giants shuffled uneasily, glancing at the frozen body of Periboia.

And why shouldn't Piper intimidate them? Aphrodite was the most ancient Olympian, born of the sea and the blood of Ouranos. She was older than Poseidon or Athena or even Zeus. And Piper was her daughter.

More than that, she was a McLean. Her father had come from nothing. Now he was known all over the world. The McLeans didn't retreat. Like all Cherokee, they knew how to endure suffering, keep their pride, and when necessary, fight back. This was the time to fight back.

Forty feet away, Percy bent over the giant king, trying to yank a sword from the braids of his hair. But Porphyrion wasn't as stunned as he let on.

"Fools!" Porphyrion backhanded Percy like a pesky fly. The son of Poseidon flew into a column with a sickening *crunch.*

Porphyrion rose. "These demigods *cannot* kill us! They do not have the help of the gods. Remember who you are!"

The giants closed in. A dozen spears were pointed at Piper's chest.

Annabeth struggled to her feet. She retrieved Periboia's hunting knife, but she could barely stand upright, much less fight. Each time a drop of her blood hit the ground it bubbled, turning from red to gold.

Percy tried to stand, but he was obviously dazed. He wouldn't be able to defend himself.

Piper's only choice was to keep the giants focused on her.

"Come on, then!" she yelled. "I'll destroy you all myself if I have to!"

A metallic smell of storm filled the air. All the hairs on Piper's arms stood up.

"The thing is," said a voice from above, "you don't have to."

Piper's heart could've floated out of her body. At the top of the nearest colonnade stood Jason, his sword gleaming gold in the sun. Frank stood at his side, his bow ready. Hazel sat astride Arion, who reared and whinnied in challenge.

With a deafening blast, a white-hot bolt arced from the sky, straight through Jason's body as he leaped, wreathed in lightning, at the giant king.

# PIPER

FOR THE NEXT THREE MINUTES, LIFE WAS GREAT.

So much happened at once that only an ADHD demigod could have kept track.

Jason fell on King Porphyrion with such force that the giant crumpled to his knees—blasted with lightning and stabbed in the neck with a golden *gladius*.

Frank unleashed a hail of arrows, driving back the giants nearest to Percy.

The *Argo II* rose above the ruins and all the ballistae and catapults fired simultaneously. Leo must have programmed the weapons with surgical precision. A wall of Greek fire roared upward all around the Parthenon. It didn't touch the interior, but in a flash most of the smaller monsters around it were incinerated.

Leo's voice boomed over the loudspeaker: *SURRENDER! YOU ARE SURROUNDED BY ONE SPANKING HOT WAR MACHINE!*

The giant Enceladus howled in outrage. "Valdez!"

*WHAT'S UP, ENCHILADAS?* Leo's voice roared back. *NICE DAGGER IN YOUR FOREHEAD.*

"GAH!" The giant pulled Katoptris out of his head. "Monsters: destroy that ship!"

The remaining forces tried their best. A flock of gryphons rose to attack. Festus the figurehead blew flames and charbroiled them out of the sky. A few Earthborn launched a volley of rocks, but from the sides of the hull a dozen Archimedes spheres sprayed out, intercepting the boulders and blasting them to dust.

"PUT SOME CLOTHES ON!" Buford ordered.

Hazel spurred Arion off the colonnade and they leaped into battle. The forty-foot fall would have broken any other horse's legs, but Arion hit the ground running. Hazel zipped from giant to giant, stinging them with the blade of her *spatha*.

With extremely bad timing, Kekrops and his snake people chose that moment to join the fight. In four or five places around the ruins, the ground turned to green goo and armed *gemini* burst forth, Kekrops himself in the lead.

"Kill the demigods!" he hissed. "Kill the tricksters!"

Before many of his warriors could follow, Hazel pointed her blade at the nearest tunnel. The ground rumbled. All the gooey membranes popped and the tunnels collapsed, billowing plumes of dust. Kekrops looked around at his army, now reduced to six guys.

"SLITHER AWAY!" he ordered.

Frank's arrows cut them down as they tried to retreat.

The giantess Periboia had thawed with alarming speed.

She tried to grab Annabeth, but despite her bad leg, Annabeth was standing her ground. She stabbed at the giantess with her own hunting knife and led her in a deadly game of tag around the throne.

Percy was back on his feet, Riptide once again in his hands. He still looked dazed. His nose was bleeding. But he seemed to be holding his own against the old giant Thoon, who had somehow reattached his hand and found his meat cleaver.

Piper stood back to back with Jason, fighting every giant who dared to come close. For a moment she felt elated. They were actually winning!

But too soon, their element of surprise faded. The giants overcame their confusion.

Frank ran out of arrows. He changed into a rhinoceros and leaped into battle, but as fast as he could knock down the giants, they got up again. Their wounds seemed to be healing faster.

Annabeth lost ground against Periboia. Hazel was knocked out of her saddle at sixty miles an hour. Jason summoned another lightning strike, but this time Porphyrion simply deflected it off the tip of his spear.

The giants were bigger, stronger, and more numerous. They couldn't be killed without the help of the gods. And they didn't seem to be tiring.

The six demigods were forced into a defensive ring.

Another volley of Earthborn rocks hit the *Argo II.* This time Leo couldn't return fire fast enough. Rows of oars were sheared off. The ship shuddered and tilted in the sky.

Then Enceladus threw his fiery spear. It pierced the ship's

hull and exploded inside, sending spouts of fire through the oar openings. An ominous black cloud billowed from the deck. The *Argo II* began to sink.

"Leo!" Jason cried.

Porphyrion laughed. "You demigods have learned nothing. There are no gods to aid you. We need only one more thing from you to make our victory complete."

The giant king smiled expectantly. He seemed to be looking at Percy Jackson.

Piper glanced over. Percy's nose was still bleeding. He seemed unaware that a trickle of blood had made its way down his face to the end of his chin.

"Percy, look out . . ." Piper tried to say, but for once her voice failed her.

A single drop of blood fell from his chin. It hit the ground between his feet and sizzled like water on a frying pan.

The blood of Olympus watered the ancient stones.

The Acropolis groaned and shifted as the Earth Mother woke.

# X L V

# NICO

**ABOUT FIVE MILES EAST OF CAMP,** a black SUV was parked on the beach.

They tied up the boat at a private dock. Nico helped Dakota and Leila haul Michael Kahale ashore. The big guy was still only half-conscious, mumbling what Nico assumed were football calls: "Red twelve. Right thirty-one. Hike." Then he giggled uncontrollably.

"We'll leave him here," Leila said. "Just don't bind him. Poor guy . . ."

"What about the car?" Dakota asked. "The keys are in the glove compartment, but, uh, can you drive?"

Leila frowned. "I thought *you* could drive. Aren't you seventeen?"

"I never learned!" Dakota said. "I was busy."

"I've got it covered," Nico promised.

They both looked at him.

"You're, like, fourteen," Leila said.

Nico enjoyed how nervous the Romans acted around him, even though they were older and bigger and more experienced fighters. "I didn't say I would be behind the wheel."

He knelt and placed his hand on the ground. He felt the nearest graves, the bones of forgotten humans buried and scattered. He searched deeper, extending his senses into the Underworld. "Jules-Albert. Let's go."

The ground split. A zombie in a ragged nineteenth-century motoring outfit clawed his way to the surface. Leila stepped back. Dakota screamed like a kindergartner.

"What is *that*, man?" Dakota protested.

"This is my driver," Nico said. "Jules-Albert finished first in the Paris-Rouen motorcar race back in 1895, but he wasn't awarded the prize because his steam car used a stoker."

Leila stared at him. "What are you even talking about?"

"He's a restless soul, always looking for another chance to drive," Nico said. "The last few years, he's been my driver whenever I need one."

"You have a zombie chauffeur," Leila said.

"I call shotgun." Nico got in on the passenger's side. Reluctantly, the Romans climbed in back.

One thing about Jules-Albert: he never got emotional. He could sit in crosstown traffic all day without losing his patience. He was immune to road rage. He could even drive straight up to an encampment of wild centaurs and navigate through them without getting nervous.

The centaurs were like nothing Nico had ever seen. They

had back ends like palominos, tattoos all over their hairy arms and chests, and bullish horns protruding from their foreheads. Nico doubted they could blend in with humans as easily as Chiron did.

At least two hundred were sparring restlessly with swords and spears, or roasting animal carcasses over open fires (carnivorous centaurs . . . the idea made Nico shudder). Their camp spilled across the farm road that meandered around Camp Half-Blood's southeast perimeter.

The SUV nudged its way through, honking when necessary. Occasionally a centaur glared through the driver's side window, saw the zombie driver, and backed away in shock.

"Pluto's pauldrons," Dakota muttered. "Even more centaurs arrived overnight."

"Don't make eye contact," Leila warned. "They take that as a challenge for a duel to the death."

Nico stared straight ahead as the SUV pushed through. His heart was pounding, but he wasn't scared. He was angry. Octavian had surrounded Camp Half-Blood with monsters.

Sure, Nico had mixed emotions about the camp. He'd felt rejected there, out of place, unwanted and unloved . . . but now that it was on the verge of destruction, he realized how much it meant to him. This was the last place Bianca and he had shared as a home—the only place they'd ever felt safe, even if only temporarily.

They rounded a bend in the road and Nico's fists clenched. More monsters . . . *hundreds* more. Dog-headed men prowled in packs, their poleaxes gleaming in the light of campfires.

Beyond that milled a tribe of two-headed men dressed in rags and blankets like homeless guys, armed with a haphazard collection of slings, clubs, and metal pipes.

"Octavian is an idiot," Nico hissed. "He thinks he can control these creatures?"

"They just kept showing up," Leila said. "Before we knew it . . . well, look."

The legion was arrayed at the base of Half-Blood Hill, its five cohorts in perfect order, its standards bright and proud. Giant eagles circled overhead. The siege weapons—six golden onagers the size of houses—were arrayed behind in a loose semicircle, three on each flank. But for all its impressive discipline, the Twelfth Legion looked pitifully small, a splotch of demigod valor in a sea of ravenous monsters.

Nico wished he still had the scepter of Diocletian, but he doubted a legion of dead warriors would make a dent in this army. Even the *Argo II* couldn't do much against this kind of strength.

"I have to disable the onagers," Nico said. "We don't have much time."

"You'll never get close to them," Leila warned. "Even if we get the entire Fourth and Fifth Cohorts to follow us, the other cohorts will try to stop us. And those siege weapons are manned by Octavian's most loyal followers."

"We won't get close by force," Nico agreed. "But alone, I can do it. Dakota, Leila—Jules-Albert will drive you to the legion lines. Get out, talk to your troops, convince them to follow your lead. I'll need a distraction."

Dakota frowned. "All right, but I'm not hurting any of my fellow legionnaires."

"No one's asking you to," Nico growled. "But if we don't stop this war, the *entire* legion will be wiped out. You said the monster tribes take insult easily?"

"Yes," Dakota said. "I mean, for instance, you make *any* comment to those two-headed guys about the way they smell and . . . oh." He grinned. "If we started a brawl, by accident of course . . ."

"I'll be counting on you," Nico said.

Leila frowned. "But how will you—"

"I'm going dark," Nico said. And he faded into the shadows.

He thought he was prepared.

He wasn't.

Even after three days of rest and the wondrous healing properties of Coach Hedge's gooey brown gunk, Nico started to dissolve the moment he shadow-jumped.

His limbs turned to vapor. Cold seeped into his chest. Voices of spirits whispered in his ears: *Help us. Remember us. Join us.*

He hadn't realized how much he had relied on Reyna. Without her strength, he felt as weak as a newborn colt, wobbling dangerously, ready to fall at every step.

*No,* he told himself. *I am Nico di Angelo, son of Hades. I control the shadows. They do not control me.*

He stumbled back into the mortal world at the crest of Half-Blood Hill.

He fell to his knees, hugging Thalia's pine tree for support. The Golden Fleece was no longer in its branches. The guardian dragon was gone. Perhaps they'd been moved to a safer spot with the battle so close. Nico wasn't sure. But looking down at the Roman forces arrayed outside the valley, his spirits wavered.

The nearest onager was a hundred yards downhill, encircled in spiked trenches and guarded by a dozen demigods. The machine was primed, ready to fire. Its huge sling cupped a projectile the size of a Honda Civic, glowing with flecks of gold.

With icy certainty, Nico realized what Octavian was up to. The projectile was a mixture of incendiaries and Imperial gold. Even a small amount of Imperial gold could be incredibly volatile. Exposed to too much heat or pressure, the stuff would explode with devastating impact, and of course it was deadly to demigods as well as monsters. If that onager scored a hit on Camp Half-Blood, anything in the blast zone would be annihilated—vaporized by the heat, or disintegrated by the shrapnel. And the Romans had six onagers, all stocked with piles of ammunition.

"Evil," Nico said. "This is evil."

He tried to think. Dawn was breaking. He couldn't possibly take down all six weapons before the attack began, even if he found the strength to shadow-travel that many times. If he managed it once more, it would be a miracle.

He spotted the Roman command tent—behind and to the left of the legion. Octavian would probably be there, enjoying breakfast at a safe distance from the fighting. He wouldn't lead his troops into battle. The little scumbag would hope to destroy the Greek camp from a distance, wait for the flames to die down, then march in unopposed.

Nico's throat constricted with hate. He concentrated on that tent, envisioning his next jump. If he could assassinate Octavian, that might solve the problem. The order to attack might never be given. Nico was about to attempt it when a voice behind him said, "Nico?"

He spun, his sword instantly in his hand, and almost decapitated Will Solace.

"Put that down!" Will hissed. "What are you *doing* here?"

Nico was dumbstruck. Will and two other campers were crouched in the grass, binoculars around their necks and daggers at their side. They wore black jeans and T-shirts, with black grease paint on their faces like commandos.

*"Me?"* Nico asked. "What are *you* doing? Getting yourselves killed?"

Will scowled. "Hey, we're scouting the enemy. We took precautions."

"You dressed in black," Nico noted, "with the sun coming up. You painted your face but didn't cover that mop of blond hair. You might as well be waving a yellow flag."

Will's ears reddened. "Lou Ellen wrapped some Mist around us too."

"Hi." The girl next to him wriggled her fingers. She looked a little flustered. "You're Nico, right? I've heard a lot about you. And this is Cecil from Hermes cabin."

Nico knelt next to them. "Did Coach Hedge make it to camp?"

Lou Ellen giggled nervously. "Did he *ever.*"

Will elbowed her. "Yeah. Hedge is fine. He made it just in time for the baby's birth."

"The baby!" Nico grinned, which hurt his face muscles. He wasn't used to making that expression. "Mellie and the kid are all right?"

"Fine. A very cute little satyr boy." Will shuddered. "But I delivered it. Have you ever delivered a baby?"

"Um, no."

"I had to get some fresh air. That's why I volunteered for this mission. Gods of Olympus, my hands are still shaking. See?"

He took Nico's hand, which sent an electric current down Nico's spine. He quickly withdrew. "Whatever," he snapped. "We don't have time for chitchat. The Romans are attacking at dawn and I've got to—"

"We know," Will said. "But if you're planning to shadow-travel to that command tent, forget it."

Nico glared at him. "Excuse me?"

He expected Will to flinch or look away. Most people did. But Will's blue eyes stayed fixed on his—annoyingly determined. "Coach Hedge told me all about your shadow-travel. You *can't* try that again."

"I just *did* try it again, Solace. I'm fine."

"No, you're not. I'm a healer. I could feel the darkness in your hand as soon as I touched it. Even if you made it to that tent, you'd be in no shape to fight. But you *wouldn't* make it. One more slip, and you won't come back. You are *not* shadow-traveling. Doctor's orders."

"The camp is about to be destroyed—"

"And we'll stop the Romans," Will said. "But we'll do it our way. Lou Ellen will control the Mist. We'll sneak around, do as much damage as we can to those onagers. But *no* shadow-travel."

"But—"

"*No.*"

Lou Ellen's and Cecil's heads swiveled back and forth like they were watching a really intense tennis match.

Nico sighed in exasperation. He hated working with other people. They were always cramping his style, making him uncomfortable. And Will Solace . . . Nico revised his impression of the son of Apollo. He'd always thought of Will as easygoing and laid back. Apparently he could also be stubborn and aggravating.

Nico gazed down at Camp Half-Blood, where the rest of the Greeks were preparing for war. Past the troops and ballistae, the canoe lake glittered pink in the first light of dawn. Nico remembered the first time he'd arrived at Camp Half-Blood, crash-landing in Apollo's sun car, which had been converted into a fiery school bus.

He remembered Apollo, smiling and tan and completely cool in his shades.

Thalia had said, *He's hot.*

*He's the sun god,* Percy replied.

*That's not what I meant.*

Why was Nico thinking about that now? The random memory irritated him, made him feel jittery.

He had arrived at Camp Half-Blood thanks to Apollo.

Now, on what would likely be his last day at camp, he was stuck with a son of Apollo.

"Whatever," Nico said. "But we have to hurry. And you'll follow *my* lead."

"Fine," Will said. "Just don't ask me to deliver any more satyr babies and we'll get along great."

# XLVI

# NICO

**THEY MADE IT TO THE FIRST ONAGER** just as chaos broke loose in the legion.

On the far end of the line, cries went up from the Fifth Cohort. Legionnaires scattered and dropped their *pila*. A dozen centaurs barreled through the ranks, yelling and waving their clubs, followed by a horde of two-headed men banging on trash can lids.

"What's going on down there?" Lou Ellen asked.

"That's my distraction," Nico said. "Come on."

All the guards had clustered on the right side of the onager, trying to see what was going on down the ranks, which gave Nico and his comrades a clear shot to the left. They passed within a few feet of the nearest Roman, but the legionnaire didn't notice them. Lou Ellen's Mist magic seemed to be working.

They jumped the spiked trench and reached the machine.

"I brought some Greek fire," Cecil whispered.

"No," Nico said. "If we make the damage too obvious, we'll never get to the other ones in time. Can you recalibrate the aim—like, toward the other onagers' firing lines?"

Cecil grinned. "Oh, I like the way you think. They sent me because I excel at messing things up."

He went to work while Nico and the others stood guard.

Meanwhile the Fifth Cohort was brawling with the two-headed men. The Fourth Cohort moved in to help. The other three cohorts held their positions, but the officers were having trouble keeping order.

"All right," Cecil announced. "Let's move."

They shuffled across the hillside toward the next onager.

This time the Mist didn't work so well. One of the onager guards yelled, "Hey!"

"Got this." Will sprinted off—which was possibly the stupidest diversion Nico could imagine—and six of the guards chased after him.

The other Romans advanced on Nico, but Lou Ellen appeared out of the Mist and yelled, "Hey, catch!"

She lobbed a white ball the size of an apple. The Roman in the middle caught it instinctively. A twenty-foot sphere of powder exploded outward. When the dust settled, all six Romans were squealing pink piglets.

"Nice work," Nico said.

Lou Ellen blushed. "Well, it's the only pig ball I have. So don't ask for an encore."

"And, uh"—Cecil pointed—"somebody better help Will."

Even in their armor, the Romans were starting to gain on Solace. Nico cursed and raced after them.

He didn't want to kill other demigods if he could avoid it. Fortunately, he didn't need to. He tripped the Roman in the back and the others turned. Nico jumped into the crowd, kicking groins, smacking faces with the flat of his blade, bashing helmets with his pommel. In ten seconds, the Romans all lay groaning and dazed on the ground.

Will punched his shoulder. "Thanks for the assist. Six at once isn't bad."

*"Not bad?"* Nico glared at him. "Next time I'll just let them run you down, Solace."

"Ah, they'd never catch me."

Cecil waved at them from the onager, signaling that his job was done.

They all moved toward the third siege machine.

In the legion ranks, everything was still in chaos, but the officers were starting to reassert control. The Fifth and Fourth Cohorts regrouped while the Second and Third acted as riot police, shoving centaurs and *cynocephali* and two-headed men back into their respective camps. The First Cohort stood closest to the onager—a little *too* close for Nico's comfort—but they seemed occupied by a couple of officers parading in front of them, shouting orders.

Nico hoped they could sneak up on the third siege machine. One more onager redirected and they might stand a chance.

Unfortunately, the guards spotted them from twenty yards away. One yelled, "There!"

Lou Ellen cursed. "They're *expecting* an attack now. The Mist doesn't work well against alert enemies. Do we run?"

"No," Nico said. "Let's give them what they expect."

He spread his hands. In front of the Romans, the ground erupted. Five skeletons clawed out of the earth. Cecil and Lou Ellen charged in to help. Nico tried to follow, but he would've fallen on his face if Will hadn't caught him.

"You idiot." Will put an arm around him. "I told you no more of that Underworld magic."

"I'm fine."

"Shut up. You're not." From his pocket, Will dug out a pack of gum.

Nico wanted to pull away. He hated physical contact. But Will was a lot stronger than he looked. Nico found himself leaning against him, relying on his support.

"Take this," Will said.

"You want me to chew gum?"

"It's medicinal. Should keep you alive and alert for a few more hours."

Nico shoved a stick of gum into his mouth. "Tastes like tar and dirt."

"Stop complaining."

"Hey." Cecil limped over, looking like he'd pulled a muscle. "You guys kind of missed the fight."

Lou Ellen followed, grinning. Behind them, all the Roman guards were tangled in a weird assortment of ropes and bones.

"Thanks for the skeletons," she said. "Great trick."

"Which he *won't* be doing again," Will said.

Nico realized he was still leaning against Will. He pushed him away and stood on his own two feet. "I'll do what I need to."

Will rolled his eyes. "Fine, Death Boy. If you want to get yourself killed—"

"Do *not* call me *Death Boy!*"

Lou Ellen cleared her throat. "Um, guys—"

"DROP YOUR WEAPONS!"

Nico turned. The fight at the third onager had not gone unnoticed.

The entire First Cohort was advancing on them, spears leveled, shields locked. In front of them marched Octavian, purple robes over his armor, Imperial gold jewelry glittering on his neck and arms, and a crown of laurels on his head as if he'd already won the battle. Next to him was the legion's standard-bearer, Jacob, holding the golden eagle, and six huge *cynocephali*, their canine teeth bared, their swords glowing red.

"Well," Octavian snarled, "*Graecus* saboteurs." He turned to his dog-headed warriors. "Tear them apart."

# XLVII

# NICO

NICO WASN'T SURE whether to kick himself or Will Solace.

If he hadn't been so distracted bickering with the son of Apollo, he would never have allowed the enemy to get so close.

As the dog-headed men barreled forward, Nico raised his sword. He doubted he had the strength left to win, but before he could attack them, Will let out a piercing taxicab whistle.

All six dog-men dropped their weapons, grabbed their ears, and fell down in agony.

"Dude." Cecil opened his mouth to pop his ears. "What the actual Hades? A little warning next time."

"It's even worse for the dogs." Will shrugged. "One of my few musical talents. I do a really *awful* ultrasonic whistle."

Nico didn't complain. He waded through the dog-men, jabbing them with his sword. They dissolved into shadows.

Octavian and the other Romans seemed too stunned to react.

"My—my elite guard!" Octavian looked around for sympathy. "Did you *see* what he did to my elite guard?"

"Some dogs need to be put down." Nico took a step forward. "Like you."

For one beautiful moment, the entire First Cohort wavered. Then they remembered themselves and leveled their *pila.*

"You will be destroyed!" Octavian shrieked. "You *Graeci* sneak around, sabotaging our weapons, attacking our men—"

"You mean the weapons you were about to fire at us?" Cecil asked.

"And the men who were about to burn our camp to ashes?" added Lou Ellen.

"Just like a Greek!" Octavian yelled. "Trying to twist things around! Well, it won't work!" He pointed to the nearest legionnaires. "You, you, you, and you. Check all the onagers. Make sure they're operational. I want them fired simultaneously as soon as possible. Go!"

The four Romans ran.

Nico tried to keep his expression neutral.

Please don't check the firing trajectory, he thought.

He hoped Cecil had done his work well. It was one thing to screw up a huge weapon. It was another thing to screw it up so subtly that no one noticed until it was too late. But if anyone had that skill, it would be a child of Hermes, god of trickery.

Octavian marched up to Nico. To his credit, the augur didn't seem afraid, though his only weapon was a dagger. He stopped so close, Nico could see the bloodshot veins in his pale watery eyes. His face was gaunt. His hair was the color of overcooked spaghetti.

Nico knew Octavian was a legacy—a descendant of Apollo many generations removed. Now, he couldn't help thinking that Octavian looked like a watered-down, unhealthy version of Will Solace—like a photo that had been copied too many times. Whatever made a child of Apollo special, Octavian didn't have it.

"Tell me, son of Pluto," the augur hissed, "why are you helping the Greeks? What have they ever done for you?"

Nico was itching to stab Octavian in the chest. He'd been dreaming of that ever since Bryce Lawrence had attacked them in South Carolina. But now that they were face-to-face, Nico hesitated. He had no doubt he could kill Octavian before the First Cohort intervened. Nor did Nico particularly care if he died for his actions. The trade-off would be worth it.

But, after what happened with Bryce, the idea of cutting down another demigod in cold blood—even Octavian— didn't sit well. Nor did it seem right to sentence Cecil, Lou Ellen, and Will to die with him.

It doesn't seem *right*? Another part of him wondered, *Since when do I worry about what's right?*

"I'm helping the Greeks *and* the Romans," Nico said.

Octavian laughed. "Don't try to con me. What have they offered you—a place in their camp? They won't honor their agreement."

"I don't *want* a place in their camp," Nico snarled. "Or in yours. When this war is over, I'm leaving both camps for good."

Will Solace made a sound like he'd been punched. "Why would you do that?"

Nico scowled. "It's none of your business, but I don't belong. That's obvious. No one wants me. I'm a child of—"

"Oh, please." Will sounded unusually angry. "Nobody at Camp Half-Blood ever pushed you away. You have friends— or at least, people who would *like* to be your friend. You pushed yourself away. If you'd get your head out of that brooding cloud of yours for once—"

"Enough!" Octavian snapped. "Di Angelo, I can beat any offer the Greeks could make. I always thought you would make a powerful ally. I see the ruthlessness in you, and I appreciate that. I can assure you a place in New Rome. All you have to do is step aside and allow the Romans to win. The god Apollo has shown me the future—"

"No!" Will Solace shoved Nico out of the way and got in Octavian's face. "*I* am a son of Apollo, you anemic loser. My father hasn't shown anyone the future, because the power of prophecy isn't working. But this—" He waved loosely at the assembled legion, the hordes of monstrous armies spread across the hillside. "This is *not* what Apollo would want!"

Octavian's lip curled. "You lie. The god told me *personally* that I would be remembered as the savior of Rome. I will lead the legion to victory, and I will start by—"

Nico felt the sound before he heard it—*thunk-thunk-thunk* reverberating through the earth, like the massive gears of a drawbridge. All the onagers fired at once, and six golden comets billowed into the sky.

"By destroying the Greeks!" Octavian cried with glee. "The days of Camp Half-Blood are over!"

• • •

Nico couldn't think of anything more beautiful than an off-course projectile. At least, not today. From the three sabotaged machines, the payloads veered sideways, arcing toward the barrage from the other three onagers.

The fireballs didn't collide directly. They didn't need to. As soon as the missiles got close to one another, all six warheads detonated in midair, spraying a dome of gold and fire that sucked the oxygen right out of the sky.

The heat stung Nico's face. The grass hissed. The tops of the trees steamed. But when the fireworks faded, no serious damage had been done.

Octavian reacted first. He stomped his feet and yelled, "NO! NO, NO! RELOAD!"

No one in the First Cohort moved. Nico heard the tromping of boots to his right. The Fifth Cohort was marching toward them double-time, Dakota in the lead.

Further downhill, the rest of the legion was trying to form up, but the Second, Third, and Fourth Cohorts were now surrounded by a sea of ill-tempered monstrous allies. The *auxilia* forces didn't look happy about the explosion overhead. No doubt they'd been waiting for Camp Half-Blood to go up in flames so they'd get charbroiled demigod for breakfast.

"Octavian!" Dakota called. "We have new orders."

Octavian's left eye twitched so violently it looked like it might explode. "Orders? From whom? Not from me!"

"From Reyna," Dakota said, loud enough to make sure everyone in the First Cohort could hear. "She's ordered us to stand down."

"Reyna?" Octavian laughed, though no one seemed to get

the joke. "You mean the outlaw I sent you to arrest? The *ex-praetor* who conspired to betray her own people with this *Graecus*?" He jabbed his finger in Nico's chest. "You're taking orders from her?"

The Fifth Cohort formed up behind their centurion, uneasily facing their comrades in the First.

Dakota crossed his arms stubbornly. "Reyna is the praetor until voted otherwise by the Senate."

"This is war!" Octavian yelled. "I've brought you to the brink of ultimate victory and you want to give up? First Cohort: arrest Centurion Dakota and any who stand with him. Fifth Cohort: remember your vows to Rome and the legion. You will obey *me*!"

Will Solace shook his head. "Don't do this, Octavian. Don't force your people to choose. This is your last chance."

"*My* last chance?" Octavian grinned, madness glinting in his eyes. "I will SAVE ROME! Now, Romans, follow my orders! Arrest Dakota. Destroy these *Graecus* scum. And reload those onagers!"

What the Romans would have done left to their own devices, Nico didn't know.

But he hadn't counted on the Greeks.

At that moment, the entire army of Camp Half-Blood appeared on the crest of Half-Blood Hill. Clarisse La Rue rode in the lead, on a red war chariot pulled by metal horses. A hundred demigods fanned out around her, with twice that many satyrs and nature spirits led by Grover Underwood. Tyson lumbered forward with six other Cyclopes. Chiron stood in full white stallion mode, his bow drawn.

It was an impressive sight, but all Nico could think was: *No. Not now.*

Clarisse yelled, "Romans, you have fired on our camp! Withdraw or be destroyed!"

Octavian wheeled on his troops. "You see? It was a trick! They divided us so they could launch a surprise attack. Legion, *cuneum formate*! CHARGE!"

# XLVIII

# NICO

NICO WANTED TO YELL: *Time out! Hold it! Freeze!*

But he knew it wouldn't do any good. After weeks of waiting, agonizing, and steaming, the Greeks and Romans wanted blood. Trying to stop the battle now would be like trying to push back a flood after the dam broke.

Will Solace saved the day.

He put his fingers in his mouth and did a taxicab whistle even more horrible than the last. Several Greeks dropped their swords. A ripple went through the Roman line like the entire First Cohort was shuddering.

"DON'T BE STUPID!" Will yelled. "LOOK!"

He pointed to the north, and Nico grinned from ear to ear. He decided there *was* something more beautiful than an off-course projectile: the Athena Parthenos gleaming in the sunrise, flying in from the coast, suspended from the tethers of six winged horses. Roman eagles circled but did not attack. A few of them even swooped in, grabbed the cables, and helped carry the statue.

Nico didn't see Blackjack, which worried him, but Reyna Ramírez-Arellano rode on Guido's back. Her sword was held high. Her purple cloak glittered strangely, catching the sunlight.

Both armies stared, dumbfounded, as the forty-foot-tall gold and ivory statue came in for a landing.

"GREEK DEMIGODS!" Reyna's voice boomed as if projected from the statue itself, like the Athena Parthenos had become a stack of concert speakers. "Behold your most sacred statue, the Athena Parthenos, wrongly taken by the Romans. I return it to you now as a gesture of peace!"

The statue settled on the crest of the hill, about twenty feet away from Thalia's pine tree. Instantly gold light rippled across the ground, into the valley of Camp Half-Blood and down the opposite side through the Roman ranks. Warmth seeped into Nico's bones—a comforting, peaceful sensation he hadn't had since . . . he couldn't even remember. A voice inside him seemed to whisper: *You are not alone. You are part of the Olympian family. The gods have not abandoned you.*

"Romans!" Reyna yelled. "I do this for the good of the legion, for the good of Rome. We must stand together with our Greek brethren!"

"Listen to her!" Nico marched forward.

He wasn't even sure why he did it. Why would either side listen to him? He was the worst speaker, the worst ambassador ever.

Yet he strode between the battle lines, his black sword in

his hand. "Reyna risked her life for all of you! We brought this statue halfway across the world, Roman and Greek working together, because we *must* join forces. Gaea is rising. If we don't work together—"

*YOU WILL DIE.*

The voice shook the earth. Nico's feeling of peace and safety instantly vanished. Wind swept across the hillside. The ground itself became fluid and sticky, the grass pulling at Nico's boots.

*A FUTILE GESTURE.*

Nico felt as if he was standing on the goddess's throat—as if the entire length of Long Island resonated with her vocal cords.

*BUT IF IT MAKES YOU HAPPY, YOU MAY DIE TOGETHER.*

"No . . ." Octavian scrambled backward. "No, no . . ." He broke and ran, pushing through his own troops.

"CLOSE RANKS!" Reyna yelled.

The Greeks and Romans moved together, standing shoulder to shoulder as all around them the earth shook.

Octavian's *auxilia* troops surged forward, surrounding the demigods. Both camps put together were a minuscule dot in a sea of enemies. They would make their final stand on Half-Blood Hill, with the Athena Parthenos as their rallying point.

But even here, they stood on enemy ground. Because Gaea *was* the earth, and the earth was awake.

# XLIX

# JASON

JASON HAD HEARD OF someone's life flashing before his eyes. But he didn't think it would be like this.

Standing with his friends in a defensive ring, surrounded by giants, then looking up at an impossible vision in the sky—Jason could very clearly picture himself fifty years in the future.

He was sitting in a rocking chair on the front porch of a house on the California coast. Piper was serving lemonade. Her hair was gray. Deep lines etched the corners of her eyes, but she was still as beautiful as ever. Jason's grandchildren sat around his feet, and he was trying to explain to them what had happened on this day in Athens.

*No, I'm serious,* he said. *Just six demigods on the ground, and one more in a burning ship above the Acropolis. We were surrounded by thirty-foot-tall giants who were about to kill us. Then the sky opened up, and the gods descended!*

*Granddad,* the kids said, *you are full of schist.*

*I'm not kidding!* he protested. *The Olympian gods came charging out of the heavens on their war chariots, trumpets blaring, swords flaming. And your great-grandfather, the king of the gods, led the charge, a javelin of pure electricity crackling in his hand!*

His grandkids laughed at him. And Piper glanced over, smiling, like *Would* you *believe it, if you hadn't been there?*

But Jason *was* there. He looked up as the clouds parted over the Acropolis, and he almost doubted the new prescription lenses Asclepius had given him. Instead of blue skies, he saw black space spangled with stars, the palaces of Mount Olympus gleaming silver and gold in the background. And an army of gods charged down from on high.

It was too much to process. And it was probably better for his health that he didn't see it all. Only later would Jason be able to remember bits and pieces.

There was supersized Jupiter—no, this was *Zeus*, his original form—riding into battle in a golden chariot, a lightning bolt the size of a telephone pole crackling in one hand. Pulling his chariot were four horses made of wind, each constantly shifting from equine to human form, trying to break free. For a split second, one took on the icy visage of Boreas. Another wore Notus's swirling crown of fire and steam. A third flashed the smug lazy smile of Zephyrus. Zeus had bound and harnessed the four wind gods themselves.

On the underbelly of the *Argo II*, the glass bay doors split open. The goddess Nike tumbled out, free from her golden net. She spread her glittering wings and soared to Zeus's side, taking her rightful place as his charioteer.

"MY MIND IS RESTORED!" she roared. "VICTORY TO THE GODS!"

At Zeus's left flank rode Hera, her chariot pulled by enormous peacocks, their rainbow-colored plumage so bright it gave Jason the spins.

Ares bellowed with glee as he thundered down on the back of a fire-breathing horse. His spear glistened red.

In the last second, before the gods reached the Parthenon, they seemed to displace themselves, like they'd jumped through hyperspace. The chariots disappeared. Suddenly Jason and his friends were surrounded by the Olympians, now human-sized, tiny next to the giants, but glowing with power.

Jason shouted and charged Porphyrion.

His friends joined in the carnage.

The fighting ranged all over the Parthenon and spilled across the Acropolis. Out of the corner of his eye, Jason saw Annabeth fighting Enceladus. At her side stood a woman with long dark hair and golden armor over her white robes. The goddess thrust her spear at the giant, then brandished her shield with the fearsome bronzed visage of Medusa. Together, Athena and Annabeth drove Enceladus back into the nearest wall of metal scaffolding, which collapsed on top of him.

On the opposite side of the temple, Frank Zhang and the god Ares smashed through an entire phalanx of giants—Ares with his spear and shield, Frank (as an African elephant) with his trunk and feet. The war god laughed and stabbed and disemboweled like a kid destroying piñatas.

Hazel raced through the battle on Arion's back,

disappearing in the Mist whenever a giant came close, then appearing behind him and stabbing him in the back. The goddess Hecate danced in her wake, setting fire to their enemies with two blazing torches. Jason didn't see Hades, but whenever a giant stumbled and fell, the ground broke open and the giant was snapped up and swallowed.

Percy battled the giant twins, Otis and Ephialtes, while at his side fought a bearded man with a trident and a loud Hawaiian shirt. The twin giants stumbled. Poseidon's trident morphed into a fire hose, and the god sprayed the giants out of the Parthenon with a high-powered blast in the shape of wild horses.

Piper was maybe the most impressive. She fenced with the giantess Periboia, sword against sword. Despite the fact that her opponent was five times larger, Piper seemed to be holding her own. The goddess Aphrodite floated around them on a small white cloud, strewing rose petals in the giantess's eyes and calling encouragement to Piper. "Lovely, my dear. Yes, good. Hit her again!"

Whenever Periboia tried to strike, doves rose up from nowhere and fluttered in the giantess's face.

As for Leo, he was racing across the deck of the *Argo II*, shooting ballistae, dropping hammers on the giants' heads, and blowtorching their loincloths. Behind him at the helm, a burly bearded guy in a mechanic's uniform was tinkering with the controls, furiously trying to keep the ship aloft.

The strangest sight was the old giant Thoon, who was getting bludgeoned to death by three old ladies with brass clubs—the Fates, armed for war. Jason decided there was nothing in the world scarier than a gang of bat-wielding grannies.

He noticed all of these things, and a dozen other melees in progress, but most of his attention was fixed on the enemy before him—Porphyrion, the giant king—and on the god who fought by Jason's side: Zeus.

*My father,* Jason thought in disbelief.

Porphyrion didn't give him much chance to savor the moment. The giant used his spear in a whirlwind of swipes, jabs, and slashes. It was all Jason could do to stay alive.

Still . . . Zeus's presence felt reassuringly familiar. Even though Jason had never met his father, he was reminded of all his happiest moments—his birthday picnic with Piper in Rome; the day Lupa showed him Camp Jupiter for the first time; his games of hide-and-seek with Thalia in their apartment when he was tiny; an afternoon on the beach when his mother had picked him up, kissed him, and showed him an oncoming storm. *Never be afraid of a thunderstorm, Jason. That is your father, letting you know he loves you.*

Zeus smelled of rain and clean wind. He made the air burn with energy. Up close, his lightning bolt appeared as a bronze rod a meter long, pointed on both ends, with blades of energy extending from both sides to form a javelin of white electricity. He slashed across the giant's path and Porphyrion collapsed into his makeshift throne, which crumbled under the giant's weight.

"No throne for you," Zeus growled. "Not here. Not *ever.*"

"You *cannot* stop us!" the giant yelled. "It is *done*! The Earth Mother is awake!"

In answer, Zeus blasted the throne to rubble. The giant king flew backward out of the temple and Jason ran after him, his father at his heels.

They backed Porphyrion to the edge of the cliffs, the whole of modern Athens spread out below. Lightning had melted all the weapons in the giant's hair. Molten Celestial bronze dripped through his dreadlocks like caramel. His skin steamed and blistered.

Porphyrion snarled and raised his spear. "Your cause is lost, Zeus. Even if you defeat me, the Earth Mother shall simply raise me again!"

"Then perhaps," Zeus said, "you should not die in the embrace of Gaea. Jason, my son . . ."

Jason had never felt so good, so *recognized*, as when he father said his name. It was like last winter at Camp Half-Blood, when his erased memories finally returned. Jason suddenly understood another layer of his existence—a part of his identity that had been cloudy before.

Now he had no doubt: he was the son of Jupiter, god of the sky. He was his father's child.

Jason advanced.

Porphyrion lashed out wildly with his spear, but Jason cut it in half with his *gladius*. He charged in, jabbing his sword through the giant's breastplate, then summoned the winds and blasted Porphyrion off the edge of the cliff.

As the giant fell, screaming, Zeus pointed his lightning

bolt. An arc of pure white heat vaporized Porphyrion in mid-air. His ashes drifted down in a gentle cloud, dusting the tops of the olive trees on the slopes of the Acropolis.

Zeus turned to Jason. His lightning bolt flickered off, and Zeus clipped the Celestial bronze rod to his belt. The god's eyes were stormy gray. His salt-and-pepper hair and his beard looked like stratus clouds. Jason found it strange that the lord of the universe, king of Olympus, was only a few inches taller than he was.

"My son." Zeus clasped Jason's shoulder. "There is so much I would like to tell you . . ."

The god took a heavy breath, making the air crackle and Jason's new glasses fog up. "Alas, as king of the gods, I must not show favoritism to my children. When we return to the other Olympians, I will not be able to praise you as much as I would like, or give you as much credit as you deserve."

"I don't want praise." Jason's voice quavered. "Just a little time together would be nice. I mean, I don't even know you."

Zeus's gaze was as far away as the ozone layer. "I am always with you, Jason. I have watched your progress with pride, but it will never be possible for us to be . . ."

He curled his fingers, as if trying to pluck the right words out of the air. *Close. Normal. A true father and son.* "From birth, you were destined to be Hera's—to appease her wrath. Even your name, Jason, was her choice. You did not ask for this. I did not want it. But when I gave you over to her . . . I had no idea what a good man you would become. Your journey has shaped you, made you both kind and great. Whatever happens when we return to the Parthenon, know that I do *not* hold you accountable. You have proven yourself a true hero."

Jason's emotions were a jumble in his chest. "What do you mean . . . *whatever happens?*"

"The worst is not over," Zeus warned. "And someone must take the blame for what has happened. Come."

# L

# JASON

NOTHING WAS LEFT OF THE GIANTS except heaps of ash, a few spears, and some burning dreadlocks.

The *Argo II* was still aloft, barely, moored to the top of the Parthenon. Half the ship's oars were broken off or tangled. Smoke streamed from several large splits in the hull. The sails were peppered with burning holes.

Leo looked almost as bad. He stood in the midst of the temple with the other crewmembers, his face covered in soot, his clothes smoldering.

The gods fanned out in a semicircle as Zeus approached. None of them seemed particularly joyful about their victory.

Apollo and Artemis stood together in the shadow of a column, as if trying to hide. Hera and Poseidon were having an intense discussion with another goddess in green and gold robes—perhaps Demeter. Nike tried to put a golden laurel wreath on Hecate's head, but the goddess of magic swatted it away. Hermes sneaked close to Athena, attempting to put his arm around her. Athena turned her *aegis* shield his way and Hermes scuffled off.

The only Olympian who seemed in a good mood was Ares. He laughed and pantomimed gutting an enemy while Frank listened, his expression polite but queasy.

"Brethren," Zeus said, "we are healed, thanks to the work of these demigods. The Athena Parthenos, which once stood in this temple, now stands at Camp Half-Blood. It has united our offspring, and thus our own essences."

"Lord Zeus," Piper spoke up, "is Reyna okay? Nico and Coach Hedge?"

Jason couldn't quite believe Piper was asking after Reyna's health, but it made him glad.

Zeus knit his cloud-colored eyebrows. "They succeeded in their mission. As of this moment they are alive. Whether or not they are *okay*—"

"There is still work to be done," Queen Hera interrupted. She spread her arms like she wanted a group hug. "But my heroes . . . you have triumphed over the giants as I knew you would. My plan succeeded beautifully."

Zeus turned on his wife. Thunder shook the Acropolis. "Hera, do not *dare* take credit! You have caused *at least* as many problems as you fixed!"

The queen of heaven blanched. "Husband, surely you see now—this was the only way."

"There is never only *one* way!" Zeus bellowed. "That is why there are *three* Fates, not one. Is this not so?"

By the ruins of the giant king's throne, the three old ladies silently bowed their heads in recognition. Jason noticed that the other gods stayed well away from the Fates and their gleaming brass clubs.

"Please, husband." Hera tried for a smile, but she was so clearly frightened that Jason almost felt sorry for her. "I only did what I—"

"Silence!" Zeus snapped. "You disobeyed my orders. Nevertheless . . . I recognize that you acted with honest intentions. The valor of these seven heroes has proven that you were not entirely without wisdom."

Hera looked like she wanted to argue, but she kept her mouth shut.

"Apollo, however . . ." Zeus glared into the shadows where the twins were standing. "My son, come here."

Apollo inched forward like he was walking the plank. He looked so much like a teenage demigod it was unnerving—no more than seventeen, wearing jeans and a Camp Half-Blood T-shirt, with a bow over his shoulder and a sword at his belt. With his tousled blond hair and blue eyes, he might've been Jason's brother on the mortal side as well as the godly side.

Jason wondered if Apollo had assumed this form to be inconspicuous, or to look pitiable to his father. The fear in Apollo's face certainly looked real, and also very human.

The Three Fates gathered around the god, circling him, their withered hands raised.

"Twice you have defied me," Zeus said.

Apollo moistened his lips. "My—my lord—"

"You neglected your duties. You succumbed to flattery and

vanity. You encouraged your descendant Octavian to follow his dangerous path, and you prematurely revealed a prophecy that may *yet* destroy us all."

"But—"

"Enough!" Zeus boomed. "We will speak of your punishment later. For now, you will wait on Olympus."

Zeus flicked his hand, and Apollo turned into a cloud of glitter. The Fates swirled around him, dissolving into air, and the glittery whirlwind shot into the sky.

"What will happen to him?" Jason asked.

The gods stared at him, but Jason didn't care. Having actually met Zeus, he had a newfound sympathy for Apollo.

"It is not your concern," Zeus said. "We have other problems to address."

An uncomfortable silence settled over the Parthenon.

It didn't feel right to let the matter go. Jason didn't see how Apollo deserved to be singled out for punishment.

*Someone must take the blame,* Zeus had said.

But why?

"Father," Jason said, "I made a vow to honor all the gods. I promised Kymopoleia that once this war is over, none of the gods would be without shrines at the camps."

Zeus scowled. "That's fine. But . . . Kym who?"

Poseidon coughed into his fist. "She's one of mine."

"My point," Jason said, "is that blaming each other isn't going solve anything. That's how the Romans and Greeks got divided in the first place."

The air became dangerously ionized. Jason's scalp tingled.

He realized he was risking his father's wrath. He might get turned into glitter or blasted off the Acropolis. He'd known his dad for five minutes and made a good impression. Now he was throwing it away.

A good Roman wouldn't keep talking.

Jason kept talking. "Apollo wasn't the problem. To punish him for Gaea waking is—" He wanted to say *stupid*, but he caught himself. "—unwise."

"Unwise." Zeus's voice was almost a whisper. "Before the assembled gods, you would call me *unwise*."

Jason's friends watched on full alert. Percy looked like he was ready to jump in and fight at his side.

Then Artemis stepped out of the shadows. "Father, this hero has fought long and hard for our cause. His nerves are frayed. We should take that into account."

Jason started to protest, but Artemis stopped him with a glance. Her expression sent a message so clear she might have been speaking in his mind: *Thank you, demigod. But do not press this. I will reason with Zeus when he is calmer.*

"Surely, Father," the goddess continued, "we should attend to our more pressing problems, as you pointed out."

"Gaea," Annabeth chimed in, clearly anxious to change the topic. "She's awake, isn't she?"

Zeus turned toward her. Around Jason, the air molecules stopped humming. His skull felt like it had just come out of the microwave.

"That is correct," Zeus said. "The blood of Olympus was spilled. She is fully conscious."

"Oh, come on!" Percy complained. "I get a little nosebleed and I wake up the entire Earth? That's not fair!"

Athena shouldered her *aegis*. "Complaining of unfairness is like assigning blame, Percy Jackson. It does no one any good." She gave Jason an approving glance. "Now you must move quickly. Gaea rises to destroy your camp."

Poseidon leaned on his trident. "For once, Athena is right."

*"For once?"* Athena protested.

"Why would Gaea be back at camp?" Leo asked. "Percy's nosebleed was here."

"Dude," Percy said, "first off, you heard Athena—don't blame my nose. Second, Gaea's the *earth*. She can pop up anywhere she wants. Besides, she *told* us she was going to do this. She said the first thing on her to-do list was destroying our camp. Question is, how do we stop her?"

Frank looked at Zeus. "Um, sir, Your Majesty, can't you gods just pop over there with us? You've got the chariots and the magic powers and whatnot."

"Yes!" Hazel said. "We defeated the giants together in two seconds. Let's all go—"

"No," Zeus said flatly.

"No?" Jason asked. "But, Father—"

Zeus's eyes sparked with power, and Jason realized he'd pushed his dad as far as he could for today . . . and maybe for the next few centuries.

"That's the problem with prophecies," Zeus growled. "When Apollo allowed the Prophecy of Seven to be spoken, and when Hera took it upon herself to interpret the words, the Fates wove the future in such a way that it had only so many possible outcomes, so many solutions. You seven, the demigods, are destined to defeat Gaea. We, the gods, *cannot.*"

"I don't get it," Piper said. "What's the point of being gods if you have to rely on puny mortals to do your bidding?"

All the gods exchanged dark looks. Aphrodite, however, laughed gently and kissed her daughter. "My dear Piper, don't you think we've been asking *ourselves* that question for thousands of years? But it is what binds us together, keeps us eternal. We need you mortals as much as you need us. Annoying as that may be, it's the truth."

Frank shuffled uncomfortably, like he missed being an elephant. "So how can we possibly get to Camp Half-Blood in time to save it? It took us months to reach Greece."

"The winds," Jason said. "Father, can't you unleash the winds to send our ship back?"

Zeus glowered. "I could slap you back to Long Island."

"Um, was that a joke, or a threat, or—"

"No," Zeus said, "I mean it quite literally. I could *slap* your ship back to Camp Half-Blood, but the force involved . . ."

Over by the ruined giant throne, the grungy god in the mechanic's uniform shook his head. "My boy Leo built a good ship, but it won't sustain that kind of stress. It would break apart as soon as it arrived, maybe sooner."

Leo straightened his tool belt. "The *Argo II* can make it. It only has to stay in one piece long enough to get us back home. Once there, we can abandon ship."

"Dangerous," warned Hephaestus. "Perhaps fatal."

The goddess Nike twirled a laurel wreath on her finger. "Victory is always dangerous. And it often requires sacrifice. Leo Valdez and I have discussed this." She stared pointedly at Leo.

Jason didn't like that at all. He remembered Asclepius's grim expression when the doctor had examined Leo. *Oh, my. Oh, I see . . .* Jason knew what they had to do to defeat Gaea. He knew the risks. But he wanted to take those risks himself, not put them on Leo.

*Piper will have the physician's cure,* he told himself. *She'll keep us both covered.*

"Leo," Annabeth said, "what is Nike talking about?"

Leo waved off the question. "The usual. Victory. Sacrifice. Blah, blah, blah. Doesn't matter. We can do this, guys. We *have* to do this."

A feeling of dread settled over Jason. Zeus was correct about one thing: the worst was yet to come.

*When the choice comes,* Notus the South Wind had told him, *storm or fire, do not despair.*

Jason made the choice. "Leo's right. All aboard for one last trip."

# JASON

SO MUCH FOR A TENDER FAREWELL.

The last Jason saw of his dad, Zeus was a hundred feet tall, holding the *Argo II* by its prow. He boomed, *HOLD ON!*

Then he tossed the ship up and spiked it overhand like a volleyball.

If Jason hadn't been strapped to the mast with one of Leo's twenty-point safety harnesses, he would have disintegrated. As it was, his stomach tried to stay behind in Greece and all the air was sucked out of his lungs.

The sky turned black. The ship rattled and creaked. The deck cracked like thin ice under Jason's legs, and with a sonic boom, the *Argo II* hurtled out of the clouds.

"Jason!" Leo shouted. "Hurry!"

His fingers felt like melted plastic, but Jason managed to undo the straps.

Leo was lashed to the control console, desperately trying

to right the ship as they spiraled downward in free fall. The sails were on fire. Festus creaked in alarm. A catapult peeled away and lifted into the air. Centrifugal force sent the shields flying off the railings like metal Frisbees.

Wider cracks opened in the deck as Jason staggered toward the hold, using the winds to keep himself anchored.

If he couldn't make it to the others . . .

Then the hatch burst open. Frank and Hazel stumbled through, pulling on the guide rope they'd attached to the mast. Piper, Annabeth, and Percy followed, all of them looking disoriented.

"Go!" Leo yelled. "Go, go, go!"

For once, Leo's tone was deadly serious.

They'd talked through their evacuation plan, but that slap across the world had made Jason's mind sluggish. Judging from the others' expressions, they weren't in much better shape.

Buford the table saved them. He clattered across the deck with his holographic Hedge blaring, "LET'S GO! MOVE IT! CUT THAT OUT!"

Then his tabletop split into helicopter blades and Buford buzzed away.

Frank changed form. Instead of a dazed demigod, he was now a dazed gray dragon. Hazel climbed onto his neck. Frank grabbed Percy and Annabeth in his front claws, then spread his wings and soared away.

Jason held Piper by the waist, ready to fly, but he made the mistake of glancing down. The view was a spinning kaleidoscope of sky, earth, sky, earth. The ground was getting awfully close.

"Leo, you won't make it!" Jason shouted. "Come with us!"

"No! Get out of here!"

"Leo!" Piper tried. "Please—"

"Save your charmspeak, Pipes! I told you, I've got a plan. Now shoo!"

Jason took a last look at the splintering ship.

The *Argo II* had been their home for so long. Now they were abandoning it for good—and leaving Leo behind.

Jason hated it, but he saw the determination in Leo's eyes. Just like the visit with his father, Zeus, there was no time for a proper good-bye.

Jason harnessed the winds, and he and Piper shot into the sky.

The ground wasn't much less chaotic.

As they plummeted down, Jason saw a vast army of monsters spread across the hills—*cynocephali*, two-headed men, wild centaurs, ogres, and others he couldn't even name— surrounding two tiny islands of demigods. At the crest of Half-Blood Hill, gathered at the feet of the Athena Parthenos, was the main force of Camp Half-Blood along with the First and Fifth Cohorts, rallied around the golden eagle of the legion. The other three Roman cohorts were in a defensive formation several hundred yards away and seemed to be taking the brunt of the attack.

Giant eagles circled Jason, screeching urgently, as if looking for orders.

Frank the gray dragon flew alongside with his passengers.
"Hazel!" Jason yelled. "Those three cohorts are in trouble!
If they don't merge with the rest of the demigods—"

"On it!" Hazel said. "Go, Frank!"

Dragon Frank veered to the left with Annabeth in one
claw yelling, "Let's get 'em!" and Percy in the other claw
screaming, "I hate flying!"

Piper and Jason veered right toward the summit of Half-
Blood Hill.

Jason's heart lifted when he saw Nico di Angelo on the
front lines with the Greeks, slashing his way through a crowd
of two-headed men. A few feet away, Reyna sat astride a new
pegasus, her sword drawn. She shouted orders at the legion,
and the Romans obeyed without question, as if she'd never
been away.

Jason didn't see Octavian anywhere. Good. Neither did he
see a colossal earth goddess laying waste to the world. Very
good. Perhaps Gaea had risen, taken one look at the modern
world, and decided to go back to sleep. Jason wished they
could be that lucky, but he doubted it.

He and Piper landed on the hill, their swords drawn, and
a cheer went up from the Greeks and the Romans.

"About time!" Reyna called. "Glad you could join us!"

With a start, Jason realized she was addressing Piper, not
him.

Piper grinned. "We had some giants to kill!"

"Excellent!" Reyna returned the smile. "Help yourself to
some barbarians."

"Why, thank you!"

The two girls launched into battle side by side.

Nico nodded to Jason as if they'd just seen each other five minutes ago, then went back to turning two-headed men into no-headed corpses. "Good timing. Where's the ship?"

Jason pointed. The *Argo II* streaked across the sky in a ball of fire, shedding burning chunks of mast, hull, and armament. Jason didn't see how even fireproof Leo could survive in that inferno, but he had to hope.

"Gods," Nico said. "Is everyone okay?"

"Leo . . ." Jason's voice broke. "He said he had a plan."

The comet disappeared behind the western hills. Jason waited with dread for the sound of an explosion, but he heard nothing over the roar of battle.

Nico met his eyes. "He'll be fine."

"Sure."

"But just in case . . . For Leo."

"For Leo," Jason agreed. They charged into the fight.

Jason's anger gave him renewed strength. The Greeks and Romans slowly pushed back the enemies. Wild centaurs toppled. Wolf-headed men howled as they were cut to ashes.

More monsters kept appearing—*karpoi* grain spirits swirling out of the grass, gryphons diving from the sky, lumpy clay humanoids that made Jason think of evil Play-Doh men.

"They're ghosts with earthen shells!" Nico warned. "Don't let them hit you!"

Obviously Gaea had kept some surprises in reserve.

At one point, Will Solace, the lead camper for Apollo, ran

up to Nico and said something in his ear. Over the yelling and clashing of blades, Jason couldn't hear the words.

"Jason, I have to go!" Nico said.

Jason didn't really understand, but he nodded, and Will and Nico dashed off into the fray.

A moment later, a squad of Hermes campers gathered around Jason for no apparent reason.

Connor Stoll grinned. "What's up, Grace?"

"I'm good," Jason said. "You?"

Connor dodged an ogre club and stabbed a grain spirit, which exploded in a cloud of wheat. "Yeah, can't complain. Nice day for it."

Reyna yelled, *"Eiaculare flammas!"* and a wave of flaming arrows arced over the legion's shield wall, destroying a platoon of ogres. The Roman ranks moved forward, impaling centaurs and trampling wounded ogres under their bronze-tipped boots.

Somewhere downhill, Jason heard Frank Zhang yell in Latin: *"Repellere equites!"*

A massive herd of centaurs parted in a panic as the legion's other three cohorts plowed through in perfect formation, their spears bright with monster blood. Frank marched before them. On the left flank, riding Arion, Hazel beamed with pride.

*"Ave,* Praetor Zhang!" Reyna called.

*"Ave,* Praetor Ramírez-Arellano!" Frank said. "Let's do this. Legion, CLOSE RANKS!"

A cheer went up among the Romans as the five cohorts

melded into one massive killing machine. Frank pointed his sword forward, and from the golden eagle standard, tendrils of lightning swept across the enemy, turning several hundred monsters to toast.

"Legion, *cuneum formate!*" Reyna yelled. "Advance!"

Another cheer on Jason's right as Percy and Annabeth reunited with the forces of Camp Half-Blood.

"Greeks!" Percy yelled. "Let's, um, fight stuff!"

They yelled like banshees and charged.

Jason grinned. He loved the Greeks. They had no organization whatsoever, but they made up for it with enthusiasm.

Jason was feeling good about the battle, except for two big questions: Where was Leo? And where was Gaea?

Unfortunately, he got the second answer first.

Under his feet, the earth rippled as if Half-Blood Hill had become a giant water mattress. Demigods fell. Ogres slipped. Centaurs charged face-first into the grass.

*AWAKE,* a voice boomed all around them.

A hundred yards away, at the crest of the next hill, the grass and dirt swirled upward like the point of a massive drill. The column of earth thickened into the twenty-foot-tall figure of a woman—her dress woven from blades of grass, her skin as white as quartz, her hair brown and tangled like tree roots.

"*Little fools.*" Gaea the Earth Mother opened her pure green eyes. "*The paltry magic of your statue cannot contain me.*"

As she said it, Jason realized why Gaea hadn't appeared until now. The Athena Parthenos had been protecting the demigods, holding back the wrath of the earth, but even

Athena's might could only last so long against a primordial goddess.

Fear as palpable as a cold front washed over the demigod army.

"Stand fast!" Piper shouted, her charmspeak clear and loud. "Greeks and Romans, we can fight her together!"

Gaea laughed. She spread her arms and the earth bent toward her—trees tilting, bedrock groaning, soil rippling in waves. Jason rose on the wind, but all around him, monsters and demigods alike started to sink into the ground. One of Octavian's onagers capsized and disappeared into the side of the hill.

*"The whole earth is my body,"* Gaea boomed. *"How would you fight the goddess of—"*

*FOOOOMP!*

In a flash of bronze, Gaea was swept off the hillside, snarled in the claws of a fifty-ton metal dragon.

Festus, reborn, rose into the sky on gleaming wings, spewing fire from his maw triumphantly. As he ascended, the rider on his back got smaller and more difficult to discern, but Leo's grin was unmistakable.

"Pipes! Jason!" he shouted down. "You coming? The fight is up here!"

# L I I

# JASON

As SOON AS GAEA ACHIEVED LIFTOFF, the ground solidified.

Demigods stopped sinking, though many were still buried up to their waists. Sadly, the monsters seemed to be digging themselves out more quickly. They charged the Greek and Roman ranks, taking advantage of the demigods' disorganization.

Jason put his arms around Piper's waist. He was about to take off when Percy yelled, "Wait! Frank can fly the rest of us up there! We can all—"

"No, man," Jason said. "They need you here. There's still an army to defeat. Besides, the prophecy—"

"He's right." Frank gripped Percy's arm. "You have to let them do this, Percy. It's like Annabeth's quest in Rome. Or Hazel at the Doors of Death. This part can only be them."

Percy obviously didn't like it, but at that moment a flood of monsters swept over the Greek forces. Annabeth called to him, "Hey! Problem over here!" Percy ran to join her.

Frank and Hazel turned to Jason. They raised their arms in the Roman salute, then ran off to regroup the legion.

Jason and Piper spiraled upward on the wind.

"I've got the cure," Piper murmured like a chant. "It'll be fine. I've got the cure."

Jason realized she'd lost her sword somehow during the battle, but he doubted it would matter. Against Gaea, a sword would do no good. This was about storm and fire . . . and a third power, Piper's charmspeak, which would hold them together. Last winter, Piper had slowed the power of Gaea at the Wolf House, helping to free Hera from a cage of earth. Now she would have an even bigger job.

As they ascended, Jason gathered the wind and clouds around him. The sky responded with frightening speed. Soon they were in the eye of a maelstrom. Lightning burned his eyes. Thunder made his teeth vibrate.

Directly above them, Festus grappled with the earth goddess. Gaea kept disintegrating, trying to trickle back to the ground, but the winds kept her aloft. Festus sprayed her with flames, which seemed to force her into solid form. Meanwhile, from Festus's back, Leo blasted the goddess with flames of his own and hurled insults. "Potty Sludge! Dirt Face! THIS IS FOR MY MOTHER, ESPERANZA VALDEZ!"

His whole body was wreathed in fire. Rain hung in the stormy air, but it only sizzled and steamed around him.

Jason zoomed toward them.

Gaea turned into loose white sand, but Jason summoned a squadron of *venti* who churned around her, constraining her in a cocoon of wind.

Gaea fought back. When she wasn't disintegrating, she lashed out with shrapnel blasts of stone and soil that Jason barely deflected. Stoking the storm, containing Gaea, keeping himself and Piper aloft . . . Jason had never done anything so difficult. He felt like he was covered in lead weights, trying to swim with only his legs while holding a car over his head. But he *had* to keep Gaea off the ground.

That was the secret Kym had hinted at when they spoke at the bottom of the sea.

Long ago, Ouranos the sky god had been tricked down to the earth by Gaea and the Titans. They'd held him on the ground so he couldn't escape and, with his powers weakened from being so far from his home territory, they'd been able to cut him apart.

Now Jason, Leo, and Piper had to reverse that scenario. They had to keep Gaea away from her source of power—the earth—and weaken her until she could be defeated.

Together they rose. Festus creaked and groaned with the effort, but he continued to gain altitude. Jason still didn't understand how Leo had managed to remake the dragon. Then he recalled all the hours Leo had spent working inside the hull over the last few weeks. Leo must have been planning this all along, and building a new body for Festus within the framework of the ship.

He must have known in his gut that the *Argo II* would eventually fall apart. A ship turning into a dragon . . . Jason supposed it was no more amazing than the dragon turning into a suitcase back in Quebec.

However it had happened, Jason was elated to see their old friend in action once more.

*"YOU CANNOT DEFEAT ME!"* Gaea crumbled to sand, only to get blasted by more flames. Her body melted into a lump of glass, shattered, then re-formed again as human. *"I AM ETERNAL!"*

"Eternally annoying!" Leo yelled, and he urged Festus higher.

Jason and Piper rose with them.

"Get me closer," Piper urged. "I need to be next to her."

"Piper, the flames and the shrapnel—"

"I know."

Jason moved in until they were right next to Gaea. The winds encased the goddess, keeping her solid, but it was all Jason could do to contain her blasts of sand and soil. Her eyes were solid green, like all nature had been condensed into a few spoonfuls of organic matter.

*"FOOLISH CHILDREN!"* Her face contorted with miniature earthquakes and mudslides.

"You are so weary," Piper told the goddess, her voice radiating kindness and sympathy. "Eons of pain and disappointment weigh on you."

*"SILENCE!"*

The force of Gaea's anger was so great, Jason momentarily lost control of the wind. He would've dropped into free fall, but Festus caught him and Piper in his other huge claw.

Amazingly, Piper kept her focus. "Millennia of sorrow," she told Gaea. "Your husband Ouranos was abusive. Your grandchildren the gods overthrew your beloved children the Titans. Your other children, the Cyclopes and the Hundred-Handed Ones, were thrown into Tartarus. You are so tired of heartache."

*"LIES!"* Gaea crumbled into a tornado of soil and grass, but her essence seemed to churn more sluggishly.

If they gained any more altitude, the air would be too thin to breathe. Jason would be too weak to control it. Piper's talk of exhaustion affected him, too, sapping his strength, making his body feel heavy.

"What you want," Piper continued, "more than victory, more than revenge . . . you want *rest*. You are so weary, so incomprehensibly tired of the ungrateful mortals and immortals."

*"I—YOU DO NOT SPEAK FOR ME—YOU CANNOT—"*

"You want one thing," Piper said soothingly, her voice resonating through Jason's bones. "One word. You want permission to close your eyes and forget your troubles. You—want—SLEEP."

Gaea solidified into human form. Her head lolled, her eyes closed, and she went limp in Festus's claw.

Unfortunately, Jason started to black out too.

The wind was dying. The storm dissipated. Dark spots danced in his eyes.

"Leo!" Piper gasped for breath. "We only have a few seconds. My charmspeak won't—"

"I know!" Leo looked like he was *made* of fire. Flames rippled beneath his skin, illuminating his skull. Festus steamed and glowed, his claws burning through Jason's shirt. "I can't contain the fire much longer. I'll vaporize her. Don't worry. But you guys need to leave."

"No!" Jason said. "We have to stay with you. Piper's got the cure. Leo, you can't—"

"Hey." Leo grinned, which was unnerving in the flames, his teeth like molten silver ingots. "I told you I had a plan. When are you going to trust me? And by the way—I love you guys."

Festus's claw opened, and Jason and Piper fell.

Jason had no strength to stop it. He held on to Piper as she cried Leo's name, and they plummeted earthward.

Festus became an indistinct ball of fire in the sky—a second sun—growing smaller and hotter. Then, in the corner of Jason's eye, a blazing comet streaked upward from the ground with a high-pitched, almost human scream. Just before Jason blacked out, the comet intercepted the ball of fire above them.

The explosion turned the entire sky gold.

# NICO

NICO HAD WITNESSED MANY FORMS OF DEATH. He didn't think anything could surprise him anymore.

He was wrong.

In the middle of the battle, Will Solace ran up to him and said one word in his ear: "Octavian."

That got Nico's full attention. He had hesitated when he'd had the chance to kill Octavian, but there was no way Nico would let that scumbag augur escape justice. "Where?"

"Come on," Will said. "Hurry."

Nico turned to Jason, who was fighting next to him. "Jason, I have to go."

Then he plunged into the chaos, following Will. They passed Tyson and his Cyclopes, who were bellowing, "Bad dog! Bad dog!" as they bashed the heads of the *cynocephali*. Grover Underwood and a team of satyrs danced around with their panpipes, playing harmonies so dissonant that the earthen-shelled ghosts cracked apart. Travis Stoll ran past, arguing with his brother. "What do you *mean* we set the land mines on the wrong hill?"

Nico and Will were halfway down the hill when the ground trembled under their feet. Like everyone else—monster and demigod alike—they froze in horror and watched as the whirling column of earth erupted from the top of the next hill, and Gaea appeared in all her glory.

Then something large and bronze swooped out the sky.

*FOOOOMP!*

Festus the bronze dragon snatched up the Earth Mother soared away with her.

"What—how—?" Nico stammered.

"I don't know," Will said. "But I doubt there's much we can do about *that.* We have other problems."

Will sprinted toward the nearest onager. As they got closer, Nico spotted Octavian furiously readjusting the machine's targeting levers. The throwing arm was already primed with a full payload of Imperial gold and explosives. The augur rushed about, tripping over gears and anchor spikes, fumbling with the ropes. Every so often he glanced up at Festus the dragon.

"Octavian!" Nico yelled.

The augur spun, then backed up against the huge sphere of ammunition. His fine purple robes snagged on the trigger rope, but Octavian didn't notice. Fumes from the payload curled about him as if drawn to the Imperial gold jewelry around his arms and neck, the golden wreath in his hair.

"Oh, I see!" Octavian's laughter was brittle and quite

insane. "Trying to steal my glory, eh? No, no, son of Pluto. I am the savior of Rome. I was promised!"

Will raised his hands in a placating gesture. "Octavian, get away from the onager. That isn't safe."

"Of course it's not! I will shoot Gaea down with this machine!"

Out of the corner of his eye, Nico saw Jason Grace rocket into the sky with Piper in his arms, flying straight toward Festus.

Around the son of Jupiter, storm clouds gathered, swirling into a hurricane. Thunder boomed.

"You see?" Octavian cried. The gold on his body was definitely smoking now, attracted to the catapult's payload like iron to a giant magnet. "The gods approve of my actions!"

"Jason is making that storm," Nico said. "If you fire the onager, you'll kill him, and Piper, and—"

"Good!" Octavian yelled. "They're traitors! All traitors!"

"Listen to me," Will tried again. "This is *not* what Apollo would want. Besides, your robes are—"

"You know nothing, *Graecus*!" Octavian wrapped his hand around the release lever. "I must act before they get any higher. Only an onager such as this can make the shot. I will singlehandedly—"

"Centurion," said a voice behind him.

From the back of the siege engine, Michael Kahale appeared. He had a large red knot on his forehead where Tyson had bonked him unconscious. He stumbled as he walked. But somehow he had found his way here from the shore, and along the way, he'd picked up a sword and shield.

"Michael!" Octavian shrieked with glee. "Excellent! Guard me while I fire this onager. Then we will kill these *Graeci* together!"

Michael Kahale took in the scene—his boss's robes tangled in the trigger rope, Octavian's jewelry fuming from proximity to the Imperial gold ammunition. He glanced up at the dragon, now high in the air, surrounded by rings of storm clouds like the circles of an archery target. Then he scowled at Nico.

Nico readied his own sword.

Surely Michael Kahale would warn his leader to step away from the onager. Surely he would attack.

"Are you certain, Octavian?" asked the son of Venus.

"Yes!"

"Are you absolutely certain?"

"Yes, you fool! I will be remembered as the savior of Rome. Now keep them away while I destroy Gaea!"

"Octavian, don't," Will pleaded. "We can't allow you—"

"Will," Nico said, "we can't stop him."

Solace stared at him in disbelief, but Nico remembered his father's words in the Chapel of Bones: *Some deaths cannot be prevented.*

Octavian's eyes gleamed. "That's right, son of Pluto. You are helpless to stop me! It is my destiny! Kahale, stand guard!"

"As you wish." Michael moved in front of the machine, interposing himself between Octavian and the two Greek demigods. "Centurion, do what you must."

Octavian turned to release the catch. "A good friend to the last."

Nico almost lost his nerve. If the onager really *did* fire true—if it scored a hit on Festus the dragon, and Nico allowed his friends to be hurt or killed . . . But he stayed where he was. For once, he decided to trust the wisdom of his father. *Some deaths* should not *be prevented.*

"Good-bye, Gaea!" Octavian yelled. "Good-bye, Jason Grace the traitor!"

Octavian cut the release wire with his augur's knife.

And he disappeared.

The catapult arm sprang upward faster than Nico's eye could follow, launching Octavian along with the ammunition. The augur's scream faded until he was simply part of the fiery comet soaring skyward.

"Good-bye, Octavian," Michael Kahale said.

He glared at Will and Nico one last time, as if daring them to speak. Then he turned his back and trudged away.

Nico could have lived with Octavian's end.

He might even have said *good riddance.*

But his heart sank as the comet kept gaining altitude. It disappeared into the storm clouds, and the sky exploded in a dome of fire.

# LIV

# NICO

THE NEXT DAY, THERE WEREN'T MANY ANSWERS.

After the explosion, Piper and Jason—free-falling and unconscious—were plucked out of the sky by giant eagles and brought to safety, but Leo did not reappear. The entire Hephaestus cabin scoured the valley, finding bits and pieces of the *Argo II*'s broken hull, but no sign of Festus the dragon or his master.

All the monsters had been destroyed or scattered. Greek and Roman casualties were heavy, but not nearly as bad as they might have been.

Overnight, the satyrs and nymphs disappeared into the woods for a convocation of the Cloven Elders. In the morning, Grover Underwood reappeared to announce that they could not sense the Earth Mother's presence. Nature was more or less back to normal. Apparently, Jason, Piper, and Leo's plan worked. Gaea had been separated from her source of power, charmed to sleep, and then atomized in the combined explosion of Leo's fire and Octavian's manmade comet.

An immortal could never die, but now Gaea would be like her husband, Ouranos. The earth would continue to function as normal, just as the sky did, but Gaea was now so dispersed and powerless that she could never again form a consciousness.

At least, that was the hope. . . .

Octavian would be remembered for saving Rome by hurling himself into the sky in a fiery ball of death. But it was Leo Valdez who had made the *real* sacrifice.

The victory celebration at camp was muted, due to grief—not just for Leo, but also for the many others who had died in battle. Shrouded demigods, both Greek and Roman, were burned at the campfire, and Chiron asked Nico to oversee the burial rites.

Nico agreed immediately. He was grateful for the opportunity to honor the dead. Even the hundreds of spectators didn't bother him.

The hardest part was afterward, when Nico and the six demigods from the *Argo II* met on the porch of the Big House.

Jason hung his head, even his glasses lost in shadow. "We should have been there at the end. We could've helped Leo."

"It's not right," Piper agreed, wiping away her tears. "All that work getting the physician's cure, for *nothing*."

Hazel broke down crying. "Piper, where's the cure? Bring it out."

Bewildered, Piper reached into her belt pouch. She

produced the chamois cloth package, but when she unfolded the cloth, it was empty.

All eyes turned to Hazel.

"How?" Annabeth asked.

Frank put his arm around Hazel. "In Delos, Leo pulled the two of us aside. He pleaded with us to help him."

Through her tears, Hazel explained how she had switched the physician's cure for an illusion—a trick of the Mist—so that Leo could keep the real vial. Frank told them about Leo's plan to destroy a weakened Gaea with one massive fiery explosion. After talking with Nike and Apollo, Leo had been certain that such an explosion would kill any mortal within a quarter mile, so he knew he would have to get far away from everyone.

"He wanted to do it alone," Frank said. "He thought there would be a slim chance that he, a son of Hephaestus, could survive the fire, but if anyone was with him . . . He said that Hazel and I, being Roman, would understand about sacrifice. But he knew the rest of you would never allow it."

At first the others looked angry, like they wanted to scream and throw things. But as Frank and Hazel talked, the group's rage seemed to dissipate. It was hard to be mad at Frank and Hazel when they were both crying. Also . . . the plan sounded exactly like the sneaky, twisted, ridiculously annoying and noble sort of thing Leo Valdez would do.

Finally Piper let out a sound somewhere between a sob and a laugh. "If he were here right now, I would *kill* him. How was he planning to take the cure? He was *alone!*"

"Maybe he found a way," Percy said. "This is Leo we're talking about. He might come back any minute. Then we can take turns strangling him."

Nico and Hazel exchanged looks. They both knew better, but they said nothing.

The next day, the second since the battle, Romans and Greeks worked side by side to clean up the warzone and tend the wounded. Blackjack the pegasus was recovering nicely from his arrow wound. Guido had decided to adopt Reyna as his human. Reluctantly, Lou Ellen had agreed to turn her new pet piglets back into Romans.

Will Solace hadn't spoken with Nico since the encounter at the onager. The son of Apollo spent most of his time in the infirmary, but whenever Nico saw him running across camp to fetch more medical supplies or make a house call on some wounded demigod, he felt a strange twinge of melancholy. No doubt Will Solace thought Nico was a monster now, for letting Octavian kill himself.

The Romans bivouacked next to the strawberry fields, where they insisted on building their standard field camp. The Greeks pitched in to help them raise the dirt walls and dig the trenches. Nico had never seen anything stranger or cooler. Dakota shared Kool-Aid with the kids from the Dionysus cabin. The children of Hermes and Mercury laughed and told stories and brazenly stole things from just about everyone. Reyna, Annabeth, and Piper were inseparable, roaming the camp as a trio to check on the progress of the repairs. Chiron, escorted by Frank and Hazel, inspected the Roman troops and praised them for their bravery.

By evening, the general mood had improved somewhat. The dining hall pavilion had never been so crowded. The Romans were welcomed like old friends. Coach Hedge roamed among the demigods, beaming and holding his baby boy and saying, "Hey, you want to meet Chuck? This is my boy, Chuck!"

The Aphrodite and Athena girls alike cooed over the feisty little satyr baby, who waved his pudgy fists, kicked his tiny hooves, and bleated, "Baaaa! Baaaa!"

Clarisse, who had been named the baby's godmother, trailed behind the coach like a bodyguard and occasionally muttered, "All right, all right. Give the kid some space."

At announcement time, Chiron stepped forward and raised his goblet.

"Out of every tragedy," he said, "comes new strength. Today, we thank the gods for this victory. To the gods!"

The demigods all joined the toast, but their enthusiasm seemed muted. Nico understood the feeling: *We saved the gods again, and now we're supposed to thank them?*

Then Chiron said, "And to new friends!"

"TO NEW FRIENDS!"

Hundreds of demigod voices echoed across the hills.

At the campfire, everyone kept looking at the stars, as if they expected Leo to come back in some dramatic, last-minute surprise. Maybe he'd swoop in, jump off Festus's back, and launch into corny jokes. It didn't happen.

After a few songs, Reyna and Frank were called to the front. They got a thunderous round of applause from both the Greeks and Romans. Up on Half-Blood Hill, the Athena Parthenos glowed more brightly in moonlight, as if to signal: *These kids are all right.*

"Tomorrow," Reyna said, "we Romans must return home. We appreciate your hospitality, especially since we almost killed you—"

"You almost *got* killed," Annabeth corrected.

"Whatever, Chase."

*Oooooohhhhh!* the crowd said as one. Then everybody started laughing and pushing each other around. Even Nico had to smile.

"Anyway," Frank took over, "Reyna and I agree this marks a new era of friendship between the camps."

Reyna clapped him on the back. "That's right. For hundreds of years, the gods tried to separate us to keep us from fighting. But there's a better kind of peace—cooperation."

Piper stood up from the audience. "Are you sure your mom is a *war* goddess?"

"Yes, McLean," Reyna said. "I still intend to fight *a lot* of battles. But from now on, we fight *together*!"

That got a big cheer.

Zhang raised his hand for quiet. "You'll all be welcome at Camp Jupiter. We've come to an agreement with Chiron: a free exchange between the camps—weekend visits, training programs, and of course, emergency aid in times of need—"

"And parties?" asked Dakota.

"Hear, hear!" said Conner Stoll.

Reyna spread her arms. "That goes without saying. We Romans invented parties."

Another big *Oooohhhhhhh!*

"So thank you," Reyna concluded. "All of you. We could've chosen hatred and war. Instead we found acceptance and friendship."

Then she did something so unexpected Nico would later think he dreamed it. She walked up to Nico, who was standing to one side in the shadows, as usual. She grabbed his hand and pulled him gently into the firelight.

"We had one home," she said. "Now we have two."

She gave Nico a big hug and the crowd roared with approval. For once, Nico didn't feel like pulling away. He buried his face in Reyna's shoulder and blinked the tears out of his eyes.

# LV

# NICO

THAT NIGHT, NICO SLEPT IN THE HADES CABIN.

He'd never had any desire to use the place before, but now he shared it with Hazel, which made all the difference.

It made him happy to live with a sister again—even if it was a only for a few days, and even if Hazel insisted on partitioning her side of the room with sheets for privacy so it looked like a quarantine zone.

Just before curfew, Frank came to visit and spent a few minutes talking with Hazel in hushed tones.

Nico tried to ignore them. He stretched out in his bunk, which resembled a coffin—a polished mahogany frame, brass railings, bloodred velvet pillows and blankets. Nico hadn't been present when they built this cabin. He definitely had *not* suggested these bunks. Apparently somebody thought the children of Hades were vampires, not demigods.

Finally Frank knocked on the wall next to Nico's bed.

Nico looked over. Zhang stood so tall now. He seemed so . . . *Roman*.

"Hey," Frank said. "We'll be leaving in the morning. Just wanted to tell you thanks."

Nico sat up in his bunk. "You did great, Frank. It's been an honor."

Frank smiled. "Honestly, I'm kind of surprised I lived through it. The whole magic firewood thing . . ."

Nico nodded. Hazel had told him all about the piece of firewood that controlled Frank's lifeline. Nico took it as a good sign that Frank could talk about it openly now.

"I can't see the future," Nico told him, "but I can often tell when people are close to death. You're not. I don't know when that piece of firewood will burn up. Eventually, we *all* run out of firewood. But it won't be soon, Praetor Zhang. You and Hazel . . . you've got a lot more adventures ahead of you. You're just getting started. Be good to my sister, okay?"

Hazel walked up next to Frank and laced her hand with his. "Nico, you're not threatening my boyfriend, are you?"

The two of them looked so comfortable together it made Nico glad. But it also it caused an ache in his heart—a ghostly pain, like an old war wound throbbing in bad weather.

"No need for threats," Nico said. "Frank's a good guy. Or bear. Or bulldog. Or—"

"Oh, stop." Hazel laughed. Then she kissed Frank. "See you in the morning."

"Yeah," Frank said. "Nico . . . you sure you won't come with us? You'll always have a place in New Rome."

"Thanks, Praetor. Reyna said the same thing. But . . . no."

"I hope I'll see you again?"

"Oh, you will," Nico promised. "I'm going to be the flower boy at your wedding, right?"

"Um . . ." Frank got flustered, cleared his throat, and shuffled off, running into the doorjamb on the way out.

Hazel crossed her arms. "You just *had* to tease him about that."

She sat on Nico's bunk. For a while they just stayed there in comfortable silence . . . siblings, children from the past, children of the Underworld.

"I'm going to miss you," Nico said.

Hazel leaned over and rested her head on his shoulder. "You too, big brother. You *will* visit."

He tapped the new officer's badge that gleamed on her shirt. "Centurion of the Fifth Cohort now. Congratulations. Are there rules against centurions dating praetors?"

"Shhh," Hazel said. "It'll be a lot of work getting the legion back in shape, repairing the damage Octavian did. Dating regulations will be the least of my worries."

"You've come so far. You're not the same girl I brought to Camp Jupiter. Your power with the Mist, your confidence—"

"It's all thanks to you."

"No," Nico said. "Getting a second life is one thing. Making it a *better* life, that's the trick."

As soon as he said it, Nico realized he could've been talking about himself. He decided not to bring that up.

Hazel sighed. "A second life. I just wish . . ."

She didn't need to finish her thought. For the past two

days, Leo's disappearance had hovered like a cloud over the whole camp. Hazel and Nico had been reluctant to join the speculation about what had happened to him.

"You felt his death, didn't you?" Hazel's eyes were watery. Her voice was small.

"Yeah," Nico admitted. "But I don't know, Hazel. Something about it was . . . different."

"He couldn't have taken the physician's cure. Nothing could have survived that explosion. I thought . . . I thought I was helping Leo. I messed up."

"No. It is *not* your fault." But Nico wasn't quite so ready to forgive himself. He'd spent the last forty-eight hours replaying the scene with Octavian at the catapult, wondering if he'd done wrong thing. Perhaps the explosive power of that projectile had helped destroy Gaea. Or perhaps it had unnecessarily cost Leo Valdez his life.

"I just wish he hadn't died alone," Hazel murmured. "There was no one with him, no one to give him that cure. There's not even a body to bury. . . ."

Her voice broke. Nico put his arm around her.

He held her as she wept. Eventually she fell asleep from exhaustion. Nico tucked her into his own bed and kissed her forehead. Then he went to the shrine of Hades in the corner—a little table decorated with bones and jewels.

"I suppose," he said, "there's a first time for everything."

He knelt and prayed silently for his father's guidance.

# LVI

# NICO

AT DAWN, HE WAS STILL AWAKE when someone rapped at the door.

He turned, registering a face with blond hair, and for a split second he thought it was Will Solace. When Nico realized it was Jason, he was disappointed. Then he felt angry with himself for feeling that way.

He hadn't talked to Will since the battle. The Apollo kids had been too busy with the injured. Besides, Will probably blamed Nico for what happened to Octavian. Why wouldn't he? Nico had basically permitted . . . whatever that was. Murder by consensus. A gruesome suicide. By now, Will Solace realized just how creepy and revolting Nico di Angelo was. Of course, Nico didn't care what he thought. But still . . .

"You okay?" Jason asked. "You look—"

"Fine," Nico snapped. Then he softened his tone. "If you're looking for Hazel, she's still asleep."

Jason mouthed *Oh*, and gestured for Nico to come outside.

Nico stepped into the sunlight, blinking and disoriented. *Ugh* . . . Perhaps the cabin's designers had been right about the children of Hades being like vampires. He was *not* a morning person.

Jason didn't look as though he'd slept any better. His hair had a cowlick on one side and his new glasses sat crookedly on his nose. Nico resisted the urge to reach out and straighten them.

Jason pointed to the strawberry fields, where the Romans were breaking camp. "It was strange to see them here. Now it'll be strange *not* seeing them."

"Do you regret not going with them?" Nico asked.

Jason's smile was lopsided. "A little. But I'll be going back and forth between the camps a lot. I have some shrines to build."

"I heard. The Senate plans to elect you *pontifex maximus*."

Jason shrugged. "I don't care about the title so much. I *do* care about making sure the gods are remembered. I don't want them fighting out of jealousy anymore, or taking out their frustrations on demigods."

"They're gods," Nico said. "That's their nature."

"Maybe, but I can try to make it better. I guess Leo would say I'm acting like a mechanic, doing preventative maintenance."

Nico sensed Jason's sorrow like an oncoming storm. "You know, you couldn't have stopped Leo. There's nothing you could have done differently. He knew what had to happen."

"I—I guess. I don't suppose you can tell if he's still—"

"He's gone," Nico said. "I'm sorry. I wish I could tell you otherwise, but I *sensed* his death."

Jason stared into the distance.

Nico felt guilty for squashing his hopes. He was almost tempted to mention his own doubts . . . what a *different* sensation Leo's death had given him, as if Leo's soul had invented its own way into the Underworld, something that involved lots of gears, levers, and steam-powered pistons.

Nevertheless, Nico was sure Leo Valdez had died. And death was death. It wouldn't be fair to give Jason false expectations.

In the distance, the Romans were picking up their gear and toting it across the hill. On the other side, so Nico had heard, a fleet of black SUVs waited to transport the legion cross-country back to California. Nico guessed that would be an interesting road trip. He imagined the entire Twelfth Legion in the drive-through lane at Burger King. He imagined some hapless monster terrorizing a random demigod in Kansas, only to find itself surrounded by several dozen carloads of heavily armored Romans.

"Ella the harpy is going with them, you know," Jason said. "She and Tyson. Even Rachel Elizabeth Dare. They're going to work together to try to reconstruct the Sibylline Books."

"That should be interesting."

"Could take years," Jason said. "But with the voice of Delphi extinguished . . ."

"Rachel still can't see the future?"

Jason shook his head. "I wish I knew what happened to

Apollo in Athens. Maybe Artemis will get him out of trouble with Zeus and the power of prophecy will work again. But for now, those Sibylline Books might be our only way to get guidance for quests."

"Personally," Nico said, "I could do without prophecies or quests for a while."

"You've got a point." He straightened his glasses. "Look, Nico, the reason I wanted to talk to you . . . I know what you said back at Auster's palace. I know you already turned down a place at Camp Jupiter. I—I probably can't change your mind about leaving Camp Half-Blood, but I have to—"

"I'm staying."

Jason blinked. "What?"

"At Camp Half-Blood. The Hades cabin needs a head counselor. Have you seen the decor? It's disgusting. I'll have to remodel. And someone needs to do the burial rites properly, since demigods insist on dying heroically."

"That's—that's fantastic! Dude!" Jason opened his arms for a hug, then froze. "Right. No touching. Sorry."

Nico grunted. "I suppose we can make an exception."

Jason squeezed him so hard Nico thought his ribs would crack.

"Oh, man," Jason said. "Wait till I tell Piper. Hey, since I'm all alone in my cabin too, you and I can share a table in the dining hall. We can team up for capture the flag and sing-along contests and—"

"Are you *trying* to scare me away?"

"Sorry. Sorry. Whatever you say, Nico. I'm just glad."

The funny thing was, Nico believed him.

Nico happened to glance toward the cabins and saw someone waving at him. Will Solace stood in the doorway of the Apollo cabin, a stern look on his face. He pointed to the ground at his feet like *You. Here. Now.*

"Jason," Nico said, "would you excuse me?"

"So where were you?" Will demanded. He was wearing a green surgeon's shirt with jeans and flip-flops, which was probably not standard hospital protocol.

"What do you mean?" Nico asked.

"I've been stuck in the infirmary for, like, two days. You don't come by. You don't offer to help."

"I . . . what? Why would you want a son of Hades in the same room with people you're trying to heal? Why would *anyone* want that?"

"You can't help out a friend? Maybe cut bandages? Bring me a soda or a snack? Or just a simple *How's it going, Will?* You don't think I could stand to see a friendly face?"

"What . . . *my* face?"

The words simply didn't make sense together: *Friendly face. Nico di Angelo.*

"You're so dense," Will noted. "I hope you got over that nonsense about leaving Camp Half-Blood."

"I—yeah. I did. I mean, I'm staying."

"Good. So you may be dense, but you're not an idiot."

"How can you even talk to me like that? Don't you know I can summon zombies and skeletons and—"

"Right now you couldn't summon a wishbone without melting into a puddle of darkness, di Angelo," Will said. "I told you, no more Underworld-y stuff, doctor's orders. You owe me at least three days of rest in the infirmary. Starting *now*."

Nico felt like a hundred skeletal butterflies were resurrecting in his stomach. "Three days? I—I suppose that would be okay."

"Good. Now—"

A loud *whoop!* cut through the air.

Over by the hearth in the center of the common, Percy was grinning at something Annabeth had just told him. Annabeth laughed and playfully slapped his arm.

"I'll be right back," Nico told Will. "Promise on the Styx and everything."

He walked over to Percy and Annabeth, who were both still grinning like crazy.

"Hey, man," Percy said. "Annabeth just told me some good news. Sorry if I got a little loud."

"We're going to spend our senior year together," Annabeth explained, "here in New York. And after graduation—"

"College in New Rome!" Percy pumped his fist like he was blowing a truck horn. "Four years with no monsters to fight, no battles, no stupid prophecies. Just me and Annabeth, getting our degrees, hanging out at cafés, enjoying California—"

"And after that . . ." Annabeth kissed Percy on the cheek. "Well, Reyna and Frank said we could live in New Rome as long as we like."

"That's great," Nico said. He was a little surprised to find that he meant it. "I'm staying too, here at Camp Half-Blood."

"Awesome!" Percy said.

Nico studied his face—his sea green eyes, his grin, his ruffled black hair. Somehow Percy Jackson seemed like a regular guy now, not a mythical figure. Not someone to idolize or crush on.

"So," Nico said, "since we're going to be spending at least a year seeing each other at camp, I think I should clear the air."

Percy's smile wavered. "What do you mean?"

"For a long time," Nico said, "I had a crush on you. I just wanted you to know."

Percy looked at Nico. Then at Annabeth, as if to check that he'd heard correctly. Then back at Nico. "You—"

"Yeah," Nico said. "You're a great person. But I'm over that. I'm happy for you guys."

"You . . . so you mean—"

"Right."

Annabeth's gray eyes started to sparkle. She gave Nico a sideways smile.

"Wait," Percy said. "So you mean—"

"Right," Nico said again. "But it's cool. We're cool. I mean, I see now . . . you're cute, but you're not my type."

"I'm not your type . . . Wait. So—"

"See you around, Percy," Nico said. "Annabeth."

She raised her hand for a high five.

Nico obliged. Then he walked back across the green, where Will Solace was waiting.

# PIPER

PIPER WISHED SHE COULD CHARM HERSELF TO SLEEP.

It may have worked on Gaea, but the last two nights she'd hardly gotten a wink.

The days were fine. She loved being back with her friends Lacy and Mitchell and all the other Aphrodite kids. Even her bratty second-in-command, Drew Tanaka, seemed relieved, probably because Piper could run things and give Drew more time for gossip and in-cabin beauty treatments.

Piper kept busy helping Reyna and Annabeth coordinate between the Greeks and Romans. To Piper's surprise, the other two girls valued her skills as a go-between to smooth over any conflicts. There weren't many, but Piper did manage to return some Roman helmets that mysteriously made their way into the camp store. She also kept a fight from breaking out between the children of Mars and the children of Ares over the best way to kill a hydra.

On the morning the Romans were scheduled to leave, Piper was sitting on the pier at the canoe lake, trying to placate the naiads. Some of the lake spirits thought the Roman guys were so hot that they, too, wanted to leave for Camp Jupiter. They were demanding a giant portable fish tank for the journey west. Piper had just concluded negotiations when Reyna found her.

The praetor sat next to her on the dock. "Hard work?"

Piper blew a strand of hair out of her eyes. "Naiads can be challenging. I think we have a deal. If they still want to go at the end of the summer, we'll work out the details then. But naiads, uh, tend to forget things in about five seconds."

Reyna traced her fingertips across the water. "Sometimes I wish I could forget things that quickly."

Piper studied the praetor's face. Reyna was one demigod who hadn't seemed to change during the war with the giants . . . at least not on the outside. She still had the same strong, unstoppable gaze, the same regal, beautiful face. She wore her armor and purple cloak as easily as most people would wear shorts and a T-shirt.

Piper couldn't understand how anyone could take so much pain, shoulder so much responsibility, without breaking. She wondered if Reyna ever had anyone to confide in.

"You did so much," Piper said. "For both camps. Without you, none of it would've been possible."

"All of us played a part."

"Sure. But you . . . I just wish you got more credit."

Reyna laughed gently. "Thank you, Piper. But I don't want attention. You understand what that's like, don't you?"

Piper did. They were so different, but she understood not wanting to attract attention. Piper had wished for that her whole life, with her dad's fame, the paparazzi, the photos and scandal stories in the press. She met so many people who said, *Oh, I want to be famous! That would be so great!* But they had no idea what it was really like. She'd seen the toll it took on her father. Piper wanted nothing to do with it.

She could understand the appeal of the Roman way too— to blend in, be one of the team, work as a part of a well-oiled machine. Even so, Reyna had risen to the top. She couldn't stay hidden.

"Your power from your mom . . ." Piper said. "You can lend strength to others?"

Reyna pursed her lips. "Nico told you?"

"No. I just sensed it, watching you lead the legion. That must drain you. How do you . . . you know, get that strength back?"

"When I get the strength back, I'll let you know."

She said it like a joke, but Piper sensed the sadness behind her words.

"You're always welcome here," Piper said. "If you need to take a break, get away . . . you've got Frank now—he could assume more responsibility for a while. It might do you good to make some time for yourself, when nobody is going to be looking at you as praetor."

Reyna met her eyes, as if trying to gauge how serious the offer was. "Would I be expected to sing that odd song about how Grandma puts on her armor?"

"Not unless you really want to. But we might have to ban

you from capture the flag. I have a feeling you could go against the entire camp solo and still beat us."

Reyna smirked. "I'll consider the offer. Thank you." She adjusted her dagger, and for a moment Piper thought about her own blade, Katoptris, which was now locked in her hope chest in her cabin. Ever since Athens, when she'd used the blade to stab the giant Enceladus, its visions had stopped completely.

"I wonder . . ." Reyna said. "You're a child of Venus. I mean Aphrodite. Perhaps—perhaps you could explain something your mother said."

"I'm honored. I'll try, but I have to warn you: my mom doesn't make sense to *me* a lot of the time."

"Once in Charleston, Venus told me something. She said: *You will not find love where you wish or where you hope. No demigod shall heal your heart.* I—I have struggled with that for . . ." Her words broke.

Piper had a strong urge to find her mother and punch her. She *hated* how Aphrodite could mess up someone's life with just a short conversation.

"Reyna," she said, "I don't know what she meant, but I do know this: you are an incredible person. There is someone out there for you. Maybe it's not a demigod. Maybe it's a mortal or . . . or I don't know. But when it's meant to happen, it will. And until it does, hey, you have friends. Lots of friends, both Greek and Roman. The thing about you being everyone's source of strength, sometimes you might forget that *you* need to draw strength from others. I'm here for you."

Reyna stared across the lake. "Piper McLean, you have a way with words."

"I'm not charmspeaking, I promise."

"No charmspeak required." Reyna offered her hand. "I have a feeling we'll see each other again."

They shook, and after Reyna left, Piper knew that Reyna was right. They would meet again, because Reyna was no longer a rival, no longer a stranger or a potential enemy. She was a friend. She was family.

That night the camp felt empty without the Romans. Piper already missed Hazel. She missed the creaking timbers of the *Argo II*, and the constellations her lamp used to make against the ceiling of her cabin aboard the ship.

Lying in her bunk in Cabin Ten, she felt so restless she knew she wouldn't be able to doze off. She kept thinking about Leo. Again and again she replayed what had happened in the fight against Gaea, trying to figure out how she could have failed Leo so badly.

Around two in the morning, she gave up trying to sleep. She sat up in bed and gazed out the window. Moonlight turned the woods silver. The smells of the sea and the strawberry fields wafted on the breeze. She couldn't believe that just a few days ago the Earth Mother had awoken and almost destroyed everything Piper held dear. Tonight seemed so peaceful . . . so normal.

*Tap, tap, tap.*

Piper nearly hit the top of her bunk. Jason was standing

outside the window, rapping on the frame. He grinned. "Come on."

"What are you doing here?" she whispered. "It's after cur-few. The patrol harpies will *shred* you!"

"Just come on."

Her heart racing, she took his hand and climbed out the window. He led her to Cabin One and took her inside, where the huge statue of Hippie Zeus glowered in the dim light.

"Um, Jason . . . what exactly . . . ?"

"Check it out." He showed her one of the marble columns that ringed the circular chamber. On the back, almost hid-den against the wall, iron rungs led upward—a ladder. "Can't believe I didn't notice this sooner. Wait till you see!"

He began to climb. Piper wasn't sure why she felt so ner-vous, but her hands were shaking. She followed him up. At the top, Jason pushed open a small trapdoor.

They emerged on the side of the domed roof, on a flat ledge, facing north. The whole of Long Island Sound spread out to the horizon. They were so far up, and at such an angle, that nobody below could possibly see them. The patrol harpies never flew this high.

"Look." Jason pointed at the stars, which made a splash of diamonds across the sky—better jewels than even Hazel Levesque could have summoned.

"Beautiful." Piper snuggled up against Jason and he put his arm around her. "But aren't you going to get in trouble?"

"Who cares?" Jason asked.

Piper laughed quietly. "Who *are* you?"

He turned, his glasses pale bronze in starlight. "Jason Grace. Pleased to meet you."

He kissed her, and . . . okay, they had kissed before. But this was different. Piper felt like a toaster. All her coils heated to red-hot. Any more warmth and she'd start smelling like burned toast.

Jason pulled away enough to look in her eyes. "That night at the Wilderness School, our first kiss under the stars . . ."

"The memory," Piper said. "The one that never happened."

"Well . . . now it's real." He made the ward-against-evil symbol, the same one he'd used to dispel his mother's ghost, and pushed at the sky. "From this point on, we're writing our own story, with a fresh start. And we just had our first kiss."

"I'm afraid to tell you this after just one kiss," Piper said. "But gods of Olympus, I love you."

"Love you too, Pipes."

She didn't want to ruin the moment, but she couldn't stop thinking of Leo, and how he would never have a fresh start.

Jason must have sensed her feelings.

"Hey," he said. "Leo is okay."

"How can you believe that? He didn't get the cure. Nico *said* he died."

"You once woke up a dragon with just your voice," Jason reminded her. "You *believed* the dragon should be alive, right?"

"Yes, but—"

"We have to believe in Leo. There is no way he would die so easily. He's a tough guy."

"Right." Piper tried to steady her heart. "So we believe. Leo *has* to be alive."

"You remember the time in Detroit, when he flattened Ma Gasket with a car engine?"

"Or those dwarfs in Bologna. Leo took them down with a homemade smoke grenade made from toothpaste."

"Commander Tool Belt," Jason said.

"Bad Boy Supreme," Piper said.

"Chef Leo the Tofu Taco Expert."

They laughed and told stories about Leo Valdez, their best friend. They stayed on the roof until dawn rose, and Piper started to believe they *could* have a fresh start. It might even be possible to tell a new story in which Leo was still out there. Somewhere . . .

# LVIII

# LEO

**LEO WAS DEAD.**

He knew that with absolute certainty. He just didn't understand why it *hurt* so much. He felt like every cell in his body had exploded. Now his consciousness was trapped inside a charred crispy husk of demigod roadkill. The nausea was worse than any carsickness he'd ever had. He couldn't move. He couldn't see or hear. He could only feel pain.

He started to panic, thinking maybe this was his eternal punishment.

Then somebody put jumper cables on his brain and restarted his life.

He gasped and sat up.

The first thing he felt was the wind in his face, then the searing pain in his right arm. He was still on Festus's back, still in the air. His eyes started to work again, and he noticed the large hypodermic needle retracting from his forearm. The empty injector buzzed, whirred, and retreated into a panel on Festus's neck.

"Thanks, buddy." Leo groaned. "Man, being dead sucked. But that physician's cure? That stuff is *worse*."

Festus clicked and clattered in Morse code.

"No, man, I'm not serious," Leo said. "I'm glad to be alive. And, yeah, I love you too. You did awesome."

A metallic purr ran the length of the dragon's body.

First things first: Leo scanned the dragon for signs of damage. Festus's wings were working properly, though his left *medius* membrane was shot full of holes. His neck plating was partially fused, melted from the explosion, but the dragon didn't seem to be in danger of crashing immediately.

Leo tried to remember what had happened. He was pretty sure he had defeated Gaea, but he had no idea how his friends were doing back at Camp Half-Blood. Hopefully Jason and Piper had gotten clear of the blast. Leo had a weird memory of a missile hurtling toward him and screaming like a little girl . . . what the heck had that been about?

Once he landed, he'd have to check Festus's underbelly. The most serious damage would probably be in that area, where the dragon had courageously grappled with Gaea while they blowtorched the sludge out of her. There was no telling how long Festus had been aloft. He'd need to set down soon.

Which raised the question: where were they?

Below was a solid white blanket of clouds. The sun shone directly overhead in a brilliant blue sky. So it was about noon . . . but of which day? How long had Leo been dead?

He opened the access panel in Festus's neck. The astrolabe was humming away, the crystal pulsing like a neon heart. Leo checked his compass and GPS, and a grin spread across his face.

"Festus, good news!" he shouted. "Our navigation readings are *completely* messed up!"

Festus said, *Creak?*

"Yeah! Descend! Get us below these clouds and maybe—"

The dragon plummeted so fast, the breath was sucked out of Leo's lungs.

They broke through the blanket of white and there, below them, was a single green island in a vast blue sea.

Leo whooped so loudly they probably heard him in China. "YEAH! WHO DIED? WHO CAME BACK? WHO'S YOUR FREAKIN' SUPERSIZED McSHIZZLE NOW, BABY? Wooooooooo!"

They spiraled toward Ogygia, the warm wind in Leo's hair. He realized his clothes were in tatters, despite the magic they'd been woven with. His arms were covered in a fine layer of soot, like he'd just died in a massive fire . . . which, of course, he had.

But he couldn't worry about any of that.

She was standing on the beach, wearing jeans and a white blouse, her amber hair pulled back.

Festus spread his wings and landed with a stumble. Apparently one of his legs was broken. The dragon pitched sideways and catapulted Leo face-first into the sand.

So much for a heroic entrance.

Leo spit a piece of seaweed out of his mouth. Festus dragged himself down the beach, made clacking noises that meant *Ow, ow, ow.*

Leo looked up. Calypso stood over him, her arms crossed, her eyebrows arched.

"You're late," she announced. Her eyes gleamed.

"Sorry, Sunshine," Leo said. "Traffic was murder."

"You are covered with soot," she noted. "And you managed to ruin the clothes I made for you, which were impossible to ruin."

"Well, you know." Leo shrugged. Somebody had released a hundred pachinko balls in his chest. "I'm all about doing the impossible."

She offered her hand and helped him up. They stood nose-to-nose as she studied his condition. She smelled like cinnamon. Had she always had that tiny freckle next to her left eye? Leo really wanted to touch it.

She wrinkled her nose. "You smell—"

"I know. Like I've been dead. Probably because I have been. *Oath to keep with a final breath* and all, but I'm better now—"

She stopped him with a kiss.

The pachinko balls slammed around inside him. He felt so happy he had to make a conscious effort not to burst into flames.

When she finally let him go, her face was covered in soot smudges. She didn't seem to care. She traced her thumb across his cheekbone.

"Leo Valdez," she said.

Nothing else—just his name, as if it were something magical.

"That's me," he said, his voice ragged. "So, um . . . you want to get off this island?"

Calypso stepped back. She raised one hand and the winds swirled. Her invisible servants brought two suitcases and set them at her feet. "What gave you that idea?"

Leo grinned. "Packed for a long trip, huh?"

"I don't plan on coming back." Calypso glanced over her shoulder, at the path that led to her garden and her cavern home. "Where will you take me, Leo?"

"Somewhere to fix my dragon, first," he decided. "And then . . . wherever you want. How long was I gone, seriously?"

"Time is difficult on Ogygia," Calypso said. "It felt like forever."

Leo had a stab of doubt. He hoped his friends were okay. He hoped a hundred years hadn't passed while he was flying around dead and Festus searched for Ogygia.

He would have to find out. He needed to let Jason and Piper and the others know he was okay. But right now . . . priorities. Calypso was a priority.

"So once you leave Ogygia," he said, "do you stay immortal or what?"

"I have no idea."

"And you're okay with that?"

"More than okay."

"Well, then!" He turned toward his dragon. "Buddy, you up for another flight to nowhere in particular?"

Festus blew fire and limped around.

"So we take off with no plan," Calypso said. "No idea where we'll go or what problems await beyond this island. Many questions, and no tidy answers?"

Leo turned up his palms. "That's how I fly, Sunshine. Can I get your bags?"

"Absolutely."

Five minutes later, with Calypso's arms around his waist, Leo spurred Festus into flight. The bronze dragon spread his wings, and they soared into the unknown.

# Glossary

**Acropolis**   the ancient citadel of Athens, Greece, containing the oldest temples to the gods

**Actaeon**   a hunter who spied Artemis while she was bathing. She was so angered by the idea of a mortal seeing her naked that she turned him into a stag.

***Ad aciem***   Latin for *assume battle stance*

**Aeolus**   lord of all winds

**Alcyoneus**   the eldest of the giants born to Gaea, destined to fight Pluto

**amphora**   a tall ceramic wine jar

**Antinous**   the leader of the suitors for Odysseus's wife, Queen Penelope. Odysseus killed him by shooting him through the neck with an arrow.

**Aphrodite**   the Greek goddess of love and beauty. She was married to Hephaestus, but she loved Ares, the god of war. Roman form: Venus

**Apollo**   the Greek god of the sun, prophecy, music, and healing; the son of Zeus, and the twin of Artemis. Roman form: Apollo

**Aquilo**   Roman god of the north wind. Greek form: Boreas

**Ares**   the Greek god of war; the son of Zeus and Hera, and half brother to Athena. Roman form: Mars

**Artemis**   the Greek goddess of nature and hunting; the daughter of Zeus and Hera, and twin to Apollo. Roman form: Diana

**Asclepeion**   a hospital and medical school in Ancient Greece

**Asclepius**   the healing god; son of Apollo; his temple was the healing center of Ancient Greece

**Athena**   the Greek goddess of wisdom. Roman form: Minerva

**Augustus**   the founder of the Roman Empire and its first Emperor, ruling from 27 BCE until his death in 14 CE

*auxilia*   Latin for *helps*; the standing non-citizen corps of the Imperial Roman army

*Ave Romae*   Latin for *Hail, Romans*

**Bacchus**   the Roman god of wine and revelry. Greek form: Dionysus

**Banastre Tarleton**   a British commander in the American Revolution who gained infamy for his part in the slaughter of surrendering Continental Army troops during the Battle of Waxhaws

**Barrachina**   a restaurant in San Juan, Puerto Rico; birthplace of the piña colada

**Bellona**   a Roman goddess of war

*bifurcum*   Latin for *private parts*

**Boreas**   god of the north wind. Roman form: Aquilo

**Briares**   older brother of the Titans and Cyclopes; son of Gaea and Ouranos. The last of the Hundred-Handed Ones still alive.

**Bythos**   combat trainer at an underwater camp for mer-heroes; half brother of Chiron

**Calypso**   the goddess nymph of the mythical island of Ogygia; a daughter of the Titan Atlas. She detained the hero Odysseus for many years.

**Ceres**   the Roman goddess of agriculture. Greek form: Demeter

*chlamys*   a Greek garment; a white wool cloak loosely wrapped and pinned at the shoulder

**Circe**   a Greek sorceress who once turned Odysseus's men into pigs

**Clytius**   a giant created by Gaea to absorb and defeat all of Hecate's magic

*coquí*   the common name for several species of small frogs indigenous to Puerto Rico

*cuneum formate*   a Roman military maneuver in which infantry formed a wedge to charge and break enemy lines

**Cupid**   Roman god of love. Greek form: Eros

**Cyclops (Cyclopes, pl.)**   a member of a primordial race of giants, each with a single eye in the middle of his or her forehead

*Cynocephali* (*Cynocephalus*, **sing.**)   dog-headed monsters

**Damasen**   giant son of Tartarus and Gaea; created to oppose Ares; condemned to Tartarus for slaying a drakon that was ravaging the land

**Deimos**  fear, the twin of Phobos (panic), son of Ares and Aphrodite

**Delos**  the island birthplace of Apollo and Artemis in Greece

**Demeter**  the Greek goddess of agriculture, a daughter of the Titans Rhea and Kronos. Roman form: Ceres

**Diana**  the Roman goddess of nature and hunting. Greek form: Artemis

**Dies**  Roman goddess of the day. Greek form: Hemera

**Diocletian**  the last great pagan emperor, and the first to retire peacefully; a demigod (son of Jupiter). According to legend, his scepter could raise a ghost army.

**Dionysus**  the Greek god of wine and revelry, a son of Zeus. Roman form: Bacchus

*dracaena* (*dracanae*, **pl.**)  female reptilian humanoids with snake trunks instead of legs

**Earthborn**  *Gegenees* in Greek; monsters with six arms that wear only a loincloth

*Eiaculare flammas*  Latin for *Launch flaming arrows*

**Enceladus**  a giant created by Gaea specifically to destroy the goddess Athena

**Ephialtes**  a giant created by Gaea specifically to destroy the god Dionysus/Bacchus; twin brother of Otis

**Epidaurus**  a Greek coastal town where the sanctuary of the physician god Asclepius was located

**Epirus**  a region presently in northwestern Greece, site of the House of Hades

**Erechtheion**  the temple to both Athena and Poseidon in Athens

**Eros**   Greek god of love. Roman form: Cupid

**espresso**   strong coffee made by forcing steam through finely ground dark-roast coffee beans

**Eurymachus**   one of the suitors of Odysseus's wife, Queen Penelope

**Evora**   a Portuguese city still partially enclosed by medieval walls, with a large number of historic monuments, including a Roman temple

*fartura*   a Portuguese pastry

**Field of Mars**   a publicly owned area of ancient Rome; also the practice field at Camp Jupiter

*filia Romana*   girl of Rome

*frigidarium*   a room in a Roman bath with cold water

**Furies**   Roman goddesses of vengeance; usually characterized as three sisters—Alecto, Tisiphone, and Magaera; the children of Gaia and Uranus. They reside in the Underworld, tormenting evildoers and sinners. Greek form: the Erinyes

**Gaea**   the Greek earth goddess; mother of Titans, giants, Cyclopes, and other monsters. Roman form: Terra

**Gaius Vitellius Reticulus**   a member of the Roman legion when it was first created; a medic during the time of Julius Caesar; now a Lar (ghost) at Camp Jupiter

*geminus* (*gemini*, pl.)   half human, half snake; the original Athenians

**Hades**   the Greek god of death and riches. Roman form: Pluto

**Hasdrubal of Carthage**   king of Ancient Carthage, in present day Tunisia, from 530 to 510 BCE;  he was elected as "king" eleven times and was granted a triumph four times, the only Carthaginian ever to receive this honor

**Hebe**   the Greek goddess of youth; daughter of Zeus and Hera. Roman form: Juventas

**Hecate**   goddess of magic and crossroads; controls the Mist; daughter of Titans Perses and Asteria

**Hemera**   Greek goddess of day; daughter of Erebos (darkness) and Nyx (night). Roman form: Dies

**Hephaestus**   the Greek god of fire and crafts and of blacksmiths; the son of Zeus and Hera, and married to Aphrodite. Roman form: Vulcan

**Hera**   the Greek goddess of marriage; Zeus's wife and sister. Roman form: Juno

**Hermes**   Greek god of travelers; guide to spirits of the dead; god of communication. Roman form: Mercury

**Hippias**   a tyrant of Athens who, after he was deposed, sided with the Persians against his own people

**Hippodrome**   an oval stadium for horse and chariot races in ancient Greece

**Hippolytus**   a giant created to be the bane of Hermes

**House of Hades**   a place in the Underworld where Hades, the Greek god of death, and his wife, Persephone, rule over the souls of the departed; also the name of an old temple in Epirus in Greece

**Hundred-Handed Ones**   children of Gaea and Ouranos with one hundred hands and fifty faces; elder brothers of the Cyclopes; primeval gods of violent storms

**Hygeia**   goddess of health, cleanliness, and sanitation; daughter of the god of medicine, Asclepius

**Hypnos**   Greek god of sleep. Roman form: Somnus

**Invidia**   the Roman goddess of revenge. Greek form: Nemesis

**Iris**   goddess of the rainbow, and a messenger of the gods

**Iros**   an old man who ran errands for the suitors for Odysseus's wife, Queen Penelope, in exchange for scraps of food

**Ithaca**   a Greek island and home to Odysseus's palace, which the Greek hero had to rid of suitors for his queen after the Trojan War

**Janus**   Roman god of doorways, beginnings, and transitions; depicted as having two faces, because he looks to the future and to the past

**Juno**   the Roman goddess of women, marriage, and fertility; sister and wife of Jupiter; mother of Mars. Greek form: Hera

**Jupiter**   the Roman king of the gods; also called Jupiter Optimus Maximus (the best and the greatest). Greek form: Zeus

**Juventas**   the Roman goddess of youth; daughter of Zeus and Hera. Greek form: Hebe

**Kekrops**   leader of the *gemini*—half human, half snake. He was the founder of Athens and judged the dispute between Athena and Poseidon. He chose Athena as the city's patron and was the first to build a shrine to her.

**Kerkopes**   a pair of chimpanzee-like dwarfs who steal shiny things and create chaos

**Keto**   an ancient marine goddess and the mother of most sea monsters; daughter of Pontus and Gaea; sister of Phorcys

**Khione**   the Greek goddess of snow; daughter of Boreas

**Khios**   the fifth largest of the Greek islands, in the Aegean Sea, off the west coast of Turkey

**Kronos**   the youngest of the twelve Titans; the son of Ouranos and Gaea; the father of Zeus. He killed his father at this mother's bidding. Titan lord of fate, harvest, justice, and time. Roman form: Saturn

**Kymopoleia**   minor Greek goddess of violent sea storms; nymph daughter of Poseidon and wife of Briares, a Hundred-Handed One.

**Laistrygonian ogre**   a monster giant cannibal from the far north

**Little Tiber**   a river that flows in Camp Jupiter. Though not as large as the original Tiber River in Rome, it flows with as much power and is able to wash away Greek blessings.

**Lupa**   the sacred Roman she-wolf that nursed the foundling twins Romulus and Remus

**Lycaon**   a king of Arcadia who tested Zeus's omniscience by serving him the roasted flesh of a guest. Zeus punished him by transforming him into a wolf.

*makhai*   the spirits of battle and combat

*mania*   a Greek spirit of insanity

**manticore**   a creature with a human head, a lion's body, and a scorpion's tail

**Mars**   the Roman god of war; also called Mars Ultor. Patron of the empire; divine father of Romulus and Remus. Greek form: Ares.

*medius*   Latin for *middle*

**Medusa**  a priestess whom Athena turned into a gorgon when she caught Medusa with Poseidon in Athena's temple. Medusa has snakes for hair and can turn people to stone if they look directly into her eyes.

**Mercury**  Roman messenger of the gods; god of trade, profit, and commerce. Greek form: Hermes

**Merope**  one of the seven Pleiades, star-nymph daughters of the Titan Atlas

**Mimas**  a giant created to be the bane of Ares

**Minerva**  the Roman goddess of wisdom. Greek form: Athena

*mofongo*  a fried plantain-based dish from Puerto Rico

**Mykonos**  a Greek island, part of the Cyclades, lying between Tinos, Syros, Paros, and Naxos

**Nemesis**  the Greek goddess of revenge. Roman form: Invidia

**Neptune**  the Roman god of the sea. Greek form: Poseidon

**Nereids**  fifty female sea spirits; patrons of sailors and fishermen and caretakers of the sea's bounty

**Nestor's Cave**  the spot where Hermes hid the cattle he stole from Apollo

**Nike**  the Greek goddess of strength, speed, and victory. Roman form: Victoria

*Numina montanum*  Roman mountain god. Greek form: *Ourae*

**Nyx**  goddess of night, one of the ancient, firstborn elemental gods

**Odysseus**  legendary Greek king of Ithaca and the hero of Homer's epic poem *The Odyssey*. Roman form: Ulysses

**Olympia**   the most ancient and probably most famous sanctuary in Greece, and home of the Olympic Games. Located in the western region of the Peloponnese.

**onager**   a giant siege weapon

**Oracle of Delphi**   a speaker of the prophecies of Apollo. The current Oracle is Rachel Elizabeth Dare.

***Orbem formate!***   At this command, Roman legionnaires assumed a circle-like formation with archers placed among and behind them to provide missile fire support.

**Orcus**   the Underworld god of eternal punishment and broken vows

**Orion**   a giant huntsman who became the most loyal and valued of Artemis's attendants. In a jealous rage, Apollo drove Orion mad with bloodlust until the giant was slain by a scorpion. Heartbroken, Artemis transformed her beloved hunting companion into a constellation to honor his memory.

**Otis**   a giant created by Gaea specifically to destroy the god Dionysus/Bacchus; twin brother of Ephialtes

***Ourae***   Greek for mountain gods. Roman form: *Numina montanum*

**Ouranos**   father of the Titans; the sky god. The Titans defeated him by calling him down to the earth. They got him away from his home territory, ambushed him, held him down, and cut him up.

***panadería***   Spanish for *bakery*

**Parthenon**   a temple on the Athenian Acropolis, Greece, dedicated to the goddess Athena. Its construction began in 447 BCE, when the Athenian Empire was at the height of its power.

**Pegasus**   a winged divine horse; sired by Poseidon in his role as horse god, and foaled by the Gorgon Medusa; the brother of Chrysaor

**Pelopion**   a funerary monument to Pelops located in Olympia, Greece

**Peloponnese**   a large peninsula and geographic region in southern Greece, separated from the northern part of the country by the Gulf of Corinth

**Pelops**   According to Greek myth, the son of Tantalus and the grandson of Zeus. When he was a boy, his father cut him into pieces, cooked him, and served him as a feast for the gods. The gods detected the trick and restored him to life.

**Penelope**   Queen of Ithaca and Odysseus's wife. During her husband's twenty-year absence, she remained faithful to him, fending off a hundred arrogant suitors.

**Periboia**   a giantess; the youngest daughter of Porphyrion, the king of the giants

**Phobos**   panic, the twin of Deimos (fear), son of Ares and Aphrodite

**Philip of Macedonia**   a king of the Greek kingdom of Macedon from 359 BCE until his assassination in 336 BCE. He was the father of Alexander the Great and Philip III.

**Phlegethon**   the River of Fire that flows from Hades's realm down into Tartarus; it keeps the wicked alive so they can endure the torments of the Field of Punishment

**Phorcys**  a primordial god of the dangers of the sea; son of Gaea; brother-husband of Keto

*piragua*  a frozen treat made of shaved ice and covered with fruit flavored syrup, from Puerto Rico

**Pluto**  the Roman god of death and riches. Greek form: Hades

**Polybotes**  the giant son of Gaea, the Earth Mother; born to kill Poseidon

**Pompeii**  In 79 CE, this Roman town near modern Naples was destroyed when the volcano Mount Vesuvius erupted and covered it in ash, killing thousands of people.

*pontifex maximus*  Roman high priest to the gods

**Porphyrion**  the king of the Giants in Greek and Roman mythology

**Poseidon**  the Greek god of the sea; son of the Titans Kronos and Rhea, and brother of Zeus and Hades. Roman form: Neptune

**propylon**  an outer monumental gateway standing before a main gateway (as of a temple)

**Pylos**  a town in Messenia, Peloponnese, Greece

**Python**  a monstrous serpent that Gaea appointed to guard the oracle at Delphi

*Repellere equites*  Latin for *repel horsemen*; a square formation used by Roman infantry to resist cavalry

*retiarius*  a gladiator who uses a trident and a weighted net

**Romulus and Remus**  the twin sons of Mars and the priestess Rhea Silvia. They were thrown into the River Tiber by their human father, Amulius, and rescued and raised by a she-wolf. Upon reaching adulthood, they founded Rome.

**Somnus** Roman god of sleep. Greek form: Hypnos

**Spartans** citizens of the Greek city Sparta; soldiers of ancient Sparta, especially its renowned infantry

**Spes** goddess of hope; the Feast of Spes, the Day of Hope, falls on August 1

**Straits of Corinth** a shipping canal that connects the Gulf of Corinth with the Saronic Gulf in the Aegean Sea

**Tartarus** husband of Gaea; spirit of the abyss; father of the giants; also the lowest part of the Underworld

**Terminus** the Roman god of boundaries and landmarks

**Terra** the Roman goddess of the Earth. Greek form: Gaea

**Thoon** a giant born to kill the Three Fates

**Three Fates** Even before there were gods there were the Fates: Clotho, who spins the thread of life; Lachesis, the measurer, who determines how long a life will be; and Atropos, who cuts the thread of life with her shears.

**Titans** a race of powerful Greek deities, descendants of Ouranos and Gaea, who ruled during the Golden Age and were overthrown by a race of younger gods, the Olympians

**Ulysses** Roman form of Odysseus

**Venus** the Roman goddess of love and beauty. She was married to Vulcan, but she loved Mars, the god of war. Greek form: Aphrodite

**Victoria** the Roman goddess of strength, speed, and victory. Greek form: Nike

**Vulcan** the Roman god of fire and crafts and of blacksmiths; the son of Jupiter and Juno, and married to Venus. Greek form: Hephaestus

**Zeus**   Greek god of the sky and king of the gods. Roman
form: Jupiter

**Zoë Nightshade**   a daughter of Atlas who was exiled and
later joined the Hunters of Artemis, becoming the loyal
lieutenant of Artemis

*Coming in May 2016*

The Trials Of Apollo,
Book One

THE HIDDEN ORACLE